THE QUIET SUN

NOÉMI RUSSELL

CONTENTS

CONTENT WARNING

Dear reader, this book contains death of a loved one, profanity, PTSD, sexual assault, suicidal thoughts, torture, and vomiting. I trust you know your triggers before moving along.

In Case I Fall for You
Black Sea Dahu

To my brother, Jonam, who never made it back home from across
seas.
May his name always be remembered.

PART I
CAPTURED

Chapter One

I couldn't breathe.

I stood there, staring at the near-lifeless woman lying in front of me on the cot in the apothecary as every part of my body screamed for me to look anywhere but her.

What have I done?

Looking down at the last, now shattered bottle of medicine I had, this was a healer's nightmare come true. I tried to swallow the lump that rose in my throat.

The woman in front of me was so pale. She had lost almost all her color in the last hour. Just a moment ago, she started struggling, moving her head in a hasty discomfort, nearly choking on her own dark-colored tongue. I had been rationing the last of her medicine, but at her rapid decline, in the midst of panic, I rushed and shattered what could have helped her last until tomorrow.

Without waiting another moment, I rushed out of the apothecary to find another bottle of medicine. Sprinting down the cobblestone streets, passing the occasional glare and hiss, I couldn't help the tears running down my face and the slight tremble in my legs as they drove me to the only place I could hope for.

After what felt like an eternity, I reached the worn-down red door and pounded on it with my fist.

The wooden door creaked open, and a tall man with peppery hair stood in the way. "What did I tell you last time you came by, witch?" he spat.

If only he were right. Maybe then I could heal this woman who lay in the apothecary nearly lifeless, breaths shallowing every second I wasn't with her.

"Away from here!"

He was about to slam the door in my face before I placed my palm on it. "Please, you have to help me. Shipment isn't arriving until tomorrow, and I need laudanum. She isn't going to make it to tomorrow," I pleaded, barely holding it together.

The man lowered his brows and clicked his tongue. "Tell Fenrah we don't have any more. The last bottle was used two nights ago on a crying babe. You'll have to wait until—"

"She won't make—"

"There's nothing I can do to help." The man took a step back. "I suggest you leave at once. Don't come back, she-devil. This is your last and final warning."

The door slammed, air hitting the tip of my nose.

The store across the street was no different. The owner shook his head. They didn't have any. Although, even if they did, I didn't think they would tell me.

I was breathless by the time I stepped back into the apothecary, but I halted as soon as I did.

Fenrah.

My mentor and owner of this apothecary was cleaning the shattered pieces of the broken bottle on the floor. She had an apron wrapped around her middle, her brown hair with white streaking at the roots pulled into a neat braid. Fenrah was the age my mother would have been, but the years had nothing on Fenrah. She was vigorous to a fault.

"Here, let me." I sniffled, grabbing what was left of the glass. "Is there anything I can do?"

Fenrah knew what I was asking but shook her head with pursed lips. My chest tightened even more, feeling like there wasn't enough air in this room. I couldn't tell what she was thinking. She must be disappointed in me. No one had died under her care in many years. She had trusted in me.

Death was approaching this apothecary. And as the village healer's apprentice, it was my fault.

After cleaning the mess I had made, I stood by the cot.

For the thirtieth time today, I went over my options. I kept coming to the same conclusion Fenrah had: there weren't any.

I couldn't do anything but hold the woman's hand and stare at her. It made this moment of death ten times worse. Waiting for something so cold and inevitable. Her eyelids were weak, neither lifted nor closed. Though she wasn't past her thirties yet, her time was coming, and it was coming quick. I swallowed the painful lump at the back of my throat.

I couldn't help but think about the deaths of my own family, though their deaths were not the same as this dying woman's.

I missed them in a body-aching, gut wrenching way. I'd been living a life without my family for several years, and I still hadn't quite grasped the true concept of me being alone in this world. Maybe it was because I was truly afraid to admit it out loud. It didn't feel right. It was not fair I was living and breathing but my mother, father, sister, and brother were gone—dead.

The woman's chest rose and fell softly. Too softly. I doubted she had many more breaths left in her. Mine painfully faded alongside hers. My hand trembled as I lifted the damp towel and pressed it to her forehead, trying to do as much as I could to make her comfortable before she left this world.

I did this to her.

"These things happen, Solei." My name rolled off Fenrah's tongue, and it was strange to hear it. My parents named me Solei, after the sun, because of my bright copper hair, but most people in my village called me "girl," "witch," "wench," "her," sometimes even "it."

Looking over my shoulder, I found Fenrah now sitting on a hard wood chair nearby, waiting with me. Dark, heavy air filled the apothecary. Though this day had not turned out the way I had expected, I was grateful for Fenrah and for her guidance and presence in my life.

My family was the only thing in my life that had ever felt *normal*. They never saw me as different; they treated me the same as they would anyone else, or better, because I meant something to them. I was family.

Now, the only time I felt normal was at Fenrah's apothecary working with medicine grown straight from the land. The regular customers were wise enough to know I wasn't a witch or a she-devil, and they treated me as any other healer. Well, maybe there was a touch of skepticism. Sometimes they'd smile at me, and I'd smile back. I hated to admit it, but it would always make my entire week. I lived for those moments—the moments where they would see me as an actual person. That feeling was like finally letting out a deep breath after holding it in for eternity.

I glanced back at the woman lying on the cot. I didn't think I'd ever feel the same way about that cot now. And if that made me weak, so be it. That was my favorite cot, and I had the best sleep on it. It was far more comfortable and inviting than the thin cot I slept on at home, a tiny space shared with two other women, Kryst and Brijet, neither of whom cared for me. And we all shared *one* cot.

But how could I feel the same way after this?

My chin quivered, my eyes stung and begged to release a few tears. But I couldn't—it wasn't professional.

After some time, Fenrah stood beside the woman as she let out her last breath.

I let out a silent sob as men came to take the lifeless woman's body away. I couldn't keep it in anymore. In my eyes, it was *my* fault that the woman died. I had failed her.

Fenrah smacked my cheek. "Stop crying, child! You stop crying, or else it *will* get worse."

My eyes widened. I cradled my cheek as it stung, but I held back the tears that screamed to be freed. I stared into her cold, brown eyes. I was speechless.

"You did the best you could with the tools you had in front of you. We are healers, not miracle workers." Fenrah glowered. "Don't let this eat you alive, or you won't be able to heal anyone else again."

Chapter Two

I brushed my copper hair back, fighting through the knots. *Stupid brush.*

Frustrated, I chucked it across the empty cot. After a slow, dreadful week following the incident, I realized Fenrah was right; it had eaten me alive. And every time it did, my hands shook uncontrollably, and I lost all of what little confidence I had. It was a constant battle in my head. I would tell myself it wasn't my fault, but then the next moment, I'd hate myself for not being able to save that woman's life.

I was exhausted. I woke up almost every morning feeling like I hardly slept. But it wasn't only because of the crowded cot or what had happened last week. It was because it didn't feel safe as a home should feel when there was no love there.

I stared at the wooden brush lying on our ripped blanket, silently cursing it and wishing I could cast some sort of spell on it. When the brush miraculously *didn't* change into a magical new bone brush, I snapped my head back to the blurry mirror. *No brushing for today, it is,* I thought, narrowing my livid green eyes in the reflection and staring at my red curls...angry that the rumors weren't true.

Just for a moment, I wished they were. That I was a witch who could cast a spell on anyone or anything I wanted—wishing I could change stale bread into a warm, fluffy baguette or that I could transform into another being just so I didn't have to live through another day of hateful glances and cursed words. I studied my pale, freckled body...

Since I could remember, I'd been branded as a witch. For so long I blamed my copper-colored hair for all the attention it had brought me. It made it impossible to avoid attention. Perhaps there would be a day when people didn't associate hair color with superstition. But today was not that day. Some had hated me for looking different, some because they thought me a child of the devil, and some lusted for me in ways that made my stomach churn.

My mother used to tell me there were people who looked like me in faraway lands in the north, but I'd never met anyone else who looked like me besides my brother. He had shaved his head as often as he could, which helped to a certain extent. I often wondered what life would look like if I were up north. I wondered if I'd still feel lonely or if I would feel like I belonged.

If I were being honest with myself, it wasn't just today that I wished for that. It was every damn day of my life. Well, ever since my family left.

My brother was the first of us to leave this world. He died in the previous war with an overseas country, Wendlen, that we'd been fighting with since the beginning of time. There was no body recovered. No body to grieve over. I never got to say goodbye to him. His friend brought the news upon his return home from the war across the seas. After my brother's death, we watched my father fade in result of it. It was almost as if he died long before a plague took his life. He didn't want to live anymore; guilt had swallowed him whole, and his life force depleted quickly—no longer caring for his breathing family. I closed my eyes and quickly shook my head to stop the memories from flowing.

The crisp summer winds slammed into my face as I left the tavern that swarmed with crowded bodies and muddied boots. I rushed down the steps, not bothering to look at anyone who entered for their daily murky cup of coffee ale. The weather in the Western Sea Islands, especially in Prustan, was always like this in the summer. I didn't mind the whispers of cold in the weather; it was a pleasant contrast to the heat of the sun as it lifted itself into the sky.

I continued my way through the village, walking through puddles of gods knows what, towards the cliffside that looked over the Western Sea. For the most part, the cliffside was vacant from visitors. Most people didn't want to trek the difficult path that was necessary to reach it. But it was worth it. The view was always worth it. I liked to imagine that one day when I had enough coin saved up, I would build a lovely cottage by the cliffside. It sent a bolt of tingles down my spine just thinking about it.

I kept my head down, focusing on where my leather boots hit the cobblestoned streets as I imagined my cottage in the woods and its—

"Witch!" A young boy appeared in front of me. His eyes darted briefly to my hair, but there was no fear in them.

I stopped and placed my hands on my hips. I leaned forward, and his voice lowered as he made his daily request.

"Did you turn my flower into a sweet almond overnight?" Tristan asked, eyes sparkling.

These were the moments I cherished and kept tucked away deep in my heart for the rainy days when life didn't seem worth living. These small moments were worth everything to me.

My lips curved into a slow smile. I whispered, "Why, yes, I did, young Tristan. What's the secret passcode?"

"Solei's the best healer in the village." He scanned our surroundings to ensure no one heard the super-secret passcode he swore up and down he'd never, ever share with anyone.

I opened my palm, like I did almost every day, and revealed a sugar-coated almond I purchased earlier. I knew my coin purse was light and held hardly any savings for the cottage I dreamed of having one day, but if his smile and happiness at one sweet almond meant my dreams would wait just a little longer, then it was worth it. Plus, the flower he gave me yesterday expecting a sweet almond this morning was on my bed stand, and it made me smile. Today's flower was going to add to the collection for the week before they wilted and died. We traded, and the moment the almond hit the young boy's palm, he was sprinting off across the cobblestones towards his friends, beaming with excitement.

Lifting the daisy to my nose and inhaling its sweet, fresh scent, I smiled and resumed my walk towards the west woods and up the mountain until I'd eventually reach the sea. The village, Prustan, stretched through the small valley and was bordered with sparse woods and shrubs. Predictable in the sweetest yet most annoying ways, my life here in the village seemed clear.

"Hey, cherry, how much for a fair trade?" a man asked in a low, sultry voice, leaning on a brick building outside a closed tavern as I passed.

I regrettably lifted my gaze and saw he had a hanging pot belly that reflected the amount of ale he consumed, matched by a balding head and patchy beard. My stomach roiled, and I refused to lift my gaze any more from the stone ground. I finally rounded the corner away from the reeking man.

As a woman and child passed me, she grabbed the back of her young daughter's dress, glaring at me as she warned, "Careful, sweetheart. Look at her hair. Do you see how unnatural that is?"

The little girl nodded her head nervously, terror filling her eyes.

"That's the witchcraft at work! You are to never go near her, do you hear me?" The woman pulled her even closer to her bosom.

Even though I was used to their fearful, wandering eyes, relentless hisses, and insults, it still crushed my heart. The little girl couldn't be more frightened of me. If I had bent down and told her it was all a lie, that I carried no magic and I was the same as her, they would scream and believe they'd just been cursed by me.

That afternoon, after visiting my family's four small graves near the forest edge, I sat at the edge of the cliffside gazing out at the Western Sea, feeling the cool breeze on my cheeks. The cliffs went on for miles and miles. They were the largest on the island, known for their treacherous falls. For some reason, I had never been afraid of these cliffs. The sun was finally dipping below pink-tinted waves crashing into the soft sand bed below.

After waiting here for hours, I closed my eyes for a moment, feeling a heavy, unbearable weight on my chest. Swallowing the tightness in my throat, I eventually opened my stinging eyes.

I breathed in the salt in the air and searched the seas.

I searched the skies, too.

Anyone who saw me on this cliffside wouldn't know. They wouldn't understand my searching. They couldn't possibly know what was on my mind.

He was out there. I knew he was.

My brother would be coming back for me.

Chapter Three

My eyes fluttered open as I heard ear-piercing screams coming from outside the cottage windows.

It took me a moment to remember where I was. I blinked back the blurriness that came from my interrupted sleep and pulled myself from Fenrah's cot in the apothecary. I had a few moments to spare in between mixing herbs and tinctures because today had been, oddly enough, much quieter. I didn't hesitate to take a little cat nap.

Before I reached the window, I could smell the smoke that seeped underneath the threshold of the cottage door. It was so dense that it masked the lavender and rosemary-filled jars that I prepared earlier this morning. It now filled the cottage with an acrid smell.

My feet moved on their own to the window, the glass fogged with that same smoke. Cautiously, I pulled the thin cotton curtains back so I could see what the commotion was about. The smog was so thick in the air, I could barely make out anything.

Until a young woman—Brijet—darted by with a man in hot pursuit of her. My trembling fingers clamped my open mouth to quiet the shriek that begged to be let out. I nearly forgot to breathe as I watched with wide eyes while Brijet was flung back when a savage man grabbed the back of her hair. A man I'd never seen before, in a strange soldier's uniform.

The village was in chaos. I saw more and more villagers running for safety from soldiers—soldiers that were not from our lands. They were grabbing women and hauling them away to gods knows where.

A horse dashed by my window, galloping with drool dripping from his large white foaming mouth. My eyes darted to a townsman brave enough to fight the horseman before being slaughtered—helpless as his wife and children were taken in front of his fading eyes.

"Edward, *no!*" the woman screeched, frantic tears falling.

All I heard were the desperate screams. A shiver ran down my spine.

Everything was in flames.

My eyes were pulled towards a large, tan man on the white horse who barked orders to the soldiers. He towered above the chaos, wielding a sword as long as I was tall in one hand and covered in swirling black tattoos. Leather straps crisscrossed his large chest that held several more weapons. Left and right he swung his deadly, clashing sword, pointing at the building across the street from where I kneeled hiding behind the curtain. Metal meeting metal, the screeching sound filled the musky air. My world stopped spinning and focused on the rider. I couldn't peel my eyes away from the tattooed man as he thrust a knife into one of the farmers that I'd come to know in the last few years.

My heart pounded inside my chest. I barred the entrance by sliding a large shelf in front of the door. It was small and barely holding up. *Like that will do much,* I thought to myself. My body trembled, but I reminded myself that I was prepared for this. I'd dreamt about it almost every other night. Nightmares had plagued my mind of a dark figure attacking me, and I wasn't able to move no matter how hard I tried to wake; all I could do was wait until it left.

I closed the curtains and blew out the candles. Quietly, I hid under the cot, my back pressed up against the dirt and straw. I clutched a small knife to my chest that was used for our herbs, squeezing it until my knuckles turned white.

I wondered for a moment where Fenrah was. If she was safe and hiding or if she was dead somewhere on the cold, muddy ground...A warm, bitter liquid burned in the back of my throat. No, *no*, I couldn't think about that right now.

Okay, breathe. I knew that my time had probably come. I was ready, ready to fight and ready to die. I knew I wasn't strong enough to withhold and protect myself from bloodthirsty, primal men.

More ear-shattering screams sliced through the air.

I was ready. With my eyes slammed shut, I took another breath to try to calm my nerves.

There was nothing I could do but breathe. I looked at the barred door. It was the only door to come in and out of this place. There was nothing else I could do to protect myself. I had to stay put.

I clutched the knife tightly, praying to the gods above, even though I wasn't much of a religious person. Hugging my knees to my chest, I rocked myself gently, my hair falling in front of my eyes, obscuring my vision.

Stupid hair. And there was *so* much of it. I considered for a moment shaving it like my brother did...but then I'd really get more stares.

There were fewer screams now.

I wasn't sure how much time had passed. That happened a lot. My mind often wandered, lost in my thoughts. Time and space became obsolete. Nour, my sister, would laugh if she were here. She always did the talking, and I always did the thinking. We were the perfect pair of sisters. A small smile formed as I thought about her, and my chest tightened.

I didn't hear any more screams.

Maybe the soldiers left and continued their rampage in other villages and towns? Maybe they overlooked this place. Maybe I wouldn't need to die today. I rose just enough to peer through the cotton curtains.

Thick, dark smoke had filled the town, no sun or blue sky in sight. All was quiet. As my hopes grew—

CRASH!

The wooden shelf exploded, and the door came along with it. Crashing into all the precious vials, tinctures, and potted plants.

A towering, ominous man crossed the threshold while splinters of wood were still falling to the ground, blood trailing from his thick sword. Through the haze of smoke, the cold amber of his eyes dropped my heart to the floor. He saw me, and I scrambled to the furthest part underneath the cot.

But he was faster, and his rough, large hand wrapped around my ankle, yanking me from the floor so fast I couldn't even let out a scream. My head snapped back and hit the cold stone floor.

I only saw darkness enveloping my existence.

Chapter Four

The swaying of the cart rumbling over stones and dirt woke me. My eyes squinted against the bright new light as they tried to open. I struggled to swallow, but my mouth felt as if twenty cotton balls had been stuffed down my throat. I coughed up a cloud of dust. I wondered how long I had been out for.

Sitting up, I found I was surrounded by several women and children, somehow all packed into this tiny cart. The same woman who called me a witch the day before was now huddled in the corner of our makeshift cage, her arms surrounding her terrified child. With every bump and jolt of the cart, our dirty, bloodied bodies swayed and knocked against each other, sending fresh pain exploding through my skull. I reached up to find blood leaking down my face and soaking my hair.

Instinctively, I searched for the knife, my last futile hope, only to find it gone.

Of course, they took it from me, I thought grimly.

Dust circled the cart as the women and children searched...searching for something I knew was not going to come. We were captives, prisoners of war—I was sure of it. Destined to be sold off in some foreign land like cattle. Mindlessly, I twisted my hands against each other. I felt like my ribs were too close together. I couldn't expand them right—I couldn't breathe right.

A group of mounted soldiers guarded us on either side.

Growing up, we were educated on our enemies in Wendlen—the same ones who killed my brother in battle. These men did not resemble our enemies. Rather, they had dark, tan skin and were far stronger than any I'd seen before. My pulse raced, and my stomach twisted in a sickening way as I remembered the stories told to us as children. Stories of vicious warriors across the Eastern Sea.

My eyes caught a symbol on one of their massive swords, a red snake wrapped around its grip. The warriors we were told about slaughtered, pillaged, and conquered countless towns and territories, but they never once ventured across the sea. Even so, their strength was renowned—and feared. The prisoners of war would die in brutal living conditions, in cages, or they would die from extensive, long hours of labor. The symbol on their swords shook me far more than the unsteady cart could. If these truly were Strokan warriors, then that would mean they would have had to rampage and defeat countless lands to get to the Western Sea—to Prustan.

It couldn't be.

I pulled my knees up to my chest and wrapped my arms around them. At least I wasn't shackled.

The cart swayed and jolted aggressively for what seemed like hours. I dared a glance at the warrior riding next to my corner of the cart.

It was the man who attacked me.

He wore light armor, revealing his massive muscular arms and chest. Swirling tattoos ran from his fingers to his wrists, to his shoulders, chest—and perhaps elsewhere. Scars of various sizes and severity covered his body and face. Dark, unwashed hair stopped above his shoulders. I'd never seen a warrior so beastly.

The soldiers from our lands were much paler from being close to the mountains. Their builds were also slenderer; no doubt their training was much less rigorous than the Strokans'. Maybe that was why we were defeated—*obliterated* was more like it. We had weak men. I was weak too. Pathetic.

Except for my brother. He was the best soldier and quickly went up in rank. And I wasn't saying that because he died. He truly was. Maybe that was why we lost to these savages, because my brother wasn't here.

The man must have felt eyes on him because he glanced over, and we locked eyes for a moment. He was beautiful and massive...and terrifying.

I looked away and scolded myself for being so curious. It could cost me my life, whatever was left of it anyway.

Despite my better judgment, I discreetly observed the other warriors. They all seemed to look the same—scary, mysterious, and beastly. Their vicious grunts gave way to their savagery, and their angular, sharp features hid any gentle bone they might have.

Hours went by hearing only the rumbling wheels on dirt and stone, and the sun started setting. I wondered how long we had been in this cage when the steel cart finally slowed to a stop. Straightening my spine, I glanced around the new landscape. There were war tents—hundreds of war tents...and hundreds of warriors.

Holy shit.

They were invading our lands. Home, despite what I thought of it in the recent few years, wouldn't be home anymore. It would all be part of the Strokan Empire. A place of death and darkness. Evil and immoral. From the looks of it, the stories we were told as children held true.

For a moment, I was glad my family wasn't here to experience this atrocity. I was glad it was me experiencing the end of our home and not them. That same sickening deep-rooted feeling rose again in my chest—the feeling that I was cursed.

The steel door to the cart creaked open. Without warning, I was yanked out as my captor grabbed my arm. I stumbled to the ground, my hands plunging into the mud. The rest of the women and children followed, being pulled onto the cold, wet ground as we huddled together for security. The smoke in the air caught in my throat, and I coughed violently.

It smelled like *death*. I knew the acrid scent well. The twisted symphony of rot, embers, and blood was the song of death.

The other women and children were herded into a group, but a shout pulled our attention as a man on a white horse barked orders nearby.

It was the same man I saw outside Fenrah's apothecary window. A shiver ran down my spine, remembering his ruthlessness. He wore the same light armor as the rest of the warriors, but slightly different, more subtle. He reeked of beauty and power.

Even though I was a distance away with the rest of the women and children, I could see—I could *feel* the rage in his wild and dark eyes. The veins of his neck bulged as he commanded the warriors.

"Where is he?" he roared.

One of the warriors nearby grabbed onto his white horse's reins as another shouted, "Over there, Emperor Aris!"

My heart stopped. He was an emperor. But I didn't recognize his name. I clawed the inside of my mind for a memory, but nothing came.

The emperor flung himself from his white horse and charged off. I felt the attention from the women around me turn towards this man who disappeared into one of the tents bordering us. Not a minute later, the emperor dragged a warrior by the nape of his neck.

"My Lord—please, *please*!" the warrior screamed, and his hands grappled, clawing onto the emperor's arm for release.

The emperor walked to the clearing, dragging the warrior away from the tent. I could see the panic in the warrior's eyes, and he looked for ways to get out of this. He seemed to be one of them—not a prisoner.

"I beg of you—don't do this, My Lord!" the warrior pleaded.

"I didn't ask you to speak, *traitor*," the emperor spat and twisted the warrior onto the ground in front of him, releasing his hold on his neck. The man tumbled onto his knees, tears slipping past his dirt-filled cheeks as he stayed put. "You've already spoken your last words to the man you murdered in his sleep. You're a coward. You're nothing. Your words have gone to waste."

The man shook his head, sobbing into his hands. He looked up with glistening eyes, eyes that begged for another chance.

Emperor Aris' rage rippled amongst us. "You die a dishonorable death."

A warrior near us whistled low.

Two women behind me discussed the events taking place. "I heard a dishonorable death is when they rip their hearts out of their chests, so their souls no longer travel to the next life."

The younger woman whispered, "But that's cruel. How—"

"It's for the worst of sins. It's not a death taken lightly in the East," the older woman warned.

The man gripped the dirt that turned into paste with his tears. The hairs on the back of my neck stood.

"I wonder what happened," another whispered behind me.

The emperor's voice was cold and merciless. "You thought you were the law itself. You killed your own kin. You're a traitor to your family, to your brothers, to your *country* and to *me*."

The man sobbed, sniveled in the dirt, and begged for his life.

The emperor unsheathed the sword attached to his hip and took a deep, controlled breath. "No man is law itself except for me and my sword. This brings me no pleasure. You die knowing the choices you made brought you here."

The world seemed to stand still for a moment. He was going to die in front of us.

I wanted to grab the children near me and show them a way out, but there wasn't one. We were all forced to stare while we held our breaths, fearful of what was to come. My eyes were glued to this pleading man who had now soiled his trousers.

Without a moment of hesitation, the emperor lifted his sword with pure, lethal rage and slashed the man's neck without completely decapitating him. I flinched as I saw the accused murderer's eyes grow wider and wider. The blood from his neck spilled like water, and the emperor was at his side, kicking him to the ground.

The emperor grabbed the man's jaw and kept it above ground, so the man's gurgling noises echoed as he choked on his own blood. The man's eyes never left the emperor's as he sputtered the blood out of his mouth and choked to his last dying breath.

My mouth grew warm with bile pressing to be released. I pressed my trembling hand over my mouth. I could smell vomit from some of the women who had already freed the entirety of their stomach contents.

The emperor rose from the ground, his upper lip raised. One moment he kept his eyes on the dead man's and the next he dropped his sword and grabbed a knife from the leather strapped around his chest. He raised the knife, glittering in the afternoon light, and penetrated the man's chest. With almost no effort, he dragged the knife down, ripping the man's chest wide open.

The bones in my body rattled. My eyes—they wouldn't look away. My heart was going to burst with the way it was pounding against my ribs.

The emperor shoved his hand into the man's chest and wrenched something—

His heart.

The emperor held the man's heart, blood spilling all over his hand.

He raised the heart, tilted his head back towards the sky—towards the dead man's heart—and squeezed it until blood poured onto his face, down his neck, and onto his body.

Without another moment to spare, the emperor hurled the dead man's beating heart into the woods, far, far away from his body.

A dishonorable death for a murderer, a traitor.

I tried to swallow, but my throat felt like sandpaper, and my knees locked. I hadn't realized how tense my body felt until now.

The emperor looked at the surrounding warriors near him, breathing heavily. "I have zero tolerance for murderers," he rasped and spat on the warrior's empty chest. He snapped at some nearby warriors, "Take it somewhere the animals will feed off it."

It. My heart pounded as he barked orders to the others.

His eyes darted around, and I watched as a sea of heads bowed in submission, perhaps afraid he'd lunge with lethal rage and kill us too. I could sense the warriors near me stiffen. They were all on edge after this.

The emperor swung himself onto his white horse and galloped back towards what I imagined was the front of this camp.

Even though I had been brought to the most lethal camp, I couldn't seem to draw my mind away from the thought of that man's beating heart in the emperor's cold, unforgiving hands.

Savages. That was what the Eastern warriors were. Brutal, ruthless, merciless savages.

Tilting my head, I noticed for a moment the warriors who were once surrounding the emperor wore small yellow sashes around their waists that ran along the leather armor, their demeanor slightly more sophisticated. The warriors guarding us wore crimson sashes.

Death seemed more real than before. It seemed closer. Like any moment, a beast-like warrior could snap on me and rip my heart out too.

My captor and the other warriors glanced around at all the women shifting nervously. It seemed as if they were looking for something...or someone. They paced aggressively back and forth around us. I observed the other women and children, their eyes wide and faces pale, unsure of what lay ahead.

A shriek split the air as one of the young women was pulled out into the open. I inhaled sharply. I knew her. Klawdia.

She was one of the prettier maidens in our village besides my sister. Klawdia had full red lips, luscious black locks, and eyes that sparkled wildly. When we were younger, she occasionally bullied me, tugged on my red hair, spat in my face, and told me how disgusting I was. Nour would often follow close behind me, full of rage. They'd fight and claw at each other's throats like wild cats. But there was always something about Klawdia that made my bones creak.

Nour never had a problem with getting in people's faces and showing her true wild colors. It always took me by surprise, but I admired it. She had the most ridiculous amount of confidence and didn't care what people thought or said about her. She was one of the happiest, most free-spirited people I had ever known. While she looked everyone straight in the eye, I kept my eyes glued to the floor. I hated the attention. I was afraid of it. Even more now after what happened to Nour and Mother.

Now, these women were dragged through this gods-awful, reeking mud. They heaved another woman out. She was also young and beautiful, though smaller than Klawdia. Another woman, Maeri, was pushed next to the other two, knees deep in the muck, tears rolling down her sweet face. She knew my family as well. She begged the warriors to let her go, but they slapped her into submission on the wet ground.

Why were they singled out? Then I realized that all of these women had something in common.

I lowered my head behind the others.

These men preyed upon women who looked young and healthy, with full curves and strong bones. In fact, I'd never heard of a place where pretty girls *weren't* targeted. It was dangerous for women to be attractive, and that was why I had always done what I had to do to avoid attention.

I tightly wrapped a ripped-up cloth from my dress around my hair, hiding my face behind shadows.

I heard the women nearest to me wailing and pleading for the warriors to bring back their women, when suddenly my body was aggressively hauled out in front of everyone. My captor's hand tightened on my arm to the point of pain as he jerked me close to him.

Stupid piece of cloth. It did nothing to hide my hair or my face.

Before releasing me beside Klawdia and the other girls, my captor ripped the cloth from my head, leaving my bright red curls exposed. He cursed and gave me a smirk that made my body rigid.

"I won't ask you again," he hissed. "How old are you?"

I didn't hear him the first time amidst the commotion. I desperately wanted my lips to let the words out that I was twenty-three to save myself further pain. They remained glued together. He shook me violently, and all it did was further push those words back down my throat.

"What, are you mute?" he demanded. The sheer confusion and haze over my eyes answered for me. "Fuck's sake." He shoved me toward Klawdia and the rest of the young women.

I kept my head low and stood with the others.

There were several of us. Maybe seven or eight, but I refused to look too much with my wandering eyes. My eyes were too green for a place like this. A place that was colorless. Only darkness and smoke lingered here.

I didn't see what happened to the rest of the women and children from the village. As I walked with the small group of women, including Klawdia and Maeri, the warriors would push us back in line when we lingered too far behind.

Even in the darkest hour, women distanced themselves from me, which was nothing new. I wrapped my arms around myself from the cold. It had been this way too long to get emotional about it anymore. I had to find a way out of this shithole or else I would die in more ways than I could count.

My taunting thoughts were cut short when we came to a stop in front of the largest war tent we'd yet passed. My captor left our group and entered through the thin flaps. I saw red and yellow banners with a curling snake flying above the tent.

Before I had time to figure out what was happening, my captor motioned the warriors to bring forward the women.

"Are you sure it's a good time, Tobias? The emperor seems to be dealing with his advisors," the warrior behind me said.

"A good time as any—he's always planning something," Tobias, my captor, muttered to the warrior.

A pair of rough hands shoved me forward. I glanced over to find the man giving me a conniving smirk that made the hairs of my neck rise. I swore silently. Shadows of evil spread through this camp, and no amount of shuddering would shake it from my shoulders.

As we entered the large tent, I noticed the beautiful white and tan sheep skins that were draped on the floor, the chairs, and the bed.

Oh, Erus.

The emperor stood by a wooden desk in the center of the tent and spoke in quick, hushed words to others who sat in the sheep-skinned chairs. He was the definition of darkness.

My dread grew more prominently now that I was in closer proximity.

The emperor, whom everyone had their eyes on, stopped pacing for a moment to listen to Tobias, who spoke in a low voice. Tobias motioned towards us with a smug little smile on his face that made me want to slap it off him. The emperor seemed frustrated, glanced at us, and went on speaking in hushed tones with the men who were seated. Just as clearly as the emperor was disinterested in Tobias' words, he was equally indifferent about who we were—the women from the village they just destroyed.

Tobias' jaw tightened. It didn't go as he expected...or did it?

He reached the other warriors surrounding us.

"Take the women with us. Leave the witch here," he ordered. "I'm sure the emperor can handle her—he might enjoy the challenge." He chuckled sarcastically.

I dared to look up at him, and I narrowed my eyes in a threatening manner. He raised his hand and swung his palm across my cheek. I held my stinging cheek as my eyes pricked with tears.

"Give me that look one more time, and I don't care how pretty you are, it'll be the end for you, she-devil." He frowned in bitter disgust, but I saw it—the fear in his eyes and in his voice. This wasn't the first time someone was afraid of me, afraid that I had cursed them silently. The rest of the warriors followed his orders, giving me strange, nervous looks.

They most likely had never met a redhead with eyes the color of jade before and didn't know what to think or do about it.

Frustration begins when knowledge ends, my mother had cautioned me.

The women walked out with the warriors escorting them. I was left in the middle of the tent, still holding my cheek from the burning sting knowing that it would likely bruise the next day. The rest of my family had tan skin and could easily hide any blemish. My pale skin hated me and wanted everyone to know what happened—insufferable.

I looked around my new surroundings. The emperor was still in deep conversation. The other men began to rise from their chairs as their conversation faded. I cautiously walked to the side of the tent where chests were laid out. I curled up on the floor near a chest, trying to hide most of my body and existence. My eyes darted for any sort of weapon that could protect me at this time.

They didn't seem to care that I was here. Maybe I wasn't cursed. Maybe the gods favored me.

I might just be able to escape. I'd find an abandoned cottage somewhere, rebuild it, and live the rest of my life in total peace. Just me and the land.

I scanned the tent for any way out. There were no openings in the back or side. It appeared the only way out was through the entrance.

The men got closer to the entrance of the tent, now in visible sight of me hiding near the chest that was double my size. One must have noticed because they made their way over, their boots scuffing up the floor as they stopped before me.

A weight settled in my chest with the bitter taste of defeat replacing the sweetness of hope I'd been forced to swallow.

"What do you have here, Emperor?" one of the men questioned in amusement.

"What are you talking about, Ryle?" The emperor walked over, noticing me for the first time. Sensing his compelling gaze, I couldn't resist looking up to meet his eyes.

My eyes widened in fear. They were dark and wild, like pools of black ink that threatened to swallow you under. I dropped my stare to hide behind my lashes.

"Ah, Tobias. Of course, he can't think of anything else but women," the emperor scoffed.

"I'm sure he wanted you to have warmth in your bed tonight, My Lord. How thoughtful," Ryle suggested with a smirk.

"Or he wanted you cursed. I remember seeing a few of these up north," said another man who was by far the oldest in the group.

The emperor rolled his eyes and snickered. "Don't believe those silly superstitions, old man. They don't do anything but cause pointless distractions."

The emperor left the men and went further into the tent. I hid a smile. It was rare to meet someone who didn't believe in superstitions. Most people didn't question tradition.

The old man stomped over, and I pressed my body into the corner, paralyzed with fear. He grabbed a handful of my hair and forced my face to look up at him.

"I'd be careful about what you do to my emperor, you hear?" the old man warned while I looked into his wrinkled, threatening eyes.

"Ralius, don't you have more important things to do than to bother yourself with a captive?" the emperor drawled from across the tent.

Ralius released me with repugnance.

"Take her to Camilla," the emperor said to no one in particular.

Ryle stepped forward and grabbed my arm, pulling me from the ground. He had dark stubble across his face with streaks of white flared through his hair. The clouds of smoke didn't help our vision in the darkness, and the corners of his brown eyes crinkled as he squinted through the dim pathways. Though he was not particularly rough, we walked at a fast pace through the camp.

I needed to get out of here. My legs trembled uncontrollably in my gray dress, secretly thankful I hadn't relieved myself yet.

I could hardly survive in this world—how could I survive this? These foreign warriors walked on this ground with such darkness, as if their bodies were indeed empty and soulless. They could devour me in a moment's time, and I'd be left with nothing.

Perhaps I'd even forget who I was in a place like *this,* surrounded by people like *them.*

A few minutes later, we appeared in front of a much smaller tent with pale lilac veils draped over the entrance.

"Camilla, it's your father. May I come in?" Ryle waited by my side.

"What is it?"

A moment later, a tall woman came through the veils. My breath caught in my throat. She was beautiful. She had long dark hair to her hips and dark almond-shaped brown eyes. Her crimson dress brushed against the mud as she stepped out of the tent. What was she doing in a place like this?

The moment her eyes landed on me, her face crinkled as if I smelled like soured milk.

"Emperor Aris wanted me to bring her. He thought she could be of use to you here," Ryle stated.

"Didn't the emperor wish to see me himself?" Her brows furrowed slightly.

"He didn't mention it, Camilla. I tried telling you before," Ryle grunted impatiently, "but this is no place for a woman. I don't care what you are to him, but he's got greater issues to handle in a place like this than tending to you."

"I didn't ask what you thought, Father, or else I would have asked that *before* I traveled here!" she snapped.

Tension filled the heavy air.

"Take the girl." Ryle shoved me towards the entrance.

As soon as Ryle disappeared down the dark path, Camilla and I entered her tent. It was simple but clean. Her bed was at the back of the tent and had a few large chests to each side. A beautiful swirling red rug was spread on the floor protecting her long dress from unwanted mud.

"You are to stay there." She pointed to a corner, dropping a sheep skin near it. "If you so much as move without me asking, I'll have your back flayed, do you hear me?"

My jaw dropped slightly. I was about to say something, but Camilla spoke again before I could.

"Don't you think of doing anything stupid. I know your kind," she muttered.

I snapped my jaw shut. Camilla regarded me warily, like she didn't know what to think of me.

But I knew she was more afraid of me than I was of her.

CHAPTER FIVE

At first light I found myself once again in the lingering, unwelcoming hands of yet another warrior—one that had been in the emperor's tent last night. One that heard me ordered to Camilla's side. I had woken up this morning after a fitful night of sleep to find Camilla gone. Naturally, a moment of hope for escape rose, and I silently peeked my head out of the tent. I was immediately recognized.

Altis, son of Erus, did not favor me on this day. My eyes darted up into the gray sky. *Why?*

"Camilla is with Emperor Aris. This way," the warrior grunted. "She usually is this early in the morning or late at night," the warrior added without me asking. He had a thick scar across his cheek that met his upper lip.

As we walked through the narrow muddy pathways, I kept wondering how that happened and if I would have been able to fix a wound like that. I wondered if my brother had any scars similar to this when he was in battle. I looked around for a moment, at this gruesome smoke-filled camp. I wondered if he lived in a place like this before he died.

The last time I saw him, he promised he'd be there for my birthday. Instead, we buried an empty box in his stead.

It had been hard to breathe freely after that.

I was thankful to be out of the warrior's hands when he shoved me into the emperor's tent. They lingered on my body longer than I'd have liked.

As soon as I walked in, my eyes fell on Camilla, who was sitting on the emperor's bed, the bedding wrapped loosely around her naked body. The emperor was also sitting on the bed, shirtless and his pants sitting loose on his hips. It seemed a sin to stare at his sculpted body as Camilla toyed with his necklace. I dropped my gaze.

Camilla giggled. Clearly, she had won her conquest and seduced the emperor. I had never in my life witnessed a woman *happy* after bedding someone. All the women I had ever known expressed to me that sex was something only men enjoyed. Even my own mother, though she loved my father in her own way, didn't seem to talk particularly highly about sex. She made it sound like a chore that had to be done for two reasons: to please your man and to produce children.

I tried to hide my wonder and confusion, but my brows furrowed. These were strange warriors...and even stranger women.

"Wench, here," Camilla ordered me forward to where they were sitting on the bed. "Take this. Wash it." She threw a small towel at my chest.

The emperor's face was almost expressionless aside from his jaw that ticked, causing me to feel he had a certain disdain for me. He was older than me by several years—most likely around his late twenties or early thirties, but still, he seemed young for a ruler.

Afraid of what he might do if I lingered much longer, I quickened my pace. I took the towel in my hand and went to a water bowl across the tent. As I cleaned the towel of its contents, I glanced up at the mirror in front of me and noticed that the emperor was looking my way. His dark, lingering eyes pierced through my body. I shuddered.

"Where did your head go?" Camilla cooed to the emperor, pulling his face closer to hers.

The emperor jerked his face away and threw a glare at her.

Oh, he didn't like that.

"What is it?" Camilla pried, and her voice switched an octave higher. She reached over between his legs with a sweet smile on her pretty face, and the emperor snatched her wrist from his body.

"Not now, Camilla," the emperor scolded as he let her wrist go.

"My Lord? Is it because of this presence that lurks in your bedroom?" Her voice was low, but she threw a fearful glance my way.

The emperor chuckled as he gazed at me.

"Are you not afraid of what she might do to you?" Camilla whispered in hushed tones, seemingly forgetting about her previous intention with the emperor. I almost felt bad for her, for all the false superstitions she believed so much.

"I don't remember what fear feels like anymore," the emperor stated plainly. He rose from his bed, buckled his pants, and threw a white drawstring tunic on. I'd never seen so many tattoos. I wondered what they—

"Well, regardless of what she is...I appreciate the gesture that you thought of me," Camilla spoke softly. When the emperor didn't respond and continued adjusting his clothes, she added, "It seems you need some help here, as well. I wouldn't mind sharing the help."

No. My heart pounded violently against my ribcage.

"That's fine. This place can use it." The emperor scanned the tent.

"Girl, change the chamber pot," Camilla directed towards me. Much better than *wench*.

Without sparing another moment, I did as I was told. Chamber pot in hand, I left the tent, taking my time since I dreaded going back to the emperor's ominous presence. I released the contents in a nearby hole and walked back. The smoke had doubled in the time I'd arrived in this gods-forsaken place—no doubt from the wind that pushed the dark smoke from the recent pillaged villages. Coughing violently, I could taste the ash that flew in the air.

I stepped through the entrance of the tent, my eyes darting around. Camilla was gone. I was *alone* with the emperor.

Subtly, I rubbed a clammy hand down my linen dress, and swallowed dryly.

Even if Camilla was not so sure of me, I felt safer when I was around her. There was something about being in the presence of a woman that felt comforting...even if they were my enemy. Something about being alone with a man made me uneasy. Placing the chamber pot where it belonged, I thought of ways I could get out of here quickly and unseen. Standing against the wall of the tent, my eyes flitted around, looking for any possible ways to escape this place when the opportunity rose.

The emperor was on the other side of the tent, fixing his tunic in the mirror. His muscled arms rippled underneath the fabric, and I wondered how many people he'd killed with them. Chills ran through my body. I watched as he washed his angular face in the water basin and dried it with a clean towel. Anticipating my duties, I walked over to his table and took the water bowl and wet towel.

Again, his eyes followed my every movement. I could *feel* them studying me. I couldn't breathe, knowing that any mistake I made could cost me my life.

Without warning, Tobias stormed into the tent, causing me to flinch and spill some of the bowl's contents on the emperor. The emperor jumped back as the water seeped through his trousers and onto the floor. My heart stopped as I froze.

With heavy steps, Tobias barged his way towards me and raised the back of his hand to strike. I flung my hand out for cover, but the emperor caught Tobias' wrist midair.

"Emperor?" Tobias questioned, brows brought together.

"Don't touch her," the emperor ordered Tobias.

Air returned to my lungs. *What's happening?*

"She cannot go unpunished," Tobias insisted.

"Tobias, it was nothing." The emperor released his wrist. "It's water. It's not going to hurt me." His brows lifted slightly at Tobias.

"Emperor Aris, if you'll allow me, I'll find another, maybe one that is more useful for you," he suggested with a look of disgust. "One that understands how to do things properly, instead of adding more work. We can get rid of her at once."

"I like her. She doesn't talk as much as you do." The emperor, *Aris*, sat in his wooly seat next to the wooden table. He shuffled some papers around, ignoring us both.

"Does she even talk at all?" Tobias asked while inspecting me.

"That's a good question." Aris, the emperor, turned his head toward me.

I shifted my glance to the floor, praying that talking didn't have anything to do with my duties. Gods, I *hated* talking. I'd realized that

I could live more peacefully if I took the time to listen more and talk less.

"She might be a mute," Tobias suggested.

Aris rose from his seat and sauntered towards me. I could feel the power radiating from his body as he approached. It was like death itself. I took a step back, slowly and cautiously, my boots rubbing along the rug.

He reached where I stood, placed a rough hand on my neck, lifting my chin up with his thumb. I wanted more than anything to close my eyes and pretend the emperor was not touching me, but instead, I swallowed, forcing my fears down, and lifted my eyes to meet his. Dark as the night, his eyes pierced into my being—observing me, reading me. Every cell in my body screamed for me to *run*.

Aris narrowed his eyes slightly, as if he were trying to find some answer in me.

I heard Tobias' boots shuffle and the tapping of a cane as another man I hadn't seen yet entered.

"Aris, my nephew!" the man with the cane called out. Aris released his hold on me. "It's time we talk about the voyage back home."

"Uncle Helon!" Aris turned away from me and strode towards his uncle to greet him.

"I've come to remind you how important it is that we return to our home before those around us suspect you've deserted your people," Helon said.

"That won't be happening. I have it under control, Uncle. No need to fear," Aris stated matter-of-factly as he sat regally on his wooden table. "We'll be leaving after the next battle."

Helon and Aris continued their conversation around the wooden table as Tobias came to my side and pushed me towards the entrance of the tent.

"Get some food for the emperor, girl," he ordered.

I stumbled as I rushed out of the tent.

With all the commotion from this morning, I hadn't realized the pounding in my head from the day before. I hurried my pace to where meals were placed out for the warriors and grabbed some fruit and cheese. Picking up a silver spoon, I noticed my appearance in its reflection. Light purple like lavender spread across my cheek bone. A layer of dirt covered every inch of my skin, and dried blood was caked onto my head and the side of my cheek. I didn't necessarily care how I looked. Honestly, the uglier I looked, the better for me, but the wound concerned me.

I snatched a cloth nearby to clean up the dried blood and contemplated using another linen cloth to wrap my hair in. The last one had been yanked from my head, unable to cover the vibrant color from this barbaric camp.

The feeling of the emperor's hand on me lingered, and the thought of how quickly he could snap my neck sent shudders down my spine.

Shaking the thought from my mind, I used this opportunity to get an understanding of the camp's layout. Through the dark and murky smoke, I looked around. Past several large paths behind the emperor's tent, I spotted the tops of trees, with patches of other white tents scattered within it. Perfect. I was close to the edge of the camp. The gods did indeed favor me. Maybe I wasn't cursed after all.

I remembered the path the warrior and I took this morning to get to the emperor's tent. I knew exactly how to get from his tent into the woods. Before they returned to their lands, I would escape. It would be quieter—with fewer warriors walking about. And being quiet was something I felt confident in.

Taking more time than I ought to get my bearings, I brought the plates of food back to the emperor's tent. My stomach growled. How long had it been since I last ate? Making sure no one saw, I snuck one piece of bread from the plate, slipping it into my pocket. I had to save food if I were to escape and survive. I stopped dead in my tracks as I recognized an herb that was growing near the base of the tents.

Creosote. Perfect for my head wound, I thought.

Fenrah once told me it helped with inflammation and heat in the body. I grabbed a handful of the herb and stuffed it into my pocket.

Time must have flown by because the emperor was carefully putting his leather armor on when I entered the tent. I placed the plates of food on the wooden table, and his uncle, Helon, began to devour his plate. He moaned as he ate his food with his mouth open and grapes sputtered out of his mouth. It made me want to vomit. The grape juices left a trail on his unwashed beard and his red tunic. My hunger left me. Helon threw the chicken bones on the ground. I tried not to stare, but he was acting as if he were an animal with no manners.

"Aris, come and eat. You need the energy for the next few days," Helon urged.

I went to the side of the tent to await my orders. The emperor, ignoring his uncle, finished placing on his light armor, then sat down and ate in silence. His chiseled jaw was tense as he chewed gracefully.

He seemed to be contemplating something, because he suddenly stopped chewing. He threw a glance in my direction. Eyes locked.

Shit.

I looked down at the floor. My cheeks flushed.

The emperor returned to his food and then rose to finish preparing for the next battle. Tobias, Helon, and Aris left shortly thereafter. Tobias mentioned that they would be back before nightfall. Half of the warriors seemed to be gone for this next battle, but there were still many strutting around the camp. I sat next to the large chest on the side of the tent that offered some protection.

Gods, how am I going to make it out?

Chapter Six

I was abruptly awoken by multiple warriors stumbling as they helped the emperor into his tent. It was the darkest part of the night, and blood leaked from his chest and stomach. I felt my insides turn when I saw the wound that cut deep into his flesh. I frowned. What was I doing here? I clawed my mind for my last memory, and, ah. Of course, I was tempted for a quick nap while the emperor was gone.

My breath hitched, and my heart raced, realizing that this could be my way out of this dreadful place if the emperor was gravely injured. The other warriors were also wounded but not as severely as the emperor. Aris drew in a sharp breath when they placed him on his bed, grimacing from the pain.

"Leave!" he commanded.

The warriors obeyed and scurried to leave, not noticing I was crouched near the large chest. Aris grabbed one of the linen cloths I had laid out and held it to his wound in an attempt to stop the bleeding.

How long was I asleep? Nighttime was filled with danger, and I knew I couldn't linger here. But I also couldn't risk walking back to my tent now... I heard the crackling of a large fire nearby and some of the warriors outside the tent cheering in victory.

Idiot. I shook my head.

As I contemplated my dilemma, the thought of staying in the emperor's tent seemed utterly imprudent. He lay wounded on his bed. A low groan escaped his lips, and his eyes now fluttered closed. I should be heading back to Camilla's tent. Where I would be safe—for the most part. I looked over at the emperor, oblivious to me watching him.

Flashbacks to the woman dying in the apothecary danced across my mind. It was my fault. She wouldn't have died if I hadn't been so clumsy, if I had a steadier hand when I gripped that bottle that might have saved her. I took her life and—

Just this once, I would help him. Life had given me another opportunity to save a life. And I would help give his life back into his hands. Not only did I feel obligated to make this heavy, suffocating guilt right within my heart, but he chose to protect me from Tobias.

Utterly unaware of my presence, I silently approached the sleeping emperor. My heart crashed against my ribcage, knowing that my life depended on staying unnoticed.

I stared at the emperor—completely vulnerable. My sister would kill him if she were in my position. She wouldn't even bat an eye. But I was weak and pathetic, nothing like her. I grabbed a fresh cloth and plunged it into the water bowl next to his bed.

It was hard to tell if he was asleep or unconscious from the pain and blood loss.

This is dangerous, Solei, I thought to myself.

I carefully lifted his arms away from his wound and placed them by his side. With gentle and hesitant hands, I cleaned his wound and rinsed the excess blood away. The wound was undeniably deep. He definitely needed stitches.

Moving swiftly, I searched the tent for any slender objects that would work as a needle. My hands settled on the thinnest bones I could find scattered on the floor. Remembering Helon's sputtering mouth all over the chicken bones, I cleaned them thoroughly. I ground the bones together until they formed a point that was thin enough to penetrate through skin. I carved a small hole at the other end. After preparing my makeshift needle, I tore a loose thread from my dress.

Droplets of sweat formed at the back of my neck as I crept to the emperor's bed. I'd done this process many times before; I knew exactly what I was doing, but a tremor ran through me as I realized the position I was in. He might wake up and find me harming him instead of healing him. He might blame me if the infection grew worse and then kill me. I would be touching the emperor in his sleep without his permission—that alone was cause for punishment. So many things could go wrong.

I had to try; it was an oath I made when I became a healer. I wouldn't make the same mistake of letting someone die in my hands if I could help it. I drew a breath as I pierced his skin and weaved the thread through.

His breath remained steady.

I continued.

Stitch by stitch.

The last thread went through effortlessly, and I completed the procedure with a rigid knot, ensuring any rough movements would keep the stitches intact. I grabbed another clean linen, drenched it with fresh water, and performed a final cleaning.

I looked at Aris. How innocent someone could appear when they were completely unconscious...yet when they were awake, they were responsible for death and misery. Shaking the confusion from my head, my hand went into my pocket to find the medicinal herbs I had stashed earlier. I placed some across his now-closed wound. The herbs soaked in and clung to his stitches.

Perfect. I smiled proudly.

As I picked up the needle and thread, I heard the flaps of the tent open. I whirled towards the entrance to find a healer, dressed in a long black tunic, and multiple warriors accompanying him.

Oh, no.

"You! Who is this intruder?" shouted the healer, his voice filling the tent.

My scrambled thoughts left me speechless and wide-eyed as I stepped away from the emperor. Frozen in shock, the needle slipped from my fingers and fell to the floor.

The healer stalked toward me. "Answer us immediately, child!"

Out of the corner of my eye, I noticed the emperor stirring from the commotion.

This is bad. Think. Think!

One of the warriors rushed towards me. I recognized him from before. His eyes narrowed.

"You witch!" the warrior shouted. "She is the emperor's pet. Tobias left her here for Aris' pleasure," the warrior explained to the healer. He seized my arm as I attempted to pull away from his harsh hold.

"What has she done to you, My Lord?" the healer muttered as he examined my procedure. "Witchcraft," the healer hissed as he inhaled sharply.

Stitching was a relatively new procedure Fenrah had taught me. It was not widely accepted yet and most likely would be frowned upon—especially by those from the Eastern Sea. My employer warned me to choose wisely whom to heal with this new technique.

I was a fool.

The emperor finally lifted his heavy eyelids and rested his sleepy gaze upon the healer.

The healer bowed his head. "My emperor."

The emperor slowly sat up, grimacing from the pain. He propped his elbows up on the pillows and analyzed the situation. As he surveyed his closed wound, wrapped in herbs, the healer eagerly explained, "I came as quickly as I heard you were wounded, Master. But the witch found you first, planning for your death before we reached you."

The emperor focused on the healer, listening and contemplating.

The healer continued, "I've heard of procedures such as this in the West, and the infection spreads within. It suffocates the healing. We need to leave it open and cauterize the wound. I have no doubt the witch secretly enclosed your wound, knowing you'd grow weak from infection."

The emperor glanced at me, his eyes darker than I'd remembered. I shifted, barely able to move from the warrior's tight grip around me. He held one arm around my waist and the other on my mouth—probably afraid I would try to cast a spell on them.

"My emperor, allow me to continue this procedure the correct way. I will need to reopen and clean the wound out properly," the healer suggested. He looked at the warrior who controlled me. "You, take the witch and dispose of her immediately for putting him in danger. Now, let me see this—"

"No—not tonight, Oleo. Leave it."

The warrior pulled me towards the entrance. I fought and struggled against his grip. I regretted not walking back to my tent earlier and leaving the emperor wounded in his bed.

"We can't wait too long, My Emperor," Oleo warned Emperor Aris.

Their voices faded as the warrior's tight grip pulled me towards dark-lit paths. The crackling fires nearby and the cheering voices faded as I could only hear the beating of my pounding heart.

Everything seemed a blur before I was thrown into a cage, tall enough for a small being like me but wide enough to fit a few more. The warrior slammed the door in my face, locked the cage, and left with a grunt.

My world stopped spinning as realization sunk in.

I frantically looked around me. I'd heard of these infamous Strokan cages before. War prisoners, criminals and captives were held in these barbaric cages. Known for its cruel isolation, most people would lose themselves before slowly dying from the lack of food and clean water.

They'd become *Insulatus*.

No. There was no way out. I wrapped my fingers around the cage door, leaning my forehead on its cool bars.

I cursed myself for trying to help the emperor—my enemy! How could I?

Why I cared at all perplexed me. Although many in my life had chosen to keep me at distance for different reasons, it was difficult for me to not care how others thought of me. My mother would often regard me with such weariness and tell me I was too sensitive for the world we lived in. She was convinced I was born at the wrong time and wouldn't hesitate to let me know that, too. I knew that my mother would also have stabbed the emperor in the heart for what he had done to our village, and she would have died happily for her people. She was bold like that.

I slumped into mud in the corner of the cage. I, on the other hand, was not convinced yet by aggression or hatred. But maybe I should be. Maybe then I wouldn't be in *this* mess.

My mother would tell me it was because I was young, inexperienced, and had never been hurt by anyone or anything, but I thought being ignored and bullied my entire life was something that normal people would grow a thick skin for.

I took a long, shaky breath. This was going to be a long night.

Chapter Seven

I was wondering where you'd gone." Camilla stood in front of the cage, brows furrowed. "Not that I minded. What happened, girl? What did you do?"

Camilla placed her hands on her hips, waiting for me to answer. I couldn't muster up the energy to speak. After spending an entire day in this cage on an empty stomach, it was impossible for me to even try to explain that I attempted to heal her emperor but got accused of witchcraft.

"Speak when you're spoken to!" Camilla demanded.

I tilted my head, forming my thoughts before Tobias, appeared. He wore a dark red tunic, and stubble imprinted his sharp face.

"She's a mute, we've realized," he grunted and turned to Camilla. There went my answer. "Isn't that perfect for us?"

Camilla's lips twitched up in greeting. "Tobias. Nice to see you, as always. Quite perfect, actually. Hopefully they don't decide to get rid of her. She'd be useful for me since she can't speak ill. What is she accused of?"

It took all the willpower I possessed not to furrow my brows and remain undisturbed by her words. This just got a lot more interesting. Why would someone speak ill of her?

"Witchcraft."

"Do you believe she's a witch?"

"Who knows." Tobias shrugged. "Do you have any news for me?"

Something flickered across Camilla's face. "No, not yet, Tobias. Give me time," she muttered. "My Lord notices everything."

Tobias scoffed. "I'll see you tonight." He walked towards what I figured was the emperor's tent.

Camilla lingered for a moment, staring into or through me. I stared back. Who was she?

"You and I are not so different after all."

That did it. I couldn't stop from pressing my brows together. We could not be more different from each other.

I could see something in her face, pity in the form of fear I saw in her eyes the day before. Strange. She strode toward the opposite direction of Tobias, the bottom of her crimson dress brushing against mud.

Evening came when I found myself leaning against the ice-cold bars, observing the camp. Warriors passed by with wary glances. Some smirked. Some tried to grab me through the bars and laughed when I pulled away. But the most interesting part of observing these warriors was the tension between some of them. It was almost like they fought together in battle, but they were at war with each other at camp. Occasionally, fights broke out between the warriors, making the day go by swiftly.

In a way, I felt safer in this cage away from the unknown dangers that lay outside. I hadn't seen the emperor all day and wondered if the wound was infected or in fact, healing. Maybe I had killed him like I did that woman. Maybe I didn't have a healer's touch after all.

Regardless of his condition, it didn't seem likely that I would survive this situation. If I did manage to heal him and they decided not to execute me, I'd still lose my mind and body in this cage.

A chuckle pulled my eyes toward a certain healer. Oleo.

Oh, no. My legs went weak, but I managed to back away from the door.

Oleo's fingers wrapped around the bars of the cage as he leaned forward. "I saw right through your ruse, mute," he spat in my face. "You won't survive another day here. I ordered your execution tomorrow for what you did to my emperor."

My breath faltered and stopped. So the emperor was in a worse condition. I was not able to further his healing. I had failed. Again. Oleo's eyes felt like fire burning through mine, and I couldn't pull away from him or the truth that he sang.

"I will not stand for witchcraft. I've done this before to your kind—in fact, many of you. I know one when I see one."

I slid another shaky step back. I was going to die. Realization sunk into my chest and captured my breath.

Oleo laughed softly as he pushed against the bars. "See you at first light, she-devil." And then Oleo waltzed away.

The world around me slowed down. I was afraid, but then I wasn't. I was more afraid of the unknown, not necessarily the act of death itself.

Could it be possible I would see my family in such a short time from now? My brother could be holding me and welcoming me in Hevan by first light. Or wherever he'd be.

My brother and I were not religious like the rest of my family was. It was comical since we were the only redheads. Maybe these people who accused me of witchery made a point. If he ended up in Hevan, then I would, but if he didn't, then I'd be wherever he was. And that made my heart happy.

I wouldn't be alone. We'd finally be together again. A sense of peace flowed through my chest.

After many hours of watching fire burn and drunken warriors stumble by, exhaustion hit me, and darkness swept through.

Movement in front of the cage probed my eyes open.

Oleo. He was dressed in a long black tunic with a warrior by his side. An executioner, no doubt.

This was my time.

The door to the cage creaked open, and naturally, I stumbled back. Maybe I wasn't ready like I thought I was.

The warrior slammed his elbow across my head and sent me sprawling onto the muddy ground, my trembling hands barely catching my fall.

My chest heaved as I fought for air through my lungs from the impact. I looked at the demented healer, his eyes filled with raging vengeance. His lean body loomed above me, casting a shadow from the rising sun with terrifying malice. I crawled backward further into the cage, but the healer stepped forward and grabbed the front of my linen dress, dragging me up to my feet once more.

"Your time is here, witch," Oleo hissed and rammed his iron fist into my empty stomach.

My breath was knocked out of me, and I coughed.

The warrior grabbed a hold of my arm in a tight grip and pulled me out. I tripped into the mud, but the warrior dragged me through the pathway into a clearing.

"Live no more, she-devil. The world will be a better place without you in it." The healer scowled as he walked behind us.

The warrior stopped and drew a knife from his hip. My heart pounded violently against my chest.

I didn't have enough time to ask Erus to take me wherever my brother was. I shouldn't have slept last night. What was I thinking? I didn't have time. Not now. Not ever.

Oleo stepped in front of me as the knife pressed against my throat. "I will never have a *woman* ruin my reputation."

"Stop this," a voice thundered across the small clearing.

The warrior with the knife against my throat hesitated. The healer whirled and faced the emperor, who approached us.

I gasped silently. The emperor didn't look gravely ill, though I couldn't see the wound that hid under his black tunic. His face was slightly paler than his usual tan and—because I was a healer and knew the signs of the body fighting for healing—I noticed moisture at the top of his forehead. But besides that, he looked to be fine.

Oleo's face paled. "My Lord, she has done great damage," the healer pressed.

"Release her," the emperor ordered the warrior.

Without waiting another second, the warrior obeyed and released his deadly hold on me. I stumbled in the mud as I tried to gain my balance. My heart thundered loudly knowing how close I was to kissing the face of death moments before.

"Master, y—you need to understand—" Oleo stuttered.

"Leave." The emperor focused his gaze on the healer.

In astonishment, the healer choked. "My Emperor—"

"Now." The emperor raised his voice.

The healer bowed his head without any more questioning. As Oleo scurried through the reeking mud, he gave me a glare that sent shivers down my spine.

The warrior near me, asked quietly, "What would you like me to do with her?"

"You may go."

The warrior gave a concerned look before he sheathed his knife in his leather strap across his chest and uncertainly walked in the same direction as Oleo. I couldn't decide if I'd rather go with the warrior or the healer. Both, just a moment prior, were about to execute me, but I knew this was the last place I wanted to be: in the emperor's hands.

The emperor stepped forward. "You treated my wound." His gentle tone caught me off guard. His obsidian eyes peered into mine, and he tilted his head. "Why did you do it?"

My heart sprinted. He knew I wasn't trying to hurt him or spread infection like the healer insisted. I wondered how his wound was healing. I didn't know how to answer his question as I stumbled to find the words.

He didn't wait for me to answer, as he turned on his heel and called over his shoulder, "Follow me."

I swallowed. He saved my life and didn't seem to want to end it any time soon. If I fled from here, no doubt he'd outrun me, then I'd be dead for sure. I followed him back to his tent, praying to Erus he wasn't going to rip my heart out of my chest.

"I will need some food and drink for the morning. I have a long day ahead of me, and I'll need all the energy I can get," the emperor ordered while he stepped away to his chests across the room and prepared for the day.

Bringing the emperor's food and drink didn't take much time. My heart and mind were still catching up to the fact that I didn't die this morning. Though there wasn't much to it before, I missed the life I lived just four days prior, and my chest tightened knowing I'd never see that village again. The peaceful time I spent alone in Fenrah's apothecary, focused on herbs and medicine. Would I ever see Fenrah again?

How long until I found my freedom? *If* I found my freedom. Perhaps, I'd find solace in a humble cottage tucked away in a peaceful meadow, surrounded by trees and most importantly, far away from everything and everyone.

I decided to grab some more creosote near his tent to help the healing of his wounds and mine. It didn't take long before I found exactly what I needed. I scanned the area for more herbs that would be useful and settled on a large bushel that was between two white tents. I heard warriors walk past me in serious conversation about how their blade was sharper than the other's. I hunched over to the bush, feeling a sense of familiarity.

After I snapped the healthiest herbs and pocketed all but one, I walked back, observing the natural curvature of the herb and occasionally darting my eyes about, ensuring Oleo wasn't about to stab my back.

I heard a twig snap and rushed to the entrance of the tent. I slammed into a hard body, nearly losing my balance. I looked up and found Helon, the emperor's uncle, smiling down at me with recognition from the day before written across his face.

"Oh, it's you, again." Helon smirked.

I glanced toward the front to find the emperor there with his arms crossed over his chest, his stance strong, and looking more annoyed than ever before. Helon's hand remained upon the small of my back to ensure my balance.

"Quiet little thing, aren't you?" Helon murmured. His voice and touch were so foreign to me; most men were repulsed by my presence. But there were some that liked to play with the she-devil—and those were the worst types of men. Which was Helon?

"Girl, fetch some water for another cleaning." The emperor gave me a bored glance.

So, I did help his wound, and he wanted me to continue dressing his wound. I felt a wave of relief crash over my body. Helon's arm dropped, and I bowed my head as I left for my task, releasing a quiet exhale.

I managed to clean my face of the dirt and blood that accumulated from the healer's pursuit before returning to the emperor's tent with his fresh bowl of water. I noticed, through a small mirror that appeared near the water source, a red mark was left on my cheek from the brutal elbow earlier today. I gently touched my fingers to my face. It was sore but would heal just fine.

I walked back and entered the tent. Ryle, Helon, and others among the emperor stood near the wooden table. I placed the fresh bowl of water near his bed and stepped to the side of the tent.

"Then it's settled, Aris. We'll be heading back to our homeland in the next two days," Helon stated to the emperor.

Nods of agreement traveled across the room.

Ryle rose from his chair. "I understand we're all eager to return, Helon, but we have worked too long to conquer these lands. There are enough warriors among us to stay behind and ensure the lands are secured. This will allow us to head back to our homeland without worrying about losing what we've fought long for."

"Ryle, you will stay behind and ensure the lands. Helon, be ready in two days. We're heading back," the emperor concluded.

"Two days will give us time to finish the last of the lands," Ryle contemplated. "That's good. The rest will remain secure with me until we've been established here." He walked towards the sheer flaps at the entrance and nodded to the emperor. "Emperor Aris, I'll meet you at midday."

The rest of the group followed Ryle, with Helon being the last to leave.

The emperor walked to his bedside near the water bowl I placed and slowly took his tunic off, careful not to rupture the stitches. My heart skipped a beat as his long, thin sleeve slid off his strong, sculpted shoulders.

I kept my eyes on the floor as I stepped to the water bowl with a fresh linen in my hand. Carefully, I soaked the linen and braced myself as I picked off the old herbs from the suture. I reminded myself I'd done this before, demanding my hands to stop trembling before he noticed.

His abdominal muscles clenched as my fingers touched near his wound. I glanced up to ensure he wanted me to continue. He locked his eyes with mine and gave me a silent nod. My breath hitched as his face was too close to mine. He was beautiful, but in the darkest way possible. It felt terribly wrong to be this close to evil. I could feel it pulling me in deeper into its darkness.

Once all the herbs had been cleared from his stitches, I reached for the linen that had been soaking. I squeezed the excess water and gently placed the wet cloth on the suture. His abdominal muscles tightened even more, and his breathing deepened as I cleaned his wound of any blood that seeped through. I tried my hardest to prevent skin-to-skin contact, and every time I did touch him, a sharp flutter kicked in my stomach, and I flinched. He seemed to notice that too.

His wound seemed to be healing the way it should. As I finished cleaning it, I placed fresh and healthy herbs on top of it, watching them settle in place.

Reaching for a longer linen that I had brought, I wrapped it around his naked torso to keep the herbs intact. My face came close to his, and though I was used to healing others and being in their personal space, I couldn't stop the heat that rose through my neck and settled in my ears. He was watching me so intensely, I had to force myself not to meet his gaze.

I quickened my pace, and so did my heart.

Finally, I tied the linen at the front and went to release my hands, but the emperor held my hand on the knot. I was startled from the touch and instinctively looked up. His dark eyes were upon me.

"Thank you," he said softly. His touch burned through my hand. It was the only thing I could concentrate on.

I lowered my head, and he released my hand.

In silence, I demanded my heart to even itself instantly as I stepped to the side of the tent, watching him leave shortly after.

The fact that I was nervous as a healer led me to wonder if I was truly meant to heal others.

Chapter Eight

The following morning was quiet as I helped Camilla tie the corset on her back. She was clothed in beautiful blue silks with gold threads, and she wore sparkling gold jewelry to match.

"I have to say, I'm glad you haven't died yet. It's not easy to be a woman in a place like this," she said softly, almost like there was a heavy weight to her words. I was thankful she couldn't see my eyes widen. Was she being nice to me? "We'll be heading over to Aris' tent. On the way there, you can grab My Lord and me our breakfast. We'll take it together."

And I did just that. Not caring to hurry back to the emperor's tent, I snatched pieces of bread and nuts for myself when I knew no one was looking. The plan for escape hadn't completely gone from my mind. This stash should be plenty for the escape and my way back home if I conserved it. There was a slight bulge in the side of my dress, but it was hardly noticeable. Our enemies fed us, though it wasn't much. My stomach growled violently, reminding me the last time I ate was last night.

On my way, another familiar face stumbled past me with warriors surrounding her. Klawdia. Our eyes locked in recognition. Her face said it all; she was looking for a way out. She was barely surviving.

Her arms were marked up and down with bruises. My heart fluttered in sympathy, wondering if she'd had a similar fate as mine or worse.

As soon as I entered the tent, Camilla's strong lavender scent wafted to me. Camilla was gracefully perched on his wooden table, her legs crossed, and her voice filling the air. Her dark straight hair fell over one of her tan shoulders. I tried not to stare, but it was difficult. It was like seeing a goddess in the darkest pits of Erus' wrath.

Silently, I moved across the tent and placed the plates of food near the emperor, who was seated on his sheep-skinned chair. For a moment, I almost pitied him, as it seemed he carried the weight of the world on his shoulders. Camilla's hands held the emperor's while she spoke. But he seemed far away from here.

After a few moments, Camilla rose and sat on a chair next to the emperor as they ate in silence. I wondered how long they had been together, or how long Camilla had thought they had been together.

They finished quickly and placed the utensils to the side. Reaching over, she cupped her jeweled hands around his face. Again, it was hard not to stare, but I'd never really seen anything like their dynamic before. It was interesting how she seemed to want his attention in an intimate way.

He glanced over to her but then fluttered his eyes across the room to where I stood. Eyes locked with his obsidian darkness. I lowered my gaze. Being curious always got me into trouble.

Camilla must have felt his attention leave her once more. "Leave us, girl. Wait outside," she ordered me.

I obeyed her instructions and waited at the entrance. I could hear her whispers to the emperor about how they never had a moment of privacy and how she couldn't wait to get away from here.

Warriors walked past me. Some with prurient, curious gazes. I diverted my body so that I was least exposed to unwanted attention.

I could hear Camilla's boisterous laughter throughout the tent and a sound as if she collapsed on the emperor's bed. I was aware I remained visible to some degree by the sheer flaps, which made me uncomfortable. If I could disappear for just a little while and come back without drawing any attention, I would. But I also didn't feel so confident away from the emperor's tent while Oleo might be lurking nearby.

I heard a shriek from Camilla, and without thinking, I glanced towards the flaps.

Camilla was sprawled on the emperor's bed below him, smiling and laughing into submission. She melted into his bed, her body claiming the bed as fully hers. He lowered his head to whisper in her ear as she intertwined her long fingers through his black hair. She brought his head even closer to hers as their lips touched and parted.

The emperor smiled at something Camilla said, and it might have made my stomach flutter. I tilted my head slightly at the way the emperor touched her. He lowered his hips above Camilla's, and for a moment, lifted his head from her face and glanced up. Our eyes locked.

Shit.

Fuck.

I whirled from the sheer flaps. Heat flushed my cheeks and neck. All I wanted to do was hide under a bed and slam my head against the ground. *Why do I have to be so damn curious all the time?* I scolded myself.

With a heavy sigh, I looked further towards the war tents to distract myself.

There was one thing I was certain of: I would never let a man touch me before my spirit left my body. I would at no time ever carry a child, and on no occasion enjoy the company of a man. I'd vowed it to myself when a man tore my mother and sister apart, and I would uphold that vow until I joined them in Hevan. That was, if Erus and his son, Altis accepted me. Maybe the gods were superstitious as well—I wouldn't know. I did know that it wouldn't be fair to bring children into a world where I couldn't guarantee their safety. I'd rather end my life than meet the same fate as my family.

In the beginning, my father worried about how curious I was. He was afraid and sheltered my mind and body. Maybe that was one of the reasons why I vowed celibacy because I knew I was quick to do things that would be troublesome for me. I needed to cage myself in a way, just as my father did. It was for the best.

But witnessing all of this now, I wondered, for a moment, if I had been wrong.

Unexpectedly, I heard a different commotion in the room, like a conversation that wasn't going well with hushed voices. I glanced and saw the emperor standing and lacing his dark tunic. Camilla reached for him to join her again, but instead he said something and turned his back to her, clearly not having it.

At once, I looked away towards the war tents before he caught me again. For a moment, I remembered what Camilla told Tobias, how the emperor noticed everything.

I couldn't agree more.

As I searched for nothing in particular in the distance, I squinted and noticed someone approaching the emperor's tent. Ryle, the advisor from earlier. I didn't stop him as he passed the flaps and entered the tent.

"Camilla, get up!" Ryle said in an agitated tone.

"Father." Camilla jumped off the bed and tightened her dress around her chest as the laces had gotten looser.

"Leave. We have important things to discuss," Ryle commanded Camilla.

She hastily slipped her sandals on and stormed out of the tent with her brows furrowed. I could almost see the steam coming from her ears.

Camilla and I could hear Ryle from outside the entrance flaps.

"I apologize, Aris. I know how she can be."

The emperor and Ryle's voices faded, and Camilla rolled her eyes. "The emperor told me his wound doesn't feel worse, maybe slightly better than before. You're to stay here and clean it once more before he leaves for the last battle today. Come straight to my tent after. I'll be in need of you."

Camilla stormed down the dirt paths in between white tents, her gold jewels flashing in the bright sun just when Tobias turned a corner and matched his pace with Camilla's. They walked together until I couldn't see them any longer.

I heard Ryle and the emperor mutter about what their plans would consist of once they reached the front line today. It was the same as it always had been in war; they were conquering more lands and killing more of our people. I imagined my sister walking through the afterlife back into this life and shaking me until I had the strength to make a difference in this world.

Lost in thought about my sister, time flew by until Ryle finally stepped out and followed the same direction as Camilla. I bowed my head, avoiding any attention.

"Girl, bring me some food. I'm still famished," the emperor called out from behind me.

On my way back to the emperor's tent, I snatched more herbs for him and extra for my journey back home. I barely knew where I was in the world, but I would rather be in control of my life and lost than captive in a foreign land I grew up learning and fearing about. The things that they told us sent shivers down my spine. It was rare that anyone survived a place like theirs.

My fear of ending up like people in the stories I had been told pushed me to finish my escape plans. I couldn't wait around to find out if that would also be my fate.

Using the opportunity that the emperor was heading to the front line of the battle, bringing with him most of his men, I planned my escape for when they would be gone. By the time they arrived back, I would be long gone before anyone, especially Camilla, realized I'd left.

As I walked through the flaps of his tent, the emperor was laying his fighting leathers out on his bed ready to be worn. I placed his plated meat on the wooden table and waited patiently for him. Refusing to be curious again, I kept my eyes glued to the floor.

As soon as he finished, I went to the freshwater bowl near his bedside. Without a word, he sat on his bed as I peeled the wilted herbs one by one from his skin. I reached for the wet cloth and began to clean his wound. It looked like it was healing perfectly. I gave myself a slight smile. Just as I was about to retreat, he took my hand in an iron hold I could not escape.

"I saw you earlier." The emperor peered into my eyes.

My heart thundered in my chest. My gaze dropped to where his hand held mine. I knew exactly what moment he was referring to.

I attempted to regain control of my hand and wrist but to no avail. His strength was overpowering.

He placed a finger under my chin and lifted it so that my eyes met his. "You look familiar..."

I swallowed, and warmth rushed to my face.

His eyes grew darker and narrowed as he searched my soul intently.

In that moment, I wanted to dig a hole and bury myself in it—preferably very far away from him. I tried to pull my face away. He finally released me and chuckled softly.

I stepped to the side of the tent while he buckled his leather armor across his chest. He left shortly after without so much as a glance my way. My eyes followed his powerful body out of the tent, knowing he probably felt them on him.

Little did he know, he'd never see me again.

Chapter Nine

The sky was gloomier than the previous days and chillier than I expected it to be. Rain was just around the corner; I could feel it in my bones. I scanned the nearly empty paths around the war tents and noticed half as many warriors walking about as I stepped towards the one that would take me to the edge of the war camps.

I took a deep breath. I could almost *feel* the freedom in my grasp, just waiting for me. Looking down at my dress, I made sure I had everything I needed: bread, nuts, cheese, herbs, and fresh water in the skin I stole. I even grabbed several short and long linens for the journey back home in case I'd need extra coverage.

Passing several drunk and wounded warriors, I moved swiftly and quietly. My ears twitched when I heard their bursts of laughter and felt their curious gaze follow my body. I took short pathways and cut corners, getting closer and closer to the edge of the war camp.

The sun had set the previous hour, and darkness crept through the war camps. My heart raced, and so did my legs. The smoke from the camp was being blown away by the wind that grew stronger with each hour. I could smell the rain preparing itself to scatter through the valley.

Out of nowhere, a hand encircled my wrist and jolted me to the side of one of the tents. A hint of rosemary wafted in the air as I gasped, stumbling to find my balance.

I looked up to see Klawdia. She kept one finger on her lips as she yanked me further between two tents. I moved my feet to keep up with her pull but knew the longer I was in this camp, the sooner the emperor and the others would arrive to find me gone.

Klawdia whirled around to face me. "You have to take me with you," she pleaded with wide eyes, tightening her grip on my arm.

"What do you mean?" My voice was hoarse.

"I know exactly what you're doing, Solei." She grabbed my shoulders, and her brown eyes glistened.

I swallowed and stared at her bruised and cut face. Everything in me was telling me to rip myself out of her grasp and leave her to a fate she deserved, but a nagging feeling reminded me that no one truly deserved that fate.

"I see the food you pocketed, and I know where you're heading, so don't try to convince me otherwise," she whispered.

"Klawdia—"

"*Please*! I'm begging you," Klawdia cried. "I can't survive this—no one can!"

A moment went by.

"Okay," I agreed reluctantly. "But come quickly." I freed my arm from her hold.

We stepped back on the dirt path and walked discreetly, but swiftly.

"Do you have enough for yourself, or do we need to get more supplies?" I murmured.

Klawdia knew what I was referring to: food. I wasn't about to give her all my supplies even though she'd most likely steal them anyway.

"We can stop here." She pointed across the pathway to another red tent. "There's a cook there who's been kind. I'll ask for some extra portions. Wait here. I'll be back." Her voice trailed off as she darted towards the red tent. Every part of my body told me to run, not just from these war camps and warriors but from *her* as well.

There was barely any light out anymore. Whether it worked in our favor or not, I was unsure. My feet tapped fervently. Something in my bones didn't feel right.

Hurry. Hurry, I thought in my head.

I looked at my surroundings and caught the eyes of some of the warriors across my path. They were mumbling to themselves and laughing from the flagons of ale they downed earlier. They could barely hold themselves up. I diverted my gaze, wiped my brow and waited. My stomach twisted against itself, and though night was approaching, my skin began to feel feverish.

Where is she? I couldn't stop my fingers from strangling each other as I waited for Klawdia.

Darkness was appearing, and I wondered if I should leave without her. Regardless, at some point, I'd need to leave her. There was no way I was going stay with her after escaping.

What's taking her so long?

Finally, Klawdia emerged from the red tent and crossed over to where I waited. We walked together towards the edge of the camp with our supplies intact. Our legs moved faster as we got closer.

Step by step, we went down the pathway.

Klawdia and I reached the edge of the woods after what seemed like a thousand miles. The trees were tall and dark. They had a different type of mystery about them that made me uneasy. We weren't in the clear just yet as there were more white tents scattered throughout the edge of the woods, but at least our chances of being seen were significantly lower.

We saw a few warriors hunched over a fire, too busy in their drunken conversations to notice two captives escaping through the woods.

My own heart felt like it might escape from my chest as it raged against my ribs. I felt like every breath I took was too loud. That perhaps they could hear my breathing or even sense the fear of losing my chance at freedom.

Faster, we walked.

With each step my worry grew, and so did my hope.

I scoured the area we were walking and made sure there weren't any warriors ahead. The empty woods lay in front of us, beckoning us to move forward.

We were careful where we placed our steps in fear of making too much noise. Slowly, but quickly enough that we could make the escape. Even the leaves crunching underneath our steps were *too* loud.

I could hear Klawdia's breathing behind me as I pushed a branch from the pathway.

Constantly checking over my shoulder to ensure no one was following our steps, my heart raced faster and faster as we got closer to freedom.

"Just past these boulders ahead, and we should be in the clear." Klawdia's voice grew in confidence the further we got from our captors. I wanted to shake her shoulders and scream for her to *shut up*.

Light raindrops fell from the sky, and the further we walked into the woods, the harder it was to see ahead. We had only heard the soft crunch of our boots hitting the ground until we finally passed the large boulders—

"Hey! Stop there!" a warrior shouted in our general direction.

Whirling around, a warrior marched towards us at a distance, pointing a finger straight at us.

"I see you! Don't move!" he roared.

They found us.

No, this can't be it.

"They're coming for us." Klawdia faced the warrior quickly approaching us.

There were now multiple warriors following the first man and rushing towards us.

"*Run,*" I cried out, daring a moment more before I sprinted into a run. I no longer cared about the steps crunching on broken twigs and leaves. I ran as fast as I could. I heard Klawdia behind me, but I focused on the path ahead.

This was it. This was my chance.

Branches ripped my face as I burrowed my way through the woods, my dress catching on thorns and branches.

Run, I told myself. *Run.*

The warriors were getting closer.

I only heard the sound of my breath, my heaving, until I heard her screams.

No. Klawdia.

I looked over my shoulder, but I didn't see her or the warriors. Her screams echoed through the woods. They caught her.

I froze in my tracks, my thoughts scattered, wondering what I should do.

Before I could decide, a hand from behind went over my mouth. Before I could react, another arm went around my waist and dragged me behind a wide boulder.

"Don't even think about it," a rough voice said in my ear. "You'll never make it out of here."

Chapter Ten

He flattened his body against the boulder and held me tightly to his solid chest. Keeping my body barely lifted from the ground, powerless against his constricting hold. My chest heaved deeply, unable to control itself. I knew exactly who held me against my will.

Aris.

I went for a jab in the only place I knew would hurt him severely—his wound. Just as I threw an elbow behind me to puncture his cut, he squeezed my arm to my side, hardly impacting his wound. It was as if he knew exactly what I intended to do.

He chuckled in my hair near my ear. Shivers went down my body. My breath sprinted faster than before.

Oh, gods. I was caught. *I'm going to die.*

"You don't understand." He kept his voice low as he spoke near my neck. "*Listen.*"

At first, there was silence. The beating of my pounding heart and his breath. Then, I heard the pouring of the rain bouncing off the ground.

After a few moments of listening, I heard it.

Screaming. It was Klawdia. My mouth went dry. They were the worst screams I'd ever heard. I almost let out a sob. They were dreadful, murderous screams.

What have I done? I brought this upon us. My eyes turned vacant as I listened to her screams.

What was going to happen to her—to me? My chin trembled, but I refused to give in. Was the emperor going to kill me? Would he rip my heart out, too?

Hesitantly, the emperor released his hand over my mouth, allowing me to breathe more freely. I couldn't believe it. Klawdia had been captured, and who knew what the warriors were doing to her for her attempted escape. Unspeakable things.

The screams continued and grew louder, echoing in my ears. They were all I could hear now. Why did he pull me away when he did?

"These warriors have no mercy for captives and prisoners of war. They'll make a lesson out of her to the others for disobeying and trying to escape." His grip around me didn't waver.

The screams were further and further away now. I was sure they were back at the base of the war camps. The emperor loosened his grip on my waist but kept his arms secured around me.

"There's nothing left for you here."

He loosened his hold as the illusion of escape faded, and with it the last hope I had. There was nothing left here of my land because he and his warriors took that from me. Everything that I had ever known, they took it from me and squashed it.

The emperor pushed himself off the boulder and prowled around to face me. He observed me through the twilight, his gaze not faltering from the rain. I kept my vacant eyes upon him as I pulled my fingers into a fist and felt my knuckles go white.

He was playing with his food. I wondered how long he'd play with me until he devoured and killed me.

I took a step back to provide more distance between us.

"Don't have any more thoughts of escaping. It's not going to happen." He took a slow step towards me, calculating my movements.

I saw how this was going to be. I swallowed, taking another step backward, and found the slick boulder pressed against my back. My heart was pounding so loudly, I was sure the emperor could hear it himself.

I had to try. I couldn't accept this life. I would have to make a break for it through the side of the boulder.

The emperor must have read my mind because he looked to my side and back to me. It was going to be a deadly dance between an emperor and his prisoner.

I took a cautious sidestep. He followed my exact movement and smiled, amusement flooding his face. "The fact that you think you have a chance of escaping when I'm right here is pretty comical, I have to admit."

He made a fair point, but that wasn't going to stop me from trying. What, was I supposed to sit idly waiting for my fate to come to me?

Slowly, I moved another step along the wet boulder. Again, he followed my movement. His eyes locked on me. I was the prey, and he the predator.

Without another moment, I made a break for it. I sprinted faster than I knew possible, my legs burning. As I willed myself to run faster through the dark and wet woods, I could hear the emperor's footsteps directly behind me.

Branches grabbed at my clothes and hair as I fought my way through the underbrush. The trees above me were too thick for the moonlight to reach my path. Thorns cut my cheek as I dashed through the trees. Faster and faster, I ran.

What was I thinking? He was the emperor of one of the strongest empires in the world. How would I outrun his strength and training? Or was this part of his ruthless game?

I didn't care. I had to keep trying. As far as I knew, this was my only moment to fight for my freedom and *my life*.

It was close—so close. My freedom right at my fingertips, just me and my cottage.

Run faster! I screamed in my head.

Just as I thought I couldn't hear him anymore, he was running alongside me and pulled my body into his as our legs tumbled with each other's, and we plummeted into the wet grass near some trees.

His body landed on top of mine, and his hand covered my mouth before I could make a sound or move. I might have panicked and struggled against his weight if I didn't hear something else.

"Did you hear it this way?" I heard a warrior ask nearby.

"Yeah, I heard something come through here. If there's another bitch around, she'll have it coming," another warrior mumbled.

My heart rate caught up to my breathing as the emperor's body crushed mine, his large hand still covering my mouth ensuring I wouldn't make another sound.

"Maybe it was that pretty little redhead that's been walking about."

"I sure hope so. I'd love to watch her squirm beneath me."

They both chuckled. My body froze in the emperor's arms as the warriors' conversation faded.

Once they were completely out of sight and no longer within hearing, the emperor moved his head in front of mine so that our eyes met. The emperor could surely feel my body shake uncontrollably beneath him. How was I ever going to escape?

He must have seen through the darkness because he whispered, "It'll be safer where I'll take you."

And for a moment, I believed him.

In that moment, I knew that my life would never look the same as it did before in my village. I'd never again wake up in that crowded cot, looking forward to mixing herbs with Fenrah. I'd never again be able to walk to my garden or the woods knowing that I was safe to do so. I'd never have that cottage in the middle of nowhere surrounded by the woods and my gardens. I'd never again have the freedom to plan my life the way I chose, but instead would be subject to someone else's will. I belonged to another.

My eyes watered, but I stopped them from overflowing and demanded strength from within.

Chapter Eleven

The emperor must have known I wasn't going to run from him again when we walked quietly back to the war camp. He didn't grab my arm or put a hand behind my back to ensure I followed him; he merely strolled ahead, shoulders back.

His confidence sent boiling rage coursing through my body.

The moon was well above us by the time he brought me to Camilla's tent. He turned around and held my gaze. He was more than a head taller than me, so my neck craned to meet his scrutiny.

"The others wouldn't have been so kind," he whispered.

My eyes fluttered to anywhere but his scrutiny, knowing he most likely felt the heat burning my cheeks. I rushed into Camilla's tent, and I didn't have to look up to know he was walking back toward his tent.

He was right.

Gods, he was so right.

In that moment, I sent a prayer to Altis, hoping Klawdia wasn't dead. My heart ached for what could or perhaps had already happened.

I crumpled in my usual corner while Camilla lightly snored in her bed. I never thought I would say this, but I missed the cot that I shared with Kryst and Brijet.

My head was spinning. I was sick to my stomach, and not just from the lack of food I'd had the last few days.

Not to mention the emperor's actions didn't make any sense. He and his own warriors were the cause of my pain and suffering, so why did he keep his own warriors from finding me?

The morning came and with it the pouring of the sky, the cleansing of the ages. I knew that the gods above were in mourning for those who died brutally at the hands of these foreign warriors. Pathways were running rivers with murky water. The entirety of my clothes leached onto my body. My hair clung to my skin and clothes. The captives and servants were gathered deep in the center of the camp far from where I tried to escape the night before with Klawdia.

Speaking of the actual devil, in the middle guarded by several warriors with red sashes along with their leather armor, was Klawdia. Her arms were tied around a large wood pole that was dug deep in the mud. Her face was more colorful than it was the night before. My stomach twisted. Poor girl. Just as the emperor said, she was to be a lesson for all who disobeyed.

Warriors, captives, and servants all gathered around Klawdia. I could tell they were servants because they weren't treated like they were an enemy. I saw them as they helped with the cooks. They spoke to the warriors as if they were on the same side, which they were.

Alongside me was Maeri. We'd given each other a few kind glances and silent words since our village was seized. It was nice to have a familiar face so far from home. She was slightly taller than most women and had sharp but stunning facial features. Regardless of how intense she looked, there was something warm about Maeri. On my other side was a cook, most likely the same one that gave the extra servings to Klawdia the day before. She was plumper than the rest of the servants and had soft facial features with a pout to her lips. With narrowed eyes, she kept her intense gaze on Klawdia.

"The emperor would never allow this in our homeland." The cook clicked her tongue and shook her head in disappointment.

Maeri and I glanced at each other, making sure we heard the same words.

"The emperor wouldn't *allow* this?" Maeri asked for the both of us.

The cook faced us with her brows furrowed. "Of course." She stared as if we should have already known this. The cook released her brows as realization washed over her, and her eyes softened. "This is not his doing."

"Then why doesn't he stop this from happening, Finny?" Maeri questioned.

"Because this is the doing of the Strokan's emperor, Malakar—the Emperor of Emperors. He has power everywhere even if you can't see it," Finny whispered as she nervously looked about. "He is the one who is behind all of this." She waved her hand around the camp, towards Klawdia. "And he controls the emperors who govern his territories. He is fear itself."

I glanced at Maeri once more. If this was the doing of Stroka's emperor, Malakar, then who was this emperor here with us? Who was the emperor that led these warriors?

Finny glanced to where Klawdia was thrown to the ground and on her knees. I could only imagine what last night looked like for her. Her eyes were swollen shut, but I saw tears rolling down her face. Klawdia shook her head as she looked up, begging the warriors to stop and release her. My chest ached, and it was getting harder to breathe watching her suffer.

"This captive tried to escape in the night and for that, she'll receive thirty lashes!" one of the warriors walking around Klawdia said to the crowd.

The sounds of gasps and whispers spread amongst the people.

My face turned in the direction my eyes felt pulled to, and they met the emperor's to the side of the gathering, near us. He wore a dark hood and cloak that protected his body from the rain. He leaned on one of the large sturdy tents, and his arms crossed against his chest as he locked eyes with mine. I knew exactly what he was thinking.

That could have been me.

"Who is he?" Maeri followed my gaze and asked no one in particular.

Finny answered Maeri, "He is the emperor of Siniya. My emperor, Aris." She looked back at Klawdia. "He is bound by servitude, as are the rest of the emperors from the east, to Malakar. Emperor Aris is forced to fight Stroka's battles as Malakar's best weapon against his conquests."

My world shifted. This wasn't completely Emperor Aris' doing, I processed, possibly not at all. Was that why he protected me against other warriors that were not, in fact, his own?

Klawdia's shrieks broke into my thoughts as she took her first lash. My face crumpled as I heard her piercing cries with each lash. Her dress was becoming bloody shreds. Shaking my head, I couldn't look anymore. The guilt swallowed me whole, and my heart squeezed in my chest.

It should have been me.

The silver rain was relentless as it poured from the dark sky and into the arena. We barely heard anything else besides its heavy drops and the screams that left Klawdia's blood-stained lips.

Aris' jaw hardened, and his nostrils flared as he watched every lash given to Klawdia.

"Isn't there anything he can do to stop this?" Maeri asked the cook.

"They would not listen even if he tried. Those are not his warriors. Aris is only here to ensure the conquest of these western lands for Malakar. The girl is Malakar's prisoner."

"Where will we go? Who do we belong to?" Maeri whispered the question I'd been wondering since we were taken.

Finny tore her eyes from Klawdia, who had received her final lash, and regarded Maeri with sadness. "You belong to Malakar. Aris does not take captives, from what I have seen."

I stared off into the distance, my trembling hand reaching my throat.

"Where will we go?" Maeri croaked, her voice rough and heavy.

Finny shook her head, eyes softening. "I'm not sure, child. Most of the captives will stay here where the new Stroka land will be built. People like you are not common in Siniya. As I said, Aris mostly has servants, those he pays for their work and have freedom to do as they please."

I began to tremble, and it wasn't from the rain, the cold wind, or the cracking lashes.

Once the warriors left Klawdia in the rain, her arms drooped around the stake, knees in the puddled ground, looking completely demoralized. The cook uncrossed her arms and trudged through the mud toward Klawdia. I wasn't sure if she was conscious anymore, but the extra herbs in my pocket should help the swelling on her bleeding back.

When I began to follow Finny's footsteps to help Klawdia, I was pulled back by one of the warriors. They took ahold of Maeri as well.

We were pushed towards the front of the camp by a group of warriors dragging only a handful of us: Maeri, another slave, and myself. I could barely see which path we were taking as it was hard to see through the pouring rain and the sound it made in my ears.

Were they taking us back to the villages—to the new Stroka? Glancing behind me, their sizes were intimidating; just the weight of one of their bodies could crush me to death. Their faces held vacant stares that sent a shiver down my spine. I swallowed. They were not men. They were beasts.

The path we walked between the white tents finally came to a clearing at the front camp, and there were large horses, carts, and warriors scattered around. They were preparing to head out.

Emperor Aris appeared, trotting on a large white horse towards the warriors that surrounded us. The rain slid along his tan arms and face, glistening with every drop. His horse didn't seem to enjoy the rain with his hooves stomping in the mud. Once we came to a stop, I realized that the warriors who guarded us had a wolf insignia on their sheathed swords.

One of the warriors bowed his head. "My Lord."

"Kallen," Aris greeted, shouting through the rain. "We head out now. The rain will continue to pour. The storm's coming in strong. Gather up the rest."

"Yes, Emperor Aris." Kallen nodded.

Aris rode off to where I imagined the front was, the white horse kicking mud behind him. His legion seemed to span for miles ahead.

Finny, the cook, met us at the end of the legion. She seemed surprised to see Maeri and I again. With her hand on the horse's reins, she led a cart full of supplies near us.

"Where are we heading to?" Maeri dared ask Finny near the warriors.

The cook looked up to us, but it was the warrior, Kallen near me who answered, "You'll be going to Siniya with us." He clicked his horse to follow his pace.

"I thought the emperor did not take captives," Maeri whispered to him.

The warrior gave us a blank stare. "Malakar insisted he take some back to Siniya, to help establish the prisoners equally across the empire. If you're lucky enough in a few years, Aris could grant your freedom like he has done for many in the past through servitude. But it would be an insult or rebellious to Malakar if Aris rejected you all." I belonged to Malakar, and he gave me to Aris. At this point, I wanted to vomit from how much I had been passed around. Kallen continued, "He's taking as few of you as he possibly can without upsetting Malakar—he's not someone you want to rattle."

"What will happen to the rest of us?" Maeri asked.

"Nothing good happens in Stroka. Those who survive the journey could be used for labor in Stroka. Some of them will be left in prison camps, but most... I'm afraid most die from the conditions they put them in Stroka."

After a moment, I realized that Kallen wore slightly different attire than the warriors I'd noticed around the camp. He still had leather straps across his chest, still looked like a beast with massive arms, unwashed long hair, but different somehow. I couldn't place my finger on it.

"Where are you from?" Maeri asked.

"Siniya."

Chapter Twelve

I could tell we weren't near Prustan anymore by the landscape that surrounded us. Instead of the occasional trees and shrubs scattered through my village, the wide road we walked on was nestled deep into the thick woods.

"What do you think it'll be like in Siniya?" Maeri broke the silence while we walked a ways behind the warriors.

I didn't feel like talking, but this was the first time Maeri had tried sparking a conversation with me since this journey. She knew me and my family, of course, so I couldn't mask the fact that I wasn't a mute around her.

"I'm not entirely sure. I've been wondering the same thing," I said hoarsely.

The weather had taken a turn. For better or worse, I wasn't sure. I didn't care anymore. Nothing affected me as much as not being able to have any control over my being. I had stopped counting the days that went by, I stopped counting the blisters along my foot, and I stopped thinking about what my future might look like from here on out. It felt like weeks had gone by. I wouldn't know. The only thing keeping me from giving up and going insane was watching my foot walk in front of the other, over and over again. Step by step, I walked with Maeri mostly by my side.

Sometimes, I'd gaze up to look ahead of me. I'd see the backs of the warriors and their heads bobbing up and down as they rode their horses. It was safe to assume that Emperor Aris' wounds were healing just fine as I hadn't seen him since we left the war camp. I figured he was at the front leading this legion to Siniya. Hundreds and hundreds of warriors, some servants and a few captives marching towards the Eastern lands, a part of the world I'd only heard in tales when I was a child. Ones that kept me wide awake at night, unable to sleep, wondering if the monsters would come and capture me.

Never did I imagine my worst childhood fears coming true.

One of the stories that I remembered was about an Eastern emperor named Gretum, who made it his life's purpose to ensure unity in his country. Unity meant there would be no quarrels, no disagreements, and everyone looked and dressed the same. Everyone had the same amount of work to do along with the same amount of food. If one didn't fit in this perfect box he created, they were considered corrupted or spoiled. They were the lowest of low-borns and would eventually die off from starvation or neglect from the community.

"Solei?" Maeri interrupted my thoughts again. I raised my brows in silent question. "I said I heard Stroka's skies are filled with smoke and darkness. Nothing grows there. Nothing's alive there. People barely live since the crops are weak. Maybe Siniya is like that, too."

"Maybe," I muttered.

"Have you ever heard of Siniya before?"

"Never, actually. Have you?"

"Yes. In fact, I have heard of the infamous Aris, too..." Maeri whispered.

My ears perked. "What have you heard?"

"Only that as a warrior he became quickly known for his brutality and conquests for Malakar."

"Oh?" I inquired. That would make sense as to why I felt the urge to run every time I was near him. The memory of Emperor Aris crushing the man's heart lingered in my mind. But then why did he protect me from the Strokan warriors that night I tried to escape? I couldn't figure him out, and that bothered me.

"One of those conquests was Siniya, which now he is emperor of—under Malakar's rule, of course. The basics, you know?"

"No, I don't know." I chuckled softly. "What have you heard of Malakar?" His name on my lips made me skip a heartbeat.

"Nothing good," Maeri muttered. "I heard that he is Strokan's god. There is no religion but him. There is no law but him. He tortures and toys with those who disobey him until they lose themselves. No one so much as thinks of disobeying in fear that their own neighbor will report their thoughts. That's what I heard in the war camp from the other women."

I gazed at my feet, one step after the other. Was Siniya similar to Stroka?

A few moments went by in peace and quiet, moments I thrived in. But Maeri spoke again.

"I'm sorry about what happened to your sister—and your mother."

My world stopped spinning, and walking suddenly seemed too difficult. Memories flooded my head, and I pushed and shoved them away into the darkest corners of my mind. Not having the energy to get emotional, I shrugged. I didn't have the words to spin lies. I just hoped Maeri would stop talking about them.

"It was brutal, Solei. I considered Nour my friend at one point. She was one of those girls you just knew could get whatever she wanted and wouldn't stop until she had it." Maeri smiled as if remembering what Nour was like. "She was such an inspiration to so many of us."

My eyes stung, and I blamed it on the dust in the air. I turned my head to hide my teary-eyed face.

I knew Maeri wasn't going to change the subject, so I did. "What do you think happened to Klawdia?" That question had eaten me alive. My chest tightened once more—that question didn't help this pain. *Idiot*.

"Apparently, she's been with us since...that last moment at the camp. She's further up in the legion. I saw her pass by when I was talking to Finny the other day. She looked better. At least she's alive. And coming to Siniya with us."

"I hope I see her sometime soon so I can treat her wounds."

"It's been a couple weeks since the lashes...I'm sure it's scarred by now. What would you treat her with anyhow?"

"I'm sure I could find some herbs nearby," I muttered and looked around the road we walked. The trees from the woods seemed to cave toward us.

"Don't you think that would be like finding a needle in a haystack?" Maeri furrowed her brows in disbelief.

"The land gives us what we need in order to survive."

Maeri laughed, but that didn't stop her from pointing at random plants and asking their benefit.

After some time, the legion and its horses ahead of us slowed to a stop. Maeri and I steered to the side of the road where the trees gave us some coverage from the sun. We shared the little water we were offered by Finny.

With the scorching sun came dehydration. I lacked water, and my lips broke in absence of it. My energy and life force slowly dripped out of my body one bead of sweat at a time.

"We'll rest here for the night," ordered one of the leaders.

The sun was already setting behind us while Maeri and I found a spot near the edge of the woods to lay our heads for the night. My stomach growled at me, but I refused to pay attention to it. I curled my body into a fetal position behind Maeri, who did the same.

That night, I learned I liked having Maeri around. Even though the circumstances were nothing but unsustainable, I realized she gave me strength by keeping me outside my head.

The sleepless night left as quickly as it came.

Or that was how it felt when a voice startled me awake.

"*You!*"

A figure loomed over my body. The morning sunlight was about to release itself through the woods, but there was enough light that I could make out who was in front of me.

"Klawdia," I breathed.

Chapter Thirteen

H ow are you still here?" Klawdia lingered above me, gaping at me as if I were a ghost. Her rosemary scent wafted through the morning air.

"I never made it out," I whispered, supporting myself on my elbows. My eyes were still adjusting.

"You lie! Or else you would have been whipped like I was." Her voice turned louder.

I heard people rustling nearby, and my heart began to race. What was she implying? "I am not, Klawdia. The emperor found me." I kept my voice low, hoping she got the hint to calm down.

"If you hadn't left me behind, if you hadn't deserted me—we might have had a chance!" She took a step closer. It was as if she didn't hear a word I was saying.

She was almost unrecognizable. I rose from where I lay and said softly, "I was captured as well."

"You *lie*," she spat. "Is that what you've been telling yourself? Why didn't they punish you for the same crime I did?" She gave a raspy chuckle. "You knew they were coming and planned this because of what I did to you and Nour. This is all your fault. Look at me!"

She twisted around, and my eyes widened.

Her back showed several marks from the lashes she received. They were not completely healed but were already scarring—she'd be scarred for life. Her skin had been mutilated. Her dress was ripped in several areas from the leather whip.

"Look at my body—my *face*," she hissed. She turned back around and faced me with eyes that had gone wild.

I took a cautious step back, unsure where this was going. Klawdia took a step towards me.

"I didn't leave you, Klawdia. The emperor brought me back," I defended myself.

"The emperor would have never let you go—he would have killed you if he found you himself!" she insisted.

I shook my head and took several steps back as she advanced towards me. What did she want? I looked around, and warriors were stirring awake.

"What's going on?" Maeri croaked from being half asleep.

"*You* did this," she growled. "You deserved to die with your sister and mother. It should have been you, just like it should have been *you* they captured—"

She lunged for me. Before she reached me, I whirled and scurried in the opposite direction through the woods. I passed several sleeping warriors. I glanced back—she had a thin leather strap wrapped around her hand as she came for me. A branch slapped my cheek as I maneuvered through the trees.

Run, run, run. My legs burned and felt like pillars of bricks, but I forced them forward. As Klawdia chased me down, I heard her steps closing in on me—

She took a fistful of my hair and yanked me towards her. When I fell on my back, she attempted to grab ahold of me, but I scrambled to my feet and pushed myself away from her grasp. I felt my hairs being ripped from my scalp. Her hands clawed my face and neck, trying to grab ahold of me. I stumbled backward, fumbled on my knees, and lifted myself, attempting to gain distance.

I felt a pull at my ankle and crashed into the mossy ground. I crawled on my hands and knees away from her, but out of nowhere the leather strap was wrapped around my neck.

She crawled on top of my back, her legs straddling me. The strap squeezed my throat, and my hands flew up to free myself. I couldn't breathe out. I couldn't breathe in.

I tried to call out her name, but nothing came.

Klawdia yanked the strap behind me tighter. "You did this, you cursed witch," she spat. "You're going to wish you were dead along with your sister."

I tried to tell her to stop.

My fingers clawed to find leverage against the rope crushing my throat, desperate for air as darkness closed in around me. She was killing me, but this wasn't the end for me. I refused this death. I wasn't going to leave this world from a leather strap.

My fingers let go of the strap and reached behind me to where I felt her. They found her face and clawed against her mouth and eyes. I heard her growling from the scrapes. I thrashed as hard as I could.

For a moment, she loosened her hold on the strap just enough for me to take a breath. That was all I needed. I thrusted an elbow into her face. Her shoulders went flying off my back, and I scrambled onto my feet, coughing as air entered my chest.

Klawdia screamed from the stinging abrasions to her eyes and cheeks. Without wasting another moment, I ran as quickly as my short legs would allow.

I looked back to see Klawdia trailing behind me, relentless. She had eyes of murder. My body rammed into another's, and I looked up. A warrior had his arms wrapped around mine.

"What is going on here?" His brows drew together, and his head tilted while he stared at my neck.

I couldn't stop heaving, begging for air to live inside me again. I couldn't speak even if I tried.

"I saw her." Kallen appeared alongside Maeri, both panting, as if they'd been chasing us all along. "She attacked this girl. I ran as quickly as I could."

The warrior I'd never met released me and walked to Klawdia. My eyes followed her, making sure there was a safe distance between herself and I. Her eyes went from murderous to fearful real quick. I could see her body trembling from where I stood. Actually, I was barely standing—my hands leaned on my knees to catch an ounce of breath.

"No! She did *this* to me!" Klawdia screamed. The warrior who had caught me had a hand around her arm, pulling her out of the woods. "Let go of me!"

I shook my head, not registering completely what just occurred. I didn't mean for that to happen. I felt like I was just asleep less than five minutes ago in dreamland. I tried to pay attention to the conversation ahead of me. My breathing slowed, air filling my lungs more naturally now.

"Shut it!" The warrior tightened his grip on Klawdia. "Do you know where we send violent people in our country?" He paused. "We send them to Stroka."

Klawdia's eyes widened, her face turning ashen.

"What's your plan with the girl?" Kallen asked, his panting slowing down, mirroring my own.

"Seems like the both of them need a lesson on how to deal with conflict. We don't have time for this nonsense. We'll send them both to Stroka."

My lips parted. *No.*

Kallen's back stiffened. "I'm not sure if that's the wisest choice. This one"—Kallen pointed at me—"healed some of Emperor Aris' wounds. He might not take it too fondly if he found we sent a healer back. We might want to bring him in on this decision."

"No, no need to bother him with trivial matters. We'll just send this one back to Stroka. She's been a constant nuisance anyway," the warrior grunted. He pulled Klawdia with him.

"You can't possibly. Please, I beg of you!" Klawdia cried, attempting to pull her arm free of his grasp.

"That's where you'll be sent as punishment..." The warrior's voice faded along with their presence.

But I had a feeling this wouldn't be her last effort to end my existence.

Maeri was across from me and she stared with wide eyes. I was sure she was wondering what happened, but she didn't intrude. I felt a burning, stinging sensation around my neck. My hand went to the raw, open, and inflamed skin that encircled my throat. I flinched at the touch.

I hadn't noticed until now that my limbs were shaking uncontrollably. I had gone into survival mode, though it didn't feel much different from the last couple weeks. Perhaps, I was just getting used to the feeling that every day depended on how much I wanted to live it.

If I gave up just a little, I'd die.

Looking towards the edge of the woods where Klawdia disappeared, the rest of the woken up warriors around began to pack their belongings and we began our journey to Siniya once more.

I now focused on my breath, my steps, and my pain. The burn around my neck, in a way, felt like company. I finally felt something; pain replaced the numb feeling that once filled me. I thought perhaps I was losing my mind, because it felt comforting to have something that caused me to feel something.

Chapter Fourteen

Nirelle was her name. The third slave Maeri and I traveled with.

She was quiet, but not as quiet as me. She was young and cheerful, petite—a far comparison from Maeri. Nirelle felt like home in some way. Familiar. Maybe it was her soft brown eyes and her round face, but she felt safe. Maybe it was the way she'd distract us from where we were heading to with her sweet outbursts of random things she wanted us to know. One moment it was to vent about a certain boy who was most likely dead, and the next it would be how her hair was getting tangled up with pines in the dirt during our sleep. Out of the three of us, she seemed to not have a care in the world and enjoyed even the darkest of moments. She would tilt her head up to the sky, smile, and say there was something for us to learn today. Her presence felt like a warm hug.

I would comment every now and then, but mostly Maeri and Nirelle spoke while I stayed in my own world. Both of them didn't mention to anyone else that I was not, in fact, a mute and completely capable of speaking for myself. I felt like I could trust them in this small way. I thought, in my mind, this was my own way of surviving in this new, treacherous world.

Tonight I felt the tables turning in our favor when Nirelle, Maeri, and I came upon two large trees. This was to be our bed tonight, and it happened to be near an abandoned fire most likely from some drunken warriors. We didn't know where they went off to, but if we had only a little time near the fire, it was worth it.

As Nirelle and I lay together in front of the fire, I stared into the flames, begging for it to show the course of the rest of my life. My long red hair spread ahead of me on the dirt in loose waves, now reflecting the red flames. Funny how fire illuminated a path, yet many believed hell was filled with fire. It made no sense. How could something so full of light be filled with so much darkness?

I took a deep breath, the clean, moist air filling my lungs, and for a moment, I felt at peace being so close to the earth. I could almost feel the earth breathing along with me, as if it were comforting me, letting me know I wasn't alone. We each had a long, dark linen given to us by the cook that didn't give us any warmth but gave us a false sense of safety. Regardless, I was grateful for it.

Days were long, but the nights were no different. We spent most of our nights searching for warmth between ourselves and the earth under the open sky, surrounded by the woods. Sleep was a luxury in a predicament like ours, as we tossed and turned, aware of all the footsteps nearby. We would pick large trunks to sleep nearby that would offer some sort of coverage between us and the prowling predators in the dark. They allowed us some freedom to choose where we slept, but the reality was there were only a few of us and a multitude of them. We were surrounded at all times. None of us dared to escape with the repercussion of Klawdia's lashes still fresh in our minds.

"Good night, ladies," Nirelle whispered sweetly between us.

"Night," mumbled Maeri, half asleep already.

I hoped I would find rest tonight. My body ached for it. I was so tired.

My body felt heavy and hard to hold up from the lack of rest. Finny fed us when she could, and the creek we came across replenished our thirst and bathing needs, but my body ached from the constant journey. My wound had gotten infected several times despite the washing I'd give it and the herbs I'd found.

Taking a deeper breath in and releasing it, I felt myself drifting off to sleep. I listened to the crickets sing to me nearby, but I also heard wild animals making sounds I couldn't quite place. Howling like a wolf, if I had to guess. Then I heard shouting and cheering from the warriors.

I opened my eyes. I looked over. Nirelle and Maeri were sound asleep. Was I hearing things in my mind? A loud *pop* vibrated through my ears, enough that I got up to see what the commotion was about. How did they not hear that?

Wrapping the dark linen around my head and shoulders, I got up to inspect the strange sounds I heard in the distance. I walked around Nirelle and Maeri, careful of where I stepped with the crushing of the leaves and rocks beneath my feet. The broad trees covered the night sky, leaving it hard to see anything ahead.

As I approached the howling sounds and loud pops in the air, I noticed a large fire further on surrounded by a crowd. It seemed to be a celebration of some sort. The fire was so large in the small clearing, it seemed almost unnatural.

As I stood on a hill, a safe distance from the commotion, I could see them dancing, waving their arms high in the sky around the fire. Shouting and chanting echoed through the canyon. Drums were being played near the fire, and there were bottles of liquor being passed amongst themselves.

A party.

This is not safe. I should not be here.

But wanting to stay and admire held stronger than what my brain was telling me: run. My eyes and ears filled with the colors, the music, the dancing, this party, celebration, whatever it was. I was hypnotized by the energy.

Another person came into the dancing circle, moving freely with her eyes high in the sky—Camilla. Beautiful Camilla. The crowd surrounding her clapped their hands to the beat of the drum as she danced around and around the growing burning fire. Her hair flowed behind her, dressed in flowers and feathers.

Without my consent, my feet began to descend the hill towards the crowd. I didn't know why I was, but I felt a pull there. It wasn't like me to do something like this at all. But I wanted a clearer view, and standing on the hill was more suspicious than being inconspicuous in the crowd, right?

I bit my lower lip. What was I doing?

I tightened my linen around my head and body as I maneuvered towards the center. I bumped into a few large warriors, but no one noticed me as I came upon the edge of the crowd near the fire.

It was warm, crackling, and beautiful.

Camilla finished her dance and fell to the ground on her back gracefully, giggling and throwing her legs seductively in the air. The drums and chanting grew louder and louder. She got onto her hands and knees and crawled captivatingly towards one side of the crowd, towards Aris.

My mind flashed back in time. His face dripping in bright red blood, holding a still-beating heart in his hands. My stomach churned, though I'd worked on erasing the memory from my mind.

I shouldn't be standing here, staring at him.

In this moment, amidst the festivities, there was something different about him. He didn't seem like the lethal predator that could kill at any moment like the first day. Aris wore his normal leather armor strapped across his chest and waist. His arms were crossed over his chest, and he looked slightly entertained by the dance. He was beautiful, like the devil. Standing there near the fire, it was hard to resist thinking otherwise. It was…tempting to continue looking at him. Memorizing his face, his body, his posture. It was hard to think in that moment someone so beautiful could lead a legion to slaughter villages. Did darkness always appear so sweet?

The fire reflected against his onyx hair and eyes, glistening. He was magnetic. Even the crowds were drawn to him and Camilla.

Camilla reached the emperor. She spread her long, elegant fingers on his legs, stabilizing herself. She held on to his legs as she wormed and swayed her hips on her way up to his face. The beating of the drums continued. She locked both hands on his neck, tiptoed to reach up, and slowly licked the side of his face, and the crowd went wild. She was claiming her territory.

Instantly, the warriors around Aris grabbed his sculpted body and hoisted him in the air. The drums continued beating, the warriors carrying him around the fire. They cheered and praised with fists in the air as they chanted.

It was the first time I heard a laugh roar from his chest. It filled the air, and it left me breathless. His grin was wide and showed his perfect set of pearly white teeth. For a moment, I forgot where I was.

I forgot how to breathe. And, for a moment, I forgot who I was as I heard Aris' laugh carry across the fire.

Eventually the warriors released Aris to the ground, tugging on him and laughing with each other. Then Aris disappeared into the large crowd. While I was standing at the edge, watching, I wondered if he didn't like the attention much. Being an emperor seemed to carry a lot of the world's attention. I wondered if it weighed heavily on him as much as the thought did in my mind.

I would have hardly considered myself anybody important before I was captured and definitely not anybody now as a captive, and that weighed heavily on my chest. The thought of being invisible, even though I thought I preferred it. I wondered what it was like to be a person everyone had their eyes on at every moment. I wondered if that felt heavy, too.

I noticed many slurring their words, bumping into each other, intoxicated, and sliding with each other's bodies into a mesmerizing dance. Without my consent, I was pulled too inward toward the fire, and I squeezed myself through the sweaty bodies so I could breathe the cleaner air on the outside of...whatever this was. I'd never been to anything like this before.

Finally, I reached the outer edge of the crowd and started to walk uphill. I sat at a nearby tree and gazed at the party.

Even though these people were the reason for my pain and suffering, it was nice to feel normal for one night. No one noticed me. I had nothing to do, and nowhere to be. It wasn't like me to find much entertainment from the dancing and the drinking, but it reminded me of something else other than war and destruction. A part of me felt guilty about that.

After a few peaceful moments, my ears perked at some sounds around the corner behind me. I tilted my head out of curiosity.

"You were one hell of an animal out there." Tobias.

Someone snickered. It was Camilla. I knew her voice.

"Dancing has been a gift of mine ever since I was a little girl," she said softly.

"Do you think he sees through it?"

"Why do you ask? Do you think he does?" Camilla asked.

"I'm not entirely sure, but if I were him, I wouldn't be able to keep my hands off you," he said, his voice low and husky.

"Well, that's why he's the emperor and you're *you*, a thirsty, barbaric warrior," she snapped. "He's got more important things to do than have sex with me. He's smart. It's going to take time. I told you this already."

Instantly, I cringed hearing their conversation, and I knew I had to get the hell out of there. How could she be with Tobias when I thought she was with the emperor? She seemed so intimate with him. And wasn't Tobias Strokan? What was he doing on this journey traveling to Siniya?

"You don't actually have feelings for him, do you?"

"He is kind to me, Tobias."

"You're a fool, Camilla, if you think this could be something more. He doesn't trust anyone," he muttered.

"Tell me something I don't know."

A moment passed.

"Well? Do you have any information for me?" Tobias grunted. "Anything that you might have seen or heard?"

"I haven't heard. I guess that's something, right? He is loyal. I am sure of it," Camilla said quietly. "Otherwise something would have come up by now."

"Trying isn't working. If you don't have anything for me soon, you're compromised. I didn't think you were foolish enough, but you're as good as dead then."

"You wouldn't dare," Camilla breathed.

"I don't give a shit," Tobias hissed.

I didn't want to hear any more of their strange conversation. I felt like I overheard something I wasn't meant to hear, and all I wanted to do was wash my ears—if that were even a thing to do. I got up as quietly as I could and walked down the hill back to where the party was. Weaving on the outskirts of the festivities, I looked for the path to Maeri and Nirelle. The air was heavy and warm with the high energy of the crowd.

Many had left the fire and were more scattered than before, grouped up in twos and threes. Those that stayed back continued the animalistic dance ritual. The bonfire was as great and mesmerizing as before, never faltering.

I kept my head wrapped tightly and my eyes glued to the ground. As I walked further, I noticed there were more smaller fires around like the one by Maeri and Nirelle. My ears heard strange moaning from beside me. I glanced up, wondering what it was.

Grinding against each other, there was a warrior and another woman with barely anything covering their naked bodies on the ground near one of the smaller fires afar. My heart sprinted. What was this? She seemed like she was in pain or suffocating but also enjoying it by the sounds that were coming from her body. Confused, I shook my head, and I quickened my pace.

That was sex. It had to be.

I had never seen or experienced anything like that before. That was nothing like what I witnessed between Camilla and Aris. They were not having sex when I saw them fooling around, though they might have if Aris hadn't stopped what they were doing once he saw me. I swallowed, remembering that moment.

A motion caught the corner of my eye, and I regretted looking when I saw a man thrusting his bare hips into a woman against the tree. Her face looked so painful, her mouth wide open and brows furrowed. Heat flushed my neck and cheeks, and I stumbled in my steps. I glanced the other way, my hand rushing to cover my mouth that had just turned warm.

A few people laughed amongst themselves at another nearby fire, causing me to flinch, afraid of what I would see next. I hadn't realized it until now, but I was full-body shaking. I told myself I was safe. There was no need to be afraid of such frivolous things. The group near me thankfully had their clothes on and were only drinking excessively.

Without thinking, my feet picked up speed. I passed the nearby fire and headed straight into the darkness. Before I knew it, I was running, and my linen tore from me. I didn't care. I had to keep running away from this place. My breath faltered, and it was getting harder to gasp for air. I needed to get away. In the darkness, my foot caught on the large root of a tree, and my hands planted on the ground as I fell forward.

I couldn't believe my eyes and what I just witnessed. Was this normal? It looked like it could be so painful for the women but oddly pleasurable as well. It was all too confusing and overwhelming. I shook the disturbing mental images from my mind.

I contemplated sleeping here in the darkness away from the fires. I was so tired. Maybe I was feeling queasy from the infection, but I barely had the energy. It was nice to feel the cool wet ground against my cheek. It calmed the warmth building up in my throat.

Something rustled just to my left. I looked up, and there was a man sitting under a nearby tree. He must have noticed me because he gradually and silently rose to his feet. Through the darkness, I could see his silhouette heading towards me. Scrambling up, I stumbled back but balanced myself for the possible attack.

As the man approached like a fox through the night, the moonlight appeared through the trees and showed his face. It was Kallen.

His brown eyes peered through the darkness. "What are you doing here?"

I swallowed the words that left me startled.

"You shouldn't be here." He stepped towards me, his voice low and nervous. That was obvious; I should not be here.

Cautiously, I took a step backward, away from him. What did he want from me? They took my body as a captive. Would he now take my vow from me too? He must have noticed the state I was in because he reached out with his hand.

Everything seemed blurry and hard to focus. Without thinking, I ran in the direction towards Maeri and Nirelle, hoping my legs wouldn't give out again. As soon as I thought he would outrun me, I heard no one around. I glanced over my shoulder. Kallen didn't follow me.

I was safe.

After what seemed like eternity, I reached their sleeping bodies. What was left of the fire at this point were small embers. It must have been early in the morning. No one claimed the fire, and since I had no linen to warm my body anymore, I decided to risk it and sleep by it.

I curled on the ground near the fire, clutching my empty core. I couldn't think of anything else but the nausea that had crept in slowly and now thrashed against my side. Nothing came up, but my eyes slammed shut from the pain that stabbed me.

At this point, there was no way I could protect myself from an intruder, from a warrior if he desired to do what I witnessed the other men do to the women. I wouldn't be able to protect myself.

CHAPTER FIFTEEN

I thought I was slowly dying. My body had been deprived of necessities. Water and food needed for a body walking miles a day were basically nonexistent. The following days were agonizing as my body raged against me. I grew weaker, weight slid off of me continuously, and yet it was so heavy carrying myself through the days and nights. I began to question my mental clarity, what I saw the other night, and wondered if it had all been a dream. A nightmare, really.

Finny must have noticed because she snuck me extra nuts and fruit behind the warriors' backs. I couldn't remember the last moment I had received such kindness, and I took it graciously, sharing as much as I could with Nirelle and Maeri. Finny was an enemy disguised as an angel.

Because that was what they were: my enemies. And always would be for what they did to me and my village. I never felt connected to the village I grew up in or to the people there, but I had felt very protective of them since the attack.

We eventually came to another stop during the day. There was talk between the warriors nearby discussing if this was a place we would stay for a night. Curious, I surveyed my new environment. I had been so focused the last few days only on my feet, step by step, I barely noticed the new greenery we had entered. The trees were more luscious, and the air seemed brighter. It was almost painful to look around.

Then, I heard it. The water near us. It was loud and completely riveting.

Everyone started setting up for the night. There were a few already stripping naked and running towards the water through the trees. The energy had picked up in the legion. Excitement and laughter filled the air.

My fingers started tingling at just the thought of taking my first proper bath in what felt like forever, but it had only been six weeks. It wasn't me who had been counting but Maeri. She was observant like that. My body needed the cleaning, ached for it. I didn't realize washing my hair and body was a luxury until recently.

Finny packed a small bag and motioned Maeri, Nirelle and I alongside her. We walked a while further in silence, to where the crowds were sparser, pulling hanging branches and leaves away from our path. The sounds of the river guided us through the lush and thick woods.

We reached a shore filled with light brown pebbles that gradually slid into a small river. I stopped in my path to pause and take in my new surroundings. The river was not as wide as I expected but deep enough for the perfect bath. I could probably swim for a few minutes and eventually reach the other side of the river. The turquoise water rippled around large rocks that lay in the riverbed that were casting a shadow around it. It was perfect.

The waters and its heavy rolling sounds were inviting, beckoning me towards it. The river continued on each side and curved where I could no longer see.

There were no others around in this small cove except for us, so I stripped myself bare and plunged into the deep crystal-green waters without thinking twice.

The waters welcomed me with a cooling and healing effect that made it feel almost magical to be in. It sparkled from the sun's reflection. I took my time as I cleaned my body, my face, my hair. I gave extra love to my throat, where the pain from the leather burn eased, with the water cooling it instantly. I was glad it was finally healing, even though it was taking its sweet time. I couldn't imagine how gruesome it must have looked.

Nirelle wrapped her arms around herself before dipping her toes and retracting them just as quickly. "The air is getting cooler. I can tell we're heading further and further north. Isn't that right, Finny?"

"Yes, child," Finny replied, and she laid out a small linen cloth scattered with nuts and fruit. With a pinched expression, she said, "But we'll be heading into warmer months before you know it. And no need to fret if you're worried about getting a chill once you've bathed; it's warm enough outside for you to be dry quickly."

Nirelle nodded. "How long will we be in winter?"

"For about two months more, maybe three depending on how the gods took our relatively long departure."

"Can you tell us what it's like in Siniya?" Maeri asked with eyes that sparkled.

I focused on rubbing my hair in the river, letting all the weeks' filth disappear in the cool, clear waters. I didn't have one ounce of care of what Siniya was like or what the people were like. I got a good idea just by traveling with them. Savages.

"What do you want to know?" Finny started taking her boots off.

"What are the people like? Are they always angry?" Maeri spoke softly.

Finny smiled, eyes distant. "My people don't keep to themselves. Everyone knows everybody's business, and that's how it's always been." Finny paused. "No, Maeri, we aren't angry people, but we're not happy either—we haven't been for a while. But we're in a much better place than where we were. We're still healing."

Nirelle crossed her arms over her chest, one eyebrow raised while her lip turned into a pout. "I don't understand any of your vague remarks."

Finny chuckled. "You don't need to."

"The water is a bit too cold. I'm not getting in just yet. I'll wait for the sun to shine brighter this afternoon." Nirelle sat down on the wet, pebbled ground.

"You stink, child. Get in and wash your hair." Finny's voice became firmer, as if Nirelle really were her child. Nirelle could have been if I didn't know any better.

Not a moment later, Maeri's voice echoed through the river. My head swung toward her as she sang the most enchanting melody. My heart skipped a beat, and my hands paused in the middle of washing. I'd never heard a voice so soft and angelic.

I used this time to dive into the river and felt the waters go over my head. I heard its echoes bouncing in my ears. Slowly approaching the other side of the river, I came up gracefully for some breath. I could still hear Maeri's sweet voice. Across the river were two large boulders near its shore, almost protecting it with its strength and presence. In between the boulders was a smaller cove, where I would be alone with my thoughts. I dove deep and swam underneath for as long as I could hold my breath.

I didn't come up until my lungs almost collapsed, and I inhaled the clean air into my chest. I had finally reached the other side of the river and noticed the bushes near the shore that overlapped the waters. As I approached, my toes touched the bottom of the riverbed, allowing me some stability once again.

Glancing up at the shrubs that extended into the river, I recognized some of them in books I used to flip through in Fenrah's cottage. They were even more beautiful in person than the drawings.

As I reached for one of the leaves, the river settled around my hips, leaving my chest exposed to the chilly air. The waters felt warmer, beckoning me to return. My wet hair reached the top of my backside as I studied the herb in front of me.

I heard some conversations along with Maeri's singing across the river, but I had no desire to look up or pay attention. For years, it'd only been mostly me and my thoughts, apart from Fenrah and occasional customers. I'd grown to like my mind and my peace. It was difficult for obvious reasons the last weeks, but one that I hadn't considered was just constantly being in the presence of people.

I twirled the leaf around my fingers, observing the light color and the sharp edges. I lifted the white bleeding leaf to my nose and inhaled its herbal scent. How nice it felt being in my own world, no matter how unimportant or small it was. I didn't matter to anyone else, and there was beauty in that.

But I did *belong* to someone else. There was no such thing as *my own world* now.

My back soaked up the warm rays of the sun as one of the girls swam near me. I felt the water splash around my hips. Maeri's voice hadn't faltered across the river, so it had to be Nirelle. I heard the water ripple more than they did before.

"Nirelle, you finally stopped complaining and decided to join me?" I turned to find Aris in the water.

There were several other men, warriors, over where Maeri, Finny and Nirelle—damn her—were, and they were munching on the food Finny had laid out.

As I realized what was happening and that half of my body was still exposed, I submerged myself in the water. My face flushed a deep shade of red and I could feel my neck burning.

"Aris, where are you going?" I heard a man shout from the shore in my direction.

The emperor had most likely seen me, regardless of him not meeting my eyes. I swallowed the lump that rose in my throat. They must have followed Maeri's voice. The rest of the warriors inhaled the food with Nirelle and Maeri, who now had stopped singing. Damn her, too.

My mind went a thousand miles per minute. *Gods, I'm such an idiot.*

Attempting to remain inconspicuous, with the hopes he didn't see me, I took a deep breath and swam towards one of the large boulders on my right. I held my breath until my pale fingers felt the mossy green boulder under the waters, and I followed around it. When I felt I was around the boulder, safe from the view of the others across the shore, I came up for air.

The fifteen-foot-high boulder covered me as I expected. I pressed my bare shoulders on the large cold rock and closed my eyes to focus on my breath. I wouldn't go back until they were gone, I decided. I was safe here, away from any attention. I sunk my feet into the sand, allowing my body to glide in the water at shoulder height. My copper hair pooled around me, at odds with the blues and greens that surrounded me.

At this distance, across the shore and away from the group, I couldn't hear their conversations anymore. It was quiet again. I smiled to myself, feeling victorious.

"I suspected it."

My eyes flew open. I saw Aris only a few feet from me, standing on the riverbed.

"You've hidden very well the fact that you can speak. I was almost convinced you were a mute. I rarely miss these things."

For a moment, I forgot how to breathe. He looked like a river god, his dark hair wet and his strong tan face peering into me. His strong, tattooed chest was well above the water, clearly too tall for a bath on this side of the river. The waters glided over his body and scars.

I felt my body tense so much I wouldn't be able move even if I wanted to. *Remember what he is*, I reminded myself. He was dangerous, murderous, destructive.

When I didn't respond, he continued, "Did you enjoy the show the other night? I didn't take you for a girl who liked parties."

I didn't. I never went to parties, but he didn't need to know that. He didn't need to know anything about me. And when did he see me the other night? Did he really have to notice everything?

"Reverting to the charade of not speaking again, are you?" Aris smirked.

I knew, then, there was no way I could continue to fool him. I felt his black eyes penetrate my soul's existence, and my heart slammed itself into starting again, not giving my heart a moment to settle.

I narrowed my eyes—but only for a moment. "I—I heard noise."

Aris' lips curved like he won the battle. My eyes fluttered to the water in front of me. I wanted to disappear under it and never return to the surface. I could feel the heat rising to the tops of my ears. We were both naked in the waters merely a few feet from each other. I was thankful for the little modesty that the waters were giving me and him. Was this normal for him? Was this normal for the Siniyan people?

"I looked for you," he said. My eyes met his. "Where did you go after?"

I contemplated his question. Where did I go? Where did he see me? At the dance circle? Was he talking about when I ran from the gathering, from people having sex? Almost puked my guts out, sick, running back to my fire?

"It was getting late," I whispered.

"It wasn't safe for you there." His voice turned dark. He took a step towards me. By impulse, I sidestepped in the water, following the rock away from Aris.

I doubt this is much safer from that night, I thought to reply—but of course, I didn't.

His eyes followed my movement. "This feels familiar." He chuckled, and it made my body instantly tingle.

Before I could even blink, he was in front of me.

He frowned, his eyes narrowing. My body froze at the sudden change, causing my chest to lift ever so slightly from the protective waters. My breathing quickened as he placed his hand under my jaw, lifting it to the side. Though his touch was gentle, I flinched, and he noticed that, too. The moment he slaughtered that warrior and ripped his heart out kept pressing on my mind.

"Who did this to you?" he asked lowly. The muscles in the sides of his neck strained against his skin.

I swallowed and closed my eyes. I couldn't think of my next choice of words. It was hard to concentrate with him so close to me.

"Who did this?" He forced my face back to meet his gaze once more.

I kept my eyes on the waters, afraid of what he'd see with those empty soul-burning eyes. I walked through my scenarios as quickly as I could. Telling him about Klawdia was pointless since she had been sent to Stroka. If punishment was what he would seek, or if he were to kill her, that would be on my conscience. I couldn't afford that. And why did he care? Wasn't he the emperor of a land of heartless people?

I attempted to lift my jaw from his hold, but he didn't give in. I clenched my teeth and pursed my lips. A muscle in his jaw twitched.

"Who?" His voice rose, which caused me to tremble, the water rippling around me.

"It was nobody. I got stuck." I lifted my eyes to his so that I looked convincing enough for him to let go of me.

That was lame, Solei. Be smarter.

"Liar."

My nostrils flared. "I don't remember who or what happened."

"You are lying." His brows lifted slightly as he stepped closer.

"Let me go," I whispered. He didn't budge. "Please."

His body was close enough that I could feel the warmth radiate from his body into mine. It was getting harder and harder to argue with him.

"I'll let you go if you answer my question."

"I told you, I don't know." I kept his gaze. "There's your answer."

Aris laughed, and his entire body shook with the waters gliding around his bare chest. It took my breath away. Damn me. I might have even forgotten who he was for a moment. He looked so human right here, right now. He didn't seem like the murderous man I had witnessed weeks ago.

"That's not an answer."

"According to who?" I asked, casting him a glance.

No longer amused, Aris' face became serious. Detached. "*Me.*"

The emperor. His eyes were vacant and cold.

"It's the best I've got to offer you." My eyes dropped as I lied—pathetically.

Aris seemed to think for a moment. "Then answer this: what's your name?"

What was it worth to him? Was this how he spoke to all captives or prisoners of war?

"My name..." I hesitated for a moment. "Is Solei."

"Solei." He tasted my name in his mouth. That shouldn't have made warmth rush across my face and down my core, but it did. "Like the sun."

I couldn't believe myself because I already knew from the others, but I asked, "Yours?"

"Aris." He didn't hesitate. He was proud. A moment passed as he seemed to be thinking deeply about something. "You remind me of someone I once knew."

Who could I possibly remind him of? I wouldn't be surprised if he had toyed with another redheaded woman in the past.

Clearly, he was happy with his one answer because he gently let go of my jaw with a smirk. He leaned back, seemingly at ease, but kept his stance close to me. I slid my shoulders back under the protective waters. Hesitating, I swam to the side of the boulder to gain more distance between us. He didn't try to stop me, his eyes following, watching my every movement.

I wondered what he was thinking about this moment. I almost felt his eyes tightening on me.

We remained in the small cove. Then, I remembered why I wanted to be as far away from him as possible now that I wasn't cornered by him like an animal. I was able to think clearly again. My stomach twisted. This didn't feel right. This wasn't normal.

He was the predator and I the prey, I reminded myself. I kept my distance, treading to stay afloat in the water. My body screamed for me to *go* now that I wasn't in his reach.

"How did you learn to use the herbs as medicine?" he asked curiously, his body turned towards me now.

"From a healer."

"And you were?"

"Her apprentice," I responded. "Not a witch, unfortunately."

Aris laughed again. My stomach flipped. "I never thought you were one."

"You would be the first." Everyone who met me immediately thought of me as dangerous and not to be trusted; even Maeri and Nirelle were skeptical at first. But in that moment, I believed him, and it felt nice to not feel like I had to explain myself—for once.

Someone saw me solely for who I was and not for who they thought I was.

He shrugged. "I don't care for superstitions."

I wondered if he cared for anything at all. Knowing I could very well get struck in the face by him, it didn't stop me from asking, "What did that man do?"

He seemed to know exactly who I was talking about. "The murderer was a gambling addict—was in significant debt. Couldn't pay it off when he bargained for more than he had. Instead of working more than he wanted to, he sold his son to Stroka for the money to repay the debt. When Ures, one of my men, found out...well, you know the rest. The traitor had to bury the evidence that would incriminate him."

That man sold his own son. "You still found out despite..." *Ures being murdered*, was what I didn't need to say.

"It's my job to."

"What would have happened to him for selling his son?" I breathed.

Aris' jaw tightened. "He wouldn't have had a home in Siniya for the crime he did to himself, to his family, and to his people."

"And his son? Is he in Stroka now, as a slave because of what his father did?" I asked.

"As for his son, I have plans on buying his freedom back from whomever was foolish enough to buy him and return him home—to Siniya, where he belongs. I'll kill those who bought him, as well. There are too many of them, anyway."

He said it so casually, I almost questioned my hearing. Gooseflesh spread throughout my skin. I hoped he didn't see, and if he did, he marked it off as the water being too cold.

"Aris!" I heard a man shout across the shore.

We couldn't see them, but I was sure they knew where we were.

"*Arriis*, come eat!" another shouted louder. They must have been his trusted warriors if they were speaking to him so informally.

Aris chuckled softly, but he seemed hesitant to leave. His chest rose as he inhaled. "Will you join me?"

I looked down toward my naked body. The only thing covering me from being fully exposed was the water surrounding me. All I wanted was my linen dress to be wrapped around me, protecting me.

"Are you hungry?" he pressed.

"I can always eat," I answered. My stomach growled, and I wondered if he could notice the weight loss in my body.

"I'm glad to hear that." He paused, seemingly contemplating something, and added, "Though, it doesn't seem that your pickpocketing took you very far, did it?" Amusement filled his voice.

I nearly smiled but refused the temptation. Refusing to entertain his tactics. So, he noticed I stuffed my pockets at the war camp. Of course, he did.

"No, it didn't," I muttered. "If you hadn't caught me, it would have."

"If I hadn't caught you, you would have been *butchered*," he snapped, and I was glad we had distance between each other to hide my recoil.

Moody, moody emperor.

I lowered my eyes from his. He did save me from the lashes that would have left scars on my back like Klawdia.

"Let's eat." He swam past me in the direction of the rest of the group. I meekly followed. As I stayed in the protective waters, I noticed how fitting Maeri seemed with the new company. She was blossoming in a way I hadn't seen before. Her cheeks flushed pink while she engaged vibrantly with the warriors, laughing and smiling.

"Ah, there you are," one of the warriors greeted Aris and left his conversation with Maeri. He was half naked, wearing only dark red pants. "How were the waters?"

"It's exactly what I needed. Especially after last night's hunt. My body's sore," Aris answered as he walked onto shore, shaking the water from his dark hair. His friend with the red pants threw him his brown trousers.

I ducked my head, not expecting to see his backside. I flushed a deep shade of red. *Does no one care for some decency in this foreign land?*

Maeri seemed to stare, biting her lower lip. The audacity and confidence of this woman reminded me of my sister. I smiled just thinking about it. No wonder they were friends at one time.

I stopped where I knew I was covered. I would not allow my body to be exposed.

I waited for Nirelle or Maeri's attention and finally caught Maeri's eyes. I gave her a look that said, *Help me before I freeze to death out here. I need my clothes.* She pulled away, laughing with the other warrior, and hurried close to where I stood and tossed me my linen dress.

My dress landed near me in the water. Close enough.

I pulled the dress over my head and walked to the shore, pulling my dress down as I walked up. The dress soaked up the water left on my skin, leaving little to the imagination. I shivered from the biting cold. My body wanted to go back into the waters, but I knew food was a dire need at this point.

I wrapped my arms around my chest as I approached the group. Walking around them, I found a midsize rock to sit on and hoped that my dress would dry soon.

Why were they here? I just wished they would all disappear and leave me alone on this rock.

"About three days' time, Beshien, and the parties will begin." The warrior near Maeri with long hair embraced Beshien in celebration.

"About damn time," Beshien with the red pants said warily.

"Tell me more about these parties. What are they like?" Maeri asked.

"I'll tell you what they're like: they're nothing like the Stroka's," Beshien replied, and laughter exploded through the warriors, including Aris and Finny. Like an inside joke that only Siniyan people would understand.

The energy shifted. It seemed like a moment where they could finally breathe freely. Maeri joined them. She was a natural actress.

"So, you're saying you're different?" Maeri continued. Was this how she always was? Asking more questions than was safe?

"Trust me, girl, it's nothing like you've ever experienced."

If they were anything like the other night, I'd stay far away from other festivities the Siniyans threw.

"I'll just be glad not to smell their stink anymore," the long-haired warrior chimed in.

"I wouldn't count on it, Justir," Beshien said. "I'm sure they'll still be around more than we'd like them to be. Like the usual. They always seem to be lurking somewhere nearby."

Justir clicked his tongue. "Fuckin' bastards."

"It is what it is." Beshien bit into a peeled orange. The orange looked deliciously sweet, my stomach agreeing.

"Don't worry about such things. Let me do the thinking, will you?" Aris said curtly and popped a few almonds in his mouth. A piece of his wet black hair curved slightly into his forehead. Aris was the tallest amongst the warriors and seemingly the strongest. His entire being was so large, I wouldn't be surprised if it took all the air around us just to supply his lung capacity. It was hard not to stare; I didn't blame Maeri and her goggling eyes.

Finny went around offering nuts to the rest of the warriors.

"You don't need to. That's why we're in your council, is it not?" Beshien smirked.

"No, that's not why, Beshien," Aris corrected him with a lethal calm, his power thundering through the group. "Better you than advisors who will constantly pester me with their inane opinions."

For a moment, it felt as though everyone held their breath. Not one warrior responded to Aris or countered his words. Maybe he *really* didn't trust anyone, like Tobias mentioned the other night. He clearly didn't trust his warriors, his own council, to give them their opinions and advice. What a lonely world he lived in for such a powerful man.

Aris turned to Finny and snapped his fingers towards me and the girls, making a silent demand to feed us. Finny bowed her head, obeying him. Nirelle took a seat next to Justir, who also shared his fill with her.

Beshien faced Aris and spoke in a low voice intended for only his ears, but I still heard it.

"You know that you don't need to carry this all on your own, Aris."

"There's nothing to carry, so drop it." Aris levelled a vacant, cold stare at Beshien. His finger tapped his crossed arm, seemingly growing more irritating by the minute. "This is what I was raised to do. I fight."

Conversation continued with Finny as she passed some food to Nirelle and Maeri.

"I haven't recognized you in months. Maybe even years," Beshien whispered to Aris.

"We all change, Beshien." Aris leaned away from his grasp. "And I think you've had too much to drink."

The men laughed except for Aris. He shook his head, popped a few more almonds in his mouth, and looked about. For a moment, he seemed like he was searching for a way to escape. I knew that it was impossible. There must have been a reaction happening from the mix of foreign fruit and almonds in my body because clearly, I wasn't seeing things correctly.

"Why are you so far from the front of the legion?" sweet Nirelle asked the long-haired man, Justir.

"We do so every now and then to get our reports and keep the warriors in check. Plus, it's a nice change of scenery. Heard some singing. Thought maybe we'd see some new faces." Justir winked at Nirelle.

She flushed beet-red and fluttered her eyes downward. "How do you like living in Siniya?" Nirelle was also relentless with these damn questions.

"It's much better than where we came from— I can tell you that. We came from Stroka— most of us did, anyway. Siniya was barely sustainable, but now with it being rebuilt, it's starting to thrive. But there are still some people who refuse to let go of traditions from Stroka."

"What kind of traditions?"

Something flickered across Justir's face. "Branding. Torture. Cages. *Slavery*, to name a few."

"You don't like those traditions?"

"Not particularly," Justir said softly. He added, "But it takes time to progress."

Chapter Sixteen

I woke up with a start, the sensation of droplets trickling onto my face. I sat up, only to be met with biting cold because the fire had diminished. Shivers ran through me as the relentless rain drummed through the dark woods. How long had I been out here in this storm?

I couldn't see anything but the embers of the fire that were fading by the second. I hadn't realized how cold the nights were when I had Nirelle and Maeri with me. It might have been genuine or a survival strategy, but they had found a place to lay other than our usual sleeping arrangements. Maeri had paired with Beshien—I could still hear their giggling in my mind—and Nirelle joined Justir. He was twice the size of Nirelle, but something about him seemed calm, genuine, and less threatening than Aris. Although I was worried about Maeri and Nirelle, I was thankful that they would have more warmth tonight than the last few weeks. I wasn't so sure about their safety. Unlike them, something in my blood told me not to trust these men.

At first, Maeri and Nirelle had seen to me having a fire nearby before they went on with their evening, which I was not going to be a part of no matter how much begging Maeri performed. They gave up only after I refused them ten times.

With the little sight the dwindling cinders gave me, I walked over to the trees that surrounded me, hoping to find coverage from their low-hanging branches and leaves. The rain had completely soaked through my linen dress, leaving my body shaking uncontrollably and my teeth rattling in my mouth.

A crashing thunder echoed in the woods. I felt the earth shake.

Pressing my hand on tree trunks to stabilize my steps, I found one that seemed large enough to have branches and leaves to cover most of the rain. I slid down to the bottom of the trunk and brought my legs to my chest. How was I going to sleep through the night with this icy rain and wind? I closed my eyes and focused on my breath.

For a moment, I wondered if I should go find Maeri and Nirelle. Maybe they had some coverage they'd be able to offer me. That moment fled as quickly as it came to mind. I realized then, I felt safer alone, and I knew this would be a short storm. This was just the peak.

But no matter how much I told my body that I was fine, it continued to shake violently against the bark of the tree. The storm had picked up, raging through the woods. I could hear the wind howling whispers of death. My teeth chattered like never before. I rubbed my arms and legs aggressively to bring back the warmth to the surface of my skin. At this point, I felt my bones were just as cold as my exterior.

Streaking blasts of lightning passed through the woods, and I could make out the wall of rain pouring through. I wasn't going to make it through the night in these conditions. My body at this point was less than ideal to handle anything other than sunny with a gentle breeze.

I felt my body freeze and empty, and my mind wondered where in the ground my brother was. I wondered if he felt just as alone and cold buried in a place where there was no love, no warmth. Was he alone and cold? Yes, he was in a place where there was no laughter to be heard, no arms that I could hold. There would never be a day where I'd see him grow old, and somehow they told me it'd all be okay. But now, would I be meeting him soon in the afterlife?

No, but he couldn't be gone. He was coming back for me. I knew he was, even after ten years. He'd find me and take me home.

The rain splattering on my face masked the tears that rolled down.

I didn't know how much time passed, but I thought it seemed strange I couldn't think straight anymore. At some point, I fell from my seated position and was soaking up the earth's puddles. I couldn't hold the weight of my body. I propped myself up against the tree, but it would just shake itself back to the ground.

Boots appeared before me, and hands slid under my body.

"Come here," I heard a voice say. "I had noticed the clouds before. It's a good thing I got some hides in time."

Who was this?

Everything seemed disoriented, and the rain pounded around us. The man grabbed ahold of my body and lifted it from the earth. He was taking me.

Oh my Erus. It was Kallen. The last time I was by myself in the woods, he had found me. Here he was again.

No. *Danger*, my mind pressed.

A flash of lightning illuminated Kallen's face. Only it wasn't Kallen.

It was Aris.

"N-n-n-n-no," I tried to object, but my rattling teeth made it difficult. What was I saying? I was literally going to die here.

"Yes, you will, or else you'll die." He read my thoughts and carried me through the woods. I lifted my eyes, but he was blurry to me.

The earth shook again, causing Aris to increase his pace.

After some time, we entered a small opening into a space that was large enough for a few Arises to fit. The rain stopped pouring on my skin and head. There were animal hides pitched over some branches on the ground that covered us from the storm and wind. He laid me on the hides that protected me against the cold earth. There was only the sound of rain against the makeshift tent and the wind howling. I closed my eyes, curled myself in a fetal position, and focused on breathing the shivers out of my body.

I heard Aris pulling more hides over the opening and bringing a thin linen quilt over my body. "Take your dress off."

Did I hear that correctly? There was no way. Even if I were to freeze to death.

"N-n-no. I-I'm f-f-f-fine."

"It's soaked from the puddle you were lying in. You'll catch a fever and die."

Why was he so pessimistic?

Even though I hardly had control over it, my body tensed. "I c-c-c-can't."

"If you can't, then I will."

My world stopped turning. "N-n-no! I c-can. I w-w-w-will." With the linen over my body, I could manage to change out of this soaking dress. Unfortunately, he was right. I could become extremely ill from the cold seeping through my bones.

I hesitated for a moment before my trembling, wrinkled fingers worked on removing my sleeves from my shoulders and scooted the dress below my frozen chest and hips, ensuring the quilt remained covering my bare body. I was able to get the dress completely off my shivering body and placed it to the side.

Aris crawled over to me and tucked the sides of the fine quilt beneath me. My mind went blank from the gentleness he was providing. He placed another large sheepskin above me and lay down under it near me.

I couldn't think of anything else besides the cold. I'd never lain with a man in my life like this, but the thought barely stuck in my mind as my brain refocused on surviving.

After some time, Aris spoke.

"I won't be able to sleep with all your chattering over there."

"I-I-I-c-can-can't-s-st-st-stop," I managed to get out.

Aris brought his hand around the quilt over my waist and pulled me to his body. It was rock-solid but warm. Too warm. Even though that was exactly what I needed.

My stomach fluttered from being so close to him. "N-n-no." I fought to get away.

This could easily end up being my worst nightmare.

"I won't touch you. Trust me, I don't want to." He pulled me even closer, not allowing me any room to wriggle out. His warmth seeped through the quilt that covered me. My racing heart and trembling body stabilized for a moment.

I hated how my body responded so well to him. *Damn you*, I said to myself.

"W-why are y-you h-helping me?"

"If I recall correctly, you helped me when I once needed it, didn't you?"

The night he got injured. I had a choice, and almost regretted it, but for some reason I didn't.

A few moments went by, and Aris continued, "I knew someone—a friend—who was important to me, but he was a prisoner of war. I did everything I could to help him, but in the end, I was too late."

"In S-Stroka?"

"Yes...he was one of the reasons I wanted to offer my newfound country something different." His voice was soothing and melted my ear and my neck.

I didn't want to admit it, but his arms around me felt nice and warm. I could feel my muscles slowly relaxing and fading deeper into his body. My breathing slowed, and my jaw eventually softened after several heartbeats. His face was near my wet hair and ear, warming my cheeks and neck. It was dangerous. To be this close to him, especially after all that I had witnessed him do. I focused on my breath once more and tried not to think about his body pressed against mine.

I didn't like it.

I didn't like how I felt.

I didn't like how much it made me feel safe.

And for a moment I forgot he was the emperor and I his captive—or prisoner. Whatever I was. *This is purely about survival,* I told myself. I wondered if he felt the same way.

"Your heart is beating fast," Aris whispered in my ear. His arm tightened around my waist.

"It t-tends to do that," I whispered back. It was so quiet now. Was it still raining? I couldn't even hear anything besides the pounding beat of my heart. My shivering slowed down as the warmth of his breath trickled above my skin.

"What are you afraid of?"

My eyes fluttered open. I stared at the hides in front of me and didn't answer.

Oddly, I wasn't afraid in this moment. I wasn't thinking clearly, obviously. Maybe the extreme cold was damaging my brain cells.

"Have you never lain with a man before?"

Heat flushed my body. I swallowed.

Oh, he was *good*. How could he notice that? I attempted to hide my astonishment. It was becoming frustrating what an open book I was and how he could see through me. Or he was exceptionally observant. Either way, this made me want to crawl away from his warmth and hide underneath the skins.

"Ah, it all makes sense." He chuckled when I didn't answer, and his body vibrated against my back. "I have to say I'm surprised I didn't see it until now, quiet one. You're an *innocent*. Don't worry, your secret's safe. You're protected with me."

My teeth clenched shut. The feverish warmth I was able to produce from my own embarrassment slammed and suffocated every shiver.

"I've managed." I twisted a bit further from him.

Aris pulled me closer. "Barely."

Chapter Seventeen

My mind woke before my eyes opened. For a moment, I felt warm—and safe, like there wasn't anything or anyone I had to run from. For a moment, I forgot that I was on a journey as a captive, taken from my village and brought to mysterious foreign lands. I wanted to sink into this feeling even further. I didn't want to wake my eyes. I didn't want to stir, afraid that this illusion of a dream would dissipate into a nightmare.

And then, I felt warmth where my dry head lay. My cheek realized this wasn't the dry ground. Nothing could compare to this warmth.

I opened my eyes. During the night, somehow, my head had landed on the emperor's massive chest, my hips and body facing him.

My eyes now were wide open. *Oh my gods!*

I froze where I lay and panicked a little in my head. I held my breath.

My pale, freckled arm had defied me through the night and appeared across his rock-hard, inked chest. My leg was wrapped between his. As if we were one, warmth covered our entire bodies. My body was now inflamed with fire that burst from my insides to the surface of my skin. My heart pounded in my chest so hard I thought it would implode.

My chest.

I was naked.

The screaming in my head hadn't stopped. In fact, if I didn't know better, I thought I would go deaf from it.

The linen barely covered me anymore. It was loose around me since the heat generated between the two of us had protected me from the cold enough through the night.

Slowly, very slowly, I went to retract my hand, finger by finger, rising from his firm abdomen, hoping not to wake him. My mind was still panicking to *get out*—but as quietly as possible. I didn't breathe as I took my time peeling my hand from him, ever so gently.

I looked up briefly and saw his dark eyes on me.

Damn him.

I diverted my gaze, face flushed and snatching my hand away.

"You sure you've never lain with a man before?" He chuckled, and his chest vibrated under my head.

I left his warmth and sat up with one hand clenching the quilt to my chest to keep it from falling. I grabbed my dress that I had thrown to the side.

Stupid, arrogant emperor.

His grin spoke loudly, like I was his source of entertainment. "Hey, no need to get serious. It was said in jest!" His arm was above him where his head lay as he spoke to me. His tattooed chest was bare from the animal skins, and I had taken the rest of the linen and wrapped it around my body trying to hide the smallest ounce of dignity I had left.

I was so flustered by his rhetorical question, I couldn't form a single word with my mouth with the humiliation that washed over my being. My fingers rushed to pull my damp dress over my head and over the linen that still covered me. I yanked the linen from underneath, causing my wet dress to cling to me.

Aris rose from the bedding, filling the tent with his presence. His head hit the top of the skins. A muscle twitched in his jaw as his eyes hovered over my body. "At least stay a while longer, until your dress dries."

I hadn't let Aris finish his sentence when I pushed one of the skins hovering over the opening aside to get out of his suffocating space. As I stumbled out, I barely noticed the clear and warm skies as I stopped in my tracks.

Aris followed me out of the tent with nothing but his trousers that were loose around his hips. He also halted abruptly, nearly colliding with me. I could feel his body tense from behind.

Standing before us were Justir and Beshien, and by the looks on their faces, they were surprised to see anyone other than Aris come out. Perhaps even more surprised it was me. Grins appeared on their faces along with their bulging eyes. Whistles and a cheer passed between the two as they looked at each other and back to me and Aris.

Kill me now. I was ready to die and be buried already and try again in the next life.

Their clear and false assumption wasn't the worst part of this moment.

It was that Camilla was there, face pale, with an incredulous stare and mouth open.

This morning officially had become a nightmare.

Aris shook his head and cursed under his breath when Beshien approached him and clapped his hand on Aris' shoulder. "We had been looking for you." He had a large grin on his face as he looked at Aris. "A mute. Why, Aris—I would never have thought—"

My face, neck, and chest flushed the deepest shade of red. The area I stood rooted in became smaller and smaller.

I couldn't hear anymore. I swallowed the rising lump in my throat and didn't wait to hear what Aris had to say. I fled from the scene.

My eyes stung and my vision became blurry once I was far enough to not hear their voices. I followed the scattered warriors who gathered their supplies until I knew I was around the end of the legion. Out of breath, I eventually found Maeri and Nirelle. Their foreheads were crinkled with concern, but they knew better than to press the matter when they saw my flushed face and pursed lips.

The next two days went by faster than before, and we were feeling more refreshed from bathing. At last, we reached the vast lands of Siniya.

By the time the end of the legion arrived, the warriors had already been welcomed by the citizens of Siniya. Tears fell down the cheeks of women and children, embracing their warriors home. The air had turned lighter and surprisingly, brighter.

Maeri, Nirelle, and I were led by Kallen through the cobblestoned streets, weaving through vivid and colorful buildings, from bright orange to dark, rich blue. The people who greeted their beloveds wore just as colorful clothing, smiles plastered on their free-spirited faces.

The air was cooler. Like Finny had said, it was their winter, but that didn't stop them from celebrating. Bright-eyed children danced, the pounding drums and flutes filling the air as we walked through the streets. Besides the fresh, clear air that surrounded the lands, the scent of fresh-baked bread and fruits I'd never seen before permeated the air, causing my stomach to growl in response.

We passed by a large, marbled building that was guarded by towering animal-shaped trees. Kallen pointed while weaving through the crowds. "This is the Vinian temple, for all the gods and goddesses that are worshiped here in Siniya. This was where Emperor Aris was crowned many years ago by the people. According to Siniyan culture, they believe him to be their living god who saved them from destruction."

Maeri and Nirelle said, "Oooh."

I refrained myself from the snort that nearly left me. They thought *Aris* was a living god? That would explain his arrogance. Soon the temple was obscured by another pink building we passed.

My lips parted as my head turned from left to right. What was this place? This was a far cry from the camp we came from. I was tempted to admit that it might be even more beautiful than my own village, but I couldn't yet admit such a blasphemous confession.

I had never stepped into a world like this before. Tingles spread on my skin, causing my breath to hitch as we moved deeper into the soul of Siniya.

PART II

SERVITUDE

Chapter Eighteen

T he wind flew through the strands of hair that parted from my linen-wrapped head. The wind spoke louder this morning, and my ears perked to listen for any hidden messages. I still wasn't used to the amount of greenery and color that filled these foreign lands.

After being here for a few months, I thought my eyes would grow bored of the winter-blue or the pink and yellow flowers that now poured from the path I took every morning. Or that I wouldn't care about the long, green grass that flooded the weaving planes with the forest surrounding the valley. It was so bright here. I thought the smell of the fresh crisp air would eventually disappear, but it was as clear as the first day I stepped foot in this land. It felt clean, fresh, unlike the village I lived in. There was a sense of regrowth—a newness here, that I hadn't experienced before.

I never thought the village I lived in was dirty or gloomy, but I hadn't ever traveled outside of it. It was all I had ever known. And this land—Siniya was not what I expected.

I walked along the narrow dirt path, my sandals crushing the soft pebbles, following a few servants that led the way towards one of the palace's many vast and luscious gardens. My fingers brushed the tops of the long grass that crowded its way towards the center of the path. My other hand carried a woven basket ready for its fill with fresh herbs and vegetables that we would be picking this morning.

The weather was perfect today. It was getting more and more perfect with each day we got closer to summer. I wished I could get used to it—so that I could hate it.

The servants and I crossed a small wooden bridge that went over a sparkling, green stream of water. The peach-colored flowers welcomed us at the end, reminding me that spring was in full blossom. It almost took my breath away as my fingers brushed against the creaking rail. I wanted to hate it, I really did but it was becoming difficult to. The rocks scattered on the bank of the stream were filled with live moss. I wondered how sweet it might feel to lay atop the cool stream, eyes closed, facing the sky and letting all the sounds disappear around me.

Particularly the sounds of the servants speaking about the palace's court drama.

When I arrived at the palace grounds with Maeri and Nirelle, it was obvious the palace keeper didn't want me to make a frequent appearance and kept me hidden in the back of the grounds on kitchen duties with the upkeep of the gardens and animals. Regardless of her intention, I preferred it. I wouldn't want to be a chambermaid in the main palace like Nirelle and Maeri were, even if they had more freedom in the afternoon to do as they pleased. Though I was content, they looked at me with pity.

The thought of running into the emperor made my heart skip a few beats. I was perfectly happy, whatever that meant these days, with planning my potential nonexistent escape from the back of the palace's buildings and knowing for the rest of my life I would never see him again. No matter how hard I tried to focus on more important things during these slow and quiet moments, flashbacks of the morning I had with Aris poured into my mind.

"Snap out of it, girl!" one of the servants, Yari, shouted ahead of me. "Focus." She pointed at the unwanted plants that invaded the large garden boxes.

Massive trees shaded some parts, the gardens filled with large boxes embedded in the ground containing plant species that even I had never heard of. Herbs that I never tasted until I arrived. This was one of my favorite gardens because of how alive it felt. Even the invasive species loved this atmosphere. Ivy spread on the trees, on the wooden boxes and every inch of this place was covered by greenery. I often caught myself frozen, in absolute awe at all of the beauty.

With clenched teeth, I obeyed her ambiguous order and plunged to my knees. I wanted to snap something smart back, but I kept quiet. She didn't deserve my words.

Today was going to be one of those days. Some days when there weren't enough hands, I would be able to pick herbs and vegetables from the gardens, which put me in a calm, relaxed state because it was familiar to me. Most days when there were plenty of hands, like today, I was ordered to clean the gardens.

My hands were sore from the latest strike of the palace keeper's correction stick. I tried not to think of the fact that at that time, I was thinking about how it felt to be in the emperor's arms, and how disgusted I was with myself—repulsed even. Those thoughts made me work a moment too slow and that moment got me bruised hands.

My fingers pulled the invasive species one by one, dirt filling under my fingernails and spilling over my brown apron. The feelings from the memory returned. Still to this day, my stomach had churned from the amount of embarrassment I felt in those moments. I had managed my entire life to live without shame from that sort of humiliation until then.

Because I would never do what they thought I did. And worse—it was with the emperor, the merciless man who led armies that pillaged my village.

I would never think to do something like that with anyone, let alone him.

I ripped roots from the ground as the memory replayed over and over in my head. Maybe if I continued digging through this dirt, I'd reach the other side of the world and be able to escape this dreadful feeling.

Yari walked over to where my knees were plunged into dirt. "Faster, girl. These plants don't pull themselves."

My fingers tightened on the plant I was about to pull.

"It doesn't matter if she finishes in time for the Tigress Festival," another servant, Rayne, said for me.

"All are invited."

I was tempted to roll my eyes.

"She is not one of us. Plus, her people are in Stroka, where they have a special day to celebrate prisoners of war." Rayne clipped herbs nearby, though her wary eyes flew in my direction. The black line that marked the top of her eye almost reached her temple. It was fascinating to look at, but I focused my attention back on the plants before me. Before I arrived here, I had never heard or seen anything like it. They created it from near-black minerals, crushed into a paste, and placed it on their eyelids.

Yari laughed in agreement and faced me. "You're really in the wrong place, girl. They have a special day just for people like you in Stroka. How thoughtful." She took a pause as she placed her hands on her hips and continued, "Though, you wouldn't enjoy being in those cages. Unless you got purchased by a handsome lord, the majority of you would be auctioned off for work in the fields. It's called the Day of the Hand."

I swallowed. I took a deep breath but tried hard to make it not too noticeable. I didn't want them thinking they affected me with their words.

"You would have most likely been snatched up quickly for your pretty little face by a sadistic person who liked to play with the she-devil, because no one, and I mean *no one*, would ever want anything to do with someone like you."

My fingers froze.

It went quiet. Even the birds singing in the air stopped. The wind flowing through the gardens stilled.

I forced my fingers to move. To work through this. I ignored their remarks that were meant to hurt me. I focused on yanking the roots from the dirt. I was used to Yari and Rayne's empty words and hateful glances.

Most days, they ignored me as much as I ignored them, but today wasn't like other days. Today was the Tigress Festival, a celebration of honor for the middle and lower class, which included the servants in the palace. It was a celebration of all humans and animals alike. We had been preparing the last two weeks for this day. I worked longer hours in the garden and in the kitchen helping the cooks with their preparations.

It was ironic the festival was to celebrate "all humans and animals alike" yet I remained unwelcomed by them. Yari and Rayne were the kind of people Justir had warned about.

"Beats me why she's here. Probably because she's secretly sleeping with Emperor Aris."

How Rayne didn't address me directly was comical, but it was probably because they thought me mute. I chose to ignore the fact that she and almost everyone at this palace had suspected me as Aris' mistress since the moment Camilla and those warriors saw me step out of his tent that morning. That rumor spread like wildfire following that day even though I hadn't encountered him since then. It was more of a jest rumor than what people actually believed, but it was still frustrating, nevertheless.

"Emperor Aris would never stoop so low, Rayne," Yari muttered in a skeptical tone.

Regardless of what Rayne said, I knew I could go to the Tigress Festival, if I cared to, as it was for everyone. The only difference between me and servants like Rayne and Yari was that I was treated differently because I was working for freedom instead of money.

It was hard to see a future for myself without freedom. Despite the papers I did not possess, I had been learning the lay of the land the last few months, searching for opportunities, like a possible escape route. I didn't know where I was in the world or how far I was from home, but I always kept an eye out for something that would bring me to my freedom faster.

Even though I contemplated my escape and freedom, my friends were becoming quite comfortable here—maybe *too* comfortable. Maeri and Nirelle came to my quarters the other evening and begged me to join them today. I told them I would, but I lied. I had no intention of going to the festival.

Even if the festival was for all, I was the lowest kind of human. Rayne was right. I did not belong here, and I never would. Since there weren't many of us, it didn't feel like a safe option to go especially during the little free time I did have.

The winds picked up and howled at us in the late morning. I cleaned the gardens in silence as the sun behind the clouds moved above me, signaling that we had been out here for hours. My hands became raw from the constant tugging and pulling of the weeds.

After noon had passed and the rest of the women left for the festival, I continued working through the gardens until the sun lowered and became soft. It was peaceful without their chaotic energy. I was able to breathe fully and deeply.

I felt a pull in my eyes, and I looked up.

Over the rolling hillside, I saw a figure walking towards me. Directly to me.

Who was he? I squinted. He was wearing a white tunic and white linen pants. He was practically glowing in the sunlight as he glided down the hillside. Then I saw his face—

My breath caught in my throat. My world stopped spinning. It stopped and started and then stopped again.

It was my brother.

He came back for me. He found me.

I blinked.

And he was gone.

Gone.

My eyes stung, and my chin trembled. I begged and searched my mind to play tricks with me once more.

Just once more, I begged my mind. *Please let me see him again. Where is he? Where is he?*

My eyes searched the edge of the woods. Through the tall grass. Searched the skies.

I swallowed the pressure that rose in my throat.

I was tired. That was all it was. I was so tired.

CHAPTER NINETEEN

I walked back to the servants quarters in meditation, feeling gratitude for the peace that my alone time had given me. There were a few people bustling around in preparation as I strode through the cold stone quarters, past the empty common area, and into my shared room. I shared the small space with five other servants, each one of us having our own straw mattress on low wooden frames. One small window to the right of the room viewed the vast green lands and the rolling hills. I had to admit, it was a much better bed situation than the one I had back home. The window also provided a direct view of the main palace, and I would find myself observing from afar, wondering what Aris was doing in that moment.

Like right now.

I averted my thoughts as quickly as they came. It brought me painful and cringe-worthy memories of the last time I saw him. Not only that, but I felt my muscles tense, reminding me of the savagery he had presented. The true colors he possessed was that of a sick person who mercilessly killed and rampaged small, vulnerable villages.

Plunging onto my thin straw mattress, I closed my eyes and smiled knowing that tonight was going to be quiet since everyone would be going to the festival and I would have this space to myself. No more thoughts of the emperor. No more thoughts of the servants. No more thoughts of home.

Just total peace in my head.

A tingling sensation fluttered in my stomach. I loved being by myself. I planned on getting the extra sleep my body so desperately—

"Are you almost ready?"

My eyes flung open. I brought myself up from my bed and gave a tight smile.

Maeri was standing in a dark red linen dress at the doorway with her arms across her chest, waiting for me.

I swore in my head. I had hoped they had forgotten about my little promise to join in on the festivities.

Nirelle was waiting by the doorway as well, dressed in an amber linen dress with a smile so large it would be painful to break the news that I lied and decided to stay in.

"I had forgotten."

"I don't believe you." Maeri raised a brow.

"I don't have anything to wear, Maeri—and I'm tired." I was throwing every excuse I had her way.

"I know, and that's why I brought something for you." She pulled a dress from her leather bag.

It was beautiful. The fabric was in the lightest shade of blue. She had made many *friends* over the few months we had been here. I knew how poor she grew up in Prustan, so I was genuinely happy for her. Yet this made my stomach feel queasy. She was wearing a new dress almost every week. I couldn't help but wonder how close these friends were with her.

"I thought it would look beautiful with your red hair." She tossed the dress on my lap as she walked over to me. "No excuses not to spend time with your only friends."

"Maeri, I won't go."

"Why not?"

"Because I don't want to."

"You can't just hide yourself from any social interaction." Maeri stood in front of me, her attitude reminding me of my sister.

"I've done it my whole life, and I'm pretty sure I can keep doing it. I'll be just fine. I hang out with you and Nirelle all the time." My voice went up an octave as I defended myself.

"Hanging out in the servants quarters is not the same thing as social interaction! Live a little!" Maeri cried.

"Why won't you come to the festival with us?" Nirelle asked softly as she stepped forward beside Maeri.

I clenched the powder-blue dress on my lap. "Because I don't belong, nor do I want to." I placed the dress next to me on my bed. I wouldn't forget what they did to my people even if Maeri could.

"This doesn't have to be about them. We can still enjoy ourselves. Come on, Solei, it'll be fun," Maeri pressed. When I didn't respond, she continued, "What are you so afraid of? You can't make decisions based on fear, or else you'll never be happy in life. There will always be a shadow behind every action, and that doesn't feel right, does it?"

I threw a glance in her direction. It stung a bit knowing she was right. "I'll never be happy here, Maeri."

"It's just one night. I'm not asking you to marry the country." Maeri raised a brow and crossed her arms.

I glanced at my bed that beckoned me to stay and sleep awhile. It looked so soft and comfy. I took a deep breath and faced Nirelle and Maeri. Their eyes were wide, bright and hopeful.

"Please, come with us." Nirelle took my hand from my lap.

They were not going to leave unless I went with them. The last place I wanted to be was at the festival, but if I could make my friends happy by joining, it was the least I could do for our friendship.

I rolled my eyes in defeat and grabbed the dress that resembled the sky.

"Yay!" Nirelle beamed.

"It'll be fun." Maeri smiled victoriously.

Nirelle helped me into the dress and tied the strings in the back. The fabric was long and soft against my skin. The front of the dress hung low, exposing my chest more than I would have liked. I tied the front knot, hoping that would give me more coverage.

"Stop that." Maeri smacked my hand away. "You're perfect this way."

And I'm not perfect if I do cover? I narrowed my eyes slightly, but I wasn't up for a fight with Maeri. I never won.

Looking into the only mirror we had in this room, I noticed the fine pale scar finally fading around my neck. I couldn't help but constantly feel Klawdia would appear and pounce on me, killing me off like she intended from the start. My fingers traced the scar. My body tensed. Why did I agree to go again?

"Perhaps we'll get to see the emperor this evening," Nirelle said while she and Maeri exchanged glances. Obviously, she had believed the rumors or were curious about them.

I chose not to respond and continued fixing my long wavy hair in the mirror.

"I heard he's finally making an appearance after all this time," Nirelle pressed, giving me a glance this time.

"Nirelle, don't believe everything you hear from the Siniyans. They like to talk. Also, I know they're easy on the eyes and their beds are freely open, but be careful tonight and don't drink too much," Maeri warned Nirelle.

"You don't have to tell me twice, but I'm hoping to see Justir tonight. I'm sure Solei would like to see the emperor, wouldn't you?" She attempted to pry information from me.

"Over my dead body," I mumbled, fixing the top of my hair in a small bun. Soft, tiny curls framed my face.

"Are you ever going to tell us what happened between you two?" Nirelle asked.

"Yes, since you asked." I paused and faced Nirelle, who looked like she was going to open the present she'd been waiting for. "Nothing happened."

Her face dropped in disappointment. "Right."

Chapter Twenty

Nirelle, Maeri, and I walked along the dirt path with multiple groups heading in the same direction. The festival was in the heart of Siniya. It spread across the land, and it was to be the biggest celebration of the year in Siniya, and it was the biggest I had ever seen.

The air was filled with scents of freshly baked pies, seasoned chicken thighs, and smoke from the fires that lit the way against the setting sun. Bonfires spread out to every corner of the festival and within. Large red tents were crowded with people selling their food, drinks, games, and activities. Even the taverns opened for music, cheer, and liquid courage. Many rushed their way through the crowds on the streets to the fires where musicians with drums and horns led the way for dancing to begin.

I noticed many covering their faces and shoulders with fur masks of tigers, wolves, and other animals I had never seen or heard of. They felt unsettling yet mesmerizing as they maneuvered their way through the crowds, cocking their animal heads to the side. They would hiss and howl, causing me to nearly trip over my blue dress. I wasn't surprised seeing these sorts of costumes since Siniya was known for its animalistic customs and their flaunty manners.

The Tigress Festival was represented by one of the Siniyan goddesses, Estar, who was the youngest child of the Gilian. She was neglected so much that she had been entirely forgotten by her family. She represented vulnerability, strength, and sacrifice. She had to start life again from the lowest levels of humankind.

From afar, I could see the interior of the festival was a large arena with a great fire in the middle, reaching as if to touch the sky. There were many games and activities, people playing with fire followed by bursts of the crowd's cheers. The sound of music seemed louder by the arena and so, along with the crowd, we headed towards the core of the festival.

We passed a tavern on the way and decided to stop for a drink. Maeri grabbed us a tin of ale. How she acquired money to buy the ale perplexed me, but I wasn't going to question it. Maeri seemed to have a way with people.

"Drink up!" Maeri handed me the tin.

I looked down at the strange amber color, my nose wrinkling at the strong smell coming from the little tin. I handed it back to her.

"What's the problem?"

"It looks and smells disgusting."

"Gods above, Solei." Maeri rolled her eyes and gestured broadly. "You're so boring. You don't like to do anything fun with us!"

My jaw dropped. "One, none of that is true. Second, I'm just being the responsible one."

"Tonight's supposed to be fun. Come on—revel in the experience!"

I stared hard into my friend's dark eyes. We fought a battle in our minds—

Do this and we'll have a good night, Maeri seemed to say.

Drop it, and we can still have a good night.

Maeri narrowed her eyes.

"Fine." I snatched the tin, kept my eyes on Maeri's, took a large gulp, and almost immediately threw it back up. I forced it down my throat for Maeri's satisfaction.

To my relief, she smiled and handed it to Nirelle, who almost drank the entire tin. I wiped my mouth with the back of my hand. That was the most disgusting thing I'd ever tasted, like bile. Some people drank this every day? Tragic.

I knew back home I wouldn't have befriended these two girls, but I was in a foreign land, and they were the nicest people I had here. I was thankful for their genuine friendship regardless of how we were nothing alike.

Maeri gave some coins for Nirelle to grab another tin. Seriously, how did she have the money?

When Nirelle came back, she beamed, tapping our forearms as she saw Justir across the street following the crowd. "Oh my gods, there he is!"

"Wow. Nirelle, you did good for yourself," Maeri muttered while we all gawked. "How does he make you feel after?"

"After?" Nirelle questioned.

"After sex, of course. Don't tell me you're a virgin. Haven't seen one since I was fifteen." Maeri snorted and laughed, and Nirelle fell into laughter with her.

My ears might have turned red, but it was from being outdoors for too long.

"He makes me feel...nice." Nirelle smiled longingly at him. "How is your lover treating you, hmm?"

"It's fun. It feels great, and it's usually quick and ends before I'm ready for it to. I guess I never really thought about it, but afterward, I'm left feeling empty most of the time. It's a wonder why I want it so badly in the first place—but I do!" Maeri chuckled at her own words, staring off into the distance.

"Yeah, I get that," Nirelle murmured.

"Interesting." *Not really*, I muttered in my head.

Nirelle and Maeri both looked at me.

"What about you? Have anyone you're interested in lately?" Nirelle waggled her brows.

"Nope." I made a loud pop with my mouth.

A small tent between two buildings across from the tavern caught my eye. I looked over to see fabrics and materials of all kinds hanging from wooden racks and told them I'd be back. I walked over and found a pair of leather gloves that seemed just small enough to fit my hands. Back home, they were always slightly larger and would be difficult to garden with, so I would use my bare hands. Carefully, I grabbed the gloves and slipped my fingers through. It felt warm and smooth against my skin.

"Look, it's that witch who I heard seduced our lord on the journey from another land."

I turned my head to the voices that spoke near me and found two elderly women gossiping around the corner, pointing at me. Unfortunately for me, some of Aris' people, despite what he thought, still believed in superstitions.

"If she's a witch and carries evil in her bones...then she belongs in Stroka." They walked by me with their fear-filled eyes and furrowed brows.

"Give me those back, girl." The merchant snatched her gloves from my hands. She waved a hand in my face. "Get!"

My eyes burned in dismay. I took a step back. *Don't let them see you break down*, I demanded myself. I took a deep breath and looked around for Maeri and Nirelle. They were nowhere to be found. There were so many people now flooding the streets, and I could barely see past the multitude of heads.

"Solei!" The distant voice sounded like Nirelle.

I stood on my tiptoes, but I couldn't see them. I whirled around and around.

"Look! Over there! It's Emperor Malakar!" A young boy near me pointed while tugging his mother towards the center.

My heart thudded.

Wait.

Emperor Malakar? The Emperor of Emperors...

I caught my breath. All thoughts of finding Nirelle and Maeri vanished for a moment as I listened.

"That's right. Behave yourself," the mother warned as she was pulled.

The sounds of the festival faded as realization washed over me. A chill went down my spine, reminding me he was the one I belonged to.

Chapter Twenty-One

My legs froze, wondering if I should follow the crowd or continue searching for Nirelle and Maeri. Knowing them, most likely they had heard the news and wanted to see Emperor Malakar for themselves. Though I typically gave into my curiosity, I wasn't sure if it were wise of me to find out who this person was. A heavy drowning-like weight settled in my chest, but I decided to follow the crowd down the path towards the arena.

"Why is Emperor Malakar here?" a man asked near me, rushing in the same direction.

"Maybe because he knew Aris would make an appearance," the other man answered his companion. "It was common knowledge."

"It doesn't matter. He shouldn't come here without an announcement." The first man shook his head. "Fucking Strokans, always barging in uninvited."

"Careful what you say out loud," the man chided his friend.

The two Siniyan men hurried past me toward the center of the festival.

A young boy ran into me, hurtling towards the crowd. It threw me off balance, and I fell to the side of the path, landing on my knees and hands. Dirt now painted the bottom of my blue dress. I got up and brushed it off my hands and dress.

After a moment, I straightened my spine.

Only because I wasn't that invested in knowing about this Malakar did I hear it. Only because I was pushed and fell to the side of the crowd did I hear the sound. Only because I listened more than I spoke. Only because I listened for threats every moment did I hear the faint scream from far down the alley.

The hairs at the back of my neck stood up. *Run. Run*, my body seemed to say. While everyone focused on the emperors ahead, I looked back towards the alley that I stood next to. It was dark and smokey, but my legs moved before I could think to stop them.

I had to *do* something.

I heard it again.

"Stop it!" I heard a woman cry out ahead in the alley. "*Please, stop!*"

My heart stopped beating for a moment as flashbacks of my mother's and sister's bodies lay in a hidden alley, much like this one. My breath caught in my throat, making it hard to breathe.

Clothes ripped, dry blood leaking down their legs, and their necks slashed in the same diagonal cut. I walked closer to their dead bodies, hands shaking, tears rolling down my dirty face as I observed the two burns that were on their upper arm, a mark from whoever did this.

I could not allow any woman to endure the same fate my family went through. I may not have considered myself brave or stood up for myself the way my sister frequently did, but I couldn't just walk away. I searched the area for something that could be used as a weapon and found an empty liquor bottle laying on the ground near one of the buildings. I grabbed it and held it tightly as I progressed between the two buildings.

Through the voices of the crowds rushing behind me, I heard muffled sounds of a woman trying to scream. I saw the end of the alley way, but no one was there. I swore I heard someone, but I couldn't see anyone through the murky darkness.

Was I hearing something that was not real?

My heart pounded as I crept through the narrow alley. I noticed on one of the buildings to the left, a door was ajar. I forced my legs to bring me closer no matter the small voices in my head that told me not to, and I opened the door.

My eyes adjusted to the dark room. My breath hitched.

Camilla.

It was Camilla that lay on her stomach atop the cot, her dress ripped apart and barely covering her hips. Her eyes were fading. She seemed almost lifeless.

Tobias fastened his belt.

My teeth clenched. I remembered, for a moment, the day in the cage when Camilla expressed we weren't so different. I wondered if Tobias was the cage she'd been living in.

"Let this be your lesson to get things done when we ask for it." His voice rumbled across the room.

I squeezed tight the cold, empty bottle that I held in my hand.

One moment, I saw Camilla, and the next I saw my sister. I saw my mother.

I blinked. My family was gone, but Camilla lay there, broken. Wet trails of tears ran past her cheeks.

I didn't care how important this monster was or if it would endanger me more, perhaps strip me of any potential freedom I might have within Stroka. I had to do something for what he did to Camilla.

Without wasting another moment, the rage that built inside of me, the rage for what my family went through, the rage inside from hundreds of generations before me caused me to lift the bottle above my head and step behind Tobias.

"Let this be your lesson to keep your mouth shut, whore. Get me what I want."

With all my strength, I drove the hard bottle into the top of his head. It shattered into a million pieces. Tobias fumbled over Camilla's body before dropping to the floor with a large *thud*. Clouds of dust flew from the ground. I dropped the top of the bottle and looked at Camilla.

Her face said it all.

Hope.

Dragging her legs from the cot, she stepped over Tobias' unconscious, fallen body to reach me. Her hair disheveled around her head, a large red mark across her cheek.

"We have to go, *now*," she whispered urgently to me with panic in her eyes. "Or else he'll find us."

Camilla grabbed my elbow and pulled me towards the door.

We heard a sound behind us.

We whirled to see—

"You *witch*." Tobias grabbed the countertop, hauling himself up as he kept his stare on me with lethal rage in his eyes. Red blood leaked from the top of his head to his temple.

Camilla did not waste another moment and bolted through the door, with me following her hurried footsteps. In the smoky darkness, we ran through the alley towards the cheers of the crowd. Once we reached the end of the alley, Camilla gave me a quick glance that almost said *run fast and run far* and sprinted against the crowd away from the festival.

Without a moment to spare, I scurried in the opposite direction with the flow of the people, rushing and pushing through the bodies to gain more distance between me and Tobias. Multiple people murmured *watch out* and *witch* as I squeezed past the crowds.

A hand grasped my hair and yanked me backwards. My head slammed into the hard stone ground as he flew above me and rammed another fist into my abdomen.

My stomach clenched, and I heaved for breath from the impact. Before I could take a breath, another strike came to the side of my face, and I swear it fractured a piece of my skull.

In the midst of my neck nearly making a full turn from Tobias' punch, my eyes locked with several men in the middle of the rushing crowd. They looked the other way and continued walking.

"You shouldn't have done that, wench." Tobias pulled my body in a general direction with just his hold of my hair.

Instinctively, my hands flew towards his grasp and attempted to twist my way out with my legs as he dragged my body through the crowd. I clawed at his arm. The hairs of my head were like pine needles about to be ripped out one by one from my skull. Some people near me shouted, and some whispered and parted from the intrusion.

"What is all this commotion?" A hefty Siniyan warrior intercepted Tobias, raising a hand to stop him.

Tobias dragged me through the crowd by my hair to the center of the festival and finally came to a halt in front of the warrior. Everything was quiet. The crowds were no longer rushing through, the activities and games ceased, there were no more cheers, no more banter or laughter. Only silence filled the air with the crackling of the great fire nearby.

Fresh blood trickled from my cheek down my neck. My head throbbed, and I could feel the liquid flowing through my hair. I grappled against his hand and pulled my feet to stabilize themselves—

"I won't allow this woman to go unpunished!" Tobias shouted to the people.

"Tobias, my most trusted and valued warrior, show me who you speak of," a powerful voice thundered across the center.

Tobias placed his hand behind my neck and yanked me in front of him. I saw an older but well-built man dressed in fine burgundy clothes. He had black hair with white streaks along the sides of his head.

Malakar.

The one who owned my life.

Standing next to Malakar was Aris. They were nearly the same size in brute strength. Our eyes locked for a brief moment.

The stupid, arrogant emperor.

Aris' face was cold, indifferent, and hard to read. My eyes fluttered to the ground, afraid Aris would recognize me. *Of course he'll recognize me. I was his laughingstock for a night.*

"This *witch*," Tobias hissed and tightened his grip on my neck, causing me to squirm under him.

I winced from the sharp pain. I attempted to yank myself from his grip, but he only gripped me harder, enough for me to barely breathe. His hand almost covered my entire throat.

"What has this woman done to you, Tobias?" Malakar questioned.

"She tried to kill me, and she'll pay for it."

Malakar gave a quick, concerned glance to Aris, who seemed colder by the minute. Was Aris going to kill me like he did his warrior? I trembled. *What have I done?*

What have I done?

Helon walked up to Aris with a cane and stood by his side.

Even though I was fighting for my life, I couldn't help the heat that rose from my neck to my cheeks as the attention was on me.

"Girl, why did you try to cause harm to my warrior?" Malakar addressed me as he stepped forward.

Aris followed suit.

Maybe if I could get Tobias to loosen his grip just a fracture, I could hide between the crowds and run. Never to return. I was small but fast.

I felt my chest collapsing. Why didn't I run from this savage place when I had the chance? Was I becoming like Nirelle and Maeri and slowing trapping myself between the vines of its beauty?

Emperor Malakar flared his nose, waiting for his response.

I contemplated the answer to his question. I thought about Camilla and why I helped her escape. Rage boiled in my blood, rage that I had not experienced quite so intensively before.

At last, I chose not to give them the luxury of hearing my thoughts. It wouldn't change anything if they knew. Not in this world. Not these men.

"She's not going to talk. She's a mute," Tobias snorted.

I dared a glance to Aris, who caught my eyes and to my surprise, didn't say otherwise despite knowing the truth. I attempted again to free his fingers, one by one, but made no progress. Tobias wrapped his hand around my throat and pressed harder. I recoiled.

"Why did she try to kill you, Tobias?" Malakar asked in a serious tone.

"I was in the middle of teaching someone a lesson. Maybe I'll teach her a special lesson too." Tobias pulled me closer to mutter his clear threat into my ear.

I would kill you before you could touch me. My eyes flickered up, and I tightened them at Tobias.

"Keep your damn eyes on the ground, you fucking witch."

"I see," Malakar rumbled through the arena. "But you are not the law here, Tobias. She is Aris' responsibility. If there is a punishment to be served, it is Aris who should deliver as we are in Siniya. Isn't that right, Aris?"

No, no, no. He'll kill me.

"Aris shouldn't need to deal with such trivial matters. I don't have a problem with taking the situation into my own hands," Tobias argued and let go of my neck.

I stumbled on to my hands, scrambling to my feet—

His arms wrapped around me, snickering, and hoisted me up in his massive arms. "This is going to end your life, filthy whore."

I thrusted my arms against his body, scratching at his arms, worming for a way out of his captivity. There was *no* way—

"I'll take it from here, Tobias. Rest assured, I will handle it," Aris' voice thundered with no room for questioning as he snapped his fingers at a nearby Siniyan warrior to approach me. He didn't glance my way. Instead he gave a blank stare to Tobias, his hands resting in his pockets. Aris narrowed his eyes slightly, but only for the briefest moment.

Tobias let me go with a silent order from Malakar. The Siniyan warrior grabbed my upper arm and pulled me towards the other end of the crowd as they parted to make room.

Oh, God. He's going to kill me as punishment. My heart pounded against my ribs. I could still see that man's heart in Aris' hand, raised over his head as a warning to all. Zero tolerances for murders.

I heard the rest of the conversation between Malakar and Aris come to an end.

"Well done, son," Malakar said to Aris.

"I'm not your son. I haven't been in over twenty-nine years." Aris strolled away towards the end of the crowd along with his Siniyan warriors and a captive.

Aris' father was Malakar.

My heart thudded.

How did I not know this?

I looked over my shoulder to Aris' and Malakar's faces. Despite their strong jaw and nose, they seemed like they could be distant relatives. I recalled, now, how Aris' demeanor was different from the Strokans and their traditions. I wondered what lay under Aris' indifferent persona. I wondered about his reasonings behind his subtle defiance against Malakar.

The Siniyan warrior pulled me through the crowd with blood dripping on the side of my face and neck. The crowd continued to provide a path for us.

"A terrible fate."

"Bastard Strokan warrior!" a man shouted.

Another man by him agreed.

I even heard a few Strokan warriors condemn me. "Death can only be the punishment for what she did to Tobias."

I threw a glare at those who dared whisper their not-so-subtle threat. Maybe I could then instill fear in their hearts from my ungifted witchery for their damnation.

"Why are they here?"

"Poor girl," Siniyan citizens whispered.

Words I'd never heard before addressed me. Something in my heart fluttered. Was it because there was a greater enemy that lurked in their shadows?

Regardless, I couldn't help but remember Maeri's statement earlier that evening.

It'll be fun, Maeri said.

It'll be fun.

Chapter Twenty-Two

The Siniyan warrior pulled me through the festival, past the crowds, past the buildings and fires. We came to the edge of the celebration where Aris whistled at the warrior, who released me without hesitation.

Aris snapped his fingers, signaling him to go back to the celebration. The warrior obeyed his command with a silent bow and continued his way with the rest of the Siniyan warriors. Without a captor, I silently but quickly took a few steps away from them in the dark, but Aris was faster on his feet and came forward, grabbing my upper arm firmly. He pulled me up a grassy hill through the darkness, the only light from the festival becoming smaller and smaller behind us.

What was he going to do to me? Where was he taking me? Was he going to kill me? Was he going to crush my beating heart?

Erus save me.

My heart pounded as I contemplated that this very well might be the last night I had in this world. I couldn't let this be my last night. I had to fight.

My hands went cold and my legs numb. I couldn't feel anything past my chest while Aris hauled me with an iron grip up the grassy hill. This was a far comparison from the last time I saw him, the last time he touched me.

Once we reached the top, nearing the edge of the woods, I attempted to yank my arm free of his icy hold. Aris' grip hardened, and his urgency intensified.

I dug my heels into the ground, pulled and yanked—

"Stop it, or you'll kill yourself," Aris growled.

I'd rather be in control of my own destiny than have my life be given to an emperor to do with what he pleased. My lips thinned, and I continued to fight and loosen his grasp on me.

"Where do you think you'll go? If you go back, they'll find you and kill you for what you did to Tobias. And I won't let you go alone into the woods where you'll be hunted." Aris turned around to face me. He took one look at me, and his face dropped to something I hadn't seen before—understanding. The column of his throat bobbed. "I'm not going to hurt you, Solei."

He remembered my name.

I demanded my tears to stop stinging my eyes. I swallowed them down, *down* until I could breathe more clearly.

"Sit with me." Aris released his hold, leaving fingerprints on my upper arm.

I rubbed the pain away. I contemplated running off but knew that would work just as well as it did last time I tried to run from Aris. After thinking about it for a moment, I realized he had never once tried to physically hurt me. I remembered the night of the storm as he carried me into shelter. A wave of relief passed through my body and settled in my stomach. He wasn't going to hurt me.

Aris was right. I had nowhere to go. Only death stood in my way of escaping tonight.

He sat alone on the hillside with one leg propped up where he rested his arm. Hesitantly, I joined a space near him, bringing both of my legs up to my chest.

Up on the grassy hillside, overlooking the festival, it would have been peaceful and quiet if I were alone. I would have liked it up here.

"What happened?"

I glanced over and met his eyes. They had grown dark and serious. I brought my attention back to the festival. I swallowed hard as my tongue became heavy.

I couldn't tell him the truth. He would know Tobias was teaching her a lesson for more information. He would know Camilla had been deceiving him, though I wasn't sure the extent of it. Maybe he would cause harm to Camilla because of me, and all of this would have been for nothing. Aris would never understand what women had to go through, how we had to survive in a predatory world like this. He would punish me for what I did to Tobias, and the commotion I caused between him and Malakar.

When I didn't answer, Aris rose from his position, walked over to me, and stood with his arms across his chest. "Don't make me ask again."

His voice, low and powerful, rippled over me, and I trembled with fear of the unknown.

"Solei," he warned.

I gripped my hands on the rough grass from shaking.

"I-I-" I breathed quickly. "Just punish me like you said and let me be."

Staring back at the festival in front of me, a burning tear rolled down my cheek, not caring if he saw or what he thought of me. I refused to admit what happened. It wasn't my story to tell.

Aris scoffed. "Your punishment is you're going to tell me what the fuck happened."

I threw a scowl at him. "You can't make me tell you anything."

The words slipped from my mouth, and I was more shocked at myself than he was, by the look on his face.

"Yes, I can." His eyes grew darker, and my heart fluttered in panic.

Camilla. Think of her, I reminded myself to stay quiet. To stay strong.

Aris stepped closer to me. I crawled backwards to higher ground to gain more distance from him. He reached me faster than I was able to distance myself, and he now stood right above me.

"O-okay, okay. I'll tell you." I retreated from his touch. My arm still felt his phantom hand on my arm.

Aris lowered himself beside me, crouching in case I changed my mind. His brows lifted. "I'm waiting."

Impatient brat.

"Tobias, he—" I swallowed hard. "He was hurting someone."

"What did he do?"

Don't! my mind screamed in my head. Aris leaned forward.

"He—he forced himself..." I couldn't finish, my breathing turning heavy and more rapid. I wiped my clammy hands on the cool grass beside me.

He seemed to realize what I meant. "On who?"

"A woman." My eyes blurred in the moonlight as I stared at Aris.

"Who?" Aris demanded, and I flinched.

Don't tell him. Don't tell him.

"Who did he force himself on?"

I squeezed my eyes, afraid of his reaction. I dragged my fingers through the dirt and grass. "Camilla."

There was a moment of silence.

"This is all my fault," Aris whispered.

My eyes flung open, and I snapped my head at Aris, who shook his.

"She asked to go to the festival with me, and I refused her," he explained with closed eyes. "Now, I know why. She was afraid of Tobias. She must have had a feeling."

His brows furrowed, and a few moments went by seemingly deep in thought.

"Wait." His eyes locked with mine, and my heart stopped. "He said he was teaching someone—Camilla, a lesson."

I looked back down at the festival, hoping he wouldn't ask me.

"What lesson?"

"How would I know?"

"What *do* you know?"

Aris crawled above me, and my upper body fell to the ground at his sudden movement. I was trapped under him.

"Tell me what you know."

"I don't—" I shook my head and couldn't finish my thought.

"You do."

His face was too close and too powerful. I closed my eyes to hide the tears that wanted to be released. *Don't let him see how weak you are.*

Tobias wanted information from Camilla, just like how Aris now wanted information from me.

My body trembled under his scrutiny.

"Solei, I'm not going to hurt you. Just tell me what you know. I *need* to know." He read my mind.

I opened my wet eyes, looked into his, and took a few more moments to absorb what he said.

"I think Tobias has something on Camilla," I admitted.

"What?"

Even though what I saw earlier frightened me to my core, I felt that perhaps Aris didn't intend anything wrong or bad. Maybe he wanted to help Camilla, not hurt her.

"I—I'm not sure. I think he was using her to get to you—maybe for some information," I whispered reluctantly.

Aris shook his head in frustration, his body and face still above mine. "I should have been there."

"You're not mad at me for what I did?" I blurted.

"Why would I be mad at you?" He lowered his brows. "I'm frustrated you don't answer when I ask a question, but I'm not mad at you for what you did. In fact, I wish you had finished him off. Tobias has always been a thorn in my side. But at least I'll have the satisfaction of ending his life, and for good reason."

My lips parted.

His hand reached for my face and softly brushed the excess blood that leaked from my cheek with his thumb. I froze, barely breathing. His hand was warm and gentle, leaving the rest of my body tingling under his touch. My chest almost touched his. He could crush me—hurt me if he wanted to, and there wouldn't be much I could do to stop him.

For some reason, it didn't quite bother me as much as I thought it should.

"How is your head feeling?"

I had to think for a moment about what he meant. "I can barely feel anything."

I wasn't lying. I couldn't concentrate on my pain since I was sorely distracted at the moment.

"I know the feeling." His lips curved. "You'll heal fast. Maybe use some of those herbs you sneak into your pockets."

"I wouldn't have needed to sneak around if—"

"Don't even think about saying it." His eyes hardened. "You'll never understand."

"Understand what?" The words barely escaped my mouth.

"Understand what it's like to be part of the Strokan Empire. Your lands don't belong to anything or anyone else besides Stroka. The sooner you realize that, the better."

My world stopped spinning. There was an emptiness in my chest that felt heavy.

I turned my head and stared into the distant hills of dark, shadowed grass. I thought about the little boy who'd stop me every other morning for his sweet almond and how I'd never see him again. Where was Fenrah? Where was my brother?

"What's on your mind right now?"

Something came over me—something I hadn't felt in my life before.

"Did you always bore Camilla with so many questions?" My heart pounded out of my chest. He could kill me right now with this insult.

But instead, his perfect lips curved, and he chuckled softly. He peered into the window of my soul. His eyes grew a shade darker as I stared back. "It wasn't my questions that bored Camilla. It was the fact that I ignored her passes, and eventually, she saw past them. Smart girl."

"I guess you and I have that in common," I whispered.

"What is that?"

"Ignoring passes." I was playing his game. I couldn't believe myself and how natural it felt to talk to this man. The way my body and mind wanted to play with him too, in a dangerous way. I'd just respond without thinking before I said it. That was so unusual for me.

Knowing where this could lead, I wriggled my way out, and Aris rose from his position, letting me go. We walked down the hill with a comfortable distance between us.

"Why do you have bruised fingers?"

I nearly stumbled in my steps. I threw a startled glance at him, but his eyes were on the festival ahead of us. How did he notice that in the dark?

"I—I... Nothing. It's nothing." What would he do if he knew the truth? The tops of my ears burned, wondering what he would think if he knew I couldn't stop thinking of that night in his arms, and that distraction caused me bruised fingers.

I hid my fingers by fisting them in my palm.

Aris scoffed, and I clenched my fingers tighter. "I sincerely doubt that."

Once we reached the bottom, he ordered a few Siniyan warriors, one of them being Kallen, to bring me to my quarters, most likely still empty from the festivities. I was relieved and thankful it was Kallen and that he was taking me back to safety. I wanted to be in my cot, tucked under heavy blankets, and cry. I was ready for this night to be over.

We walked through the festival on the cobblestone streets, but Tobias caught sight of us and stomped over with a glower. The small crowd parted for him.

My heart rate soared. His eyes were hot with rage.

"What is *she* doing here? She should be *dead* for what she tried to do to me!" Tobias snarled, flailing his arms around. "Is this how you Siniyans handle women?"

Thank the gods Malakar wasn't in sight.

"She got her punishment. Drop it, Tobias. If you have an issue with it, take it up with Malakar. I don't have time for this." Aris walked away and continued through the festival, Helon now by his side. Helon's long coat brushed the cobblestone streets ahead of me.

A Siniyan warrior put his hands on Tobias' chest to keep him from following us, but as soon as the warrior touched Tobias, he swung his elbow across the warrior's face. The warrior went sprawling across the ground.

Kallen's face paled, but he held my elbow firmly and pushed against the smothering crowd. The Siniyan warrior shoved against Tobias, and suddenly multiple Siniyan citizens were throwing hands and elbows at the Strokan warriors near Tobias.

Fights broke out in every direction.

"Fuck. Not again," Kallen grunted and hurried our steps.

Aris rushed by the fights and fought the crowd back toward Tobias. I had seen that look on his face the first day I met him.

Darkness. Pure, destructive rage.

Our steps stilled. Kallen held his breath, and I realized I was doing the same.

Tobias took a step back as Aris approached him. Aris pulled his fist back and landed it directly in Tobias' face. He didn't give Tobias a chance to regain his balance and grabbed the front of his tunic and threw another fist and then an elbow in Tobias' face.

Tobias lost his footing, stumbled on the ground, and tried to get away, but Aris was on top of him within a second.

Aris' fist did not cease its impacts on Tobias' face. Blood splattered on the cobblestone street, and the fights continued nearby. I was shoved out of Kallen's hold for a moment, but he grabbed ahold of me again. He pushed me out of sight of Tobias' limp body being struck over and over again.

A lightness settled in my chest, watching Tobias get what he deserved. I just hoped Camilla was safe. I hoped none of this escalated to something worse between Aris and his father.

I had a feeling nothing was going to be the same again after this.

Chapter Twenty-Three

Life in the quarters was slower the next morning. Either the servants were hung over, asleep, or they had found another bed to rest in for the evening. I looked in the mirror and stared at my pale face. Soft purple and blue hues appeared across my right cheek, with a small cut already scabbing from the night before. I placed a hand at the back of my head. The inflammation throbbed, but the herbs had helped from the night before. At least it was covered by my curtain of red hair.

I wondered how Camilla was this morning. Women could never be safe from the predators that roamed free. From those that deemed us an object to enjoy and punish to their liking. No matter who I was, where I lived, what I did, I would always remain the hunted.

I heard one of the servants in my room leave without saying a word to me. My cautious eyes met hers in the mirror as she left. Something strange shone across her face, but I couldn't put my finger on it.

I would not be surprised if many of the servants had seen what happened between Tobias, Malakar, Aris, and I the night before. I wondered if they expected me dead. I would have. I brushed the washed waves from my copper hair, careful not to pull too hard as my scalp felt bruised. I placed the shared brush on the table near the mirror. Looking back at my reflection, I noticed something flash within my eyes.

Damn me.

There was a part of me that didn't want to admit the encounters I had with Aris made me feel a certain way. That scared me the most. He didn't seem to care about how I looked or what people said about me. It made me feel human.

I stared at myself. I demanded my eyes return to normal like before.

Before Aris.

I braided my hair, put my beige linen dress on, and prepared for the gardens this morning. The lead servant told me I would mostly be working by myself and that I had to pick the majority of the vegetables and herbs for today.

I strolled down the dirt path alone and at peace with my thoughts. The sunlight filled the morning air, and I could see the wind blowing away the smoke from the festival. I started in the herb garden, where familiarity put me in a meditative state. I snipped the sage and rosemary to be paired with chickens for tonight's dinner at the palace.

The branch behind me made a loud *crack*.

I whirled around, but I didn't see anything or anyone.

Oh, no. This could be it. My eyes darted around the trees and the herbal boxes and down the dirt path I had walked from.

Malakar had come back to punish me, kill me, or take me away for what I did to Tobias. My heart thundered in my chest.

"Solei," I heard a young woman hiss from around the hedge's corner.

Maeri.

That was it. I was officially paranoid.

"Maeri?" I whisper-yelled.

I walked around the hedge that separated the herb garden from the rest of the gardens. I found her walking towards me in distress, face in dismay.

"What is it?" I asked. "Are you okay? What's wrong?"

"What happened to you last night?" Worry filled her eyes.

"I don't want to talk about it." I closed the question, and walking back, I resumed snipping at the herbs. "How was your night?"

"It was fine until the chaos erupted. Emperor Malakar and Aris tried to control the fights. Nirelle and I left as quickly as we could."

From where I crouched, I glanced up at her, my brows lowering. "Do you think everything's going to be okay?" What I really wanted to say was, *I hope I'm not the reason for a war between Siniya and Stroka.*

Maeri waved a hand. "Yeah, I'm sure. I heard these things happen often, and they've always had an aggressive, divided relationship between Siniya and Stroka."

"I wonder why. Do you think that's why Strokan warriors are still here, to squash any rebellion?"

"I would assume so," Maeri murmured.

I took a moment to relish in the relief of knowing that I hadn't been the reason for a great war. And another, reminding myself I was safe for the time being. That I didn't need to hide. I placed the snippers in the basket with the rest of the freshly cut herbs.

"Did you know Malakar was Aris' father?" I asked, raising myself up and brushing my hands down my dress.

"Yes, of course. Didn't you?"

More reason to stay away and unnoticed by Aris.

"No." I shook my head, dumbfounded. "I really do live in my head."

Another twig went *crack*.

Maeri and I whirled in the direction of the sound, and my heart stopped.

Siniyan warriors stood at the entrance of the herb garden, dressed in their leather armor, weapons across their back and knives hanging on their hips.

They were there for me. I knew it, in my heart.

Instinctively, I took a step back. They were here for what I had done. Aris had changed his mind. Malakar had most likely demanded that I be returned to Stroka, for a punishment far greater than Aris led me to think.

"Girl." One of the warriors pointed directly at me. "You're coming with us."

Multiple warriors came to my side, grabbing my arms and pulling me towards their path. My body tensed. I looked back at Maeri as they pulled me further away from the herb garden, the spitting image of sorrow and beauty. Her sharp brows furrowed, and her eyes filled with concern for me, for her friend.

Go, I mouthed to her. I was afraid for her. She was associated with me. Tears welling up in her eyes, her chin trembling.

I should have told her what happened. Maeri gave me the brutal truth and sometimes was harsh on my ways—she didn't care about hurting my feelings, but she was there, and most importantly she gave me a friend.

I didn't know where I was going or how long it had been as the warriors pulled me out of the herb and vegetable garden alongside paths through the luscious green hills. There were five of them. It took five warriors to find me and bring me somewhere. I must have had some incredible fighting skills I didn't know about.

With a sigh, I kept my eyes glued to the ground. The sun felt more distant than it was yesterday, almost like it had forgotten that we were meant to be in spring. The chill wind pulled strands out from the front of my face and left my skin with gooseflesh.

Eventually, both warriors let me go. This was the moment where they would execute me. I kept my head lowered, and then I made a sudden burst to the side and ran as quickly as I could.

Run, run, run. I didn't want to die.

Not a minute later, an arm wrapped around my waist and hoisted me off the ground as I thrashed and pushed—but nothing was going to make the warrior falter. I elbowed his shoulder, and it barely hurt him; in fact, it hurt me more.

They resumed their hold on both my arms when they placed me on the ground, firmer this time than the last.

I lifted my eyes and saw what lay before me. It nearly took my breath away.

I'd never seen the palace from this view before. I only had the small window in my quarters to see the palace from afar, and it was the view from the back. It had always been forbidden for any servants who weren't working directly in the palace to visit the gardens here.

At the foot of the palace, the gardens were filled with large hedges, beautiful hanging trees, and exotic flowers of all kinds I had never seen, heard, or dreamed of. As the warriors guided me towards the bottom of the hill, the sweet fragrance of the flowers filled my nose. The hedges were in the form of animals, lions, wolves, and snakes. They were strangely magnificent. The towering, weeping trees that surrounded these gardens flew in the direction of the wind, casting shadows against the scorching sun and—

A rough hand encircled my left elbow and veered me towards the side of the gardens, peeling my attention from the vibrant colors of the glowing flowers.

My eyes turned towards the palace ahead of us. Nowhere in my village, not even my lords or kings, had a structure as remarkable as this. The palace itself was glorious. The hundreds of windows that embedded the walls looked like eyes of beasts prowling ensuring that no intruder would enter. Windows upon windows upon windows, up, up, up the palace went. I craned my neck as we walked closer.

The warrior who still had his hand wrapped around my elbow yanked me to the side of the palace where we entered. I was so enthralled by all its grandeur and beauty it was difficult for me to focus on my footsteps. As the warrior pulled me inside, my foot caught on a step, causing me to fall on my knees and hands. The warrior to my right jabbed my ribs with his calf.

"Get up, wench!"

With unsteady legs, I stumbled with the warriors through the doors. We walked through the dark brown marbled hallways, which wrapped around and opened into other smaller gardens and court-yards inside the palace. The space above the small gardens showed the sky peering over the trees.

It was magical.

They pulled me into a stairwell that went up into another dark hallway, this one filled with velvety tapestries where two warriors stood at the end. I couldn't help but peer at the tall, painted ceilings and ancient tapestries on the walls. My captor gave a quick nod to both warriors ahead, which caused them to open the floor-to-ceiling double doors.

The doors opened into a bright and airy chamber. Camilla stood in a long dark blue dress on a burnt orange rug facing the door. Her black locks danced in the reflection of the light coming through the windows and hid the marks around her long neck. Her lip was swollen, but the rest of her body showed no evidence that harm had ever found her in that alley.

"Leave us," she ordered the Siniyan warriors, and they obeyed. Camilla approached me hesitantly. "You. I—I wanted to find you."

Startled by Camilla's voice, birds fluttered out of her windowsill and a gentle breeze whisked into the chambers. I didn't know what to think or what to do as she approached me.

No matter what Camilla's intentions were with Aris, no one deserved what she went through. But still, I wondered whose side she was on with this division between Siniya and Stroka even if it were as small as a crack in a potted bowl.

That bowl was bound to break. Would there be someone to hold it together once it did, or would it shatter into a thousand pieces?

"You helped me last night." Her eyes were filled with heaviness, and under them were dark smudges. She reached out and grabbed both my hands in hers which were cold and clammy. "I don't know how I'll ever thank you for what you did." She squeezed gently. "I wanted to find you to tell you that Tobias is dead."

My heart sputtered in my throat. Tobias was *dead*. Aris must have killed him last night.

"I don't know how he knew, but he knows what Tobias did to me, and I have a feeling it's because of you. I don't know how you told him, but he knew. He came to me. Last night. He ensured I was okay after everything."

Camilla swallowed audibly as tears welled up in her eyes. "And now he's gone," she said, looking down at me with a smile. "Aris took care of me—of everything. Tobias will never find me again... Thank you."

I searched her face and her dark eyes as they twinkled in tears. I wanted to tell her she didn't need to thank me, there was no need, I would have done it for anyone, but I was at a loss for words due to the kindness she was showing me. My lips parted and—

"I don't know how I ever got trapped with Tobias and the Strokans. I was so stupid—so stupid for fighting on the wrong side."

She still thought I was a mute. She wouldn't be sharing this with me if she knew I could give this information to anyone else. "Tobias made me believe that Aris was going to betray the Strokan Empire, that the downfall was going to happen to me as well if I didn't help. I was supposed to share all the information I found and give it to Tobias, and that would save me from Malakar's wrath but—but I couldn't."

Couldn't find anything or couldn't betray Aris? I wondered.

"Aris knows what is best for this country. He is a great ruler. He takes care of all of us. I was so, so foolish for believing otherwise." Camilla let go of my hands. "I think I will go back to my father's estates. Perhaps I'll even find a good Siniyan husband. I'm so tired of this deception. I want it to be over. I am safe now—*we're* safe."

I gave her a smile and tilted my head. I felt something forming between the two of us even if it was mostly a one-way road.

For a moment, I wanted to speak to her. But I realized if she knew I could talk, maybe she would have reason to kill me because I knew her secrets.

Knowing it was my cue to leave, I left Camilla's chambers, and the warriors guided me through the palace. We crossed pillars that opened to the interior garden. It was full of ferns and ivy cascading over the walls and into the open space of the palace.

We walked down the hallway, my leather sandals softly hitting the ground. It was hands down, the most beautiful place I'd ever seen.

And there, at the other end of the hallway, was Aris. Just as I thought I'd be able to leave the palace without his notice, he caught my eye.

Shit.

CHAPTER TWENTY-FOUR

The floor-to-ceiling double doors opened into a dark, bare-ly-lit study that held shelves of books upon books, with a large carved wooden desk in the center. Thick brocade curtains were drawn over the windows, barely allowing the sunlight to shine through.

Aris wore a dark blue button-up tunic with his long sleeves rolled near his elbows and black trousers that led to his black boots. It was so dim in this room that the candles' reflected off his black hair.

Aris ordered his warriors to leave after bringing me into the study while two guards remained outside. My breaths turned shallow.

As Aris approached me, it became harder and harder to breathe, like he was pulling the air straight from my lungs. How did he do that? Power radiated from him with every step he took. Mystery, wonder, curiosity. Closer and closer, there were wars in my head causing me to not think straight.

I didn't know what Aris wanted from me. The panic within me rose the more I thought about it. Maybe he was going to give me back to Malakar. Maybe he realized I caused more trouble for him than helping him as an indentured servant.

Think, think, think.

"Look at me," Aris ordered.

I clenched the side of my dress and forced myself to study the marbled umber tiles and the deep emerald rug that covered a large part of the floor. I debated his demand for a moment more and realized it was useless and obeyed, meeting his smoldering eyes.

"You are to stay near me."

I blinked.

"After what happened last night...for your safety from the Strokans..." His eyes flickered. "You're to stay in the servants quarters inside the main palace, where I know they wouldn't dare come near."

Aris placed his hands in his pockets and peered down at me. I forgot how massive he was, towering over me. "Will it always be this hard to get a response from you?"

I diverted my eyes. The hanging black velvet tapestry across the room suddenly became *very* interesting to me. *Think, think, think.*

"Do I always have to be close to get you to talk to me?" His voice dropped an octave.

My wide eyes shot up. "No!" I shook my head and took a step back, gaining more pointless distance.

Aris chuckled softly at my quick response, clearly amused. My face flushed red. *I do not want you any closer.*

I cleared my throat. "Do I have a choice in this?"

His chuckle faded. "No, you don't."

I dug my fingers into my palms. Of course, I lost my choices months ago. I was a captive, forced into servitude. "Why do you care what happens to me?"

Aris leaned a hip on his desk. "You're my responsibility."

Right. That was what Malakar told Aris I was. But I didn't want to be here, closer to Aris. That was the last thing I wanted. He was unpredictable and unreadable.

"You're to be my chambermaid. The last one died from a sickness, and I'm in need of a new one."

My jaw dropped, but I decided to give him a nod as my response, hoping that was enough. Talking was too much around him, and I wouldn't give him the easy satisfaction since he'd made my life…not so easy.

My gods, I was playing games. *What is wrong with me?*

Several moments went by where I could feel his heavy gaze penetrating through me, *reading* me. I gazed at that extremely fascinating tapestry.

Aris pushed off the desk and strolled over to me. My fingers quivered, and I crushed them again in silent demand to stop. He grabbed my jaw with his warm hand and lifted it to the side to reveal my neck. My scar barely showed anymore, but the fact he still noticed didn't surprise me. How he cared to notice—now, *that* surprised me.

"Don't think I've forgotten." His face came too close to mine. He angled his head, narrowing his eyes on my neck. His breath danced over my skin, causing it to prickle, as the warmth of his body radiated toward me. He grabbed my hand, and I could hardly breathe right as he brushed a thumb over my bruised fingers.

"I give no mercy to those who cause harm," he stated.

I gave him a cold stare for his hold on me. That was enough. He had no right to touch me like this. His touch burned through my skin. I was tired of feeling owned, that my body wasn't even mine. I was tired of having no say over what happened to me. I was tired of being pulled and dragged and pushed.

"Let go of me." I raised my arm to release his grasp, but he caught my arm with his free hand.

He tightened his grip on my jaw, and I flinched. My body was now flush with his from the sudden movement. My breath faltered. I forced the image of me curled up in his body that fretful night out of my mind.

"You're too slow."

"I'll get faster."

Aris chuckled, and my stomach flipped. His voice turned into milk and honey as he spoke. "I try to stay away from you, but you don't make it easy, do you?"

I met his obsidian eyes above mine. "I am nothing to you," I whispered, my heart beating so loudly I was sure he could hear it.

Aris shook his head, the front of his hair almost touching my face. "If you are nothing, then why do you keep appearing in my thoughts?"

Our eyes locked, and our breaths flowed into each other's mouths. He smelled of musky oak trees. My eyes lowered to his mouth. The perfect shape of lips. I felt an unfamiliar sensation tingle down my body. It was distracting.

I didn't answer.

"Are my thoughts not important?"

This was a trap. He was playing a game. His body towering over mine felt warm and protective, even though I knew he was dangerous and what he was capable of. Maybe every other girl would have fallen for his charm, his built body, his handsome face, and the fact that he had a powerful empire, but not me.

Nothing would ever tempt me from the vow I made.

When I didn't respond to his rhetorical questions, I used my free arm to push against his hold on my jaw again, but instead he released me and twisted my last free arm behind my back. My entire body was now pressed completely with his. I attempted to yank the arm behind me out, and his hold on me tightened once more in gripping punishment.

He shook his head, clicking his tongue. "It's too easy," he said with disdain. "You better learn fast in a world like ours."

His threat made my blood boil.

How dare he.

"Like I said before, I've managed." My eyes darted to his, my neck craning.

"Oh, is that so?"

"Yeah," I whispered breathlessly.

I felt his chuckle rumble against my body. "How so?"

"I keep to myself. And stay away from emperors who like to grab me."

Aris laughed deepened. "It's been pretty easy for me to grab you, quiet one. I think you've done a terrible job at that."

My face flushed red as I attempted another escape. *Stupid, arrogant emperor.*

"Maybe I shouldn't have you as my chambermaid since you're a liability."

"I wouldn't recommend it. Having a witch for your chambermaid...doesn't seem so safe." I blew a piece of hair that fell in front of my face from the movement. My breathing deepened from my exhausting and pointless attempts.

His body went still. "Is that a threat? To your emperor?"

Oh, shit. I hadn't meant it in that way. I looked up.

He must have understood the innocence in my eyes as Aris curved his lips. His warmth seeped into my body, so much so that I almost allowed myself to lean and relax into his. My eyes lifted from his mouth to his eyes. They grew a shade darker.

He leaned down, his lips close to my ear, and whispered, "Then it's a good thing I'm not afraid of you."

I smiled faintly. For the first time in...a long time.

"Are you afraid of me?" he asked.

I didn't know what came over my body, but I lost control of my words, my thoughts, and my movements as I instinctively shook my head, my face barely touching his.

"No," I whispered softly.

It was the truth. I didn't know why or how it was, but it was truth that burned into my heart. Maybe I wasn't the pathetic girl I believed myself to be. Maybe I did have some strength in me that wasn't afraid.

Aris released both my arms and took a step back. His eyes turned indifferent and distant. "You're going to have to learn quickly. I can't have my chambermaid not know how to protect herself." He went around his wooden desk and called in his guards.

My jaw tightened. He was right. I couldn't protect myself. I was tired of being under the control of others because of *my* weakness. I decided at that moment that was going to change, and I was going to find a way to fight harder and stronger. I was going to make my brother proud. The funny thing was, I was fine when people looked at me with disgust for who I was but never pity, never in a way that made me feel like the smallest person in the world.

The large double doors creaked open, and both guards entered.

Aris sat in his large wooden chair and fussed with his papers. "She is to be my new chambermaid. Show her to her new quarters."

Chapter Twenty-Five

S hame filled the empty hole in my heart as the guard walked me toward my quarters in the back of the palace. My face flushed warm and most likely was the exact shade of my hair. I should have never admitted that to him, to myself. The man who led an army to attack my village and strip away everything that I'd ever known from my life. I welcomed the shame in my face. I welcomed it into my body, into my blood. How could I be such a traitor to my people? How could I *not* be afraid of him? How could I *not* be repulsed by him? How could I ever trust a man like him?

In the back of the palace, I could smell the freshly baked loaves of bread wafting from the kitchen as we headed towards the servants quarters. The walls were cool and dark.

As we passed the kitchen, the warm spices and citrus smells grew stronger, along with the servants not being shy about their blatant stares. Some whispered to each other about what I'd been hearing the last three months.

"That's her—the girl the Strokans fought over."

"Do you really believe she could be a witch?"

I didn't care as I kept their curious stares. I didn't look down. For the first time in my life, they were the ones to look away first. Let them think I was a witch. Let them think whatever they pleased. I didn't care anymore.

As the guard led the way past the kitchen into another dark candle-lit hallway, past three doors on the left and a fourth to the right, we stopped. He opened the door into a smaller room than the one I had before, but there were only three beds in this room.

My bed was the one closest to the door and near a window on the right side of the room. It was a thicker straw mattress and on a taller wooden frame. It was perfect. It was more than perfect. It was better than the bed before and the cot I had at Fenrah's house and the one I shared back at my village. I even had a drawer next to my bed where I could put my belongings.

Hearing a commotion near the door, I whirled around to see the guard had left, and two wide-eyed women stood before me with a palace keeper behind them. Both younger women had dark hair, neatly braided, and the palace keeper had hers up in a linen.

"Hello," the young woman to the left said.

I was about to respond, but the old palace keeper spoke for me. "She's a mute. Don't bother yourself."

Thank Erus. I smiled sheepishly.

"What is she doing here then if she can't talk?"

"Hush. Talking is never part of any role. Maybe you can take some notes. She's to be the new chambermaid for Lord Aris," the palace keeper stated.

Both young women's jaws dropped, their eyes bulging wider than before. I thought they were about to pop out of their sockets. Their disbelief made me question my own reality and Aris' choice in chambermaids.

"Behave yourself! And don't question the emperor's orders." The palace keeper thinned her lips and slapped the young woman's arm. The woman hissed yet immediately closed her mouth but didn't stop staring at me like I was a fish out of water. The palace keeper looked in my direction. "Do you understand what I'm saying?"

Swallowing, I nodded. But I was laughing in my head from how long I'd been able to keep up this charade that I was a mute.

"You're to start immediately. Sebry will show you the rest of what you're to do. Breakfast is just before sunrise. You're to do your duties in the morning right after our lord leaves."

The palace keeper and the quiet woman to the right of me hurried out, leaving me with wide-eyed, curious Sebry.

"I can't believe *you're* to be his new chambermaid."

I stared back at her with my brows creased. Did I miss something? What was all the fuss about?

"The whole lot of us have fought for months and months for this position, and never heard a response from our lord. No one did!" Sebry clicked her tongue, shaking her head. "Ever since old Tracy died eight months ago. She caught a miserable cold last winter while she was away visiting her family in Stroka. Froze to death—well, basically, since she got so cold and died days later. She had been his maid his entire life, and she also nursed him, raised him, since he was a babe. He hasn't filled the position since. We all took turns when asked by our lord."

Sebry narrowed her eyes. "Why did he hire you? Oh, never mind. He didn't hire you. You're from another land, aren't you? You're a captive working for freedom. You don't look like you belong here at all with your pale skin and that red *hair*! Do all your people look like you?" She paused, giving me a contemplative perusal. "Anywho, apparently you're Aris' new chambermaid."

She rolled her eyes and waved me to follow her down the candle-lit hallway. "It just doesn't make any sense at all. He doesn't have people like you here in Siniya. For some reason Aris doesn't want slaves—or unpaid servants. He would like this country to one day be free of all slaves. We basically do the same work. I'm not complaining because I have a job here—the best job. Well, not technically. I guess you do. But it's not even a job to you because you're not getting paid—so that means I do have the best job! I've actually never seen a captive before in my life because I'm from Siniya, unlike some folks here."

Does she always talk this much?

"My mother did, though. She said that one tried to bite her for her food in Stroka—from a cage! There were *Insulatus*. You're not going to bite me, right? Because we'll feed you just fine. You're basically one of us." We crossed a dining room into another long hall just before going up a stone staircase that swirled around. "Right! I forgot you're a mute! How did that happen? Were you born that way? Right! Shoot."

I thought about putting her out of her misery, but I wondered if I started responding whether she would really not *ever* stop talking. As we climbed and climbed, up and up, around and around, I almost passed out on the stairs. We turned into another hallway, except this one was cavernous and filled with large windows on both sides of the hallway.

"I'll show you what we do in our guest rooms, show you *exactly* what you're supposed to do, so that you can do it for our lord, Aris. Have you met him yet? He is a *god*—like literally. I rarely see him, but when I do, I just can't help but stare at his *beautiful* tall body!" Sebry threw her hands left and right as she prattled on, and we continued down the hallway, past a hallway intersection into another one. "I don't think he feels that way about anyone, actually. Maybe he just loves himself and only himself. I mean, who can blame him, right?" She looked at me. "Oh, right! That's going to be hard to remember. Anyway, not many women go into his chambers, though I dream about doing so at night."

Sebry smiled at herself, flushing. "Our lord is just so busy with other important things that he's never really found a lover. Except for Camilla, but she mostly joins her father at the war camps. I hear they get it on sometimes, but that it's nothing serious. I'm not sure why. Can you believe even she's never been invited into Aris' chambers? His chambers are off-limits to most—except for servants, of course. Camilla is gorgeous, but don't let that beauty fool you." Sebry lowered her voice a few octaves as she leaned in closer to me. "I hear she kills beautiful women at night so that she remains the most beautiful of all in the Siniyan Empire. I would stay away from her if I were you. You have a pretty face and curves in the right places, despite that hair color of..."

My mind wandered to the sturdy rugs we stepped on. They were beautifully woven in gold and silver. We passed a few large sets of doors to the right.

"I'm not sure if that's true about Camilla, but that's just what I heard. I hope one day Aris notices me and invites me into his chambers. It'll be a dream come true!" Sebry giggled, and I couldn't help myself but smile.

Sebry showed me the order of cleaning a chamber and continued talking about the men she had been with, and how she felt like she needed to settle down soon. She asked if I had a lover and forgot again that I was apparently mute.

After spending the day with Sebry, I realized my shame had withered away. I stopped thinking about myself and my actions, where I was, or who I was becoming. I appreciated someone like Sebry, who distracted that part of me that hid in the shadows.

Today was not the worst day, after all.

Chapter Twenty-Six

The ringing of a bell shocked me from my sleep, the clanging reverberating in my skull.

The palace keeper, Hara, rang a large bell directly above my face, scowling. "Wake up, silent one!"

I looked over to my roommates, and they covered their ears in unison. I barely remembered falling asleep last night. The last thing I remembered was lying my head on the mattress. Next thing I knew my ears were about to bleed off.

"There's no time to waste!" she said in a sharp tone. Her foot tapped on the floor. "You have one of the most important jobs here, and you best be going!"

Hara waved her hands for me to get off the bed. Regardless of knowing I could get struck for it, I gave her a frown for her relentless demands.

"Aris is taking the day to ride and so it'll be perfect to get that room into shape. Let's go, let's go," she continued, slinging the bell around the room before she left.

I dressed myself in a light brown linen dress that was given to me last night by my other roommate, Anna. It had a U-shaped neck with a simple white lace around the top. It had no holes, no stains, and it fit perfectly.

Looking at myself in the clean mirror, I tied the strings behind my back. My breasts filled the front as I passed my hands over the few wrinkles on the linen. I brushed my red hair and braided it back.

Just before I was ready to go, my friends stood in the doorway of my shared quarters.

Maeri and Nirelle.

I flashed a genuine smile as they approached me.

"Solei!" Nirelle came over, grabbing a hold of my hand, and wrapped me in her arms. I smelled her sweet jasmine scent in her hair. "Welcome to the palace! Oh posh, Solei, don't give me that face. You'll come to learn it's the best thing that's ever happened to you since arriving in Siniya. Speaking from experience here, you know?"

"I was so worried for you when they took you. I didn't think I'd see you again. But gods, I never expected this. You're in a much better place now." Maeri scanned my quarters, and when her eyes found two other women, she smiled.

"I'm staying a few hallways away. I'm so happy we're closer now! We can hang out all the time. There's even a river nearby. I've gone a few times. It's so perfect for the summer!" Nirelle shrieked and hugged me again.

Anna passed the party happening in her quarters, cocking her head to the side.

Maeri grew serious. "What's happening?"

"Nothing. I'm the emperor's chambermaid," I admitted.

"*What*!" Nirelle, Maeri *and* Sebry exclaimed.

My head snapped in Sebry's direction.

"*You're not a mute*?" Sebry's eyes protruded as she stumbled over to me.

"No, but she doesn't talk much if that's what you're wondering," Nirelle explained.

"Thanks, Nirelle." I rolled my eyes. *I don't talk much. Why does no one seem to understand that?*

"Maeri, what's new with you? What a beautiful dress!" I exclaimed.

Maeri wore a burnt red dress with velvet blue lace at the top of her V-neckline. "Thank you. It was a gift from—"

"Your *lover*," Nirelle answered for Maeri.

Maeri slapped her arm and blushed. She changed the subject. "You have to tell us everything. What happened? How did *this* happen?" Maeri asked me.

Before I could answer, Sebry interrupted, "What are those?"

"Oh, these are Solei's belongings. I thought she might want them here since she moved quarters." Maeri handed me my things.

I gave her a smile of gratitude.

"Solei. That's your name? That's very strange. Where does it come from? Everything about you is pretty strange, and why didn't you tell me you could talk? The whole day yesterday, we could have been talking together, but instead you decided to keep your mouth shut and spoil the fun." Sebry crossed her brown, dainty arms over her small chest with a pout on her lips.

"I—"

"She prefers to listen," Nirelle explained, smiling at Sebry, who accepted it. I furrowed my brows and internally rolled my eyes again. Nirelle now turned her attention completely on Sebry. "So how long have you been working here at the palace? My name's Nirelle."

"I have to go. Thanks for bringing me my things. It was good to see you." I left the quarters towards my new task, hearing their voices fade.

Sebry had shown me where the emperor's chambers were late last night and because I listened well, I didn't have trouble finding it.

Among the many things I listened to during Sebry's ramblings yesterday was that Aris used most of his mornings either riding, hunting, or in his study, far away from people and most importantly, far away from me. I would rarely run into him, most likely never according to Sebry, and I didn't have any other servants to boss and bully me around like in my last quarters. It was a perfect win-win situation for me, and I celebrated any type of wins that came my way.

As I approached his chambers, I might have admired his enormous carved wood ceiling-to-floor double doors longer than necessary. They were the largest I'd ever seen, more than twice my height. It was majestic and also absurd.

What was absurd was the amount of sheer force I needed to pull one of the doors open, or maybe it was how weak my muscles were. As I entered his chambers, I noticed how dark and spacious it was. His oversized bed to the right side of the room had a beautiful, artistic wooden frame that cornered each end. His bed was made already, but not properly. I tried not to look at the weapons he hung to the far right of his bed, on the wall that connected to the door I just walked through. Countless exquisite carved knives, sharp swords, a bow, and other weapons I'd never seen before. I might have wondered how many deaths were caused by them. I might have cringed a little bit.

I drew the brown floor-to-ceiling curtains at the front of his bedroom to the side and opened the windows to allow fresh air in. I started cleaning his entire bedroom and dusted every shelf, nook, and cranny. I swept the vast godforsaken floors and hand washed them over and over until they gleamed once more. To the left of his room was the fireplace, where I cleaned the chimney and removed the buildup along its walls. I righted the cushions on his two large chairs near the fireplace to make it appear more alive.

I wiped the back of my hand along the top of my forehead. Then I brought his sheep-skinned rugs to the windows where I shook them out until I could get every ounce of dust out of them. I remade the attempted version of bed-making into what it should look like and neatly placed his pillows beside each other, pressing the wrinkles out like Sebry taught me.

After a few hours passed, the place was sparkly clean. It was coming alive, tidy and airy. I refreshed his water bowls, cleaned the bell that if pulled would call Hara, and organized his writing tools on the desk.

The morning chores were done. My entire body felt sore and exhausted. My legs nearly gave out. I quietly left his chambers, using all the strength I had left in me to shut those double doors, and headed back towards the servants quarters.

At least I didn't see Aris today.

And that was a very, very good thing.

Chapter Twenty-Seven

Why did he have to consume the thoughts in my head? I wanted to scream and scream in my blankets if only to get his presence out of my mind.

It had been a few weeks since I had my new task given to me by Aris. I ended up completing chores in Aris' chambers multiple times throughout the day due to Hera sticking her nose in my business, but I had learned his schedule, so I'd never have to spend more than a few minutes in the same room as him. Regardless of making efforts to ignore his glances and having more important things to think about, like my survival and safety, and regardless of whether I'd seen him or not, I'd still end the day thinking about what he was doing that night.

I wanted to yank the red hair from my head in spite of the servants who told me every day I should shave it, so that they weren't burdened by seeing it. I wanted to rub coffee bean powder over my skin so that I would be accepted by them and look more like they did. Yet no matter how much I screamed, no matter how much I wanted to shave my head and rub bean powder all over my body, I'd still be here.

I woke today just as every day, starting with a core exercise to strengthen my muscles mostly out of spite from what Aris said, but also because it might help me when I most needed it. I attempted to push my body up from the ground using my hands in front of me, hoping that I'd finally make one full movement—and I did. I attempted another and fell immediately on the floor.

Perhaps tomorrow.

I tried a few more exercises that I knew would help strengthen my upper and lower body. I improved my breath slightly with how many repetitions I was doing. Sweat accumulated on my forehead and dripped on the stone floor in front of me. This would help me get up the stairs easier and faster than the first day I was here.

I got ready for the day, rinsed my face, brushed and braided my hair, and left shortly after with a lilac-dyed dress gifted by Maeri. She said it wasn't her color. I rushed down the hallway, up and around the back staircase, controlling my breath, and crossed the larger hallways towards the emperor's doors.

I tested out my strength as I pushed the large double doors open—

That was easier than yesterday. I smiled. I looked down at my arms but didn't see any improvement in size. I shrugged.

I noticed Aris left some papers on the table to the left of the room—strange, as he always carried them with him or they were secured in his study.

With an overwhelming sense of curiosity, I approached the wall of weapons and brushed my fingers over one of the more beautifully carved metal knives. I bit my lower lip.

Tilting my head, I wondered how many people my brother killed. I wondered if he ever held a knife like this one. He told us he wanted to fight wars since he was eleven. My parents didn't take him seri-ously, but as he grew older, his dream of becoming a soldier never left. He'd say, *It's my destiny. It's what I'm meant to do with my life.* Little did he know, he'd be gone from our lives because of it. I fought the tears that stung and turned to continue my chores.

As I started on Aris' bed, my curiosity finally got the best of me, and I turned to gaze upon the weapons hanging on the wall. I shouldn't—but I *could*. No, I had to. I had to feel one in my hands.

Lifting a carved knife gently from the wall, I held it in my hand. It was heavier than it looked. I wrapped my fingers around the handle. It felt cold.

Focusing on swinging it back and forth, I felt the weight cutting through the cool air. I tried to take a lunge with the knife, realizing how utterly silly I was, stabbing the air, and laughed out loud.

"What's so funny?"

I whirled around and found Aris standing across the room near the privy chamber, and I dropped the lovely knife on the floor.

The sound echoed in the room.

Shit.

My eyes widened. "I—I'm so sorry, my lord. I—I was only—I didn't mean to..." The words escaped me. I should have known. The papers gave it away. If I only wasn't so distracted by my nonexistent muscles. *Damn you, Solei.*

Aris chuckled at my attempt to explain myself. "It's Aris," he corrected me. He crossed the room, dressed in black from head to toe, hands in his pockets. "What was so funny?"

I blinked and slowly relaxed my body. He wasn't mad at the fact that I was handling his weapons.

"The thought of striking air."

"Would you rather strike something else?" His brow lifted. A dangerous question.

"I wouldn't know."

Aris bent down and reached for the lovely carved knife, holding it in both his palms. "The air can be your friend sometimes. It helps balance the weight of the knife."

Then, he was holding it with only one finger. I felt my eyes grow wider. He held it on the tip of his finger, then flung it in the air and grabbed the handle with the other hand.

I took a step back.

His lips curved sinfully. "Are you afraid now?"

"I would rather not die from a fatal accident."

"An *accident*! Why, you insult me, Solei." His amusement mocked me, and I blushed a shade of red.

Why was he here? I wanted to finish my chores and leave this beautiful, beastly man immediately.

"There will be no accidents when my hands are around a weapon. I know exactly where it will end, every time, using precision, concentration, and will."

"Will?"

"If I will it, it will happen." I hid my shudder and didn't drop my gaze from him. "Come closer."

My heart fumbled. "Why should I?" I asked hesitantly.

"Why must you always argue with me? Come here."

"I should get back to cleaning." I swallowed, my breath caught in my throat.

"Too late for that. And don't make me ask again." His eyes, I couldn't read them. Perhaps they were cold, empty.

Reluctantly, I stepped forward, and Aris grabbed my arm and placed the knife in my hand. I wrapped my fingers around the warm handle, and he let go.

"I saw you earlier. You let the air hold the knife, but you need to control the weight. Left and right the weight of the knife carried your hand, but it's your wrist that needs to navigate the blade," he instructed. He placed his hand around my dainty, pale wrist and pressed it. My wrist stiffened, and the blade followed my weight. "Do you see?"

I nodded.

His hand pulled my wrist forward, turned me around, and he was behind me in a split second. The movement took my breath.

"Hold it strong," he insisted behind my shoulder and tested the weight of my wrist.

"I am, Aris!" I waited for a moment, holding my breath for his strike, but he did no such thing. Instead, he kept weighing my wrist, completely ignoring my retort.

"You're not! Hold it with some grit, quiet one. Like your life depends on it."

Frustrated and more willing to prove my point, I held the handle tightly, my knuckles going white.

"Not that strong."

I twirled around to face him. He towered above me. "Well, which one is it, *Aris*?"

His eyes were darker than before. "It's a fine line."

I tried to take a step back, but he was still holding my wrist near him. "Then teach me," I whispered, trying to distract myself from feeling a rush at his nearness.

First, he showed me how he held and swung the knife and then had me hold his wrist, feeling his weight on the handle. Then, he made a few gestures with the knife, and I followed his will.

"Do you hear that?" The knife split the air in half, and a whistle sounded through the room.

I nodded in amazement. Time passed by quickly as he showed me a few more moves.

"Again," he urged me.

I held the knife, and he was behind me again, wrapping his hand around my wrist.

With the weight evenly distributed, I slashed the air, and I could hear the whistle of the air.

I smiled at my success, my eyes filling up with excitement. "I did it!"

Aris' body stilled for a moment. Something gleamed in his eyes as he stared at me. He smiled and nodded. "You did indeed. Keep practicing."

He dropped his hold on my wrist and walked to the wall of weapons. I felt silly in my lilac dress, slashing a knife in the emperor's chamber, but I continued as he ordered me to. Besides the whistling air, I heard him take down another blade from the wall, but I focused on my *will*, as he taught me.

"Where did you learn how to fight so well?" I inquired.

"Besides being Malakar's son and being forced to have lessons since I was a child... I sharpened my skills with a man." He paused as if remembering something from a long time ago. "He was actually a prisoner of war my father captured. He taught me many things when I was barely a man, especially how to fight. He became like a brother to me." His eyes hollowed.

I wanted to know more, but Aris appeared in front of me. He pressed his finger upon the tip of the dagger he held in his hand. "Now, time to know where to plunge that blade when the time comes."

"When," I noted.

"With your luck, I'd assume so."

My mouth pursed, and I placed the blade on his bed.

With my luck? I scoffed and didn't respond, choosing to ignore him. I continued straightening out his bedsheets since I was behind schedule as it was.

"You'll learn this whether you want to or not."

How dare he.

I turned. "You—"

Suddenly, my back was flat on the middle of the bed, and a knife was between my neck and shoulder. My heart pounded. He was on top of me, crushing me.

"Aris, what are you—"

"I told you, you're going to learn. I can't have my chambermaid know how to hold a knife but reluctant to learn where to plunge it. That, I'm afraid, is the most important part—or else you may be putting yourself in more danger by targeting the wrong area."

The blade he held slid down my neck. I couldn't breathe, and it wasn't because of his weight pressing on my petite body. The blade felt sharp and cool against the warmth of my skin.

"You want to go for the side, between here and here. Do you understand?" His eyes were so serious.

I swallowed and nodded. For a moment, I lowered my gaze and noticed how soft his lips looked from here. My heart sputtered in my throat. How soft they might feel—

Fool, Solei. Stop thinking about such things.

"And here," he said softly as he trailed the knife down to the low spot on my shoulder near my neck.

The world stopped spinning as he lowered his gaze to my own wet lips. His face was so close. The blade lifted, and he brushed it against my lips and lifted his eyes to mine. I barely noticed how cold and hard it felt upon my lips. My breathing deepened.

"One more place where it's crucial when the time comes." He dragged the blade from my lips, down my neck, and lower. He stopped in the middle of my chest between my breasts, his hands dangerously brushing against them. "Here."

I thought I might have died. My heartbeat was nowhere around.

After a moment, I felt the weight of the blade against me as he whispered, "Are you afraid now?"

It was now or never, I told myself. I braced myself as I pushed him off my body now that he was caught off guard, wrapped my hand around the handle of the blade, and ripped it from him. I knew he had let it go just as easily as it felt.

I twisted my body so it was above his, though my body could barely cover half of his.

"Here." I placed the blade on the side of his neck. We didn't break our locked eyes. "Here." I traced the blade down his neck and onto the softest part of his shoulder. "And here." I gently pressed the blade against his lips.

He let out a gentle laugh that made my stomach flutter. "That isn't one." He shook his head, his lips curving to the side.

"Oh? You could have fooled me. You placed the blade on my lips."

"Indeed, but it wasn't a place I'd press my blade into." His eyes pierced me with obsidian darkness, and I could almost feel myself melting inside of them.

Warmth spread across my face.

"You missed the most important one." He smirked.

"No, you're wrong. I didn't miss one." I pressed the other blade I had caught from the bed deeper into his chest so he could feel it there.

I was asking for a death sentence—that was how it felt from how reckless I was becoming. I had lost all my senses. I could be hanged for what I was doing. My sister would stab him *now*. I knew she would, but the thought never crossed my mind.

His lips curled into a smile. "Impressive. You even managed to catch me off guard. Not many would be able to accomplish such a thing."

Feeling the heat of his eyes, the way he dropped his gaze to my lips, the way my body warmed on top of his, I dropped the blades to his side and slipped from his bed.

I didn't look back as I left his chambers, to be returned to once I knew for certain he had left for the day. I didn't realize it until then, but my entire body vibrated and tingled like never before. Not in the way of fear, but in excitement.

What was *wrong* with me? I stormed down the hallways. *What am I doing?* I wanted to smack my head onto the marble floor. *I'm an idiot!*

I rushed past the windowed hallways, down the stone stairs into the back of the palace, through the servants quarters, the kitchen, and into my room. I collapsed into my bed. I screamed in my linen blankets as loud as I could without anyone hearing me.

I couldn't do this anymore. The betrayal and guilt in my heart was too heavy. *I just can't. I can't. I can't.*

"Is everything okay?" I heard a small voice ask behind me.

Fuck!

It was Sebry. I could only tell because she talked my ears off every other day.

I looked up from the blankets I had just screamed in a moment ago and smiled sweetly. "Yes, of course."

Gods, I was such a liar.

"Okay, I was just making sure because it didn't seem so a moment ago. Was it hard today? I had multiple guest chambers to wash and clean, and it all went great. Have you eaten the cranberry muffins the cook made this morning? My god, it was the most..."

The next morning, I completed the same routine of exercises I did every morning and continued the constant glances into the mirror hoping for some physical progress. I could see some—maybe, or I might be imagining it. It was hard to tell but regardless, I felt better knowing that it was easier for me to run up the stairs every morning to complete my daily chores.

I was walking down Aris' hallway when he exited his chambers with a guard waiting outside his doors. He towered over that guard too in height. A flash of metal on his hip caught my eyes. He was carrying the beautiful carved knife that I practiced with yesterday.

Warmth fluttered inside me.

Respectfully, I walked to the side of the hallway and waited for him to pass. Daring myself a glance from my bowed head, Aris gave me a nod.

"Solei," he greeted.

I dropped my gaze and wanted to kick myself from the heat that rose in my neck.

"She has a name?" the guard asked as they walked by.

"Of course she does, Chaston. Everyone has a name," Aris said exasperatedly.

"Yes, but how did you find out?"

"I asked," Aris said as they continued down the hall.

Entering his chambers, I smiled. Then I scolded myself.

I looked over to that tempting wall and noticed the empty space the knife had hung in. My fingers twitched, wanting to practice on another dagger with what he taught me the day before. When I finished, I left his chambers and made my way down to the servant's quarters for lunch.

My leather flats padded against the dark marble floors as the lights bounced off the mirrored walls. I would sneak a glance or two as I walked past them, curious to how I was perceived by the rest of the world. My green eyes reflected vibrantly in the mirror, and my stubborn hair, yet again, left my now-loose braid.

I heard familiar voices in the interior garden below. Curious, I walked over to one of the pillars and leaned forward. My eyes darted, trying to find the source.

It was Camilla's.

"I can't thank you enough, My Lord," Camilla said softly.

"Don't mention it." Aris waved a hand.

My chest squeezed a bit at the sight of them. They looked like a painting, sitting together on a bench. I could see them from above through the open stone pillars. The bright green luscious gardens almost hid them as they sat in the center.

"I have been meaning to ask, how did the girl tell you?"

"She told me," Aris stated.

Camilla laughed as if not understanding his answer to her question. "I know, but how did she do it?"

It was Aris' turn to laugh at what clearly was the truth and an inside joke to us. "I suppose we all have our secrets, don't we?"

I wondered if Aris said that in part because of what I shared a few weeks ago with him in secrecy about Tobias and Camilla.

"My Lord...I haven't been completely honest with you."

"I know you haven't, Camilla." Aris stared at her, but there wasn't any rage in his face. "You don't have to explain. I know enough."

I could tell from where I stood that Camilla began to cry. Her whole body trembled. "I—I'm so sorry." She shook her head and looked at her hands twisting on her lap.

"We've all been caught in their webs at one point. I'm glad you were smart enough to make it out in time," Aris said.

"Will you forgive me?"

A long moment passed. I held my breath.

"I already have."

"I know things have never been too serious with us, but know that I care deeply for you."

"I care for you, too, Camilla. But we both knew this was never going to work."

Camilla nodded, wiping the tears from her cheeks. "I know. I remember what you said: there is no room in your life and in your heart for love...or anything like it."

"You deserve more than I can offer you." Aris' head turned slightly away.

"I am leaving for my father's estate tomorrow. You know where you can find me if you need anything, right?"

Aris nodded.

They rose and held each other. Aris pulled back and disappeared underneath the level I stood upon.

That must have completely shattered Camilla, to hear those heart-wrenching words from a lover. He had no room in his heart, he had told her.

At that moment, I knew I was right about Aris. He was the kind of predator that destroyed your village, destroyed your home, and took everything you'd ever known and killed it. He didn't look back, wouldn't look back. Didn't care enough to.

I tucked that little piece of information into my heart. I closed my eyes and smelled the fresh citrus air circling through the garden before I left to the servants' quarters. The stone walls within the quarters seemed extra cold and dark today. My heart grew heavy, and my stomach twisted itself.

A few servants passed by me, casting their displeased, cursed gazes, which caused my breath to quicken. This place felt too small for me. The walls were slowly closing in. I couldn't catch my breath, and beads of sweat dripped from my hairline to my chin. I passed the candle-lit dining room and hurried through the hallways towards my room. As soon as I stumbled inside, I dropped into my bed with my arms stretched out to the sides.

A tear escaped my eye and trailed its way on the bed. Exhaustion overcame me, and I drifted into sleep.

CHAPTER TWENTY-EIGHT

A large, callused hand enclosed my mouth, causing me to rise through my dreams and into full consciousness.

My eyes opened to find my legs and arms bound by several shadows who had snuck into the servants quarters in the darkest part of the night.

My heart raced. *What is happening?*

No air or sound escaped my mouth as I tried to scream at the top of my lungs. I elbowed one of the bodies that were close to my face only to receive a brutal jab into my ribs. I rammed my pale, naked legs against their dark silhouettes and attempted to free myself from their iron hold. They tightened their grip even more.

They hoisted my body from my wooden bed and carried me away as I attempted to yank my limbs free of their hold. Why weren't my roommates hearing this? My screams faded into the rough hand that engulfed my mouth.

Their bodies were rock-hard. No matter how much I resisted, it did nothing. Somehow, some way they had managed to wrap a thin cloth between my teeth and around my head, ensuring no sounds would come from me.

I couldn't see anything. It was so dark. I couldn't breathe.

They rushed me out of the servants quarters, into the palace gardens, and towards the woods. The dark night was chilly against my skin and short night dress, leaving me feeling more vulnerable and exposed. The men in shadows led the way with several torches and its burning light.

Through the dark, I noticed red leathers. The shadows walked and grunted in a beast-like manner.

Strokan warriors.

Of course. I could smell their stench now.

They placed me on the ground as they pushed me out of the gardens.

What did they want from me? Why did they take me? It surely was because of Tobias. It had to be. They were here for revenge.

I hadn't realized my face was wet until now. Tears had sprung from my eyes.

I was pulled further from the palace and its gardens. My hands lost feeling from the warrior's firm grip as we went up the hill and into the foreboding forest. The tall and thin trees that gave room for the moon light gave me little comfort as the energy had shifted with my circumstances. We walked further and further, and at this point, I was sure their intentions were to end my life.

I doubted the Siniyan servants would notice I was gone. No one would know if I disappeared.

Though spring was here, the nights were still chilly, but that did nothing for the sweat that accumulated on my skin. I had to get out of here if I wanted to live. I could feel my sister's presence and her disappointment seeping through me.

What a waste of life, she must be thinking. How I had failed her. Miserably.

Think, think, think. What would my brother do in this moment?

Without another thought to delay me, I thrust an elbow into the man who ensnared my wrist, but I missed. He flashed a murderous glare.

This was it. It had to be *now.*

With his shock still settling, I drove another hard elbow into his ribs, and for a moment, he released my wrists and grunted.

I yanked my arm from him. I didn't stop to think about what I was doing as I rammed my knee into the other warrior who had my other wrist, wrenching myself free.

I stumbled out of their grips and ran as quickly as my short legs would take me. I heard them shouting.

Don't look back. Keep going. I aimed for the forest edge. I would hide under a bush until morning.

My legs burned with fire as I busted through the woods, gaining more speed and more distance—

My body flung forward, falling to the cold hard ground as one of the warriors jabbed his hands into me. Before I could scramble to my feet, his foot swung into the side of my ribs, and I let out a scream as it struck me over and over again.

I let my arms guide me forward, crawling from him, but he grabbed my long hair and flung me back. I thrashed against him as he straddled his legs around my body and grabbed my arms with his hands.

No, no, no.

"You little witch. You're going to regret this," he growled. His face came close to mine, and I could see a large scar from his ear to his mouth. He raised my arms above my head, and I thrashed and flailed my legs behind him. He fumbled his free hand, ripping my night dress as I heard the other warriors catching up.

No! I wanted to sob and cry and kick and scream.

And I did. I fought with all of my strength. I hoped someone would hear me.

"Enough," the leader ordered him. "The earlier we get this done, the better we can move forward with tonight."

"A little fun—a little lesson—won't waste that much time—"

"You may do as you please *after*. Don't delay us any longer," the leader warned.

After what?

The other warriors forced me upright and pushed my shoulders forward until my bare knees hit the cold hard ground. I shook at the thought of what might have happened if they hadn't appeared at that moment.

I couldn't stop thinking of the bravery I never fought for. I could have fought harder, faster for myself. I could have lived life better for me. The moments I betrayed my own body and soul. I wasted so much time hiding and not living enough.

Now, I'd be dead before I could do anything differently. Now, I was out of time. It was too late.

A single tear fell down my cheek.

A warrior with a tattooed neck stepped to the side of my body with a torch that held the largest flame, reflecting off my pale skin. He lowered it near my shoulder.

They were going to kill me by fire.

This was how I was going to die. It was ironic. No matter how burning-red my hair was, there was no fire lit in my soul—until now. It burned bright with anger.

Anger at myself.

The leader brought forward a rod of iron. He placed it above the licking fire until it glowed red.

My breath quickened. *What are they—*

Two warriors appeared each beside me, crouching, and secured my arms firmly against themselves, keeping my body glued to the ground. They pushed me into the dirt, my cheek pressed onto the cool, moist dirt.

The leader proceeded towards me with the iron. They were going to brand me. The glowing orange rod approached faster and faster. A tear of linen exposed my left shoulder, exposing my skin to the biting cold of the night.

I wasn't going to let them hear a victim's screams.

My melting skin seared in my ear as the iron imprinted the side of my shoulder. Smoke from the contact danced in front of my eyes.

There was no sound that escaped my throat. If there was anything that I could control, it was my voice. They didn't deserve to hear my screams, to hear me beg for them to stop when they would do no such thing.

The searing flesh of my shoulder was the only thing I heard. My entire body clenched and froze in time. Then, I betrayed my body when a whimper escaped my lips as the searing rod burned until it felt like my bones were melting.

What felt like a lifetime within seconds later, the searing sound came to an end. The warrior released the iron rod from my shoulder, and the excruciating pain halted at its peak.

"You were never his. Now, you'll never question it. You're *ours*, sweetheart." The warrior to my left chuckled as he released his grip on my arm.

"This ought to teach him a lesson," the one to my right grunted, also releasing me.

My arms fell to my side, trembling on the cooling dirt ground. I couldn't move, but my arm twitched uncontrollably. My eyes focused in and out from the pain. Tears rolled down my cheek onto the pasty dirt below me. The linen wrapped around my mouth and head at some point loosened and fell around my neck.

"He won't harm another one of us again," the tattooed warrior with the torch muttered.

"Harm? Aris didn't *harm* one of us. He *killed* him," the scarred warrior spat. "This isn't to remind him of who owns these people. It's to start war."

"I don't think Malakar wants that, Jamir," the leader spoke.

Jamir stared at the leader with deadly eyes. "I say we kill the branded witch. He should have done it himself at the festival," he hissed through gritted teeth.

"Killing her won't start anything. She's nothing. It's a simple reminder. That's all. Not only to him, but to Siniya. This girl should have never gotten in Tobias' way."

"He *killed* Tobias and—"

An arrow pierced Jamir's throat, and he tumbled, thudding beside me, bleeding from his neck and mouth. The light in his eyes disappeared almost instantly.

The warriors scattered for their weapons as another arrow penetrated the leader's head. With the sudden commotion, I managed to twist my body to see a man in a dark hooded cloak slinging his bow across his chest and unsheathing his sword from his hip. He approached the warrior to my left.

"Aris—Aris, he made us—"

Aris slashed his sword clean through the man's neck and kicked the decapitated warrior's chest to the ground. He twisted around to intercept an incoming blade to his back, and with his free hand revealed a second short blade that with a powerful swift motion he stabbed into the warrior's neck—exactly as he taught me. The warrior's blade fell from his bleeding hand and on to the ground, followed shortly by his body.

I became all too aware of where I was in the midst of this chaos. I scrambled to a nearby dead warrior and ripped one of his knives attached to his hip. My shoulder felt like a thousand coals. As soon as I had the handle free, a hand wrapped around my waist—

"Come here, you wench."

The warrior with the neck tattoo was the last one remaining, and grabbed a hold of me. I managed to twist my body and by instinct, I plunged the knife into his shoulder—not exactly deep and not exactly where Aris taught me.

My eyes widened, and my hands shook when the warrior didn't release his hold.

Rage filled his eyes as he took the blade with his free hand and pulled me towards the woods.

This was exactly what Aris warned about.

I rammed an elbow into his ribcage, and his hold on me loosened. In that moment, Aris was catching up to us. I fell into the rustling leaves, and the warrior decided wisely I wasn't worth the trouble and scurried into the dark woods.

With an abnormally swift speed, Aris lunged across the empty space at the escaping warrior.

I could only hear the screams of a life ending as the sound of splattering blood echoed through the woods.

Chapter Twenty-Nine

Aris approached me with eyes darker than night, his sword dripping with blood, which he sheathed at his hip. His footsteps crunched on broken leaves underneath him, passing by the dead bodies as if he hadn't just hunted and killed them. Completely unfazed—unlike me.

My body shook and shook, and it wasn't because of the chilly night. I drew my naked legs closer to me as I attempted to rise from the cold ground using my good arm. My other arm trembled but felt numb. The searing pain came in waves.

Aris lent an arm for me to stabilize myself.

I looked up to find no life in Aris' eyes. The unearthly screeching wind in the woods had more life than he. He was soulless. A chill ran down my spine from his touch. There was no warmth in it, not like when we were playing in his bed.

Aris twisted towards the darkness, placed two fingers in his mouth, and whistled. I looked at where he faced, wondering what was out there. First, the sound of a beast echoed in the shadows, and then a large white horse emerged from the eerie woods, trotting past the dead warriors.

He placed his hands around the small of my waist and hoisted me up into the black leather saddle. The leather was cool against my inner thighs. All I could think about was how badly my left shoulder needed some cold air or a cold press—anything cold, and how relieving that would feel against this never-ending burning sensation the wound caused. I was scared to know what they seared into my flesh. *Branding me.*

It burned and burned. Aris held onto the horn of the saddle, placed his foot on the stirrup, and pulled himself up effortlessly, sitting behind me. His hard body pressed firmly against me, shielding my barely-covered body from the air. Grabbing both of the dark leather straps, he clicked his tongue once, and the white horse began its beastly movements through the darkness.

"How did you find me?" I whispered.

Aris chuckled, but it didn't sound pleasant, most likely in surprise that I even said anything. I had been given another chance at this life of mine, and I refused to be its victim anymore. I didn't want to be afraid. I didn't want to constantly be wondering if I'd survive this or that. It was exhausting, perhaps more than simply living. Fearing was more energy than living itself, I realized.

Aris cleared his throat. "I couldn't sleep... The man I told you about kept appearing in my dreams, and so I found myself sitting on my windowsill... That's when I saw the torches from afar, and I saw you under the light because no one here has your hair."

He lowered his warm lips to my ear. "You're not easy to hide. You practically glow in the dark."

His breath trickled down my neck. The burning feeling on my left shoulder was still yearning for cold, but I could barely concentrate with Aris so close to me.

My lips curved in amusement at his statement.

"You think that's funny? Because I certainly don't," Aris muttered as the horse trotted through the dark woods towards the opening of the hill.

"What am I supposed to do, rub dirt on my skin and shave my head?" I dared to ask.

"At least that would be something, and perhaps I wouldn't have to be searching for you in the middle of the night."

"I didn't ask for you to come find me," I murmured under my breath.

The horse came to a brutal halt. Aris wrapped his right arm around my waist, pressing his body closer to mine.

His voice was rougher than usual, "How would you have survived? Because I doubt they were going to let you walk after they were finished with you. You should want to fight for your life."

"I *am* fighting for my life!" My voice wavered.

"Are you? I can't tell!"

I winced. The pain came back tenfold. "Why are you so angry?"

Aris growled, tightened his grip around me, and clicked his tongue. He kicked the horse into a swift gallop down the hill, past the palace gardens and the front steps to the palace. It seemed so empty during the late night with no warriors, no footmen, no maids, no palace keeper to order the maids about.

We galloped into the closest stable to the far right of the palace, where the large trees almost hid the walls of the building. Aris threw his leg over his horse and landed on the hay-filled ground. His hand stayed on the horn of the saddle between my legs, grazing over my thigh, and he looked up.

For a moment, my full awareness turned to his hand near my thigh. I should move my thigh. I knew that, but it felt nice to have his warmth come back to me. A part of me reveled in it. And since tonight showed me that I should live a little more, I didn't remove myself from his foreign touch.

"I'm angry because I don't want this for you—for anyone." He waved his other hand at my bare shoulder, legs, and ripped dress. "It's maddening, and I'm tired of it."

I whispered through the darkness, "Much worse happened to my sister and to my mother." I paused. Aris kept my gaze as I opened a part of me to him. "It's hard in a world like this to be completely safe."

"I thought it was going to be better bringing you here."

"Better than where?"

"Than Stroka."

I swallowed. "I think it is."

"It doesn't seem like it is." His shoulder dropped slightly. "I don't know what to do with you."

I flinched. "You don't have to do anything." I remembered his responsibility weighed heavily on him. My arm throbbed, pulsating.

"What if I'm not there?"

"What do you mean?" I asked as he stepped even closer to where my leg hung from the straddle. His warmth permeated into my skin, causing a chill to skitter down my leg. A distraction that I needed from my shoulder.

"What if I'm not there the next time a Strokan gets to you, Solei?"

My heart skipped at the sound of my name on his lips. *What is wrong with me? Focus on the damn conversation, Solei.*

"Are you really trying to save every one of us out there?" I whispered.

His eyes flickered under the barely lit stables.

I pressed, "Is this because of the man who taught you how to fight?"

Aris was quiet, and then, "I'm trying to right the wrongs..."

"Of your father?"

He didn't answer.

That man must have meant a lot to Aris to change his perspective from his father's brutality. I had a feeling he wasn't going to speak about it anymore.

"For what it's worth...I did try—to fight, I mean. A part of me found the courage to fight for my life. If you hadn't been there, I'm not sure..." I shook my head slightly.

"I won't accept it." His voice dropped an octave, like he could feel my heart sputtering from his nearness.

Words came out freely before I could stop them. "Are you going to help me down, Aris, or are you going to keep talking all night about how frustrated you are with me?"

Aris chuckled, and I could have sworn the spark in his dark eyes returned, like stars in the night sky. He took a step closer, his chest grazing my naked leg as he placed both of his large hands around my waist. Suddenly, the pain in my shoulder disappeared, and all I could think about was how nice it felt to be touched by him.

"Good thing I can do both if I want to."

"I suppose you could. You are the emperor."

Aris pulled me off the saddle and towards him, my night dress lifting slightly from the movement. He placed me gently on the floor, the distance between his body and mine nonexistent.

I should take a step back.

"Would you want to stay up with me all night listening to me talk about how frustrated I am with you?" His hands remained on my waist, and I looked up to see his face close to mine.

My pulse fluttered. "I would," I whispered. *I'm a fool.*

"Because I can talk at length about exactly how frustrated I am with you."

For some reason, I knew Aris meant something entirely different than how careless I was. I parted my lips and breathed unsteadily. I raised my eyes higher to his, which had now turned darker than night. Obsidian eyes.

His fingers brushed softly up and down my waist, gently lifting my linen dress. His thumbs grazed just below my breasts, causing them to harden. It was as if he sensed it, because his chest heaved alongside mine.

Little by little, with each careful stroke, I felt a sensation between my legs I had never experienced before, and I didn't want him to stop touching me. His face lowered closer to mine. His eyes dipped to my mouth. We shared the same air.

Somewhere in my mind, a small voice hissed and thrashed at me to push him off me. To run. To hide.

His fingers crept closer and closer, higher and higher. My breasts turned harder. It felt...wonderful and nothing like I'd experienced before.

My breath deepened.

But what I wanted didn't matter. This was wrong.

"You're so sure I wouldn't fall asleep to you complaining about your *responsibilities*?" I voiced the words he spoke the day he asked me to be his chambermaid, hoping to distract whatever this could have been.

He stopped the brushing of his fingers and thought for a moment. "Responsibilities." A flash went through his eyes. A conversation that I couldn't hear. "We need to dress the wound."

He dropped his hold on my waist and took a step towards the leather straps. The instant cold from his absence snapped the pain of my shoulder back to reality. Aris seemed to have the same thought as he wrapped the straps around the interior wooden fence, grabbed my hand in his, and led me out of the stables.

His pace was longer and quicker than mine as he pulled me towards the palace steps. We rushed up and up the stairs, into the palace to be met by one of his servants, who he ordered to bring a few things to his room. I wasn't paying any attention to the orders he barked when I realized how I looked, my face flushed red. The man gave me, my open shoulder, and short night dress a quick glance with a flash of judgement. With swift obedience, the servant bowed and went on his way, giving me a look like he had heard the rumors before, and I just confirmed it.

As if the rumors couldn't get any worse from here.

Aris' hand felt warm and rough as it engulfed my small, pale hand. He pulled my good arm towards him and his large steps. We strode past the interior gardens and pillars, silently past the halls towards his doors.

Quietly, he opened the double doors, tugging me into his chambers, and bolting the doors shut behind me. I'd been here more times than I could count, but it felt different being here during the night, just him and me. Alone, again.

His room was well lit with the fire glowing strong in the fireplace.

"Here, change into this." Aris handed me a black tunic and pointed at the room divider towards the corner of his chambers. "Will you need help?"

My heart thudded. "N-no." My face burned fiercer than the brand on my arm, imagining him taking off my dress. *Control yourself, Solei.*

Tonight was already too much for my mind to handle. I couldn't linger around Aris too long as my body created sensations that were unfamiliar and could potentially be dangerous.

CHAPTER THIRTY

Aris was hooking his dark hooded cloak when I walked around the room divider. He was wearing a soft black long-sleeved shirt that caressed his strong form. I could barely concentrate while the fire burned bright and the shadows danced all around the room.

There was a knock on one of the doors that brought me back to reality. Aris rushed over, opened the door slightly enough to take two bowls and some linens. Shutting the door behind him with a kick, he walked over to the small table near the window on the other side of his room, motioning me to follow him.

For a moment, I hesitated going anywhere near him again and swallowed dryly.

"Sit down," Aris ordered, nodding to one of the sheepskin chairs.

I clenched my hands, fighting against myself. At last, I sat on the chair and crossed my ankles beneath it.

"This is going to hurt." He started unbuttoning the top of the shirt when I swatted his hand away.

"I'm not a child. I'm a healer and can do it myself." I glared at him.

He grabbed the hand I swatted at him with a firm grip. I doubted anyone had ever swatted his hand away. The emperor.

I held my breath. His immediate reaction faded and softened as he held my gaze. His grip loosened. A smirk appeared on his lips.

"Hurry up."

"Let go of me, and I will. I wouldn't want you boring me with how frustrated you are with me."

Aris laughed heartily, causing butterflies to spring inside of me from all directions. I couldn't help but smile when he let go.

"Trust me, Solei, it would not bore you." Aris winked.

It suddenly felt too hot in here. Was it because of the furnace or my burning brand?

I began at the top of the wooden buttons and made my way down just below the top of my chest where I pulled the opening around my left shoulder, exposing the wound to the warm air.

Exposing the pain, the memory. It all came flooding back.

Aris drenched a towel cloth in the large water bowl, squeezed the excess water, and handed me the linen.

Before I placed the linen on my brand, I could feel his domineering presence towering over me with his arms crossed. He reminded me of Fenrah for a moment, making sure I did this properly. I wanted to chuck this wet linen in his face, but I resisted and focused on the task at hand.

I placed the linen—

I swore profusely in my head.

My eyes were clenched shut, and the moment I opened them, I saw stars flashing.

Aris shook his head and stole the linen from my unsteady fingers.

I spun my head to him, but he had already placed the linen back on my brand, not giving me a moment—

It was excruciating. The pain soared and rippled through my body. Though it felt cool when he pressed the towel on my shoulder, temporarily alleviating the burning pain, but just the mere touch almost caused me to faint. I was seeing stars again, but I blinked them away.

Aris handed me a towel that I could clutch as he cleaned the wound multiple times with the cool water. I looked away towards the window, closed my eyes, and breathed through the pain. I held in a sob.

Out of the corner of my eyes, Aris poured something into the crisp water.

"Salt," he answered my internal question. "It'll sterilize it."

I know, I wanted to say. Instead, I nodded. I kept my gaze on the windows towards the palace gardens.

He washed the wound once more as I squeezed my eyes shut, keeping the pain within. When he was done, he grabbed a linen cloth nearby and was about to wrap my shoulder when I twisted to look at it for the first time in the light.

I lifted my elbow and stared at the letter that now burned more than ever. The world stilled. The crackling of the fire was the only sound I heard as I stopped breathing.

M.

It had a snake that curled around the *V* in the middle. I lifted a finger toward the engraved letter on my shoulder, and realized not only my finger was shaking but my entire body was. My heart squeezed in my chest, and I felt like there was no air in his chamber.

"I..." My voice was barely a whisper. "I belong to him...forever." The realization sunk in deep. I belonged to Malakar, to the Strokan

Empire. They did this so I wouldn't forget who I worked for, who owned me.

Aris, who was kneeling before me with the linen cloth, went deathly still. His energy was hard and cold. It chilled my bones.

Why should he care that I was someone else's?

I lifted my free arm to hide the tears that fell and faced the window. *You're stronger than this.* I could practically hear my sister in my head.

"You do not belong to him." Aris' voice was a lethal calm.

"I will never have any say over my body. I will never again. I'm nothing and nobody." Aris took my shaking hand that covered my face in his. "I am a *thing*, an *object*."

"This does not define you, Solei."

"*This* is the definition of what branding is, Aris." I finally faced Aris, not caring how blurry he looked because of my tears. I bunched the fabric of the tunic I wore in my free hand. "I am owned," I breathed, forcing back the sobs that wanted to come out.

"No, that's what they *want* you to think." Aris shook his head.

"You don't understand." I stared into Aris' dark eyes. "You don't understand what it feels like to not own your body. Your future, your existence. To feel like *nothing* you do is for you. Nothing you do is *yours*. It's for someone else. You don't understand, and you never will."

I saw a small window open in his eyes, where emotions existed. I saw them in a flash. They seemed soft, sweet, and warm.

"Maybe I don't understand what it feels like to walk your same steps. But a friend once told me that those who are strong in the mind"—Aris pointed to his head—"know that nothing in this world can define you. Not your family, not your friends, your people. No one can define you no matter how much they try to. They want to. Trust me, they want control over you and everyone else they see as a threat. But they'll never be able to truly control who you are. That's entirely up to you."

I snatched my hand out of his like it had stung me. My brand hurt more than ever. "You forget that *they* are also *you*."

I got up from the chair, covered my shoulder with the dark tunic, and walked towards the double doors. I needed to get out of here. He was my *enemy*. He needed to know I wouldn't forget. He was reeling me in because of his guilt, maybe because of Malakar. I didn't know, and I didn't care to. I didn't want to be part of their games.

"You don't know me. No matter what judgments and assumptions you make, you don't know what I've been through," Aris said behind me.

I stopped at the door and turned around to find him standing nearby.

"I might not know what it's like to be you, but I do know what it's like for someone to want to control you. It's an illusion, Solei."

"Is it?"

"Yes. I can assure you."

"How do you know?"

Aris unbuttoned his black shirt, revealing his strong chest and torso. He took it off his right arm while heading over to me.

Opening his right arm, displaying his inner bicep, I saw a large engraved *M* on his skin. A sharp pain curled in my chest. I swallowed the lump in my throat. I couldn't believe my own eyes.

It was brutal and thick. Like a thousand times the skin had gone over and over but never healed. My mind raced, searching for answers.

"I can still feel it sometimes." His whisper was a distant memory.

My brows drew together. Why would a father do this to his own son?

"How?" I said softly and stepped forward. Without permission, I placed gentle fingers on his inner bicep. Aris flinched from the touch but didn't move from it.

I closed my eyes for a moment and took a deep breath. Opening them again, I felt the heavily raised scar beneath my fingertips. Aris stiffened. An even deeper, longer cut marked across the letter. This had been more severe than mine. I took longer than necessary to study his healed wounds.

"I've noticed these types of scars all over your body..." I couldn't finish my thoughts.

"Let's just say Malakar likes to own people, captive or not. My father's execution of power and control is different than mine," Aris said sharply.

He snapped his shirt over his shoulder before I could observe it some more. I looked up to meet his cold eyes once again. The small window to his soul closed shut.

I was sure there was a lot more to the story I wasn't going to get. I didn't blame him. I had a hard time talking about things that had hurt me, too.

The anger I had toward him earlier faded from my heart. I felt the pre-conceived notions I had placed on him drift. I realized I couldn't have been more wrong about Aris.

This was treacherous territory I was balancing on.

Walking back towards the doors, I paused. Looking over my shoulder, I spoke my last words to Aris before shutting the door behind me: "Thank you."

CHAPTER THIRTY-ONE

The next morning was stranger than usual. Maybe it was just the feeling inside my body. Or the feeling that my arm was burning incessantly.

I kept a brown shawl wrapped around my shoulders to cover up the wound, which was painful from the friction. Even though it was frowned upon to keep my hair down, considered messy and not put together, I did so this morning—just in case. I wouldn't want anyone seeing my new mark. Through the night, I barely slept. I would hear sounds that had me lashing at my sheets thinking someone was grabbing me once again. My body sweat feverishly, but I would eventually settle before drifting into a night terror of my life ending.

"You are so terrible, Solei! Don't try to distract me. What about you and the emperor?" Maeri slapped my arm—the good one.

I winced anyway because it moved my other arm. I swore in my head. Maeri had come singing down the hallway to see me this morning and checked in on me. Hara was told I was to stay in bed due to my "sickness," and Maeri wanted to ensure I wasn't dying—though I felt I was. Aris must have told Hara not to send me in today.

"What about me and the emperor?" My muscles went taut.

"What have you two been up to?"

"I clean his chambers, and I think he runs an empire, but I'm not entirely sure."

Maeri crossed her arms over her chest. "Ha-ha. Very funny."

"You asked." I changed the subject as quickly as I could. "Sing for me. Your voice is so angelic. It made me feel better when I heard it."

Maeri lowered her face, and a flush rushed up. "I sung at a tavern the other night." She laughed nervously.

"Oh?"

"I did. I was so embarrassed at first, but then the crowd seemed to enjoy it. Or so I think." She bit her lower lip.

"I'm sure they did! I wished I could have been there and shown you my support," I said with a smile.

Maeri squeezed my hand.

"How are you and your *secret* lover?" I asked, waggling my brows.

Maeri lowered her head again, attempting to hide her eyes from telling the truth. "I don't know what you're talking about."

Though Nirelle and I made jokes and assumed Maeri had a lover, she had never outright told us about him—yet.

"Oh, come on, Maeri. I know you're getting all these pretty dresses and coins from someone. We're not idiots."

Before she could answer, a man came in my room.

A healer.

My heart stopped at the sight of Oleo, dressed in black from head to toe. My eyes widened, but then my heart started beating again. I was seeing people that weren't there.

The healer wasn't Oleo.

Relief flooded on my face.

"Solei, are you okay? Your face is paler than usual." Maeri's brows knitted.

I nodded and smiled.

The healer came to my side and had a calming energy to him, unlike Oleo. Maeri rose to leave, explaining that she felt nauseated around healers, and I gave her a look. I wondered what she thought of me.

With careful hands, the healer dressed my wound, and the movement—any movement, really— caused so much pain I felt light-headed and breathless from it. I broke out into another cold sweat.

"You are to stay in bed for another week to heal, silent one," the healer announced, and I nodded. "Then you are to find me in my office to start work immediately."

I creased my brows. Work? What was he talking about?

Hara appeared behind him. "Emperor Aris wants you to be Peter's assistant. You'll still be taking care of the lord's chambers, but your priority now...is to help Peter. This is insisted upon from our lord."

My jaw nearly dropped. How was this possible? A flutter rose within my core. I was going to touch medicine again.

"Emperor Aris has left on a journey, so you may use this time to heal and to learn as much as you can from Peter while he is away. I'm not sure how he thinks you'll be of any use to Peter, but I wasn't going to question it." I could tell there was disapproval in her tone, but it didn't matter.

I was going to heal again.

The rest of the week I lay in bed healing, with the help of Peter, though no one else knew about my brand apart from him and Aris. With Aris away, it was a nice feeling knowing I wasn't going to see him for the day, and that felt familiar. Like there wasn't something exciting to look forward to and that was something I could handle. It felt mundane and typical for my life. Normal and not at all confusing.

Eleven days went by since the last time I saw Aris. Though I thought it was ridiculous I was counting the days, I told myself it was that many days I'd gone without having a set chamber duty—or escaping death.

For a moment, I allowed myself to think about Aris and his wounds.

I wondered what kind of past he had that caused him to have a brand that had been done over and over like torture. Healing and burning, again and again. I didn't doubt that it was his own father who had done this to him. The letter *M* shone vibrantly in my memory of his inner arm. It made sense why he didn't have a relationship with Malakar. What type of father abused his son like that? I just couldn't—

"Hi, Solei!" Sebry exclaimed as she walked into our chambers, severing my thoughts. It was she and I for tonight. The rest of the girls were partying out at the nearest village square.

"Sebry." I smiled, welcoming her in.

"You're not going out tonight?"

I shook my head. *Definitely not.*

"Me neither. It can be fun, but it's just the same boring games they play when they drink, and the same conversations about who they're trying to bed that night. But really, it's all a façade, and they're never honest about who they just want to be with. It's like a twisted game of who they say they want to bed and who they actually want to bed.

It's too exhausting, you know, to try to read between the lines, so what I have learned to do is..."

On the seventeenth day, I found myself in the healer's office helping him organize dried herbs. Though I loathed myself for it, I couldn't stop my mind from thinking about Aris. I came to the realization that I did miss him. I wondered if he thought about me. And that made me sick.

Thirty-two mornings went by. I found my routine in the apothecary quietly comforting for my busy mind. It became a religion to me. Somewhere I could temporarily escape thoughts I didn't need nor want to have about a certain someone.

This morning, I looked at myself in the mirror as I pulled a thin sage dress over my shoulders. The sleeve was a quarter down my arms, which barely covered the brand, but it would do.

It was a wonder how people didn't talk about the emperor as much as I thought of him. Weren't they curious to know where he was? Or how he was doing? If he was alive? It was like it didn't matter whether he was here or not; they continued their busy lives with their busy chores.

I would find myself looking out the windows of the palace, searching for him, more times than I was comfortable to admit.

I decided this morning, I would adopt their thoughts. Where he was or if he was alive shouldn't matter to me.

I braided my copper hair back, wondering about the last time I had gotten it cut. Long and wavy, it would take me longer than I had time to dress my hair. With it pulled back in a thick braid, I could barely notice the thin scar that wrapped around my neck. It was fully healed, and eventually, I had high hopes it would disappear altogether.

Now, there was another more permanent mark that scarred my shoulder. Even though it had been over a month, I could still feel the burn of the letter penetrating my skin. I could still *feel* the heat radiating off my sleeve, begging for a cool touch. Eucalyptus and mint from the healer's apothecary helped. I noticed the smudge under my eyes. They didn't look dark like the morning before.

Since the branding, my nightmares had been worse than usual. The shadowy figures in my dream state held me down, and I couldn't move, couldn't breathe. I'd eventually pull through it but had restless sleep the rest of the night.

Stepping out of my quarters, there was a commotion that erupted in the hallways. Servants rushing past each other, and Hara shouting orders at a distance across the kitchen. I heard a servant rushing by saying, "She's here!"

The chef looked like she was about to faint from the chaos.

What was happening? I looked around for some answers. Who was *she*?

Sebry, who was behind me, touched my left shoulder, causing me to flinch from my pain. "You must make haste. Our lord is arriving this morning. With another woman."

I blinked at the words that Sebry spilled. My heart raced, flipped, and sank deep into my stomach.

"H-how come we d-didn't know or-or prepare for this?" I tried to gather my thoughts, but it came out stuttering. I brushed my moist hands on my sage linen dress.

"Because our lord likes to keep us on our toes. That's why."

Chapter Thirty-Two

Waiting on the steps of the palace among his primary servants, Hara, the guards and I watched as the emperor stepped away from his white horse. The morning was bright and strong, and the crisp spring winds had settled completely, creating a silent moment for his arrival. Even the birds had completely stilled. Standing as if we were statues of the palace, I was careful not to breathe too loud, afraid someone would hear it.

Aris was wearing all-black attire, a dark linen blouse with black riding trousers and tall leather boots. His hair had grown an inch more, and the fact that I noticed it disturbed me deeply. What else had changed since he'd been gone?

The large carriage behind him was a royal blue with gold fabric entwined throughout. The footman about to reach the door of the carriage was stopped by Aris, who had made his way to open it.

The woman who stepped out of the carriage, followed by Helon, was tall, thick around the bones, and had light brown hair wrapped around her shoulders.

My heart twisted and pulled. Who was she?

Her gown was the richest silky blue, and with an arm entwined through Aris', her hips swayed as she approached the palace stairs.

Her eyes darted over the stairs and past us all. Eyes like Aris. Wild eyes that ran dark and deep. Mesmerizing black ink framed her eyes, starting from the inner corner reaching toward her temple.

I didn't look anything like her. She carried an unholy amount of confidence and beauty. A strange sensation burned in my chest.

"Charming, darling." Her voice, like milk and honey, echoed in the silent air.

Helon appeared behind the woman and nodded at the palace keeper.

"Mother, this is Hara," Aris introduced.

Mother.

It shouldn't have made me this happy to hear the woman walking beside Aris was his mother, but it did. A lightness settled in the bottom of my stomach.

His attention moved ahead to where I stood on the steps, between two primary servants.

My heart burned and stopped beating altogether as his eyes found mine. His face softened as he locked his sight on me, and he offered me the faintest smile. It was as though he had been searching through the servants just to find my pair of eyes. It was as if he found me familiar and safe, because something opened in his eyes. They turned clear—

A throat cleared near him, and my attention broke to find his mother and Helon waiting on Aris. Her brows pressed together, and her gaze flew in my direction, wondering who—or what—took her son's attention. I lowered my head and kept my eyes glued to the floor as heat rose from my neck to my cheeks.

The rest of the servants turned my way.

My hands turned clammy, and I wanted nothing more than to hide under a bridge—possibly drown in the water. Anything, really, would be better than this.

Just end it completely. This was worse than the day Camilla saw me come out of Aris' tent.

Aris, his mother, and Helon continued their walk silently past me and through the palace doors. Aris showed his mother her new surroundings. Helon gave me a tight smile.

I looked up to find the palace keeper's impatient scrutiny on me. Her eyes narrowed—like always—as she approached me while the rest of the primary servants wisely went on to their duties.

"Did you make sure his chambers were in perfect condition?"

I nodded with a half-smile on my lips.

"Good." Hara gave me a list of chores to do, and obediently, I nodded through every demand even though I wasn't listening to a word she was saying.

Aris is home, I squealed mentally. Then I scowled at myself. I shouldn't be *this* happy.

When Hara was done with her relentless demands, I turned towards the side of the palace to continue my duties and for some strange reason, today was one of the better days I'd had in a while. My spirits were lifted, and I felt like nothing could change that.

If I didn't know better, I could sing, but I left that for Maeri since she was much better at it than I was.

With the quick and sudden celebrations that were sprung onto the staff, the entire palace had been transformed with hundreds of decorations and live music within a few hours. Ribbons entwined with flowers hung around the pillars, weaving in and out between the interior courtyard and the main hall. In the ballroom, there were different types of meat platters, pickled vegetables, hard and soft cheeses imported from lands I hadn't heard of, and there were several tables filled with fruit and cake. The one thing that really brought the palace to life was the music. The violin especially transformed this palace, and I could almost feel the walls breathing and vibrating to its magical sounds.

There were people flooding through the palace doors coming from all over the land to celebrate Aris and the arrival of his mother, Acantha. I was surprised by all the gowns and dresses that the women could find on such quick notice.

I glimpsed Camilla and her father entering the opened palace doors. She wore a purple dress laced with gold thread throughout, and her hair was dressed up, allowing full shoulder exposure.

"The celebration seems to be going well. I just wish I could be part of it." Nirelle pouted over my shoulder. We stood behind one of the pillars on the side of the ballroom, gazing at the festivities. Everyone was either laughing, dancing, or drinking.

"I can't believe they pulled it off so quickly. Do you think they were prepared for this many people?" Maeri asked, pulling her eyes from the direction where Aris and Helon stood.

"I think so. There is no way they didn't know he was on his way from Stroka," Nirelle said.

"He was in Stroka?" I asked quietly, surprised he even stepped foot there after finding out what his father did to him.

"Oh, yes. I heard that Malakar keeps Aris' mother on a tight leash, but from time to time, he allows her to visit Aris. I think since our lord's thirtieth birthday is around the corner, Malakar must have permitted Acantha to celebrate her son here."

"*Our lord*?" I muttered. I knew now where her loyalties lay.

"I—I just. I'm sorry." Splashes of red painted Nirelle's cheeks.

Instantly, I regretted my harsh words. "No—I'm sorry, Nirelle. It's just that...we can't forget who they are to us." I looked at Aris across the ballroom, who was embracing an older man with a lazy smile on his face. "I sometimes, too, forget..."

"Here, let's make a promise," Nirelle offered to Maeri and I, lifting a bottle out of nowhere. "No matter where life takes us, we will never forget who we are and where we came from."

I smiled at Nirelle, who took a swig of the bottle and handed it to me.

"I promise." Grabbing the bottle, I took a swig, and down went the burning liquid. I tensed up and made a face as I swallowed another gulp. Nirelle and Maeri giggled at my facial expression.

Maeri grasped the bottle in her hand and chugged the contents. My jaw dropped, surprised by how she could handle the liquor.

"Impressive." Nirelle regarded Maeri with amazement.

"Let's also promise that tonight will be the best night of our lives," Maeri said.

We all agreed and took a second round.

And then another.

And another.

After an hour of dancing together behind the pillars to the music we heard in the ballroom, we decided we were hungry for some extravagant food, and if we were clever enough, we'd be able to indulge in anything we wanted without anyone noticing. We took another swig of the bottle and then two more for some liquid encouragement.

I hadn't had this much fun in—well, forever.

I'd never felt like this before. Where everything seemed light and blurry at the same time. I didn't know if this was normal or not, or if this was what being drunk felt like, but it felt *amazing*.

I want to do this every single day, I thought to myself.

We made sure our dresses were in perfect condition. We wrapped my hair in linen, and decided to pretend we were one of them and walked, giggling, to one of the tables filled with cake and exotic fruit with attempted confidence.

The whole ballroom was packed with people, so the chances of us going unnoticed were in our favor. Most of the guests were surrounding Aris and Acantha, who seemed quiet and reserved. The apple didn't fall far from the tree, I saw.

The table we approached was filled with mini pink cakes and one large purple cake with white frosting weaving through the rim. There was a fruit that was large and blue, with yellow seeds in the middle. The taste burst in my mouth of sweet, juicy—

"If it isn't our little witch coming here to eat our food."

I turned around to see Kallen smirking behind me.

I giggled at being caught. Things were a little blurry, and I could smell his breath filled with strong liquor. The linen wrapped around my hair, of course, had fallen off. Kallen reached down and found my linen for me.

He laughed with brows high. "So much for trying to be concealed, though I'd much rather see your beautiful hair than a cloth wrapped around your head."

I blushed because I'd never heard someone call my hair beautiful before.

I turned to see where Nirelle and Maeri had disappeared to. They were both snatching cheeses from another table. Instead of catching their eyes, I met Aris' eyes from across the ballroom. Helon was at his side, speaking to him, but Aris didn't seem to listen to a word he was saying.

His face was stiff and emotionless. Even though things were blurrier than usual, I could see the flare of his nostrils from this distance.

Why was he angry? My brows knitted.

Helon, noticing Aris' absent mind, followed his view and met my own eyes.

Kallen's fingers wrapped around one of my face-framing curls, and I snapped my eyes back to him to tell him to back off, but then his hand was behind my head, forcing his lips upon mine.

My world spun out of control. His lips were cool and firm and tasted like fish.

Adrenaline shot through my chest. I felt as if I were being smothered and swallowed at the same time. I couldn't believe this was what a kiss felt like.

I was about to throw up all the contents of what I'd drunk in the last hour all over myself and Kallen. I attempted to yank my body away and release my lips from his when several hands wrapped around my wrist, pulling me from his grip.

"Come on, we have to get out of here," Nirelle said in a hurried tone.

"That's disgusting, Solei—" Maeri attempted to say while Nirelle laughed.

His cold phantom lips were still on me, and all I wanted to do was rub soap in and around my assaulted mouth.

"Quick. We've been caught!" Nirelle pulled me from the food and drinks.

The three of us squeezed through moving bodies.

"What was that about, Solei?" Nirelle called over her shoulder.

"Ugh, I have no idea. I think I'm going to be sick," I whimpered.

"Kissing is making you sick? My gods, I can't imagine what sex would do to you." I heard Maeri giggle behind me.

My lips tugged, threatening to break into a laugh.

"You'll be okay though. At least it was just an innocent kiss," Maeri tried to comfort me.

It didn't feel like it, I wanted to say.

"Hey! Where are you going?" Kallen called from behind us, and we quickened our pace.

I looked behind, and he was following with a determined look on his face.

"Run, run, *run!*" I whisper-yelled.

Maeri and Nirelle burst into laughter.

"*Wait!*" Nirelle stopped in her tracks behind one of the pillars. "Let me get some more drinks. Why don't we all meet in the servants quarters? We'll go for a swim!"

"This late?" I furrowed my brows. Peering over my shoulder, I didn't see where Kallen went and released an audible breath.

Chills appeared on my skin, remembering his lips on mine. *Gross.*

"*Yes!* This is going to be the best night ever, remember?"

"I wanted to grab some more of those small cakes. I'll be right behind you, Nirelle!" Maeri squealed.

Before I knew it, I was alone again, making my way to the servants' quarters when footsteps echoed behind me.

A chill prickled down my spine, and I felt a presence lurking in the shadows.

I whirled around to find Kallen.

Chapter Thirty-Three

I wasn't sure if he was intentionally following me...but I didn't take my chances. He was far enough for it not to look like I was purposefully running from him, but I definitely was.

I sprinted as fast as my legs could bring me through the palace hallways. My leather sandals slapped against the marbled floors until they reached the golden and crimson rugs in the next hallway. Rushing past the hallways on the first floor, I decided to sneak into one of the empty bed chambers.

Creaking the door closed, I waited and waited for any sign someone was stalking me. The chamber I walked into was dark with no fire in the hearth. No one was here.

I slowed down my breathing. The dizziness I felt before had completely disappeared, and my level of awareness heightened.

My survival instincts came back tenfold from the night I was captured and branded like an animal. Only I knew what had changed since then.

I wanted to protect myself.

I breathed as I peered through the cracks of the large wooden door. I couldn't see anything or anyone, so I leaned against the door frame.

It felt like hours had gone by before I unfolded my bent legs, stretching them out. I might have fallen asleep for a few minutes against this door frame.

I still felt Kallen's cool lips on mine, and every time I thought of it, bile lingered in my throat. *I will never kiss another man.*

It was the most repulsive feeling and taste I'd ever experienced. I heard voices echoing down the hallway. I looked for another doorway out of this room, and there was one to the right of me. I knew it led to another chamber since Sebry had trained me in rooms similar to this layout.

The footsteps were getting closer and closer, and I could see through the cracks they were not Kallen's. They were guests of Aris. Several other courtesans passed by the door and entered chambers across the hallway. I fumbled to my feet and quietly opened the next door to the side of the room.

I entered the empty chambers and waited for what seemed like another hour while hearing two guests doing unspeakable acts in the room I was just in. The constant moaning, the grunting, the bed frame hitting the wall that separated them and me, and the high-pitched sounds gave away what they were doing.

I swallowed the vomit that almost left my throat. I was going to be sick. This was the worst night.

Tapping the back of my head against the wall I leaned on, I reminded myself never to trust Maeri's words again. This was the second time her words found no favor in my nights. I reminded myself never to drink that much again, no matter how persuasive Nirelle could be.

After perhaps another hour or so, I decided it was safe to leave and find the servants quarters. I was sure Kallen was back where he came from. Most likely, I was being paranoid.

Cracking the door open to the hallway, I looked in both directions, and I was in the clear. I closed the door behind me, walking down the hallway towards the next. I could practically hear my heart pound out of my chest, it was so quiet.

Relax, I told myself. I was just overthinking it. Kallen wasn't following me, and he wouldn't hurt me. The celebrations must have ended hours ago. I might have accidentally slept longer than I originally thought.

My eyes darted in every direction, making sure no one was following me, and I was safe to proceed. Finally, I approached the last hallway to go towards the kitchen—

I heard footsteps in front of me, coming from the kitchen.

No time to waste. Without waiting another moment, I twirled back towards the hall I came from as quickly as my legs could carry me.

Am I going crazy? Am I hearing things?

I felt panic within me rise. This was the very reason why I'd been training my muscles; I didn't feel the quick burn just yet.

Quickly, I made a turn at the next crossway to the staircase I knew like the back of my hand. Running up and up and up, doubling the steps with my feet. I would not have been able to do this a couple months ago. I could hear footsteps on the stone stairs behind me, climbing up clearly at my heels.

I sped down the hallway I walked every morning. I was fifty feet away from it.

I want to live. I want to live. I want to live.

Faster and faster, I took another turn. I knew this was the only place Kallen would not be able to find me at this time of night. He would never expect it. Forty feet away. My legs now burned with exhaustion.

And then another turn, to the last hall I knew by heart. Every tapestry that lay on the walls, every curve of the tile that led its way, and every window that shone out toward those beautiful palace gardens. Only twenty feet more until I reached those wooden doors.

I heard voices float from a distant hall.

Just a few more feet, I was so close.

I practically ran into the double doors as I fumbled to open them. I entered the dark chambers that I cleaned every morning for months, shutting the doors behind me. I pressed my back upon them. I was out of breath, and I couldn't catch up. Noises were coming out of my throat, panic on the verge of exiting my chest.

I couldn't hear footsteps from the other side of the double doors. They must have gotten lost as I sped down the last hall. I swallowed the lump in my throat and attempted to quiet my breathing.

"You shouldn't be here," a powerful voice said across the room near the fireplace. The hearth was barely lit.

My chest heaved as I gasped for air.

Aris sat shirtless in his chair facing the door, facing me. I couldn't find his eyes as they were the color of darkness, but I could feel them on me. His fingers entwined with each other, as if he'd been thinking for hours. The small fire's shadows danced off the strength of his chest.

There was a moment when I ran into his chambers, I thought maybe he had found company for the night of his celebration somewhere else. There was a part of me that hoped he didn't.

I didn't fully understand the reason behind trusting Aris tonight. I blamed it on the alcohol. I knew I shouldn't be here, but I had to be honest with myself.

He was the safest place I could be.

I let out a shaky breath when realization washed over me. It didn't matter what he said or how he presented himself. I knew he wouldn't hurt me.

Like Camilla, I reminded myself.

There was a selfish part of me that broke when I realized he might have made several women feel safe out there—that it might not have meant anything to him, but everything for us. Was this part of his game?

"It's dangerous for you here."

"You wouldn't hurt me," I reassured myself.

"That's not what I'm referring to."

My body tingled, wondering what he was implying.

He stood from his sheepskin chair and strutted towards me in the darkness. "Who are you running from?"

I swallowed. "No one in particular. I just..." I froze when I couldn't find my lie quick enough in my mind. I couldn't tell him how I wasn't even sure someone was following me. That ever since the night I got branded, I constantly felt like something or someone was coming for me. He would think I was crazy.

"Wanted to see me?" Aris tried to answer for me and chuckled deeply. I joined with a nervous laugh. "Is it Kallen?" His predatory stance closed in. A muscle twitched in his jaw.

"No," I whispered. It could have been him or a ghost. I wasn't entirely sure. *But again, not going to explain myself.*

"You're not running from him?"

"I would...if he were chasing me."

"You don't want him? A strong warrior like him, many women would find themselves fortunate."

"Not in a million years," I blurted out, lifting my chin a little higher.

"That's not what it seemed like at the celebration. Looked like you two have gotten close since I've been gone," he said with a tone I'd never heard from him before. Was that jealousy?

"I thought you were good at noticing things," I challenged him with a half-smile.

Aris smirked. "I would say I am."

"How come you didn't notice how I don't want anything to do with him? And that I pushed him off of me?"

"That's a good question." He considered it as he took a step closer to me. His body seemed so tense I could almost feel it from where I stood. "What are you doing here if you're not running from anyone *in particular*?"

"I—I felt...safe to come here."

Our eyes locked as he appeared before me out of the darkness. The small fire glowed behind his shoulders. I could see how dark his eyes had turned and gasped softly.

I refused to step back as he prowled before me. I wasn't afraid, yet my breath quickened.

"You feel safe here?"

"Yes," I breathed.

"Unannounced?"

He was the emperor. I was his chambermaid. He had the right to be frustrated with me.

"You're asking an awful lot of questions tonight." My fingers were noticeably shaking.

"A lot has changed while I've been gone."

He didn't want me here like he had once mentioned the night he saved me from the Strokan warriors. I dropped my gaze, heat rushing to my face, a sudden, crashing feeling filling my chest.

I shook my head. "I'm sorry I came here."

I twirled around, stepped towards the double doors, and reached—

Aris' hand landed on the doors before I could open them. His towering body was behind me as his hand kept the door closed in front of me. My heart pounded up to my throat.

He leaned lower to reach my ear. "You shouldn't have come here, quiet one."

"I'm sorry. I'll leave at once if you'll allow me." I froze, not realizing what I had gotten myself into. He seemed frustrated with me in ways I couldn't recognize.

Aris wrapped his other hand around my arm, twisting me to face him. As his eyes met mine, they were wild and deep, as if they were pools of the night sky.

He released his hold on my arm and pressed his fingers on the lower part of my stomach, causing me to step back, pressing my back against the double doors. My heart rate fluttered in all directions in my chest as he stepped even closer to me.

"I don't want you to leave," Aris stated. "I like having you around."

I felt the heat rise to my cheeks. "You do?"

"Yes... You're real."

"Real. As opposed to what?"

"Someone who isn't honest about who they are. Most people hide behind masks. They hide the ugliest versions of themselves." He brushed the back of his finger on my cheek as if ensuring I was really here. "But you...you show who you are, no matter if you care or not. You're real. You remain so."

"Do you hide behind a mask, Aris?"

"I do. I don't want people to read me. I *can't* have them read me."

"Do you ever get confused about who is the real you and the version people perceive you to be?"

Aris chuckled. "That's why I like you." He tugged on one of my curls that fell into my face. "I don't have to mask myself. I forget what it's like when I'm around you. I forget what it's like to be an emperor. To be a son. To be a ruler or a warrior. With you, I'm just—"

"Aris," I whispered.

"Some people are hard to read. But you, I can easily read. And it's refreshing to not wonder if you're going to stab me in the back or not."

I laughed breathlessly, and my brows knitted. "I couldn't possibly."

What are you doing, Solei?

"Oh, I know. I found that out quickly." He leaned forward slightly. "Since the moment you chose not to kill me in my sleep but to heal me instead at the war camp."

That felt like forever ago.

"Aris, I do hide myself." I shook my head. "I can speak up and not play mute like I have been in the last year. It's easier to not talk and explain myself. We all have masks to survive the life we've been given."

"I don't blame your mask. People don't listen very well."

"I don't blame your mask either, Aris. In order to rule an empire, you need to hide the parts of yourself people would use against you. It's survival, my brother used tell me. You can't blame yourself for surviving."

Aris' gaze dropped to my lips. "Why does it feel like I don't have to survive when I'm around you?"

I felt warm and tingling sensations in my legs, and for some reason, I didn't want it to stop.

"I haven't been able to get you out of my head since I've been gone," he whispered.

His face inched closer and closer. Time slowed. "The things I want to do to you."

My heart fluttered as his face neared mine, warming my body in ways I'd never experienced before.

"I thought you didn't want to do anything to me," I murmured, reminding him of what he said in the tent during the storm he saved me from. He must have remembered exactly what was conversed between us when we were wrapped in each other's arms that night because he let out a soft chuckle.

He raised his obsidian eyes and locked them with mine. His jaw pulsed. "You had just been taken from your lands. You were frightened...and lost. I wanted to show you I wouldn't hurt you. But..." He paused, and the column of his throat moved. "I've wanted you since the moment I saw you."

My heart melted at the heat that rose in my body.

He wanted me.

I parted my lips so that I could breathe easier.

Something opened in his eyes, and I saw him, who he was. Everything within him was breathtakingly beautiful. I reached for his face and touched what I'd wanted to touch for so long. Aris moved his hands to my waist, tugging my body to his.

"I shouldn't," he said in a low, husky voice as his face came closer, but I couldn't hear him. I couldn't stop thinking about how beautiful he was and how I wanted him closer and closer.

"You should," I whispered near his lips as I tilted my head up in invitation.

Time slowed when his lips met mine. The touch of his lips caused my body to melt into his. They were warm, sweet, and his breath seeped into me.

This is what it's supposed to feel like.

Without thinking of what I was doing, my lips parted, and his tongue swept inside me. A groan came out of his mouth, his hands moving from my waist to my hips and over my backside. Our tongues danced and touched each other's.

Warmth pulsed between my legs. Thinking was out of the question. My body was doing things I'd never thought of doing. My hands drifted over his bare chest and abdomen. I couldn't get enough of him. I'd wanted to touch every part of him; I just never allowed myself to want it this much.

Aris grabbed hold of my backside, lifting me against the door, and my legs instinctively wrapped around his hips. It was as if he couldn't get enough of me either. His hands grazed higher and higher, exploring my body. I brought my fingers behind his neck and head, entwined them in his hair, as I plunged my tongue in his mouth. His hands reached higher until he found the strings that kept the top of my dress intact. He managed to unravel it as he tugged on my lower lip.

I felt his strength between my legs, and I whimpered, my entire body burning for more. I didn't want it to stop. I needed this.

His hands were moving in ways I'd never thought existed, not parting his lips once from mine. It was as if he had been imagining this for months, yearning for it. Now, unleashing his control, he pressed for more.

Aris pulled my dress down from my breast, exposing my left shoulder. He grazed his lips over my jaw, down my neck, licking and kissing. I welcomed every inch of warmth he left behind as he made his way to my upper chest. My nipples hardened, begging for attention.

His mouth trailed to my left shoulder and gently pressed on the brand that had healed over the month while he was gone.

"Forgive me, Solei," he whispered between the licks and kisses he left upon my scar.

"There's nothing to forgive, Aris." I pulled his face from my shoulder back to mine.

Our gazes met, searching the depths of each other, exploring the chasm of our souls. I opened myself fully to him, everything I was. I trusted him with my body and with my soul, like no other before.

I laced my fingers behind his neck and pulled him back to my lips. It was the most beautiful experience I'd ever had, and I didn't want it to end. His lips met mine, this time harder and more demanding, like he realized it as well.

He swore between our lips.

I couldn't control my hands. They were all over his bare shoulders and back, pressing and pulling, searching and craving. His mouth widened, his tongue teasing, a silent command for more.

And for a moment in time, I heard a small voice in my head that told me to *stop*.

I didn't want this to end. I didn't want to be the reason why his hands stopped touching me, worshiping me, but I couldn't put the small voice away from my mind.

Stop, stop, stop.

My entire being hesitated to listen.

Yet suddenly I couldn't stop thinking about who he was. The tragedy that befell my people. What my sister would think of me if she knew I was locking lips with an enemy.

My body tensed under his arms, and I thought he felt it too. But I knew I had to listen to that voice. Reluctantly, I pulled my lips from his and turned my cheek so he wouldn't continue.

Aris must have understood within that moment because he placed my body on the ground. Without once looking up to see his face, his eyes, I pulled my dress back over my shoulder and breast. I left as quickly as I could without saying another word.

I ran faster down the hall and into my quarters than when I came in.

Shame poured into every cell of my body.

I had betrayed myself.

PART III
ADDICTION

Chapter Thirty-Four

The next day was hell. The morning after, my head pounded, and I felt weak, unable to perform any of my core workout. I wondered if it were the effects of alcohol, or if it was the fact that I wanted to indeed shovel a hole and hide my shameful body in it.

Despite what I wanted to blame, I knew it wasn't the alcohol. Nirelle made sure the next morning I was alive and well, though it didn't feel like it. She expressed how confused and worried she was when they didn't find me last night like we had agreed. I made the excuse that I fell asleep in one of the guest chambers—partly true.

The rest of the week, my body dragged through every chore. There was a war inside my head keeping me from moving freely. Not only did I practically break my vow to never touch a man, but I also betrayed my village, my family, the prisoners who had been captured by Aris. I had never experienced such regret in my heart, in my soul, and in my body.

And it felt like poison. It was an agonizing tightening in my chest that no matter what I told myself, no matter how much I preoccupied myself, I felt it. It swallowed me whole.

I entered the apothecary where I had been working unusually long hours to calm my struggling mind. Picking up the knife, I started cutting the herbs' stems to prepare for tinctures.

While fighting the battles in my head, I had passed Aris a few times, and I could feel his dark eyes on me. I could *feel* him beg me to look at him.

"Be careful, silent one. You're going to hurt yourself," Peter reprimanded.

I gave him a fake sorry look, and Peter continued measuring liquids in the tinctures.

Such a talented actress, I was. I resumed the thoughts that had been on repeat in my head all week. I hated myself for believing in Aris, for thinking that maybe he was a different man than I originally thought. That maybe he'd feel differently for me than Camilla. I hated myself for not hating Aris. My heart was weak, and it wouldn't listen to my own reasoning.

How could something feel so pure yet make me feel such shame?

I chopped harder and faster, not caring.

Gods, I am so angry with myself! I knew it had only been a week since I'd spoken to Aris, but it felt like *months* had gone by since.

"Girl, someone's here for you," Peter interrupted my thoughts yet again.

I looked up and found a Siniyan guard in a commanding stance, waiting for me across the room.

"The emperor would like a word with you."

The knife grew heavy in my hand. I glanced over to Peter, who gave me a *you better go before they drag you out of here* look.

With a great sigh, I rubbed the dried herbs off of my sweaty palms on my apron before removing it, displaying my pale blue linen dress.

I followed the guard to Aris' study. I knew this day was coming, and he wouldn't take my avoidance much longer.

"Come in," Aris said when the warrior knocked on his door.

I stepped through the doors, the guard shutting it behind me.

My heart beat fiercely. It was only him and me. I refused to look at him.

"Sit."

A powerful command. The emperor's command. *My enemy*, I reminded myself in case I forgot again.

I walked over to the front of his large wooden desk and sat on one of the sheep-skinned seats. I could tell he was standing in the far corner of his study with his arms crossed, observing, noticing, like he always did.

I hope he notices how I want nothing to do with—

"Solei." He approached me.

My name on his lips disregarded any thought process I had in the moment.

"Don't," I said breathlessly, "come any closer."

He proceeded with authority, ignoring my request. "I can't go this long without speaking to you again. It's been driving me insane."

I *knew* it.

"I need to know what's going on in your head," he stated, stopping nearby. "And why you can't even look at me."

Don't let him in, Solei.

"You're afraid of me." It wasn't a question.

I looked up in surprise and found his face had softened. His eyes searched, open to receiving anything from me.

My heart squeezed. "No, I'm not."

"Then what is it? Is it the other night? I shouldn't—" He shook his head. "I shouldn't have done that to you. I took advantage of you, and I knew better."

"You didn't. I—I wanted it." *That* was the problem. My face, flushed, filled with shame and remorse.

"Then why are you being this way to me?"

To me...as if he were in pain because of me—because I was avoiding him at all costs. For some reason, hurting him was worse than the pain I felt all week. I twisted my linen dress between my hands.

My voice cracked as I admitted, "I betrayed myself."

Aris became blurry, and that was when I knew there were tears in my eyes.

Don't you dare cry.

His fuzzy figure approached and kneeled in front of my legs. "Why would you say that?"

"It's the truth, Aris. I betrayed myself. I took a vow to never be with a man because of my sister and mother. For what happened to them. I know I didn't break my vow—not fully, but I could have. That's what scares me." I inhaled shakily. "It was my way of keeping something sacred in honor of their deaths. Keeping something that was a choice, for them. Because they didn't have one." A tear finally spilled down my cheek. I didn't know why I was sharing this, but I did. "And I betrayed them, and my people, and anyone who has died fighting for us, by *whoring* myself to the one who destroyed their lives."

I couldn't breathe as I let out the tears that welled in my eyes, hiding my face in my hands. I'd never spoken so many words in one sitting in my life.

Though I could barely see, Aris had wrapped his arms around me, bringing me closer to him. I felt his warmth seep deep into my core as I felt shame tremble through my body.

I couldn't stop the feelings in my body whenever he came to my mind. They were stronger than the guilt and shame I was carrying with me. Sometimes, I'd forget—like Nirelle. I'd forget who he was to us. I liked those moments when I'd forget. Because I was free. I wasn't being held down but free to feel something so beautiful for Aris.

"I betrayed myself. I allowed myself to feel this way about you," I mumbled into his chest.

"Betraying yourself would only be if you didn't allow yourself to feel something so natural," he said in a low voice. He paused. "It's not your fault. It's mine, for making you stay when you wanted to go. For doing those things to you. I shouldn't have. I'm sorry—"

"No—no," I said between breathing in the tears. "I didn't want you to stop—and I hated myself for it."

I felt Aris' arms tighten around me, comforting me in ways I'd never felt before by a man. Not able to resist, I wrapped my arms around him. Despite what I kept telling myself, in his arms I felt warm and safe. I needed this.

He grabbed me, pulled me from my seat, and sat on the ground, leaning on his desk. I was curled in his arms, hiding my face in his body. I felt so raw and open, but it felt nice to be so close to him.

"You're not the only one."

"What do you mean?" I asked.

"I hated myself for what I did to you. This entire week, tormenting myself for having no self-control. You must have felt like you had no choice in the matter—but you did. You just didn't know."

I lifted my head to look into Aris' dark eyes. His face was too close to mine, but I didn't care.

I clenched his soft black tunic at the front of his chest. "I knew it was my choice, and I chose it, Aris."

His thumb brushed the upper part of my arm, and he brought me closer and squeezed me gently. He wiped the tears from my cheeks. It was so natural for me to lay my head on his chest.

He looked away for a moment, thinking, contemplating. "You said something the night we... I didn't know you had a brother?"

"Yes...I did. But he died." My voice turned quiet.

Aris nodded.

"Why?" I asked.

"Nothing—it's nothing." Aris paused. "How did he die?"

"He died in a war across the Western Sea. He was a soldier." My brows furrowed. I pressed, "Why?"

I felt like the floor was slipping away from me, but I wasn't sure why.

"How do you know he died if he was across the Western Sea?"

"I—I don't, actually. They told us when they brought the soldiers back home that he didn't make it. But...but I—I don't know. I always had this feeling in my heart that he was coming back. There's a part of me that just can't accept that he's gone. My brother was...invincible. It feels impossible for him to be dead."

Aris nodded again. "You're the youngest of your siblings?"

"Yes...how did you know?"

"You act like the youngest child. That's why." He was diverting my question, but a smile formed across my face.

I slapped his bicep, and he chuckled. His voice felt buttery and warm against my skin. "Why are you asking all these questions, Aris?"

The column of his throat worked, and he gazed ahead. "I knew this man. There was—" Aris paused, seemingly searching for his words. He didn't seem to be the type to struggle with words or be nervous, but here he was now. His brows lowered as he peered at me, hesitating. "What I'm trying to say is that—I—I told you about this man who changed my life and the way I regarded prisoners of war and slaves. I wanted something different for them and for our people."

I held in my breath.

"He became a friend. He—he taught me my greatest sword skills... He... There was something that reminded me of him when I met you..."

I couldn't hear anything else but his words.

"What are you saying?" My mind raced.

"I—I think that he was your..." He couldn't say the word.

The world stopped spinning, and my entire being stilled.

"What was his name, Aris?"

"Jonam."

The floor beneath me slipped. I couldn't move. My eyes stung.

"You know my brother," I whispered.

I must have whispered "how" because Aris said, "There were prisoners of war that arrived in Stroka a long time ago, maybe ten years ago. I was a young man, and my father ordered Jonam to teach me everything he knew about the Western Sea Islands. He told me about his family—about you."

My lips curved. "You know Jonam..." I didn't know how I was breathing. I couldn't wrap my mind around the fact that Aris knew my brother. A thread was tugging in my heart.

"Yes," Aris breathed, his jaw tensed. "He was my best friend—a brother to me."

Aris wiped a thumb across my cheeks, and I realized tears had fallen. "I can't believe it."

"Me neither. I had to be sure before I said anything."

"I knew there was a reason why he didn't come back home. I knew in my heart he hadn't died in Wendlen." I shook my head in disbelief. "It didn't make sense to me... He was their strongest, bravest soldier... He didn't die in Wendlen."

"No, he didn't. You're right." Aris pulled me even closer.

"Where is he? Is he still in Stroka?" I asked. My heart felt like it was about to burst with joy.

"Solei..." Aris' eyes widened as they perused my face.

"What is it?" I breathed.

"My father, he saw this all and how close we became. And he—" Aris looked pale despite his tan skin. "He took Jonam. I couldn't take it anymore after that, and I set out to change my father's empire..."

The world stopped shifting. The dark-lit room began to close in.

"*Where is he where is he where is he?*" I could barely speak from the sobs that fell.

But I knew the answer before Aris said a word.

My heart shattered. All over again. I felt the pressure of Aris' strong embrace holding me as I screamed.

"He's gone, Solei."

Everything hurt.

My heart hurt. My body shivered and ached. The beating of my heart felt like spasms, and I couldn't breathe. It hurt.

It hurt to breathe.

CHAPTER THIRTY-FIVE

I laid my head on my pillow that night, but I barely felt the softness where my cheek connected with it. I barely felt the beating of my heart. It was so soft, so distant. It felt as if it were fading with each beat.

Shortly after Aris informed me that my brother was gone, I uncurled myself from his arms and left his study despite his best efforts to have me stay.

I didn't register Sebry or Anna stepping into our chambers as I stared off into nothing. The candles they brought into the darkness didn't make this place any brighter because a dark cloud had cast over my eyes.

I knew my brother was dead, but there was a part in my heart that held on to the belief that he might be alive. Even if I were to never see him again, I wanted to believe he was breathing because I barely was.

He would want me to live. He fought for my happiness. The fact that he was close to Aris made my stomach squeeze and hurt all over again. They knew each other. They were in a way, brothers, according to Aris. That meant more to me than I could have ever imagined.

The following few weeks were the same. Peter kept sending me home after a couple hours of help, and Hara wasn't looking for extra hands either, oddly enough. I lay in bed as much as I could, hardly noticing the world around me, but there was a part of my heart that closed in a final way.

I didn't need to look anymore for my brother in the forest, in the meadows, or between bobbing heads when I walked past a crowd because he wasn't here. He would never be. He was in a place where I would meet him someday. Before then, he would have wanted me to live my life to the fullest because he did. But it felt so empty without him here telling me that.

A life, no matter how short or long, was lived fully when it was filled with love. He was loved. Jonam lived his life fearlessly with every smile and laugh he gave. He gave in fully with no lack of enthusiasm or passion.

One thing I noticed different about everything was that the brightness of life had dulled, and I saw more gray than anything. When I walked outside, I would see gray clouds or harsh rocks that scattered on my pathway. I could easily pick out the invasive plants in the gardens, and for a time I only saw the dried-out tips of the grass from the scorching sun. When I strode through the palace, my eyes would focus absently on the black threads in the tapestries I crossed. When I worked with the herbs with Peter to forget for a moment, I could barely register the smells of the tinctures. They weren't sweet and herbal anymore.

Everything seemed dead, dark, or dull to me.

Everything in my body ached. There was a pressure in my chest that would rise, filling up with sadness, and then descend in a river of tears.

I needed something to do, or else I would spiral faster than I could pick myself up. Paddling though the morning-lit hallways, I went to clean and freshen up Aris' chambers.

As soon as I walked in, I found him sitting at the small table to the left of the room where he had once cleaned my wound. His eyes met mine.

Aris drew himself from his seat, but I was already moving my legs and hands, working around his room. I felt his presence behind me as I made his bed. His hand wrapped around my elbow and pulled me into his warmth. I didn't resist it.

I needed it.

My mind calmed in his embrace, and I breathed in his oak-woodsy scent. My head curled under his chin as he rocked me gently. This was so new and so foreign to me, but I didn't question it. Not now.

He didn't pry into my thoughts for the rest of the time I kept my hands busy as he read over some papers near the fireplace.

That was how we communicated with each other for the next week. I stayed longer in his chambers than before. I wasn't quite ready to admit that his presence was everything I didn't know I needed. He was waiting for me to come to him whenever I was ready to speak again. He was letting me know he was there for me. I knew I should be grateful for the closure, and I could tell at times he doubted if he made the right decision in telling me. He did, but I didn't have the heart to say anything about it now.

The thread in my heart of my brother's existence no longer tugged and pulled. It was gone. It was heartbreaking, but it was clear again.

I laid my head on my pillow tonight, going over the day I had with Aris in my head. I stayed almost all day with him while he journaled and read. He held me for a long, sweet moment, his fingers grazing over my arm, causing my skin to wake before I left.

Here I was in my bed, promising myself that I was going to live my life and not let death bring me down like it did my father, but I was doing exactly that.

In a way, I thought I was punishing myself, holding myself back because I didn't think I deserved to be happy when I'd been in denial of my brother's death for so long.

I was grieving him all over again.

Jonam deserved more. He deserved everything.

I closed my eyes and took a deep breath. I couldn't be like that anymore. I wouldn't wither away like my father did.

Rising from my bed, I plodded to the window and pulled the curtains to the side. I looked up into the night sky. *It doesn't get any easier. Time doesn't heal this pain. Time doesn't heal this time. Time is the enemy here. Time only takes away the memory of you, the memories that we shared. Time takes away you.*

Biting my inner cheek, I glanced at my door. Sebry and Anna had been asleep for a couple hours, their soft snores echoing in our chambers. I hadn't been able to sleep.

He would want me to be happy.

I walked quietly through the dark halls in my night dress, hoping no one would see me in this state. I wanted him to know how I felt, regardless of the news he shared with me over three weeks ago. My hands knocked on the large double doors. I didn't know what I was going to say.

Aris opened his door, shirtless, and his eyes softened when he saw me. I tried hard not to rove my eyes over his body or feel the sudden rush of blood in my face. He opened the door wider and tugged me into his warm embrace, and I swore, a part of me melted. I heard the door behind me close.

This was exactly where I wanted to be. I knew it had only been half a day since I last saw him, but I missed him. I missed him while I'd been grieving.

"Hi." My voice was muffled against his hard chest.

"Hi, quiet one."

"Thank you," I whispered.

His body tensed. "For what?"

"For having the strength to tell me." I felt his arms tighten around my body, and I continued, "For having the strength to find peace in your life, to find Siniya, to build something so beautiful from the darkness."

I felt his throat work against my head.

"Thank you for believing in my own strength," I said.

His fingers weaved through my hair and my eyes fluttered closed.

"I never doubted you," he said gently.

I sighed. "Why are you so good to me?"

Aris chuckled against my hair. "Why are *you* so good to *me*? You should hate me."

I shook my head as much as I could in his embrace. "No, I could never hate you, Aris. I...feel like I can be myself, all the sides of myself, when I'm with you. That's all I can ask for. I've never had to explain myself to you from the beginning. You've always made me feel...safe. And seen. In a world where I thought I was disappearing slowly. You were right there. I couldn't hide from you." I lifted my head to meet his eyes. "You pulled me from the underworld, Aris."

His hand weaved in my hair descended to the back of my neck, holding me there. "I'll pull you from there every time."

I swallowed. The feelings I had for him were growing, and I couldn't stop them. I couldn't stop something that felt so natural.

My gaze dropped to his lips. He parted them like he wanted to say something.

For a long moment, we stared into each other's eyes. His turned darker. I traced my fingers across his lips to feel them. They were warm and soft, exactly as I imagined. It was as if our bodies had become one, and the heat began to radiate between us.

With my other hand, I brushed over his chest. I could feel the strong beat of his heart. It was beating so fast, I could almost hear it if it weren't for my own racing heart. His fingers flexed against the small of my back and tugged me closer to his hips.

"Careful, quiet one."

I stopped breathing. My entire body tensed, knowing I was the prey, and he was the hunter. It was dangerous to be this close to him. To open up to him in this way.

But the voice in the back of my head had started to fade.

"Solei, if you don't leave soon, I don't think I'll be able to let you go back. You should go," Aris warned.

Slowly, I slipped my body from his and brought myself back to my room, feeling a little lighter than before.

Her voice floated down the hallway on the second floor of the palace.

Maeri. My lips tugged into a smile. Last time Nirelle, Maeri and I got together was right after I found out about Jonam, and I wasn't able to share much with them. The weight was too much. Nirelle left me sweet notes when she could, and I responded with my own when I'd pass by a chamber she was cleaning. It was our way of communicating for now.

I followed Maeri's voice until I found her with her eyes closed in a beautiful, clean chamber with the windows open, allowing the warm breeze through. Leaning on the threshold, I listened to her angelic voice. Maeri must have sense a presence because she turned towards the door and upon seeing me, a flush went up her neck.

I beamed, "Maeri, don't be embarrassed! It was *beautiful*!"

She lowered her head. "There are much better singers out there."

"There will always be someone who we think are better than us, but that's how life pushes us forward. That shouldn't stop us from doing what we love. And you love singing. Don't let yourself be the reason why you hide it."

Maeri chuckled softly. "Thank you, Solei. That means a lot," she said as she gathered my hands in hers. "How have you been? Really."

Her eyes turned serious, and suddenly I wanted to leave the room.

"Talk to me, please," Maeri pleaded.

I took a deep breath, and we sat on the foot bench of the bed. "I thought...that maybe he was here, Maeri. And it broke me all over again when I found out I'd never, in fact, see him again." An insufferable lump rose in my throat, and I stopped talking lest I burst into tears.

Maeri leaned forward and wrapped her arms around me. "I can't imagine, Solei. I was an only child, but my heart is with you."

A moment went by, and I realized this felt nice—to talk.

"I remember your brother. I even had a crush on him when I was younger."

I burst out in laugher while wiping the tears from my face. "Oh my gods, I had no idea."

She waved her hand while laughing with me. "He didn't either. I was too young for him to notice at the time, but a girl could dream."

"He'll never have a wife or children, Maeri. He never had the chance to settle down."

She let me go and looked at me. "I don't think life ends here, Solei. He's just somewhere else. That's all."

Another breeze swept into the chambers, the curtains moving along with it. "I hope so. I can't imagine him not breathing..."

"He's breathing. Just not here." Maeri squeezed my hands.

Tears gathered in my eyes again. "It feels good to talk about him, especially with someone who knew him somewhat."

Maeri smiled. "Good. I'm glad. You can always come and talk to me literally about anything. I hope you know that."

"I do, thank you. It means a lot." I surveyed the clean chamber. It was large and looked almost like Aris'. "Is this a guest chamber?"

"No, it's not. It's chambers for his family when they're in town. I clean them from time to time," Maeri answered. "I was about to head out. Do you want to grab something to eat together?"

I nodded and followed Maeri out of the chambers.

"You know she's a witch when she needs to cover herself from the sun," Yari whispered a little too loudly to Rayne nearby. "The sun is the most natural part of this world. There should be no covering up from it unless you do evil."

All the servants including Rayne nodded in agreement.

I couldn't help but roll my eyes and shake my head, not caring if they saw or not. I was doing a lot of that lately, not caring. I supposed a month of finding out my brother was in fact, gone, just reminded me how trivial their accusations were. Though it'd been about five months since I'd arrived in Siniya, their comments were getting more annoying by the day. And today, I woke up on the right side of the bed, feeling a lot lighter than I had been recently, and I wasn't going to bottle up any more emotions.

Thankfully I wasn't spending as much time in the warm garden these days as most of my time was taken up with Peter. I still helped the kitchen staff whenever they needed it, like today. The sun was brighter this week than before, and I had to fully cover myself in fear of getting my skin burned. Freckles now dotted my cheeks.. Summer was just around the corner.

We were still in spring. Spring was technically the beginning of the year. There was a newness in it that made me smile. I could feel it in my bones.

I permitted myself to steal a few glances on Aris every now and then when our paths crossed. Greetings would be exchanged. Sometimes he'd ask me how my day was. At first, I kept our conversations short, but now I found myself wanting to ask him questions just to have him keep talking to me. My brother knowing Aris and having been so close to him caused me to finally embrace the feelings I had for him. In fact, every other time Aris was around me, the little flutters in my stomach grew stronger and stronger. Like a magnet, begging to be closer to him.

I wondered if he felt the same way or if this was normal. Did everyone feel this way?

"Do you hear that?" Rayne asked the group.

I dug into the dirt with my nails to find the deepest roots of the invasive plant. I heard the earth drumming to the beat of hooves.

"It's our lord," Yari breathed. "He's with Helon, Beshien, and Justir."

All of our heads followed Yari's pointed finger toward the hills ahead of us.

Just as Yari spoke, there he was in the distance. Aris galloped on the grassy hills on his white horse, followed by Helon, Beshien, and Justir on their horses. Aris' body was barely on the saddle as he leaned over his horse at full speed, creating more space from the others. They could barely catch up to their emperor. It was a sight to see. Aris peered over his shoulder to see them far behind him. Helon had a large smile, pride written on his face.

Aris was as beautiful as life could get.

Gods, I was hopeless.

"You all better get to work. He doesn't pay us to stand here and watch him ride all day," Rayne stated. "You, too, girl. Best get to work, or the palace keeper will be notified."

Rayne's threats were not empty. My hands ached from the memory of her rod, and it wasn't something I intended to feel again. I went back to work, pulling and digging the plants away.

It wasn't that I wasn't a fast worker, but at times—many times—I'd be wrapped up in my own thoughts and—and sometimes it was just hard to multitask when there were so many thoughts to think about.

"My emperor," Yari gasped.

I glanced up to find her for the first time since I'd met her lowering her head, greeting her lord. On his white horse, Aris and the others had approached the garden, panting from their ride. Along with the rest of the staff, we bowed our heads at the sudden appearance of the emperor. My heart went full force in its beating rhythm.

I was convinced I was going to have heart problems because of him, and as a healer in this day and age, there wasn't going to be anything I could do to cure my body from it.

"Might I ask, what we can do for you, My Lord?" a servant, Betrium, asked. "Are you looking for something to eat? We'd be more than happy to fix something up for you and the others."

Although my head was down and my eyes were on the plants I had recently pulled, I could *feel* his magnetic eyes on me. He saw me. My heart raced faster. What was he doing here?

Aris' horse whinnied as they made their way between the garden boxes past Betrium, past Yari and Rayne, past the other servants, and stopped before me.

"My Lord?" Yari asked, confused, waiting for his response.

"I won't be needing any food, thank you."

"Is there anything we can do for you, My Lord?" Yari persisted.

"No, there isn't," he grunted with an impatient tone.

Aris' horse grew restless. Then there was silence.

I dared a glance up and saw Aris' eyes locked on me. His face said it all.

Get up, was his silent command.

I rose from the ground, brushing the dirt from my brown dress when his left arm wrapped around my waist, gripping me firmly, then hoisted me up onto his horse. The jolt of the motion left me breathless. He couldn't wait a gods-damned minute. Sitting with both my legs on one side in front, his arms around me, Aris clucked his tongue, and led us galloping from the gardens. His embrace prickled a moment of hesitation, but the voice was so far away now, I leaned into his body.

Peeking behind me over Aris' shoulder, I could see all the servants' jaws drop to the very ground I had just pulled plants from minutes ago. This only confirmed their suspicions even further. I heard Betrium murmur something to Yari, but I couldn't hear against the hooves of Aris' horse.

I couldn't help but not give a damn as Aris led us towards the hills. Yet I wondered what the repercussions of this would be. All the relentless questions I'd received and perhaps even more pestering looks.

I stared up at his face and how he was concentrating on the ride. I couldn't stop the smile that appeared on my lips and the twinkle in my eye as he glanced down at me.

He was the only one I wanted to be with all the time. The only one I looked forward to seeing.

I was glad he found me.

Chapter Thirty-Six

Through the grassy hills, Aris and I rode with Pacha, the name of his horse, as I found out during the ride. We left behind Helon, who told Aris he would see him later this evening for dinner, and Beshien and Justir, who nodded their goodbyes. We had been riding for an hour, conversing comfortably over what my life was like before...everything, and I thought we might have completely left the empire of Siniya when we finally descended into a beautiful clearing. He was an attentive listener and asked thoughtful questions about myself and my family. I hadn't had the nerve just yet to ask about what his life was like in Stroka besides knowing his connection to Jonam.

"Was he happy?" I knew it was most likely a dumb question, but I had to ask.

Aris' arms tensed around mine. "I think it was important for him to know he was doing some good in this world. And he was. He changed my life and because of him, I'll be changing others' as well. I think he was as happy as he could be in a dark place like Stroka. His positivity was remarkable. I know that it affected me. It made me think differently. That perhaps no matter how dark a place might seem, there's always beauty in searching for the light, because at the end of the day that's all that matters. In the end, it's the courage one has that matters, not the way we end, but by the way we live."

"I bet you talked philosophy with him, didn't you?" I curved my lips.

Aris laughed. "Of course."

"What do you believe in?"

"I believe in the light," he said. His breath trickled down the side of my neck. "And the light always wins."

I knew his arms were around me while we rode, but his presence was like a warm hug around my heart and soul.

We were bordering a flowing, clear blue river that glittered against the bright sunlight. I was in awe of the colors and sparkle of this place Aris brought me to when he gently pulled me down from the saddle. I couldn't take my eyes off the trees that swayed in the light breeze. Even the trunks of the trees twirled and entwined with its branches. Landing on the ground, it was covered in a carpet of green grass. Without thinking, I took my leather sandals off so that I could feel the cool touch on my bare feet and the grass sliding between my toes.

I heard Aris chuckle softly behind me. Butterflies flew in all directions within my stomach.

"Do you always get this excited for grass?"

Heat rose to my cheeks. "I do," I admitted. "I can't imagine who wouldn't. It's soft and fresh. It makes me feel connected to the land somehow."

"Do you want to be connected to this land?" Aris brought down a saddle bag and placed it over his shoulder.

I took a moment to gather my thoughts. "Most people would disagree with me, but I see land as the Creator's land. It does not belong to anyone or anything. It's the people that live on the land that makes me feel welcomed or not, but the land itself...it always welcomes kindness and admiration from the people who walk on it. And I will give that to the land, no matter how its people treat me."

"You don't think this land belongs to me?" Aris asked. I caught his intense gaze, and to my surprise, I did not submit.

"No, I don't. I think you think it does and so does everyone else, but it does not belong to you nor to anyone else. The land has its own master, and it allows us to live here and take care of its beauty and feast off of it."

"A witch *and* a philosopher as well." Aris shook his head in amusement. My face deepened its color, and I hid a smile.

After Aris wrapped Pacha's leather straps around a nearby branch, he grabbed my hand and led me near the river. He let go to place an auburn blanket from the saddle bag on the grassy ground. Meanwhile, I walked barefoot to a nearby apple tree that had mesmerized me since we stopped. Its branches reached for the sky and called my name, beckoning me closer.

I decided to climb the old apple tree and find the juiciest apples. Holding a thick branch above my head with both hands, I walked my feet up the trunk and wrapped my leg over the branch. Lifting the rest of my body, crouching low, I raised my hands to the next branch above me.

I used to do this as a child. I'd play in the orchards that belonged to our neighbors. My brother, sister, and I would run to the orchard fields and fill our baskets with juicy apples, giggling at whoever got stuck with the smallest.

One of my last memories of my brother flashed in my mind.

"I don't want you to go. I'll be alone here. You know that I will. There's no one like us here. Why do you have to go?" Tears burned my eyes, threatening to be released.

"Because this is what I'm meant to do, Solei. This is where I'm meant to go. It's hard to explain... But I have a feeling—I always have. Hey, hey, don't cry. Listen, when I come back from the war, I'll purchase some land with the earnings I receive, and you and Nour can come and live with me, okay? We'll build on the new land across the s eas."

A small sniffling sound escaped my nose. "You promise?"

"Of course." His big bear hug engulfed my small body. *"I'll be back just in time for your birthday. You'll barely have time to miss me."*

The memories still fresh in my mind left my heart aching as I lifted myself up another branch. I had a feeling the ache was never really going to leave.

"With you being susceptible to danger, I wouldn't advise this!" Aris shouted from the ground with his arms across his chest.

I laughed at his worry. "Good thing I'm an expert at climbing trees."

"Is that so?"

"Maybe this will be how I plan my escape from you." I climbed a third branch, and he looked smaller and smaller from the view.

I could feel his dark eyes growing serious. "I'll find you every time."

Looking below as I climbed a fourth branch, I retorted, "I'm holding you to that."

I was playing with fire once again.

I held my stance on the fourth branch, not sure if I would dare another climb. Aris grabbed the branch and hoisted himself up without using his feet against the trunk.

Some serious abs he's got.

"I'm not letting you go that easy."

In half the time it took me to get up here, I found Aris crouched at a nearby branch across the trunk from me. He hadn't even broken out in a sweat.

Absurd. I wanted to roll my eyes. "You speak highly of yourself, Aris. You haven't even gotten me."

The challenge caused a spark in his eyes, and his mouth curved slightly.

"You are mine," he stated as he crawled towards the trunk that separated us, not dropping his gaze from mine.

A tingling sensation went down my leg as he said those words. Looking to distract myself from the feeling within me, I snatched the biggest reddest apple I could find and bit into the juiciest one I'd ever tasted. The tart juices exploded in my mouth.

I left the apple in my mouth as I grabbed the branch I crouched on, swung myself below, and landed on the branch beneath me. Taking a bite of the apple, I chewed it and looked up at Aris, who was smiling at this point.

"Then come get me."

Chucking the rest of the apple on the ground, I swung myself down the thick and steady branches. I could hear Aris doing the same, only on the other side of the old tree.

My feet landed on the soft grass as I set off into a sprint, laughing. Looking over my shoulder, Aris was catching up like a panther. I knew with speed I wasn't going to get away, but it was amusing to make him fight for it.

I almost made it to the river when his arms wrapped around my waist and lifted me off the ground. I squealed from the anticipation. It was exhilarating.

Aris' arms tightened around me as he twirled me from the river. "Nice try."

I could sense Aris smile as he let me go and plopped on the blanket with his arms behind his head. I couldn't remember the last time I had this much excitement, even when my family was alive. Being the youngest in the family, attention was hard to find. I didn't think I'd ever had this much attention from one person.

That scared me.

Was I a fool for thinking Aris might have feelings for me the way I did for him? Would he let me go the way he did with Camilla?

Ignoring the thoughts in my head, I lay near Aris, but not too close. Just close enough I could still think. And I needed to keep my head straight. It was the only thing that would keep my vow intact. After several minutes of comfortable, sweet silence listening to birds in the trees, Aris' voice filled the air.

"Tell me what your thoughts are." Aris faced me on my right. His hand propped up his head so he could see all of me, observing.

I flushed bright red. I wasn't sure if it was from the heat and the sweater I wore over my arms for protection or if it was because of the honest answer.

"You don't want to know."

"Are you questioning what I want?"

I faced him when I heard the challenge in his voice, and it almost took my breath away.

Well, if he wanted to know so badly. "I was thinking about you and Camilla."

His face turned stone-cold and lifeless.

"I told you, you didn't want to know."

"You know me so well," he said dryly.

"I wouldn't say so," I whispered, staring through the trees above.

"What do you want to know?"

I took a moment to gather my thoughts, hoping he wouldn't get upset. "How did you find Siniya when your father, Malakar, is Stroka's emperor?"

Aris lay on his back as he contemplated his answer. "I found Siniya with my father when we were conquering some lands when I was barely a man—a boy, really. Siniya was broken and desperate for someone to lead. I saw that when I was young and kept an eye on it as I grew older. I stepped in when I was old enough...after Jonam." He swallowed audibly. "I was looking for a way out, from Malakar."

I listened as he continued. "I couldn't survive there. Not after everything had happened. I don't know how my mother does it. I offered everything to her once I came into my position—protection, security, power, everything." A muscle twitched in his jaw.

"Why doesn't she come here with you?"

"She refuses to leave him. Even after everything he's done to her and to me. The countless times he'd almost crushed her skull against the wall for being careless." Aris shook his head absently. His tone turned flat. "The countless times he punished me for not seeing things when I should have. If I missed anything he'd burn me, wait for my skin to almost heal, and burn me again. Never letting me overlook a single fucking thing he asked. He'd have his entertainment showing me who had the power, how much he had of it. It was a game for him. He thought he'd craft me into some warrior god who'd see all and do all for him."

My mouth went dry. That explained how exceptionally observant he was. It was engrained by pure torture.

"I would have become a ghost if I stayed there—my soul would have disintegrated until there was nothing left. I left when I was old enough to lead. I've been finding a way to protect my mother. I'd do anything for her. She deserves a good life, far, far away from that animal." He paused and swallowed, looking into the distant sky, an empty stare, before he continued. "She's afraid. I know she is. She's in an invisible prison, forced to be his wife, his lover." He peered over at me. "An invisible slave."

I returned his glance. Listening between the words he didn't speak, I knew exactly what he meant. "You are nothing like him, Aris."

He looked back at the sky, afraid I'd see through him, but it was too late.

"I am not afraid of you." I reached my hand across the blanket but kept them from making contact. "You're not forcing me to do anything I don't want to do."

"That so? You're here, aren't you?"

"That's not because of you."

"Isn't it?"

"If I'd been left in my country, I would have died. If they took me to Stroka, what would my life be like there?"

"Not pretty." He faced me again.

I smiled at him. He showed me he cared about my well-being, and my heart swelled in response to his words. But didn't he do the same with Camilla?

"So, you're not going to escape me then?" He winked. The air turned lighter, and the dullness in his eyes was fading.

"That's for me to know and you to find out." I bit my lip. Gods, it felt nice when he did that.

Suddenly, I was overheating, my face burning up. I sat up from the blanket. Lifting my arms, I pulled my sweater off, exposing the thinnest beige dress I owned. I had put it on so I wouldn't overheat in the sweater while out in the sunny garden today. Clearly that didn't work too well.

"Good thing I won't find out too late. I always know what's coming." He observed as I rearranged my dress to be more appropriate, feeling his eyes pierce through me.

"Do you?" I leaned on my hand, palming the blanket, facing Aris. My red hair carpeted my shoulder, a long, curly mess.

"Always."

Without a second thought, I leaned forward, hoping to catch him by surprise. My heart pounded out of my chest. His body was as still as a statue as I reached closer to his face. And just when I was about to touch his lips, I teased him with a smile and looked into his eyes. Laughing heartily, I fell back on the blanket.

"Doubt you saw that coming."

Playing with the devil. I didn't know what I was doing or thinking, but my body wanted to play with his.

Aris touched my sides, brushing his fingers in a quick manner until I screamed my laughter. I couldn't handle it. I could *not* handle it. He found spots on my body I had never felt so ticklish before. Finally, with laughs rumbling all over his body, he let me go. I fell back on the blanket, out of breath with some laughter still escaping my throat.

"Who knew you'd be such a tease." He appeared above me, hovering over my body.

I attempted to slow my breath, but I couldn't with his face so close to mine. His eyes, a perfect shade of twilight darkness. Aris lowered his legs along mine, causing my dress to lift slightly. Aris looked further down my body as his hand explored down my side. A giggle escaped me for a moment, and then silence crept in.

He gazed while he felt me, and it sent my body vibrating with electricity from his soft touch. I wanted him. I wanted everything he would give me. I wanted his hands and his lips all over my body.

I swallowed and felt a slight pressure in my chest, knowing I shouldn't want this. The little voice in my mind was the most distant it had ever been. I could barely hear it.

I didn't want to feel shame for how I felt for Aris anymore.

Aris played with my dress, lifting it higher and higher from my bare leg. He let it go as his fingers trailed over my stomach onto the middle of my chest. My breathing turned unsteady. His gaze followed his fingers as he memorized my body. With his mouth, he reached for the strings that held the top of my dress, gently tugging them until they parted and fell. His fingers found the thin strap over my shoulder, pulling it down and down my arm. My body shuddered with how light and gentle his touches were.

His eyes lifted and locked with mine. I stopped breathing altogether.

Leaning down until his face was about to touch mine, he tilted his head and breathed upon my neck. My chest rose with each inhale, wanting more. His hand drifted to the other strap on my shoulder. With each gentle tug, he pulled my thin strap lower. Fingers grazed my skin, leaving warm, tingling sensations throughout my body.

"Please," I whispered. He was teasing me, as I did him. But he knew what he was doing.

He continued, not listening to my cries, and explored my hips with his fingers. Slowly, he lifted the other side of my dress and raised it to my hip.

I couldn't handle it. I wanted—needed more than this.

He was about to travel to my chest when I laid my hand under his jaw, guiding him towards me. His eyes were the darkest I'd yet seen. Hungry. Burning.

I brought his face closer to mine, and he obliged, giving in, brushing his lips upon mine and sending thousands of butterflies between my legs. His lips were soft and gentle as they pulled mine apart. He tasted like heaven would, sweet and warm.

I opened my mouth just a fragment wider, and his tongue swept in and around mine. We danced with our mouths, as his hand grazed higher on my now bare leg.

I could feel a pressure between my legs. The small voice in my head had completely disappeared along with all my cares. I wanted him.

I gasped sharply when his hand reached between my legs where no man had ever touched me before. I'd never experienced such vulnerability like this before. For a moment, Aris froze his mouth on mine and opened his eyes to make sure I was willing to go forward. That I was ready for this.

We both breathed together, moving along with nature's rhythm, and stared into each other's eyes.

"Are you okay?" he whispered against my lips.

"I—I've never—never done this." I breathed with him.

His throat worked. "Have you ever touched yourself?"

"Touched myself?" His hand barely moved, staying between my legs, and it felt comforting in a way. "Of course I have." I let out a soft laugh.

A moment or two passed by, and I couldn't read Aris' expression.

"No, what I mean is, have you pleasured yourself before?"

My brows twitched in confusion. I put two and two together, and thoughts flooded my head, but none of it made any sense. I flushed a deeper red.

"We can stop," he suggested.

I was so scared, but I wanted it more than anything. I could feel his hand completely stilled between my legs, not daring another move. It felt like it belonged there. My body pulsated, as if it were begging for him to continue.

"I don't want to stop."

"Are you sure?"

"No—maybe. Yes—yes, definitely." I sounded like an idiot. "I just don't know—how to do any of this."

"You don't need to do anything unless you want to."

His lips were so close to mine as he spoke to me, and I didn't want to talk anymore.

Grabbing the back of his head, I pulled him to my mouth.

"I don't want you to stop," I whispered between the movement of our lips.

He swore in my mouth. His hand moved higher as he tugged on my lower lip. The strength I felt from him between my legs created a burning sensation within me.

His fingers touched me, and I nearly whimpered.

He gently explored me, his tongue ceaselessly intertwining with mine until one finger slid into me. I inhaled sharply as he used another at the top of my sex, massaging it. All I could feel was my sex burning for more touch, more movement—sending thousands of sensations building upon each other with each stroke. I pulled Aris closer to me as a moan escaped my lips.

I eagerly began pulling and lifting his shirt higher and over his shoulders. He reconnected his lips with mine. Demanding more, he spread my lips until his tongue swept the entirety of my mouth.

Aris moved his mouth to my neck. It was sensitive, sending tingling sensations down my chest. My breasts were full and hard. He moved his mouth lower and lower, reaching the loose part at the top of my dress. He moved his strong finger, stroking more of my outer sex with the other.

He let out a groan of pleasure, breathing heavily. Aris pulled his head away, pulling his fingers from me. We breathed deeply against each other.

"We should stop," he rasped as he stared into me.

I nodded. I had no words to speak out loud to describe the feelings in my body and soul. It was like my body had been waiting years for these moments, and I just didn't realize it.

Looking into his eyes for what felt like the first time, they were as open as a mirror. Beautiful and clear. A perfect balance of light and darkness.

CHAPTER THIRTY-SEVEN

A woman was brought into the apothecary, nearly lifeless.

Peter moved the tinctures and our tools out of the way while raising his brows for help. I jumped onto my feet from behind the desk and helped place the rest of the dried herbs from the table onto the shelves in the back of the apothecary.

"Place her here." Peter pointed at the men who carried the woman to the large wooden table. He twisted the lever at one of the metal legs to lower the side, and I followed the same process. With all four corners of the table lowered, we were able to evaluate the woman better.

She was writhing in pain. Her light brown hair stuck to her skin. She was burning up.

Flashbacks of one of my last moments in the apothecary in Prustan crossed my mind and without permission, my fingers began to tremble.

"Girl!" Peter waved his hand in my face, and I snapped my attention to him. "Get me the poppy, and quickly!"

I focused on my steps as I reached the shelves, careful not to rush or break anything this time. Grabbing some poppy, I brought them to Peter just as the men who brought her here left the apothecary.

He placed the herb in the boiling water, while I wiped some of the wetness on her forehead off. Her eyes were closed. She looked young—about my age.

Because I had to know, I pried her inflamed mouth open. I saw the same dark-colored tongue, I froze.

"This can only help her stay calm, silent one, but I'm afraid that it's up to her whether she lives or dies."

I slid my eyes to him. "What do you mean?"

He froze and stared at me. The apothecary went still and quiet.

"You—you can speak?" Peter knitted his brows. I didn't answer the question because it was redundant. "Uh...yes, yes. The medicine can only calm her. There is nothing that will cure this illness. She will either survive it or not. It's entirely up to her body if she will survive."

"You mean that there is nothing we can do?" The question weighed on me more than I realized.

Peter pursed his lips. "No, I'm afraid not. I've seen this sickness around for many years. I've seen some survive, but most don't. The illness needs to run its course. It will either take a life or it won't. We can only try to make her as comfortable as we can."

My lips parted, and I glanced back at the near-lifeless woman. My chest crushed at the sight of her and remembering how I had suffered from believing it was my fault in Prustan, the lack of medicine to keep that woman alive. Nothing I could have done would have changed her fate. I sat on a chair near the table and watched the woman. No relief flowed through me.

That didn't make me feel better. I placed my face into my hands and took a deep breath. It was still painful to see a young life go.

Maybe I wasn't cut from a healer's cloth.

I felt a hand on my shoulder. "A good healer is one that cares, silent one," Peter murmured.

After hours of standing by, washing her body's sweat, I made myself a comfortable place to lie down and rest. I placed a blanket down on the green rugs and blew out some of the candle lights. Peter had gone home since it was well into the night, but I didn't want to return to my quarters just yet. I didn't want this woman to be alone.

My last thoughts of the night were of Aris.

It felt like he was gone much longer than five days. The day he left on his short hunting trip, he gave me a kiss on my cheek in his chamber, and it burned with a hundred sensations for the rest of the day. That was the only intimate contact he'd given me since the day we lay on the blanket under the orchard a week ago. I didn't know if what I felt was normal, but my mind was completely infatuated with him. Wondering what he was doing now, what he was thinking, what he was feeling. If he felt the same way I did about him. If he also thought of me as much as I thought of him.

I was going crazy.

The next morning, Peter walked in the apothecary with a warm mug of tea.

"I'm glad that you trusted me enough to speak yesterday and that we can converse a bit more now." His eyes were soft as he smiled. "How is she doing?"

I accepted the tea from him and said, "She's doing better. Her fever broke, and she's not in much discomfort."

Peter walked over to our patient and laid the back of his hand on her forehead. "Good, good. That's a great sign. I'll take over today. The kitchen needs you this afternoon, and I'll send word if anything changes."

The rest of the day flew by before I stopped by at the apothecary to find the woman sitting up, talking to Peter. My heart fluttered.

Peter was in the middle of the conversation while he brought a cup to her mouth.

I gave Peter a quick smile and wave before I left for my quarters. My mind wandered to where Aris was right now, and if he was enjoying himself on his hunt.

Falling on my cot, I fell asleep with the thought that I wanted to make a difference in this world. I wanted to help.

I heard a noise coming through my room.

My ears twitched, grasping for any more sounds or movement.

It was late in the night and dark outside. My heart raced violently, thundering against my ribs, telling me something was very wrong. My throat felt as if it were closing in.

No light in the room. Eyes wide open, they began to adjust to the darkness.

Someone was here. *No, not again.* Someone was here for revenge for the Strokan warriors.

My hands threw my blankets to the side of me. Flashes of the moments the Strokan warriors captured me a couple months ago burned in my memory.

I sat up, trying to find air, but I couldn't. My entire being was as tense as stale burnt bread. It took everything I had to continue forcing myself to breathe. My throat strained, and my heart pounded. I could feel it in every part of my body.

I was ready. *I trained for this*, I reminded myself. I pulled my legs from beneath me and crouched low on my bed.

Who was here who was here—

"Solei."

I recognized it instantly—

"I'm so sorry. I shouldn't have come. I don't know what I was thinking. I should have known how'd you react."

Aris' silhouette shook his head as he sat on my bed. I grabbed his arm to calm myself down from the panic attack. I didn't want to wake Sebry or any of the other girls, but the sounds that were coming from my throat were uncontrollable.

"I was just so excited to see you," he whispered as he scooped me into his arms, comforting me. He ran his hand through my hair. His breath was warm on my neck and smelled of citrus.

Was he even real? Was I dreaming of him? How was he possibly here—in my room? He wasn't supposed to return from his annual hunting trip until tomorrow morning.

"It's been five days. I didn't want to wait another minute once I arrived. I kept tossing and turning all night wondering when I'd see you again, and then I remembered I could see you anytime I wanted." He gave a breathy laugh.

It was so good to see him.

"How did you know to find me here?" I whispered once my heart calmed.

"I always know where you are, quiet one." Aris laughed quietly again.

I couldn't help but giggle with him. A moment later, I realized we were in a room full of sleeping servants. My eyes widened.

I needed to get him out of here. Immediately.

"Follow me." I grabbed his hand, slipped my shoes on, and led him off my bed.

"I need to get you into your own chamber but most importantly a comfier bed," he said dryly as he followed me reluctantly out of my chambers.

I shook my head, smiling. "I need to get you back to *your* bed. This is bad, Aris."

"Will you stay with me?" He wrapped an arm over my shoulders. He was walking straight and seemed coherent, but I was curious how much wine he'd consumed—if any.

"No, Aris. That's absurd that you'd even ask. I can't. You know that."

"Why not?"

"Because that will confirm the rumors."

"And?"

"And they'll hate me even more," I retorted. I thought of the servants' energy lately but also Sebry's. Her genuine concern just a few days prior flashed through my mind.

"I'm afraid for you, girl. Many women are already jealous of your position here, even as an unpaid worker. No one has gotten to work with him so close in his quarters, and now you've been seen riding with the lord. This isn't good for you."

Not to mention Maeri had been acting strange around me recently. She knew something, but that wasn't it. I made a point that tomorrow I was going to check in on her.

"Why?" Aris interrupted my thoughts.

"Because I have a sneaky suspicion they all want you." A corner of my mouth twitched and knew I was only feeding his ego.

"Do you want me?" Aris turned his head to me.

"That doesn't matter." I brought us around the corner of the kitchen, and I couldn't help the heat that rose to my cheeks.

"It's the *only* thing that matters. What do you mean?" He frowned and looked at me quizzically.

My heart fluttered, but I refused to respond. It was dangerous. I wanted him. But how could I allow him full access to my body and heart if there was no room in his heart for love?

He released me and took my hand as we walked up the staircase. We walked in silence together until we approached his large double doors.

"Get some sleep, Aris. I'll be back in the morning," I stated as I slipped my hand out of his.

"Where are you going?" He grabbed my arm, pulling me in close.

"I'm going to bed."

"Perfect. Let's do it together."

My heart stopped. I replayed what Sebry told me months ago. He had never invited anyone to his chambers before—in *this* type of way.

Not completely sure what he was implying, I swallowed audibly. "Goodnight."

His head lowered to mine, too close for me to remember what I was trying to do. He tilted his head, his lips inches from mine. Hesitating, he leaned further and brushed his lips against mine. Warm and soft, and citrus-tasting. I welcomed him. It felt so good to. I couldn't resist.

His kiss was deep and slow. Butterflies fluttered through my stomach and legs.

"Solei," he beckoned me greedily. My name on his lips nudged me further into his body.

I opened my mouth slightly, his tongue teasing me.

"Stay with me."

I felt lightheaded as his words touched the core of my being. I stopped thinking clearly the moment he lowered his head inches from mine. It would take every cell of my body to leave his presence. I couldn't do it. My body and soul wanted him. And he wanted me. To stay with him. Not Camilla. Not any of the other servants or ladies here. He wanted *me* to stay with him.

Though my brain tried to resist, I nodded slightly, agreeing to his request.

Aris opened the double doors and led me in, closing them behind us. It was dark and warm inside with only the fire in the furnace crackling and dancing against the wood. He was right when he said he had been tossing and turning all night; the bed sheets were rumpled.

"Come," he said as he crawled in his bed.

He had taken off his shirt but left short trousers on. Thank Erus.

I walked slowly, fingers playing with my short night dress, contemplating listening to my brain and running away with some dignity. I had made this bed every morning for months and never imagined I would be crawling into it alongside him.

And I wouldn't forgive myself if I didn't do it once more. I straightened out the bed sheets and continued to do so even when I heard Aris laugh at me.

"You're unbelievable," he mumbled with a smile.

"*You're* unbelievable!" I palmed at his sheets. "What are you doing in bed, attacking the sheets like an animal?"

He let out a full belly laugh, and with his eyes sparkling through the dark, it almost took my breath away. "Don't be afraid. I don't bite...hard." His wink and grin were full of teasing, causing my toes to curl at the sight.

After I straightened the last quilt, I finally crawled into the left side. His bed was large and plushy, causing me to sink deep. It was the finest bed I had ever lain on. Something in my stomach fluttered. I turned my head, facing him. Aris was looking straight ahead into the empty darkness. I wondered what he was thinking about because it seemed faraway and lonely.

I surprised myself when I decided to slither deeper into the covers until I found his body. I wrapped my leg around his. Laying my head on his warm bare chest, I could feel his smile on my head. It was the most perfect place to lay my head, as if this part of his body had been created and molded just for me.

"You have no idea how much I needed this." He wrapped his arm around my shoulders, pulling me closer. "How much I needed you here."

I nodded in agreement. If only he could hear the thoughts in my head, he would realize I felt the same way.

I must have drifted off into deep slumber because I woke up to him holding me from behind, mumbling something I couldn't understand. It was pitch-black outside, meaning it was still night. The fire was glowing strong and warm. I twisted slightly in his arms to see his face. He was asleep, his head so close to mine, and saying words that sounded like *forgive me*, and *don't leave*.

I reached a hand to his cheek, stroking it gently.

"I won't," I whispered softly.

He stirred for a moment as my gentle words woke him from his partial slumber and opened his eyes slightly from the movement. Our eyes locked, and he gave me a smile, tugging me closer to his body.

"My quiet sun."

My heart warmed. I closed my eyes knowing I was completely and utterly safe in his arms, and sleep overcame me once again.

Sharp morning light woke me, causing me to flutter my eyes open. Aris was behind me, holding me in his arms, his leg now wrapped around mine. I'd never shared such an intimate space with a man before, sharing his bed, spending the entire night together—our bodies intertwined. I suppose I did, in the storm with him. But this was different. It wasn't for survival. My heart skipped a beat as I realized where I was and who I was in bed with. If the servants found out, they would shun me forever. I was sure of it.

"I never want you to leave," he said, his voice low and thick.

I twisted my body to face him. His eyes were clear and vulnerable. Yet I felt something dark lingering deep in his eyes. A sadness that I couldn't quite grasp.

I never wanted to leave him, either. I wanted to be here, in his arms every night and every morning, lying together, our bodies woven with one another's, never letting each other go. If I broke my vow for him, how would I feel after? Would it be the right decision? I knew the answer, yet I refused to admit it to myself. I wanted nothing more than to be with him for the rest of my life.

In my heart, I knew that was what he also meant.

But I didn't respond to what he confessed.

He leaned down and brushed a kiss under my eye, then the tip of my nose, and under my other eye. Warm pools flowed in my stomach.

He pulled back, eyes locking with mine. "Your freckles are perfect. I want to kiss every single one."

I melted. But I knew this morning couldn't last forever. "I have to go, or else they'll be suspicious," I whispered, glancing at the door.

"The morning light is already midway. They have most likely already noticed you've been gone." He brushed my neck with his lips as he pulled me closer.

He was right.

"You should just stay here with me." He kissed my neck again. My jaw.

"I—I shouldn't."

"You should."

"I have chores to do." I breathed more quickly, my body heating without my permission. *Damn you, Solei.*

"Isn't it in this very room you're in, if I recall clearly?" He smiled as he kissed my cheeks.

"Aris," I whispered.

He pulled me closer in response, and I could feel something strong between his legs. All I wanted to do was touch it and feel it, a primal act within my core.

"I'll be back." Aris pulled his body away from mine, leaving me exposed to the cold air that swept into the space.

"Where are you going?" I regretted that I told him I had to go.

"I have something for you."

My heart leaped.

Aris got up from the bed and walked to the other side of his chambers. I could see something bulging from his black shorts, and my insides spiraled.

He grabbed some papers from the desk near his back window and walked back towards me. What was he giving to me? I sat up as he approached my side of the bed and handed me a large beige paper.

What was—

My heart stilled.

I read its contents, and my eyes filled with wonder and tears. My trembling hand went to my mouth.

They were freedom papers.

"You're a free woman of the Strokan Empire as of yesterday."

I couldn't believe it.

"How?" My throat was hoarse from the tears I forced down.

"I found a way to claim you as a citizen—I've been trying to legitimize it for months. Along with your friends' freedom. I still have more to go, but we'll get there."

I shook my head, bewildered. I had no words to describe the overwhelming feeling that grew in my chest.

"I won't allow slaves here because that's what working for free is. Freedom to do what you want is not a privilege; it's a right. And you were never a slave to me. I needed to make sure you and everyone else knew that."

He became blurry as he sat at the edge of the bed, explaining it to me. I felt my chest tightening, full of relief. Tears rolled freely down my cheeks on to the paper. I had never before been so taken care of in my life. Aris had gone out of his way to get these for me. I thought after learning about Stroka that it would almost be impossible to gain my freedom or that it would takes years and years of work. My hand shook as I laid the papers down to the side.

"I can't believe it."

"You deserve nothing less. I'm sorry it took me so long," he murmured. "Strokan laws can be such a pain."

"This is everything to me, Aris. You don't have to apologize."

He gathered me close, and in that moment, I looked up to see his face. His eyes were distant again.

"What is it?" I asked.

"You will leave me, won't you?"

My throat closed, and I shook my head. Our eyes locked with each other, and I could see the fear in his eyes. "I won't, Aris. I couldn't. I will stay."

"I want you to choose me. Not because you must, to survive, but because you truly want me."

"I choose you, every day. I want all of you, everything you'll give to me."

I reached my hand up to his face, fingers tracing his worry lines. He lowered his head inches from mine, breathing in each other's air, our words, our feelings. I leaned in further, crushing my lips to his, and he welcomed it openly.

Everything I said, I meant.

I wasn't afraid to admit it to him or to myself anymore.

I belonged to him.

CHAPTER THIRTY-EIGHT

I laid my head in my new chambers that night, as Aris promised.

The yellow bedspread caught my eyes, and then the white daisies that filled every shelf. My fingers grazed the beautiful dresses hanging behind the room divider. The fire in the hearth brightened the space, and I felt a sense of peace.

I exhaled a deep sigh.

Walking past the bed, I stood near the window that peered out into the darkness of the night sky. There was a bench with some cushions below me, a perfect seating area to read a book on a rainy day. To the right of me, my eyes took in the potted herbs. My breath caught in my throat and I walked over, my steps echoing in the room. My fingers brushed over one of the plants. This was the exact plant I was intrigued by in the river that day Aris found me bathing. I held back a sob. That had to be a coincidence. But it wasn't. Nothing was a coincidence when it came to him.

I cleaned myself in the bathing chamber to the far left, and the entire time I kept shaking my head. This was all surreal. What did this all mean from him?

After I washed myself, I pulled my nightgown over my body and crawled under the soft covers and nearly whimpered.

This was too perfect. Too soft. Too...alone.

Sleep knocked in the doorway of my mind, but my mind refused to answer and welcome it. I rubbed the inner corners of my sleepy eyes.

Before I could stop myself, I walked to Aris' chamber yet again in my nightgown. It was past midnight. He was going to laugh at me. I knew he would. This was supposed to be my first night in my new chambers, and he was going to laugh at me. I didn't want to be alone. I wanted to be with him.

Live fully, I reminded myself.

I was about to tap on his wooden doors before they disappeared before me and opened. Aris had a large grin on his face.

My jaw dropped. "How—"

"I heard you." He smirked. He was shirtless again with low-riding short trousers on his hips. Dangerously low.

"No, you *knew*."

"Maybe." He shrugged nonchalantly, and I wanted to shove him but pull him close to me at the same time. "Come here."

I stepped into his warm embrace. I could never get used to this feeling that surrounded me every time he wrapped his arms around me.

It felt safe. It felt right, as if I were meant to be here with him.

We didn't say a word as we lay in his large plush bed, entwined in each other's bodies, my head in that perfect spot beneath his shoulder, and fell into a deep slumber.

The next morning, Aris convinced me to stay in his bed instead of mine. I smiled every time he came back from his study just to assure himself of my presence. After tidying his chambers, I lounged in his space and caressed my freedom papers. I couldn't believe I was a free woman.

Though I was coming to terms with my brother's death, I was beginning to feel different with Aris. I knew from listening to other experiences and stories the way I felt about Aris wasn't anything like theirs. The feelings I felt for Aris were stronger and deeper—so much deeper than what others had described. It ran into my very core, into the cells of my being. It wove through my soul's existence and sang a song of union whenever he was near me.

Some moments, I felt as if I were dreaming, or floating by a memory in the distance and it would all disappear soon. I held on as tightly as I could, fearing it might all be swept away. I couldn't let this go, whatever we were.

Aris barged in for the fourth time today with a smile across his face. He held a few papers in one hand and in the other a package wrapped in brown paper.

"I brought you something."

My heart leaped, wondering what else it could be. He placed his papers on the table near his back window and approached me as he handed me the package.

I opened it with excited hands, allowing the brown paper to slip to the floor, and held the most beautiful green lace dress I'd ever seen.

"Aris," I said softly in astonishment. I held it up, straightening the dress so I could admire its entirety.

I had no words. No one had ever given me anything so delicate and beautiful as this. The dresses he placed in my chambers were remarkable, but this dress was priceless. My eyes stung. The light green lace covered the dark green silk layers of the skirt. It was pure perfection. I lifted my eyes to meet his, so open and clear, curious as to what I thought of it.

"Aris, this gift. It's—it's exquisite. I don't understand. Why are you—"

The double doors in his chambers opened, and in came a guard and Aris' mother. Her face dropped in hesitation when she saw me, eyes wide with wonder. She stopped in the middle of the room, her crimson dress flowing against the floor. Straightening my spine, I dropped my gaze, allowing my hair to hide a part of my face. I was in my short night dress in the emperor's room, holding an expensive dress as if I were his whore.

How awkward.

"Who is this?" Her voice was smooth and milky.

"Mother, this is my... She's the healer's assistant," Aris said carefully.

Acantha's brows knitted. "Are you ill?"

"Uh, no—no, I'm perfectly fine. Thank you for asking."

Acantha tilted her head, observing me.

Oh, she knows. She had the same look Aris did whenever he saw something between the lines.

"I am to leave in two days. Will I see you before my departure?"

He walked past me. "As you wish. Have you considered my offer?"

There was a moment between the two of them that spoke a thousand words.

"Darling...you know I can't. Let us speak of it no more. I wouldn't want to spoil the last days I have with you before returning to your father."

"He isn't my father." He shrugged. "One day you'll see he isn't much of a husband to you, either."

"Aris...enough of this," Acantha scolded. She whirled towards the doors, giving him a *look* and me a smile before departing.

Aris' shoulders dropped slightly, and he turned to face me. "I have some meetings to attend, but when I come back, I want to see this dress on you, or I'll put it on you myself."

My toes slightly curled, and my cheeks flushed pink, imagining him doing so. "Tempting."

He gently placed his hand on my cheek, brushing his thumb over my lip. "I'll be back."

Chapter Thirty-Nine

This whole day seemed to be a dream to me. Nothing felt tangible or real. I couldn't understand how and why he treated me this way. I wondered more than before, if he felt the same way about me as I did toward him.

I was willing to release my vows for him. I didn't care about a vow that kept me from fully expressing my love and my being with Aris. I didn't care about the vow I made when I was afraid of experiencing something that could be beautiful. It was fading slowly, every day. The fear no longer held strong, growing weaker with each smile Aris gave me.

Dusk was approaching as I folded the dress on top of the chest. I fed the fire more wood and placed a large cauldron on top to heat the water. With a cloth, I grabbed the cauldron and headed to his washroom around the corner. I poured the boiling water into the white marbled bath that had clean water from earlier. I placed lavender petals into the bath and inhaled the sweet scent. Slipping out of my night dress, I dared myself to take a bath knowing that Aris would be back later. I would have it washed and scrubbed as if it were never used by me.

Wrapping my hair up, I stepped in, and the warm waters engulfed my body. I let out a deep exhale. This was exactly what I needed. Imagining every worry of mine floating away from my body.

"Enjoying yourself?"

My eyes flung open, my arms covered my chest in the water. Blood rushed to my face as I faced Aris. He let out a low chuckle as if he knew I didn't intend for him to find me here.

"Don't let me stop you." His face said it all. He took off his long black coat and hung it over a short pillar.

My heart pounded. I felt so vulnerable, but I liked feeling this way around him. I wanted him to see me. And everything that I was. But there was a part of me that hesitated in this new territory I was risking everything for.

Aris approached me, and for the first time, he seemed as if he were questioning whether he should or not. I read the nervousness on his face. I'd be damned. It was a sight to see.

I loosened my embrace over my chest, a silent invitation for him to continue.

What am I doing? I was literally asking for it. My sister and mother would call me a whore. Everyone here in Siniya would do the same. But all of it didn't matter because I wanted him.

He approached, crouching near the stone bath, and all my thoughts and doubts disappeared as he stared into my eyes.

"Is it warm enough?" He dipped his fingers into the waters, testing.

"It's getting warmer."

"How is that even possible?" he asked with amusement.

"Because you're here," I said, my whole body flushing a deeper red.

"Ah, I tend to do that to women." Aris smirked.

Stupid, arrogant emperor.

Without hesitation, I splashed his face with bath water, but he grabbed my hand. I was playing with fire again. He turned my hand, palming it and raising it to his lips. My skin melted from the heat of his lips. He traced his mouth along my inner wrist to my forearm, and my breasts tightened in response just above the water line.

He laced his other hand through the back of my head as his lips and tongue reached my collarbone, tasting every inch of it. He pulled my head to his, and I wrapped my arms around his neck. The cold air hit the top of my body, and I drew myself even closer. He traced the side of my neck, and I breathed in his scent. His arm reached into the waters and wrapped around my bare waist, bringing me to him as his lips finally slanted over mine.

I must have let out a sound because his kiss became hungry and deeper, our tongues dancing with each other. His hand beneath the water explored my body and with it my skin relished in its touch. My hands pulled at his tunic until it was over his head. Aris' lips found mine, smiling smugly, as if he knew exactly what I wanted.

I could have sworn he was blushing with me.

His hand traced up my waist just below my breast. It pebbled at his touch, and he must have sensed it because he obliged and explored it—

He swore into my mouth. The waters bounced off us with our movement. Our breathing deepening, I tugged on his lip for more.

My body had completely taken over my mind and soul, as if by primal instinct it knew exactly what it wanted and how. With my hands wrapped around his neck and lifting off the bath to rise, his body followed mine. We stood both in each other's arms, me in the bath dripping wet, and him outside of it, dry with only his tunic off.

This wasn't fair.

I gave a slow smirk. My hands drifted from his neck to his strong pecs, his stomach and to his trousers. My fingers danced along the rim until they hitched just enough for me to pull them down.

"You're going into dangerous territory," he warned me.

I smiled, not having any words to describe this was exactly what I wanted and only he could give it to me.

I pulled Aris into the bath, and he obliged me. We took a moment to feel each other, to fully see each other, bare as we stood together.

"You're perfect," he whispered as his hands drifted to my hips.

I blushed a shade deeper and dipped my head just in time to notice what I'd been curious about this entire time. And I couldn't believe it—that was what could be inside me.

How is that even possible? My mouth went dry. My insides spiraled, and heat pulsated between my legs. My body knew what it wanted.

I heard Aris chuckle as he grabbed my backside and hoisted me up. With a swift motion, he brought us both down into the water where I straddled him with my legs around his waist. I could feel his strength behind me. He placed his hand behind my head and pulled me forward until our lips connected again. It felt like home. My lips and body loved this, craved it deep in my bones.

I had never felt the sensation between my legs become this immensely strong. I couldn't handle it.

"Solei," he whispered. I nearly whimpered at my name on his tongue.

Aris pulled my hair behind me until it exposed my neck to his lips and tongue. Once he had his feast, he let go of my hair and my neck and leaned into the back of the stone bath, staring and worshipping my body with his eyes as dark as the night sky.

I swallowed, waiting for the shame, that I should feel dirty, like a whore. But I didn't. And it surprised me. Nothing in my soul told me this was anything but pure and good.

He studied my eyes, with his hands on my hips. My legs were still wrapped around his waist.

"What are you thinking about?" I asked softly. The waters brushed against my waistline.

His throat moved as he contemplated his answer. "That I am completely and utterly at your mercy."

My heart stopped beating as his words washed over my being. His vulnerability touched a space in my heart and warmed it. I couldn't help but wonder if anyone had seen this side of Aris before.

"I will cherish every moment of it," I whispered.

Aris smiled at me. "It isn't just a moment." He lifted his hand and played with my damp hair in front of my chest.

"Well, whatever it is, you're safe with me." I raised my hand and placed it on his cheek. I realized it was the truth. His eyes lowered on my body and back to my eyes, full of thoughts.

"You clearly disobeyed me." His eyes filled with stars of amusement.

"How so?" My voice rose a pitch higher.

"You're naked."

"And?" I smiled, but suddenly self-conscious.

"I wanted that dress on you when I came back."

My jaw dropped. "I will not be needing your assistance, if that is what you're going to imply. I can handle that myself."

Aris chuckled, and his core moved beneath me. "You insult me. Do you question my expertise in dress handling?"

"I definitely do. And you would be nothing but a distraction, so stay out of it."

"Fair enough. I ordered dinner to be sent to my chambers. I heard the servants come in while we were..."

"You heard them?"

"Of course."

Of course. I hear and see all things, obviously, was what he didn't say.

My breathing quickened, and I wondered if any of them heard or saw what the two of us were doing.

Aris read my face. "Don't worry. We were quiet enough." His eyes grew a shade darker, and my sex pulsed beneath me as he said the next few words. "I will never allow a soul to see what is mine."

Our eyes locked with each other, and I embraced the fact that I was his, causing my toes to curl in the waters.

"Shall we eat then?" he asked.

Aris and I left the stone bath and met the biting cold air. He grabbed a large towel, covering me from behind, gently placing a kiss on my neck before he let go. He changed away from my peripheral vision and left me in the privy chamber alone.

I detangled the ends of my hair with my fingers enough that it was mostly dried in wavy auburn curls. I slid on the light green slip that came with the dress and then stepped into the lacy green gown that fitted my body like a glove. It felt like silky butter on my skin.

The sun had set, and the glow from Aris' chambers implied the fire was still burning strong.

Looking one last time in his large, clear mirror, I saw a redheaded woman, hair now at her hips. Freckles all over her face and body with a hue of pinkness. She was allowing herself to be happy, and nothing could end this joy that felt new but also eternal. That felt so safe and true.

A tinge of guilt prickled at me, and a gray wave flowed through my mind, reminding me of the last three weeks. I shook my head and released any tension in my muscles.

I stared at my reflection.

I didn't think I could ever feel at peace about my family's deaths, but I could live and live well.

Walking out of the privy, I stepped into Aris' chamber where he was feeding the fire. He looked up smiling and noticed the dress.

"Beautiful. I knew it would fit you perfectly."

I didn't even want to know how he knew what my measurements were.

We both took a seat at the table near the back window, where two sets of plates lay. The platters were filled with duck, potatoes, greens, and different types of breads and butters. I realized I hadn't eaten like this since...since I had been captured. And before then, I still didn't eat this well.

I made an observation. "There are two plates."

"Yes, there are two of us." He raised an eyebrow.

I lifted my eyes to his, picking up my fork and knife. "Do they know?"

He swallowed some food before he replied, "I'm not sure what they know or don't, but I'm assuming they know I'm not alone."

"Right. And they also know I haven't been in my room the last couple days."

"Right."

I snickered. "I'll make up a story of where I've been."

"Why?"

I nearly choked on the food I just swallowed. "Because then—then they will suspect."

"You are a free woman, Solei. You can do as you please, and you have your own chambers now. You don't need to answer to anybody." He spoke with liquid calm. It gave me shivers.

"Right."

That bit of information went over my head. I was a free woman. When would that register in my mind? And in my life? But I didn't want them to give me trouble for this. They would call me a whore and confirm my inner thoughts of myself. They would tell me what a fool I was, that I was young and didn't know what I was doing. And worst of all, he would leave me for someone else.

"If they give you any trouble, I will end it," he said as a matter of fact.

I finished swallowing my food and realized just how protective he was. I never had anyone protect me the way he had. But I also didn't wish harm on others, even if they caused harm to me. And if that made me weak, then so be it.

"Regardless of your new chambers, I want you to know you have a bed here with me."

"A bed here with you?"

"That is what I said."

I placed my fork down. My stomach felt queasy. "I won't be your whore." My voice cracked. "I...I would never forgive myself. I would never."

He lifted his eyes to meet mine. They looked like burning coals. He swallowed the rest of his food like it had turned inedible in his mouth. He placed his utensils down. "You are *not* my whore. And you never will be."

"It seems like I am—or I could be." I couldn't look at him anymore.

He stood abruptly. His anger thundered over to me. He stepped away from the table, trembling. "You are like no one I have ever been with, and I won't have you questioning it. I thought I made that clear. I thought I made it clear what you are to me—what you mean to me."

"Well, you didn't... I feel like maybe this is all too good to be true. Like it might slip away. *You* might slip from me." My eyes stung, and I shook my head. "This might not be as real to you as it is to me."

His face reddened as he regarded me with blazing eyes. "How could you say that?"

"I don't know what I am to you. My mind is consumed with wondering if you'll grow bored of me like you did with Camilla."

"*Camilla!* Camilla, Camilla." He shook his arms and head, looking up at the ceiling. He glanced back at me. "You're right. She was like those other women I grew bored of—who never meant anything to me. They knew that, too. I thought that was it for me, in my life. I never thought it could get better than that. That I could feel something deeper than something so temporary. Until I met you and I got to understand and *know* you. You have become everything to me, Solei. The thought of you not knowing this makes me sick." Aris shook his head, looking away.

"Maybe they were everything to you too, at one time," I said quietly.

"They weren't."

"How do you know?"

"Because I know what I feel."

"And what is that, exactly?" I bit my lower lip and met his gaze.

"Something I've never felt before. With anyone—ever. I feel new. I feel...alive. Like I finally woke the moment I met you, and everything made sense in the world. I tried to stay away from you, but there was this *feeling* that I couldn't just brush off. And—and these thoughts in my head that wouldn't just *shut the fuck up*. You became *everything* inside of me, my thoughts, my feelings, my actions. They all led to you."

I was trembling. Not because he was shouting but because of the words he spoke.

"How am I supposed to survive in this world where it feels like I can't even breathe when I'm without you?" He paced back and forth. "And when I *am* with you, I can't think of anything else *but* you!"

I didn't say a word as he continued.

"And I'm afraid, for the first time in my life. I'm—I'm afraid. Of what it might be like to not have you." He looked at me with his glimmering eyes. He pointed his hand to his chest. "I need you, Solei. More than I need water to drink or air to breathe."

As my throat tightened, I walked across the distance and wrapped my arms around his neck. He welcomed me, trembling.

"I need you too, Aris."

His face was warm against my neck as we held and breathed into each other. For several minutes we stood in each other's arms. And I didn't think I'd ever felt so safe until that moment.

I had never felt so seen in my life until him.

I lifted my face in time for him to grab my head and pulled me in for a kiss. It wasn't gentle. It was hard and fierce, hungry and passionate. I matched his pace. My hands and nails were all over his body, his back, his shoulders, and twined in his hair as he hoisted me up onto his hips. My dress in ruffles almost swallowed his arms entirely.

He smiled between our kisses. "Now I want this off of you."

I couldn't contain my laugh as I rolled my eyes. "So demanding! First, you want it on, then you want it off."

"I know what I want when I want it." He didn't allow his lips to part from mine.

"Stupid, arrogant emperor."

It was his turn to laugh as he placed me on the window ledge. His hand went to my neck as he pulled me back in for a kiss, placing his body between my legs. My mouth opened, welcoming his sweeping tongue. My insides burned. I felt the need in his hands as he gripped my hips with hunger. His warm calloused hands moved, raising my dress past my knees.

He hesitated for a moment and parted from our wet lips as he lifted his arms and closed the brown curtain behind me. Our eyes locked.

"I won't risk my men seeing a sacred moment between me and my woman," he said, and my breath hitched. *His woman.*

His hands resumed as his lips met my neck once more, licking and biting. I breathed his scent in. I would never forget this moment, I told myself, as time slowed. His lips were warm and soft. The crackling fire blurred in the background when suddenly my dress was loose on my body. His lips never faltered as his hands stripped the dress from my body and left me in my slip. Grabbing my bare thighs, his hands felt and explored, as did mine.

Aris traced warm kisses down the slip of my dress as he spread my legs with his knee. My breath quickened as he pressed soft and gentle kisses against my open thighs. I didn't know what to do but just allow and just be.

I didn't have the space in my mind to feel self-conscious or to question whether this was normal or not because it just *felt so good*. His hands gripped my thighs, his lips brushing higher and higher. My trembling hands held me up on the window ledge, and he raised my dress until I was completely exposed.

Aris pulled my hips closer to his mouth, causing my body to heat. Eyes closed, body trembling, the rest was a blur. It was his groan at how I tasted that created an eruption in my body that was uncontrollable, and nothing in this world had ever compared to it.

Aris gripped my quivering thighs even firmer as the sounds of my voice and his name filled the entire chamber. I couldn't control the sensations that vibrated throughout my entire existence at that moment. It was like time had stopped, and I forgot how to breathe.

What was *that*?

I trembled. My entire body and soul trembled.

Aris lifted his head from between my legs and carried my body in his arms as he brought me to his large bed. He had the most glorious smile on his face. Like he had accomplished something greater than in the battlefields.

"It's time to sleep."

My lips parted. "Please don't do this again."

"Do what?" He seemed surprised, his brows raised slightly.

"You pull away every time, and I don't want you to. Not this time. Not ever."

His face relaxed into understanding. He stood near where I lay as he explained, "For the first time in my life, I don't want to mess this up. There's no need to rush into something you're not ready for. And I feel like I might not be able to control myself. I can't—"

"I don't need nor want you to control yourself. I want all of you—of course, only if you'll have all of me." Heat rushed into my face as I laid out my heart's desire.

His eyes met mine. "I do want all of you, Solei. Every part of you."

"Then take me."

One moment Aris' eyes were as dark as the night sky, twinkling in the firelight, and the next, they were as clear as day. Not in the literal sense, but in a way that I saw all of him and everything in between. The man between emperor, warrior, and lover. The man who attacked and protected. The man who people feared but also loved and worshipped. The man who didn't let anyone in but couldn't stay away from the captive from the Western Sea Islands. The man who saw beyond what everyone else saw in a captive, in a witch, in a mute. Aris, who saw through and through Solei, for who she was and still, after it all, accepted her, held her, and wanted every part of her.

Aris inched closer to the bed, until his hands reached the hem of my slip, and he crawled above me. His legs entwined with mine, his warm calloused hands grazing underneath my slip until it was over my head and off my body.

He left just for a moment to undress himself before his lips met mine, soft and assuring. My heart pounded against my ribcage. His hands brushed along my side and reached my backside, spreading me apart. I pulled him closer and closer until every part of him was on mine. I felt his lips turn into a smile like he knew my body needed his.

I felt him hesitate at my entrance, his bare chest heaving, his eyes lifted to mine, showing the question he didn't let out.

My body trembled beneath his. "I'm yours, Aris."

That was my answer for him to finally let go and move gently inside me. We breathed deeply into each other's mouths. I let out a sharp inhale as I felt something painfully tear the moment he slid deeper, and it wasn't the vow that I shred into pieces. It wasn't even the lining that kept my virginity intact.

It was the tear that my soul had kept so tightly around the belief that life couldn't get this beautiful for me. And so, I poured myself into him, allowing it to be just as magical as it felt, meeting his every move, his every rhythm, his every thrust and sweet kisses. His hands and mouth explored my chest and neck. Caressing me, holding me, worshipping every part of me as he whispered my name in my ear as his hips moved faster and harder.

We trembled with each other as he moved inside me again and again, feeling, seeing, knowing every part of our bodies as they molded and created synchronicity.

The rest of the night felt like it never actually happened. I kept realizing I wasn't in fact in a dream state and that I had actually lost my virginity, the vow I swore I'd never break, to Aris. This was real. He was real. I was really here.

But how could something so real feel so abstract? I realized it wasn't as physical as I thought it would be or how Maeri described it. Because it felt like our souls were merging into one when our bodies moved in nature's rhythm. There was nothing physical about it.

It was nothing like Maeri had described.

Chapter Forty

My mind woke before my eyes opened.

I felt the empty sheets between my fingers. Aris had left. I fluttered my eyes open, wondering where Aris had gone. Last night—or I should say, this morning—was the sweetest moments I'd ever experienced. Not only did we make love once, twice, three times throughout the night, he had searched for me through the sheets, held me, and loved me. I smiled thinking about how much he had hesitated, his brows furrowed, expressing concern since it was my first time, but my body *needed* it like it was craving him. As if it had been starved for too long.

My face flushed from it all. I felt complete. Whole. I bit my lower lip just thinking about what he did to me, how he made me feel.

Searching for answers, I looked around until my eyes landed on a note that was left near the side of the bed I lay on. I picked up the note and read its contents:

My uncle sent for me early this morning. I didn't want to wake you. Enjoy your day.

Aris – stupid, arrogant emperor.

I let out a laugh. My toes curled under the sheets, thinking of exactly how I wanted to spend my day with him between my legs.

Immediately upon thinking of it, my body ached. Not for him, but from how much sex we had. I felt raw between my throbbing legs. A new pain I'd never experienced before. But a pain that was so, *so* worth it.

Ripping the sheets from my body, my breath caught in my throat when I saw it.

A small, stained color on the sheets. Blood. *My* blood.

A smile spread across my face. It had never felt so good to break a vow I made to myself.

Tugging all the corners of the sheets, I pulled them off for cleaning.

Shortly after, I made my way to the healer's apothecary. Slowly, I descended the stone staircase until I reached the servants quarters. It was a strange feeling *trying* to walk normally. All I wanted was to be with Aris, curled up against him between his sheets and maybe put some cool cloths between my legs.

"Solei!" Nirelle almost passed me.

I shared the news of the freedom papers with her and Maeri the day before in between Aris' visits back to his room, but nothing had changed besides them getting paid.

"I'm not sure what you're up to today but"—she gently squeezed my hands in hers—"why don't we take the day off and go to the river together? We can celebrate!"

"That would be perfect. Where is Maeri?"

"I'm not sure. I've been looking for the both of you, thinking you've been up to no good together."

It was my turn to let out a chuckle. "No, I haven't seen her."

"I have a feeling that she's with her *lover*." I gave her a raised brow in question. "I figured she's been disappearing with him." Nirelle rolled her eyes.

"Ah, the missing servant," Sebry said, turning from the kitchen. Sebry grazed her eyes up and down, causing me to mentally check in with my legs, ensuring they didn't appear as weak as they felt.

I gave her a smile in response as I finished packing our bag, ignoring her comment.

"We're heading to the river today during the celebrations for the emperor's mother. Would you like to join? There won't be any extra chores until tomorrow morning," Nirelle offered.

"Sure. Why not? They won't be noticing the difference anyway. I need the extra cleaning and sunbathing. Getting stuck in this palace for too long sometimes makes me look too pale. My parents would be appalled if they were to get a good look at me with my lighter skin." She slid her eyes to me and narrowed them. "But you have some explaining to do, silent one. Where have you been? You haven't slept in your chambers the last couple nights. The whole palace knows you haven't been here or there. Why, I wonder if you've still kept up with your usual chores in the morning for the emperor. Or should I say, *with* the emperor."

"I don't know what you're talking about, Sebry. I've been given my own private chambers as Peter's assistant since I'm rarely here with the others. But I think we should bring food. I'm famished."

We walked out together towards the kitchen as my stomach growled for breakfast.

"I wonder why," Sebry pressed. "Is it because you've been missing all the meals or is it because of certain activities that you've been up to that the whole palace can hear?"

"They did not." I whirled around, feeling the blood drain from my face.

"No, but you just answered my question." A mischievous smile spread across Sebry's face.

I clicked my tongue and elbowed her. "Sebry! That's not funny!"

Nirelle and Sebry laughed in unison as we snatched some fresh breads and roasted nuts for our river day. My face couldn't get more red.

"Not as funny as the way you're walking right now, silent one."

Nirelle burst out in laughter, filling the entire kitchen. I was completely mortified. My entire body turned as red as a berry.

The rest of the day consisted of Nirelle and Sebry teasing for my whereabouts the last couple days, but neither one of them could get it out of me no matter how accurate their assumptions were. Even though I wanted to tell them more than anything, I wasn't yet ready to let the whole world know Aris was giving me attention. I wasn't ready to let these peaceful moments between him and me go.

I wasn't ready.

As soon as we reached the quiet, vacant river and left our garments behind us, I felt a heavy silence around me. It was the way they were staring at me. I looked down at my body. Was there something that showed them I just had sex? And a lot of it?

Did I have blood running down my legs? No.

I looked behind me, and they kept staring at me.

"What?" I asked. They were making me uncomfortable. "What is it?"

"Solei..." Nirelle barely whispered.

"You're scaring me. What's wrong?" I pressed.

Sebry lowered her head. Nirelle approached me, and her eyes dropped to my left arm.

To my brand.

Oh.

Nirelle swallowed as she touched my shoulder. I flinched and looked elsewhere.

"When did this happen to you, Solei?" Nirelle spoke in soft tones.

"It's fine, Nirelle. It happened about three months ago. It's in the past now." I waved a hand and shut down the conversation. "Who's hungry?"

"No, it's not fine. What happened?" Nirelle demanded.

I could see Sebry was uncomfortable and was staying behind us. I could feel her heavy stare. I felt bad for her. She probably thought I hated them even though it had nothing to do with her people.

"The Strokans happened," I stated plainly. "They were trying to teach Aris a lesson to remind him I belong to them and them only. To teach Aris a lesson for killing Tobias. They wanted to do this so I didn't question who owned me. It was a game to them, and I was just a piece of it. Nothing more."

"But Solei..."

"I'm okay, really. You don't have anything to worry about. I barely notice it now, anyway."

Sebry stepped forward, and to my surprise, she gathered me in her arms and didn't say a word.

"I'm okay, Sebry. I—I promise. There's no need—"

Sebry tightened her embrace, and Nirelle hugged me from behind.

I almost cried, and I didn't know why. My eyes stung. I didn't realize I still felt a certain way about this brand. I had buried it deep.

I felt seen and heard beyond the lies I spilled. They saw right through me, and they didn't care if I lied. They only wanted to be there for me.

We didn't speak of it again.

On our way back, the palace glowed from afar. There were candles within illuminating the windows, and we could see the party dying down as people started to enter their carriages before departing. I smiled to myself as I walked in the direction of his room to the far right of the palace.

Entering Aris' chambers, it was warm but empty. He was still gone entertaining people and most likely spending time with his mother. I wondered how Aris felt about his mother leaving tomorrow. I wondered if it was difficult for him to see Acantha leaving, knowing she was going back to that torturous man.

Something caught my eye on the table near the back window. A stack of brown papers. Usually, he kept things like that in his study, away from prying eyes. My father hadn't been worried about my tendencies for no reason; he knew I was a curious woman.

I stepped towards the papers lying on the table near the back window where we had dinner the night before. Carefully, I glanced over the tan speckled papers knowing this was invading his private matters, and in doing so could be treason. But they were right here. In front of me. I had to look. I had to see—

My hands scattered the papers on the small table so I could see them more clearly. Heart pounding against my chest at what I saw on them. *What is he planning?*

My breath stopped, and I threw my hand up, covering my mouth.

War, war, war was scattered all over the pages.

Not just any war.

I knew I'd seen too much. I knew I wasn't intended to see this—perhaps no one was. With my hands shaking uncontrollably, I couldn't manage to place them exactly how I had found them.

Screw it. I didn't care if he knew I saw them.

My jaw clenched and I dropped the scattered papers as I fled the room. *I can never forget this.*

He wasn't for peace like he said. He wanted war and to conquer. Despite everything he had told me, he wanted more *war*.

He lied to me. The man I thought I knew was fading. All he wanted was bloodshed. He wanted death.

I would never be able to stand by this brutality.

How could he do this? I walked back on unsteady legs to my chambers for the first time in a few days. *Why would he want this?*

Sweat accumulated on my forehead. I was going to be sick. My brother died because of rivalry, bloodshed, and war. Aris and I bonded over my brother's death. I thought Aris understood what loss meant.

My stomach threatened to drop to the floor. A tear escaped my eye as I absently passed the hallways.

I didn't think I could do this anymore. I couldn't support this. I wouldn't.

Could it be I didn't know who he was? That he was an entirely different person than I had thought?

I quickened my footsteps and sprinted across the next hallway. *Gods, I was an idiot— a fool!* How could I have been so blind?

My eyes filled with tears when I turned a fuzzy corner, running into Maeri.

She caught ahold of my elbows. "Solei, there you are! I've been looking for you." Her eyes seemed to be glistening, but it was hard to see through my own blurriness. "What's wrong? What's happened?"

She pulled me down the next hallway and into an empty chamber. It was dark, and the only light came from the hallway outside. Maeri looked both ways before she shut the door. My eyes adjusted.

"What is it? Why are you crying?"

"I—I can't explain." I wiped the tears from my cheeks, but more continued to flow. "I'm just a mess. I don't—I don't understand anything, anymore."

Oh, gods. I wasn't making any sense.

"Let's sit down." Maeri pulled me to the chamber's couch in front of the unlit fireplace. "What do you not understand?"

"I don't understand him. He isn't who I thought he was or is. I...I'm so confused, Maeri." I sniffled and wiped another hand across my damp face.

"Shhh, tell me what happened, sweet Solei."

"I gave him everything. I trusted him."

"I know you did. I know." She held me, rocking me slowly for a while.

"I don't think I can even trust myself..." I broke again. "I don't know what's right and what's wrong. What's black and what's white."

Maeri squeezed my shoulders. "Sometimes we forget, but we can't blame ourselves. It's human nature. It's what keeps life interesting, right?"

Some time passed, but then Maeri's body tensed, and I could feel her heart racing. "I think maybe going away will do you some good. Just for a little while. What do you think?"

"Where would I go?" I whispered, not sure if I wanted that. Didn't Aris wonder if I was going to leave him after handing me the freedom papers? I couldn't do that to him. But then again, how could he do *this* to *me*?

"I have a friend that could take you," Maeri explained. "But they're leaving after the celebrations tonight. We'd have to rush there quickly since it's ending soon."

"Are you sure they'd take me?" My brows furrowed.

"Oh, absolutely! It's not a problem. In fact, why don't you go and meet them right now? I'll be right behind you. I'm going to pack some of your things for you," Maeri offered.

"Oh. Okay, that works."

"You should probably go now, catch them before they're gone." She squeezed my arms in reassurance.

"Alright. I'll head there now, then."

"Let's meet at the stables. I'll go get Nirelle, and we'll grab as much as we can for you. We'll say our goodbyes...for now."

"Thank you for helping me... You don't know how much this means to me."

Maeri nodded, but her eyes were glistening. "Anything for you."

"Don't cry, Maeri."

"I can't help it. You—you've been such a good friend."

"You too. The best." I wiped the last tears from my eyes so I could see her more clearly. "But this isn't a forever goodbye... It's just time for me to think for a while. You're right. I think I need this."

I wrapped my arms around her once more before we both parted ways.

It was the darkest part of the night, and the stars were glowing with no moon in sight. I heard the grass and sticks crush under my boots as I followed the path to the stables near the palace. From behind me, I could see a few guests leaving Aris' celebration on carriages. Drunken laughter pierced the air, and it sent a crawling sensation down my spine.

I should have listened to the voices... The voices in my head that told me I was going too far had left because I forced them out. He was a warrior—a deadly warrior.

My breath faltered as I carried on with weak steps towards the hidden stables. I could see Maeri through the windows in the barely lit stables inside, waiting for me.

That was quick. She must have really wanted to make sure she was here before I left. Her brows were knitted together, her cheekbones sharp against the dim torches.

She was the best friend I had ever known in my life. And here I was, leaving her for my own selfish reasons. I didn't deserve her.

Pushing the door to the side, I walked in the creaking stables, and Maeri's face was painful to look at. My lips parted. Something was wrong.

Maeri took a step forward toward me. "I—"

A noise behind me told me we weren't alone. I whirled around just in time for someone to grab my waist and another man to place a rope between my teeth. Rough, large hands gripped my arms. My eyes widened. I looked at Maeri, who was now shaking with tears pouring down her face.

"I—I'm so sorry, Solei—"

A voice thundered through the stables, interrupting Maeri. "You did exactly as I asked, Maeri. Well done, my sweet." From the darkness in the corner, a shadow approached us, and finally the starlight showed his face. "We'll handle it from here."

My breath caught in my throat.

Helon.

Chapter Forty-One

What is happening?

I attempted to free myself from the men who squeezed my arms tighter from behind me.

Why were they holding me down? Did they think I was trying to escape? But I was a free woman... Maybe they didn't know. Despite it being the palace stables, this place felt too small. There wasn't enough air and not enough room to move.

I was caught.

I asked the questions through my eyes to Maeri, who now had her hand trembling over her mouth. She was crying. Why wasn't she helping me?

"I said *enough*, my love," Helon scolded, and Maeri flinched. She took a step back. Further from me. Helon wore a crimson tunic with dark blue threads in the collar. But it was the way he touched Maeri's cheek that caused me to feel a chill, yet there was no breeze.

Holy Erus. Maeri's lover was Helon... How did I miss this?

This was the man who bought her luxurious dresses and handed her monies.

The food I ate earlier with Nirelle and Sebry threatened to escape my stomach. *What did Maeri do? What has she done?*

Maeri's shoulders slumped as she started to walk away toward the back of the stables toward the next set of doors. She disappeared into the shadows. My mouth dried. She did this to me.

Helon shouted at a nearby Strokan guard, "Pull the carriages behind the stables! We're to leave immediately. Send news to Aris tomorrow morning that we left on an early departure."

The beastly Strokan guard bowed his unwashed head and left the stables behind me in a grunt.

Helon grabbed the bag, *my* bag, that Maeri grabbed from my chambers. He lifted my freedom papers in the thick smoke-like air. "You think *these* are real? I knew you were a foolish young girl, but I didn't think you'd be that stupid."

He scoffed and shook his head, almost hiding his laughter from me, and what was left in my cracking heart disappeared.

What was he saying? Did Aris lie to me?

"You were just another woman twisted in his life—he gave you those freedom papers to have you. You were a challenge to him." He sneered at me as if I were scum. "These freedom papers don't mean anything in Stroka."

Stroka?

The sounds of a carriage pulling in front of the stables vibrated the walls.

They planned on taking me away. They were taking me to Stroka. The realization hit me instantly, and now I knew why Maeri was crying. She did this to me. *She did this to me.*

I panicked.

Maeri did this to me.

The Strokan warrior who held me in place was nearly an entire head taller and pressed his grimy fingers into my waist.

"It'll be a long journey to your rightful place, but it'll be worth it. You've caused enough troubles here in Siniya," Helon said as the Strokan guards yanked me to the metal carriage.

No. Not again.

But no matter how hard I yanked myself for my freedom and thrashed my legs in the air for leverage, I was thrown into the metal carriage. My knees scuffed unto the wooden planks below, and my head was hurled against the back of the cage, causing blood to trickle down to my jaw. I coughed from the collision, and more blood came spattering through the rope between my lips. The taste of metal filled my mouth. Before I realized what was happening, the portcullis slammed shut in my face, causing a loud ringing in my ears.

Helon stood a distance away, smirking. "Funny how it all worked out. My nephew will believe you ran away after receiving these freedom papers."

Aris wouldn't know I was taken.

I was taken because I was still owned by Stroka. Maybe Helon was telling the truth, and these freedom papers were false. Yet for some reason, I didn't care if Aris never found out his uncle stole me.

I would have never forgiven him for leading a country into bloodshed. Yearning for it, seeking it. It made me sick.

I stared into Helon's icy, vapid eyes. The carriage jolted into motion before I was ready to let those eyes go.

I cursed those dark eyes into damnation.

A flicker of fear flashed across Helon's face, as if he suspected the same. He continued to the next carriage behind him.

Down the dark road, the Strokan guards rode the rumbling metal carriage towards Stroka and its venomous lands. Through the starlight, as I sat at the back of the cage, I stared down the Strokans who controlled the carriage Helon rode in. I could tell I made them uneasy, but I didn't care.

I saw the fear in his eyes, and I was hungry for it.

Something was beginning to change me. I could feel it.

There was a part of me that didn't really care I was being taken away to the worst place in the world. There was a part of me that relished in the fact I was going to be very far away from *him*.

And that maybe, just maybe, the worst possible pains would make me forget him. Forget this country.

I might be a dreamer, but I was sure if I tried hard enough, I would forget about him, and what better way than a place where love did not exist.

I clenched my fists together, and I felt my chest tighten and harden. I felt my heart harden. Towards Stroka, towards Helon, towards Maeri, and towards the emperors that tugged a war between me. Then I tore my heart into pieces so there was nothing left of him in me anymore.

PART IV
RELEASE

Chapter Forty-Two

The weather was cooler than I was used to as we headed north. The metal cage was unsteady in its route, causing me to have headaches throughout the days and nights. It had been five nights since I last saw Maeri, since the last time I saw Aris.

I had never known what hatred felt like until now. It started small, like a chipped teacup. Then the crack grew and grew, and it was easy to spread. I felt my body ache with the pain of anger. I fueled it and fed it as much as my heart wanted. I was so angry with myself for falling for a man who only really wanted blood, death, and praise for his countless conquests of countries. I thought I saw something else in him...

I was angry he had me fooled when he gave me the freedom papers. Maybe it hadn't meant anything at all.

I was angry at Maeri and her lies and betrayal.

I was angry that I didn't see any of this coming.

Between all this anger and the parts of myself that tore my feelings apart, there was a small piece of me that did not admit it, that was angry Aris would never know the truth behind my disappearance. His fear of me leaving him was coming true, but he didn't know it was the furthest thing from the truth. He deserved to know regardless of if I would have stayed with him after seeing the war papers.

Without my mind's consent, my stomach hurled the little contents I had in it on the side of the carriage. I couldn't believe I gave him everything. I slipped so far and deep in adoration with him, I couldn't see things straight. I lost sight of who I was and what was important to me.

They barely fed me, only a few nuts here and there—just enough to keep me alive, I supposed. They pulled me out of the carriage to do my business in the woods where they stood watching, giving me no privacy.

Stupid fucks.

Thirteen days passed.

I thought the rest of my heart was left in pieces back in Siniya but at last, I wasn't filled with magic, and I wasn't a witch. I did have a heart inside my body, and it was absolutely crushed, causing chaos in my chest. None of it made sense, and I couldn't piece it together.

When I would think of him, I tried to think about his true colors and how he was bloodthirsty. I tried to think of how he was similar to his father. I tried to remember how he lied to me about the freedom papers. I tried to think about the fact that he destroyed my lands and killed my people. How he was cold and emotionless—like a true Strokan.

How could I have done this to myself? To my brother who fought for my freedom? I slept with our enemy.

No matter how much I told myself these things, it never lasted. My mind would turn against itself and would remember what it was like to be in his arms, to be wrapped up in his body. His sweet and warm kisses lingering on me. I could still feel them. He was a part of me, a part of my soul.

My mind would make excuses for him. Maybe he didn't know of a life without bloodshed and war? Maybe he had given me freedom papers, but Helon took them, anyway? Maybe he did truly want me to be a free woman.

Maybe he really did have feelings for me.

Eighteen days passed until I saw it. I could barely crawl. The fat on my bones had nearly disappeared. The linen trousers I wore were loose on my hips, and the tunic they gave me barely stayed on my shoulders. The skin on my lips peeled back and bled persistently. The water in my body was depleted; even my eyes were hard to blink since the dryness hurt every time they closed. My tongue felt like sand in my mouth. It felt harder and harder to inhale, and the sounds my throat made became music to my ears along with the rolling wheels and the hooves of the horses on the hard dirt.

But then I saw it. I swore, I saw the tinge of red in the clouds that lingered above Stroka. I might have been seeing things at that point—I didn't doubt it—but it looked real. I could barely register the fact that we were entering the darkest of lands.

It didn't matter anymore. I welcomed it all the same.

I was only a body, after all. A body that felt things that didn't have to be real unless I made it so.

I thought that was what freedom was: the ability to say whether something was a reality or not.

My eyes closed, and I thought I died. It was peacefully quiet, and darkness swaddled my existence.

But I felt hands grab at my body and pull me out of the carriage.

Like my nightmares. Except now they were real.

No. I wanted to go back *there*, in the darkness, where life didn't have to make sense.

Forcing my dry eyes to open, I saw the magnitude of Stroka, the vast amount of limestone buildings upon buildings. The city had its rolling hills, but it wasn't just hundreds and thousands of buildings that caused me to catch my breath but the people that swarmed the dirt streets. I'd never been somewhere so...massive. The gray smoke swirled as if it were a tornado in and around the city, filling its streets and above where the palace lay at the top of the hill. People rushed about as two Strokan guards dragged me by my underarms.

Stroka was ten times what Siniya was in one location.

"It's a witch!" a man shouted amongst the crowd before being shoved out of sight by another gaunt man. "They brought us a witch!"

"Don't look the devil in the eyes, child!" A mother grabbed another little one, veering him away from the main road.

I heard hissing and curses and children screaming a witch was coming through as the warriors carried me through the masses. Their faces wore frowns, almost permanently. There was no other expression I could find through this spiteful crowd. My legs trailed behind me for what felt like eternity until they thrust me into another cage, one that was attached to the ground.

My arms weren't quick enough to catch myself as my face palmed the harsh and wet ground. It smelled sour, and I shut out the thoughts of what it could be. I heard the creak of the door slam shut before I used the energy left in me to pull myself up.

I looked at my new surroundings.

It was the size of a small privy chamber but in a metal cage in the midst of a chaotic outdoor market. Vast amount of tables filled with fruits and vegetables lay in between the narrow buildings in the market, and tapestries on the dirt street displayed homemade leather goods. People flooded nearby, staring, cocking their heads to the side as if I were an exotic animal. If they wanted to see an animal, I would be one.

I hissed loudly and stepped towards them.

The people stepped back in fear, holding their children near their bodies with wide eyes. They muttered amongst themselves with assumptions of who—what I was.

"What is she doing here?" a young woman asked who seemed to be her father.

"Who is she?" a boy asked out loud.

"She won't be anyone for much longer," a woman warned the boy, hurrying deeper into the market.

What is this place?

I looked around my metal cage. The only thing inside of it was me and the straw and dirt on the ground. I looked through the bars of my cage and saw more cages lined up alongside the one I stood in. There were others inside, one for each cage. They were prisoners, slaves. Women and men dressed in gray rags, barely breathing. Some were reaching their hands through the metal bars, begging for food and water. Whoever they were, they'd been here for a long time.

Life had drained from their empty bodies. They looked as if they were dead. I wouldn't be surprised if some were.

I was now part of the renowned, infamous *Insulatus*, where one would lose their sense of self.

I expected a shiver to run down my spine, but none came. I was no longer afraid.

Stroka was filled with smoke from the hundreds and hundreds of cottages that circled the palace above the small hill. All I could smell was the smoke and urine that was definitely *not* in my cage.

More and more women and children crowded near the cages, especially near mine—but not too close. They were curious. Fascinated.

Before, I would have kept my eyes glued to the ground. Before, I would have hidden behind my hair and crawled to the corner of the cage.

But that was before.

Now, I wanted them to see what I was made of.

I looked at each and every one of them with my piercing green eyes, letting everything I felt flow from me and into them. My crazy shone through, and I loved it. I wanted them to see, to feel the pain in my eyes and in my body.

Placing my pale dirty fingers around the bars that kept me caged in like an animal, I leaned forward so they would see all of me.

I was no longer hiding.

I could sense the fear in their eyes as they stayed back, muttering cautionary words to their loved ones. *Witch, murderer, witchcraft, whore, thief.*

They said it all, the lies they believed, and I didn't care.

I didn't care if they called me a witch—maybe I was a witch. Maybe I'd burn their fucking town square to the ground. And I let them see that in me, too.

It was amusing, and it felt good to not care anymore.

Chapter Forty-Three

There is no room in my life and in my heart for love... Or anything like it.

I replayed the words over and over again. Those were the words he had spoken to Camilla.

Was it all a game for him? Did I mean anything different?

I shook my head. It didn't matter anymore. I'd never see him again.

Forget him. Forget him.

I forced the image of him out of my mind so I would forget the memories that killed me the most. That had caused more pain than any of this combined. I imagined he'd say the same to me like he did Camilla, if he were here right now, seeing me in filth and rags. I was hardly recognizable.

The clothes I came with barely stayed on my withering body. My skin wasn't pale anymore; it was black and brown from humidity that stuck in the air and the smoke and dirt that blew our way.

It had been thirty-something days since I'd been locked up in this cage, on display for all visitors who prowled about and spat in our faces. But that wasn't the only thing these people did.

The only food I ate was what was thrown from the children that mocked and laughed at us.

Us.

We were animals, in a sense. Some of us were dead, and it would be a few days until one of the guards would notice enough to drag one of our bodies out and stab them to ensure their death.

The day before, they had dragged a prisoner out, stabbed him in the gut, and the man roared his last breath. The guards weren't always accurate, so it put more pressure on others to act as if they were alive—if they wanted to live.

The old man in the cage to the left of me, I learned his name: Rubert. I heard some of the women hissing at him, calling him a thief. Regardless of why he was in here, we'd sleep near each other for warmth during the cold nights between the bars that kept us apart. We never had the energy to say more than a grunt to each other when strange things would happen like the day before. We'd give each other looks when one of us got slapped in the face with fish pieces or the like. Sometimes I'd see a smile from him, and it was the most beautiful thing I'd ever seen—I thought. I was not entirely sure.

Helon visited on more occasions than I'd care for. He bored me with his relentless bribes.

"Tell me what you know. You must have heard of *something* during all that time you spent with him distracting him, luring him. If you tell me something valuable, I'll consider freeing you from here."

I stared into his cold eyes. Was that why he brought me here? To tell him something about Aris?

Oh, I see. Camilla no longer had eyes on Aris for Stroka. Why they thought Aris needed to be watched and why they thought I would know anything valuable blew my mind, but here we were.

Weeks and months had gone by since I'd been here, and Helon stopped his occasional visits. I'd seen the full moon at least three times since I arrived.

The Day of the Hand passed the week before. Celebrating the lowest of the low class by selling us off to the highest bidders. I vaguely remembered a certain servant threatening me with that day. It seemed like years ago. Memories were becoming harder to remember.

"A dirty little witch, aren't you?" A man had appeared before me. Tall, dark, and nothing good. He seemed wealthy, his rich blue tunic shimmering in the fading sunlight.

I narrowed my threatening eyes, the same I'd always done to chase prowling predators away. They always believed the silent curse from my green eyes.

"Fiery." A slow grin appeared. "You'll do perfectly. We'll have fun, sweetheart. A much better place than this has to offer." He was one of *those* men.

I half expected me to feel sick over his words, but nothing came.

A few hours went by that day. The square was overly crowded with wealthy lords and ladies and the lower class. There was a dais in the square where they auctioned off the best slaves. Most of them were men with meat on their bones. The withering slaves and prisoners were bordering the square in their cages.

I remembered the man coming back again with a guard, who carried a set of keys.

"How much for this one?" the man had asked the guard.

"Ah, this one. I'm not sure she's for sale. She belongs to Helon," the guard murmured.

"I'll bring her back." He placed a purse filled with coins on top of the guard's gloves. "Eventually. Is this enough to keep you silent?"

The guard had only shrugged. I glanced towards Rubert, who for the first time had an expression on his face. His eyes were wide. I thought he was going to be sick.

Poor Rubert, I had thought.

The door to the cage opened, and the man stuck his arm in to retrieve me. I had fought back, but nothing seemed to work. In fact, the wealthy man seemed to enjoy it the more I wriggled from his grasp. I remembered biting his forearm as hard as I could, and he let out a scream.

I might have smiled, but he struck my cheek. My neck nearly snapped.

If I had to guess, for about a week, I was with that man in the countryside. It was chaos. It was a fight to keep that man off me. I didn't remember the specifics, but he touched me more than I liked to be touched, and I hurt him more than he liked to be hurt.

When I was thrown back into my cage, I remembered feeling out of my body. Not recognizing it more than ever.

How could I survive this?

The most unusual thing happened a few weeks ago when I was huddled against the bars of the cage, close to Rubert. I had a dream, and it had color. I saw green grass and rolling hills, and there was a cliffside looking out to the sea.

That was the last color I had seen—in my mind. I thought I remembered what it was like in my dream to see the color green, but it was fading from my mind every day that went by. Now, all I saw was gray. The sky was gray, my clothes were gray, even my skin was gray—everything was gray. An empty color. At least darkness had the color black that was filled with depth and feeling.

Gray was nothing.

I took a glance around. I could deal with the harsh stares, the name-calling in Siniya, but this—I couldn't handle it.

I lost myself.

The dream and its color were the first memory that faded from my mind, and then next were events that passed in my life. I didn't want to hold on to anything anymore. I let the people I used to know fade as well, holding onto only my family, but even that was hard to hold on to. It wasn't worth it at that point, to remember some things that caused more pain than what it felt like to barely breathe from starvation. For what reason should I remember them? It was already hard to remember their faces and who they were in a place where there was no laughter, there were no smiles, and where there was no love to remind one of what life used to look like before—

Before... Before what?

I tapped my head on the bars of the cage I lived in.

What happened before I came here?

Hurt, pain, death.

It was too much energy.

I dragged my body down near Rubert, who had his eyes closed sitting nearby. Carriages came by, causing mud to splatter on our bodies. I hissed at the reckless men who rode the carriages, and they shook in their pants at the sight of me.

"Don't go near the *Insulatus*. They'll bite your head off from hunger," one of the men said as he pulled the other wide-eyed man further from our cages.

Insulatus.

"Why are they there?" the other younger man said.

"Some are prisoners, some are slaves, and others are simply there because they disrespected the crown."

"Do they ever get out?"

"Yes." The man paused. "Once they're dead."

A young girl jumped from the open carriage and joined the two men. "They don't look human, Daddy."

"They're not anymore, sweetie. That's what happens when you don't listen to Emperor Malakar."

The child tugged on her father's tunic and pointed towards me. "But who is she?"

"She was a witch, they say. Stay away from her. She is darkness incarnate now," the father warned the girl. "If you get too close, she'll snatch you up and eat you."

The wide-eyed girl looked over to me in fear and bolted into the market after her mother who walked ahead of their clan.

I swallowed air down my sandy throat and looked over to Rubert, whose eyes were still shut. I slammed his shoulder with my fist through the bars that separated us. He gave me a grunt, and that was enough to tell me he wasn't dead.

After a few hours of watching people go by, I heard a peculiar sound.

"Don't," Rubert said in a raspy voice. I'd never heard it before. It sounded like nails on a stone. "Don't—forget."

I knew what he was implying.

Who I am? I looked towards the gray, smoky sky. *Don't forget who I am?*

Who am I? I could barely remember looking at myself in the mirror. I had red hair—I thought. Red, evil. Maybe I was a witch. I remembered I had a family, and they loved me. And I loved them. But where were they?

I loved herbs. I could remember that. Herbs and healing others.

A flash of a tan man on a bed came through my mind as I cleaned his wound on his torso. Was I a healer? Another memory of water, herbs, and he was there again. He, him—a man. He was not love. I forgot what love felt like in a place like this. It was so hard to remember more. He was not— He was...bad. Don't remember.

Who was I?

I glanced over to Rubert and gave him a look that told him I appreciated his effort. I reached my hand over to his and held it. He gave me a light squeeze for assurance.

I thought for a moment I did remember, but the memories had been pushed so far in my mind it would take too much energy and effort to recall.

There must have been a reason why I didn't remember anymore.

Maybe it was for the best that my mind was empty and alone.

Chapter Forty-Four

I stopped counting full moons, not because I forgot how to count—because I didn't—but because I forgot what the beginning was. From what point had I been counting moons? *Why* was I counting moons?

I didn't remember why, and so I stopped.

I had a life here, whatever that meant. I would see the same people walk through the markets, the same wide-eyed fearful women and children running back and forth. They'd always try to poke Rubert and I with sticks or throw stones and scraps at us.

I'd stare down at my body, as if I'd never observed it so closely before. I could clearly see my bones through my skin, the veins that flowed up and down my arms. It was interesting, in a way.

Every once in a while, there would be a clan with musicians, and I'd always loved to hear them. My body would sway with the rhythm, but it would make people uneasy, and they'd move somewhere else. Rubert would grunt at me and shake his head. I stuck my tongue out at him to mind his own business. But the sounds, the music, it sounded almost beautiful.

A flash came through my mind of two other women teaching me how to move my body. But I shoved the memory deep, deep down.

I wasn't up for exploring my mind today and receiving headaches as a consequence.

A few hours went by as I stared at the gray wall behind us, holding my arms for warmth, when a woman nearby said, "Solei."

It sounded familiar. Not what she said, but the voice.

"You witch," the voice hissed.

Ah, she's addressing me.

I turned my neck to see who dared approach an *Insulatus*. It wasn't her pretty face, but the scent that hit me first. Rosemary. Sweet.

Who was she? I cocked my head to the side, trying to gather a distant memory. Pain and death. My hand went to my throat, but nothing came to me.

I gave her an empty stare.

"You don't remember because—" The woman laughed. "Because you're gone." And laughed louder.

I hated her for it. She was right. I heard Rubert making a movement to the left of me. He could get a little defensive sometimes.

She was pretty, had scrapes on her face and whip lashings on her shoulder, but she was pretty in her own way.

"You're an *Insulatus* now. You'll get what you deserve," she said through yellow teeth. "Because I didn't forget."

It wasn't because I was weak that I didn't respond in time, but it was because I wasn't used to someone having enough balls to attack an *Insulatus*.

The woman grabbed me by my overgrown hair and pulled it through the bars. My eyebrow slammed into the metal bars, and I thrashed to get away from her.

The woman slipped something around my throat and yanked it towards her. It felt like a leather belt of some sort, depriving my throat of air.

This felt familiar.

"I will never forget, Solei. I will never forget what you did, what I endured because of you," she hissed in my ear.

I gripped for the leather strap suffocating my airflow. I'd done this before. She'd tried to kill me before.

Before.

I didn't have the energy to fight for my life. It was so hard—

And I was so tired.

I grappled for her hair behind her face and pulled as hard as I could until her head smashed the bars near mine. The woman only held onto the leather strap harder and harder when her head jerked to the left of me, flying into the bars.

My chest searched for breath as I glanced over to Rubert, who had an arm around the woman's throat, and he whispered to her. Her eyes were filled with fear, and her body trembled. She nodded her head insistently to whatever he spat in her head.

He let her go—but only for a moment, before he yanked her head back into the bars ten times stronger than I did. I heard a *crack*, and she screamed, begging for her life, until Rubert let her go.

She scrambled on the dry dirt and ran from the square as quickly as she could.

I felt something wet on my throat. Touching it, I found bright red blood that poured from my throat and dripped into my now brown tunic. I didn't realize I got injured by her. I didn't realize I was in pain. I didn't feel the pain. Rubbing the color between my fingers, I glanced at Rubert, who merely shrugged and gave another grunt.

That was exciting. I smiled to myself and to Rubert. Not because my life had become rather boring but because a name came to mind.

Klawdia.

Exhausted, I pulled my withered body to the ground near Rubert. We breathed heavily in unison from the sudden exertion. Once my breath settled, I heard Rubert's slow down even more than mine. I looked over, and his eyes were closed. I punched a fist over to his arm, and he barely gave me a grunt.

I gave him a chuckle. *Me too,* I thought. I wanted to say thank you, but I thought he understood. He saved my life. It was surprising that anyone, even someone like Rubert, felt like my life was worth saving.

I wondered for a moment if I'd do the same for him.

I would, I thought.

He was a life worth saving.

"There was a man who was here once...a long time ago. He looked like you." Rubert spoke for the first time in days.

My heart thudded. I didn't know who he spoke of, but there was a tug in my heart—I needed to know who it was.

"I—I would bring him food sometimes. He was a kind young man...." A dark shadow flickered across his eyes. "He only made it a few months before..."

Before what? I wanted to ask. But I couldn't bring myself to it. I didn't really want to know.

A few nights later, the moon had returned brighter than before. The air was cold, smelling like winter, but the smoke had disappeared for the night, and it was beautiful to watch. Rubert must have been watching too, because he reached for my frigid hand, and I obliged.

He pressed something into my hand. "Here, eat."

Looking down at my palm, I found a piece of bread filled with nuts inside. I shook my head and reached back through the bars, but he waved his hand in the air.

"A young prince"—his voice hoarse—"once gave me bread when I needed some. He had everything and saw me. He saw me." He looked into my eyes. "I have everything I need here, and I want you to have it."

I shook my head, brows furrowed. I was confused at what he was saying. I took the piece of bread with nuts inside and stuffed it in my trouser pockets. I wasn't going to argue with him. I would keep it for us on a rainy day. The blood that licked around my neck had completely dried, but somehow, I could tell the infection had started. With no clean water to sanitize the wound, I knew this was going to be a long journey—one that might end with me in the ground.

Fenrah. Another name appeared in my mind. She was the one who taught me medicine. I wondered for a moment where she was in this world—if she was even alive.

The next morning, the guards were taking their usual rounds, checking on the *Insulatus*. They were far away, but I could see they were making their way up here. They grabbed a couple of us and stabbed into their rib cages. None of them screamed; they were already dead.

Good.

I elbowed Rubert to alert him, but he didn't grunt like he always did. Sometimes this old man could sleep like a rock.

I swung another into his arm, more powerfully, and there was no sound.

Stupid fuck. What is he doing?

I slapped his face, but there was no flinch.

My breath stopped. The world stopped spinning.

I swallowed and grabbed his tunic. I pulled him close. "Wake up. I know you're awake. This isn't funny." My voice was deep and hoarse. I almost forgot what it was like to speak after so long of not doing so.

His face didn't move.

The guards were getting nearer.

"Rubert, *do not leave me here.*" I shook him. "I can't do this without you, Rubert."

No answer.

"Please." A tear rolled down my face. I began to tremble. I couldn't get a good enough grip on him. I just needed him closer so I could wake him because he was asleep. I knew he was.

I twisted my body to get a better hold on his neck and shoulders. His old, withering body wouldn't move. I panicked.

"Wake up, Rubert. I beg you—don't go." A sob came out of my hoarse throat. "I know you can hear me, *you son of a bitch,*" I nearly screamed in his ear. "Don't do this. I will *kill* you for this in the next life. I'll find you and kill you if you do this to me, Rubert. I swear it on my life."

I shook him persistently. Tears of love I didn't realize I had poured out of my eyes.

Wake up, wake up, wake up. I let out a sob, and it didn't stop.

Rubert.

You son of a bitch.

Chapter Forty-Five

It was an effort to breathe. It had to be made consciously, willingly.

Something hurt in my heart while I looked at the empty cage to the left of me. Pain, of course. This was what it felt like. I'd felt this way before. Others I had cared for, maybe even loved, had died.

Rubert was a friend to me. He saved my life. He was an angel in the darkest of moments.

And now, he was gone.

They had hauled his poor broken body out into the freezing square, away from me, and stabbed his beautiful heart until they were sure he was dead.

That happened days ago. All I'd been able to think about was no matter how my past slipped from my mind, I would never forget Rubert.

I leaned against the metal cage, staring off into the distance, contemplating what it'd be like to be stabbed alive by those guards. The skies seemed darker than usual, and the cool, crisp wind howled through the cages, making most of us groan from the shivers. The open wound now festering around my throat didn't help. It was hard to think clearly with my fading mind, and so I tried not thinking at all with how many headaches it created. The wound was persistently itchy, throbbing and painful.

Just when I was about to crawl into a corner, I heard an icy voice that perked my ears. I'd heard that voice before.

My eyes darted over the square and the streets of the market, until they landed on him. He wore a crimson tunic over white linen pants as he swept his gaze among the streets. He laughed at a local merchant who attempted to sell their rabbits. Others bowed their heads to him.

Helon. The name wasn't hard to remember. The rest was more or less blurry.

I followed his path as he made his way through the market. As the crowd parted for their royal member, his eyes glanced my way, and my heart thudded.

His eyes were pools of darkness. I swallowed air. They looked familiar.

Observing me, he made his way closer, but not too close—of course. You never know what these *Insulatus*—

"I almost didn't recognize you." His silky voice filled the air. "I haven't seen you in perhaps two, three months. To be honest, I hadn't expected you to survive this long. Not many do. I'm sure you won't last much longer."

I cocked my head to the side as he spoke to me. My blood warmed, and I felt energy rushing through my body. My mind said *run*, but my body wanted to *attack*.

"Regardless of what little importance you have, you made quite an impact on my nephew."

His nephew?

"And that couldn't happen again, you see? Not after Camilla switched over Aris' charms."

Aris. My heart fluttered in my chest, and it was the strangest feeling. It felt almost...nice.

Helon shook his head, smiling more to himself than anyone. "Smart boy, always was. He always knew who not to trust... Even with me, it was hard to gain his trust to the point where he'd tell me any future plans. I was hoping you'd come to your senses and tell us what you found."

The words barely registered in my mind. Aris, his nephew. I could hardly remember what his face looked like. Or how he felt on my body.

"But it seems I was too late. I've been in Siniya for a while, but now that I see you...it seems you've lost *your* senses," he scoffed. "Aris, of course, didn't suspect anything by me. He thought you left willingly and let you go. He has been a mess ever since, but...still hasn't shed any light on his plans for the future."

I grabbed the bars between my pale fingers, leaned forward, and glared into his eyes.

His breath caught in his throat. He flinched but didn't step back like so many others had.

"You know something," he rasped.

It was my turn to laugh. He might have seen something in my eyes, in my subconscious, that I didn't remember, but lucky for me, nothing came to mind.

"You know something that I don't. What did you see in Siniya?" Helon demanded through his teeth. "Tell me, *what did you see?*"

I laughed again, more loudly than before, my voice hoarser than with Rubert.

His face was flushed red by the time he left with his guards and disappeared into the smoke-filled market. Whatever he thought he saw in me, it was gone now. It had been gone for—

I didn't even know how long.

I pushed off the railings and continued to stare at the empty cage near me. The different shades of gray on the metal bars caught a mediocre attention from me. Was this what my life had come to?

"Solei..." a female voice murmured near me.

I turned because it felt too near to me not to. I looked at a middle-aged woman who had a neat braid pulled from her soft, tanned face. My brows knitted into contemplation. This woman... There was something about her.

"Solei, my darling..." Her voice was raspy.

I cocked my head.

She reached her hand through the bars and touched me.

My jaw nearly fell to the floor.

The woman gently grabbed my jaw as if I were a child and pulled it to the side, and her deep brown eyes perused my neck and its infection. She had a large fucking set of balls on her to be touching an *Insulatus* like me. But I let her. Why did I?

Her touched reminded me of home. But I didn't know what that meant.

"Where have you been? Why are you here?" Her voice was a little too rebuking. "I think I might have something to help with that infection," she muttered as she reached for her bag that was slung across her apron. Her voice still felt as if she were scolding, and it amused me. "Have you eaten at all? You don't look...the same."

The column of her throat worked as she brought out a skin bottle and a linen. She dampened it and reached past through the bars, again. I leaned my neck so she could have a better way with her washing.

"Here, drink the rest of this. Why aren't you saying anything?" Her brows lowered, and for a second, I thought she'd put her fists on her hips, but she kept washing my infection.

She paused and looked into my eyes, waiting for an answer.

"Because there is no reason to speak," I said so softly, I barely heard it myself.

"I wished I'd seen you earlier. I've been pulled to every corner in Stroka trying to take care of us but haven't made my way here yet. By the looks of it, you've been here for a long time, my girl. Let me have your neck again. Good." She placed some herbs on my neck, and then wrapped my neck in a long linen cloth, tying the ends tightly together. "I'll be back with some food and water, yeah? Just don't go anywhere," she growled as if I could go anywhere.

I wanted to laugh, but I didn't think she'd take it well, so I kept my mouth shut.

The woman left and trudged through the chaotic market with her herbs and linens. I felt something in my heart flutter. I almost cried out for her to stay, so I could continue to feel this way. This sense of safety.

But something in me refrained from doing so. I wanted her far, far from here.

There was no god in this place, but I prayed that she would not come back for me.

The sun was setting when I heard the guards rush through the markets in haste. Their thick legs and tall bodies made the ground beneath me waver.

The rest of the *Insulatus,* including me, came forward to see what the fuss was about. The crowds spread from the road to give room for the guards marching through.

I stopped breathing for a moment.

They were heading towards me.

What did they want now? Were they going to stab me like they did with all the other "dead" *Insulatus*? I looked down at my body to ensure I was alive—

Yes, I was still breathing and standing. What did they want from me?

They approached my cage and opened it with loud dangling keys. I withdrew into the back of the cage, legs shaking and barely keeping me up. I'd never stepped out of this cage.

Without a second to think, two beastly guards grabbed a hold of each side of my thin, weak body and pulled me from my home.

I wish I could say I fought against their rough hold, that I yanked my body left and right, thrashing and screaming, and did everything I could possibly do to free myself, but I didn't have a single ounce of energy in my body to make a difference.

As the guards dragged me through the streets of Stroka, people hissed and cursed me along the way towards what seemed to be the palace. It was rather boring and didn't look as impressive as I would have imagined it to be—though my imagination hadn't been working very well recently. It was quite large and could fit an entire army or two, but something about it was dry.

Through the gardens of thorny rose bushes and dead grass, we proceeded towards the high palace doors. They were open before we reached them. I was surprised my eyes couldn't get enough of this rather dull place.

The ceilings were tall and carved, but there was no color. I was pushed towards the cold, hard floor and craned my neck to find an older but powerful man standing on the dais near a throne.

"Well, well, what do we have here, Acantha?" his voice thundered in the large room.

"I'm not entirely sure, Malakar," Acantha breathed. A flash crossed her eyes, as if she did indeed recognize me.

The man took a step closer to me. Cocking my head, I realized I knew this man.

I belonged to him.

"She was Aris' lover. I'm sure of it." Helon stepped forward.

The powerful man, Malakar, peered into me the same as I did with him.

"She looks familiar—yes, I remember her." He stepped towards me again. Then looked at Acantha before he smacked his hand across her cheek. "You weren't sure? Is that right? I know you know better than that. You tell me the truth at all times." He lowered his hand and threw a glance at Helon. My heart, what was left of it, squeezed at the sight of Acantha's hand on her stinging cheek. "What about her, Helon?"

My brain hurt with how much it was trying to register the words they spoke about me. I remembered—but I didn't. None of it made sense.

"I couldn't get through to Aris, and I have reason to believe she might know a thing or two about him."

"Still thinking my son will betray me, Helon? What is your reasoning that she might know something we don't?"

"She and Aris spent a lot of time together, and I noticed the way he looked at her. Looked like a lovesick puppy, if you ask me."

"If I remember clearly, Tobias told us she was a mute. Before he died." Malakar's lips tightened.

My heart thundered against my ribcage. Tobias.

"I don't think that's the issue, Malakar. Anyone can talk with the right tools. She saw something, I *know* she did." Helon smirked. "And we're going to make her remember."

Chapter Forty-Six

My lungs filled with an infinite amount of water as my throat attempted to close and breathe at the same time.

I can't breathe. I can't breathe.

It was slow enough I could feel the water surge through my throat, and I kept trying to stop the flow.

Hold your breath. Hold it, I demanded myself. My bony legs and weak arms grappled against the leather straps keeping me secured on the wooden board.

My entire life came to this point of survival. Just one more breath, and I could live through this. I could do this. I wanted to live.

I want to live.

I believed there was a reason why I hadn't completely withered away and died like the rest of the prisoners around me, dropping like flies. In fact, the people caged around me were all new and fresh bodies. There was a reason why I was still alive, and I believed perhaps it was my *will* to live. It wasn't my time yet.

As my head moved left and right in search of air, I realized this had happened before. I had survived other types of torture before—deaths, heartache, abuse, trauma—to the body and mind. I wanted to live then, too.

One thing I knew in this moment was these people had hurt me before.

My lungs burned for air, my heart pounded harder than ever, and without my consent, my mouth opened for air but only found more water flooding inside.

I felt my body compulsively *beg* me to find my breath. One last search.

Just as my body had slowed into death, the board I lay on rose from the water bath. The pints of water entering my body involuntarily came up and retched over my entire being, splashing the warriors by my side. My entire body shook and trembled with water overflowing to the side of me and onto the ground. I heaved for air that now surrounded me and saw starlight fluttering around, though it wasn't dark in the room.

Their wicked, crooked faces smiled as if they'd done their job. Little did they know, I was *really* good at not talking.

I gave them a sinful smile, and theirs disappeared.

"You will answer us: what do you know of Aris and his plans for Siniya?" The tall, short-haired warrior demanded.

I focused on deep breaths, sputtering out water from my lips. Nothing came to my mind, but even if it were to, why would I ever help such a hateful group of people?

"What do you know of the emperor of Siniya?" the other warrior, who was missing a tooth, pried.

I gave them blank stares as I observed their tan, tattooed skins before a tall warrior lifted the bottom of the wooden board—

Water gushed into my throat before I was able to close my mouth.

They didn't give me any time. Goddamn these stupid, arrogant men.

A flash went through my mind as my body thrashed against the hard wood for air.

His warm, beautiful face as he laughed at me underneath wool blankets.

Stupid, arrogant...emperor.

My blood heated, and it wasn't because of this survival. Another flash of the note near my naked body. He had to go early in the morning to see his uncle—

That bastard. Helon. The one who ordered this done to me.

My mouth searched for the surface of the water, and my ribcage burst into expansion, no longer surviving the single breath I took under.

Water surged into my lungs. Air disappeared completely. My body jammed itself into the wood board, needed air— needed—

The board flipped into the room again. I threw up the water and bile that was left in my stomach, coughing for breath.

"We heard you knew Aris, intimately. What did he tell you of his plans?" the warrior missing a tooth spat in my face. The veins on his neck bulged.

I heaved for breath, focusing on the fact that it could be my last one. I thought of their question. Aris—Siniya's emperor, Helon's nephew, Malakar's son, *my lover.*

My lover. I laughed out loud and hoarsely. I felt my heart grow full of remembrance, but then I felt it crack.

"What did he plan to do with Siniya?"

Siniya?

I remembered the war papers. Why were they so concerned about these war papers unless—unless they were about...

About Stroka. Invading Stroka.

My mind searched to remember what they looked like.

Could I have been wrong? That he wasn't a bloodthirsty emperor like his father? That perhaps he was trying to stop more bloodshed by destroying the Strokan Empire?

I gave another breathy laugh, hoping that I had enough to expend so much air. Did I have it all wrong this whole time?

"Tell us what you know, now!" The tall warrior threw a fist at my jaw.

Before I had time to recognize what happened, another fist was hurled into my stomach. I heaved the rest of the water all over the side of my body, which made the other warrior step back with a snarl.

I didn't finish puking the rest of the water out of my body or catch a breath before my head was under water once more. *Stupid fucks*!

I would never tell them what I understood about Aris' war papers, those to destroy his father's empire and restore it into a better, more sustainable kingdom. Those papers were what Camilla had been searching for.

My face searched and searched for air as the water gushed into my lungs more and more. Pints and pints of water filled me as I thrust my body against the leather straps. I could feel the straps pull my skin apart as I heaved for life.

This was slow-motion death—exactly what Helon wanted.

This was all him. Everything happened because of him.

My body finally relaxed, and my heart pounding against my ribcage slowed. I felt the tip of the board lower, and my head rose to the surface.

Again, I purged the water, and what felt like my organs came out of my body. Before I could take my first breath, a fist was rammed into my side. And another.

Countless strikes, but I couldn't feel the pain as everything finally clicked into place.

Aris was fighting for peace.

Peace from Stroka.

I remembered everything. My family. Their deaths. My denial. My friends and the one who betrayed me. My sweet moments with Aris. Fenrah, the woman in the market. Fenrah was alive.

My heart split open.

With the beating from the two warriors and the countless near-drownings, I had blacked out. I woke up in my resting place, hanging from my wrists in shackles. My wrists had been bleeding prior from the leather straps and hadn't stopped since. I felt the blood trickling down my arms towards my shoulder. My arms felt numb as I didn't know how long I'd been unconscious. It might have been a few days.

I scanned my surroundings. I was in an empty chamber in the palace. I was surprised I wasn't in the dungeons, but this place would do.

"Wakey, wakey, silent whore." The voice from behind me told me I wasn't alone.

I turned my aching body as much as I could to see the two warriors from before.

"I wonder how it feels," the shorter warrior said with a sly smirk.

"Well, Evan, if Aris tried it, I'd say good enough." The tall warrior laughed. He walked around me. His hands grabbed the top of my torn-up dress and ripped it open.

I kneed him between his legs.

He bent forward and grunted in pain. He looked up with rage in his eyes. They'd been mocking my body since I got here, tearing me apart until there was nothing left.

"He always had such a weak spot for the helpless, Melvin. Especially the slaves here," Evan, the shorter warrior, replied regardless of Melvin's current position. "I'll be happy when he's gone for good. No more mercy for the *Insulatus* and slaves."

"Are you ready to talk?" Melvin, the tall warrior, prowled towards me, his greasy wet fingers grabbing my chin. "Helon won't be too happy if he doesn't get answers soon."

I yanked my chin from his fingers, and he lowered his hold to my throat.

"Malakar did say she's a mute," Evan muttered.

"That's right. He did say that. And how do you get a mute to talk?" Melvin eyed Evan, showing he had the answer. "You get them to write."

"Do you suppose she knows how to?"

Melvin shrugged. "Prustan taught them all how to write when they were young."

"How did you know that?"

"I traveled to Prustan about six, maybe seven years ago. Had my fun there." Melvin paused and continued to stare at me. "Actually, the women I enjoyed looked just like you, accept for the red hair."

I stopped breathing.

"Yes, yes." Melvin laughed, clearly down memory lane. "There was this mother and daughter about your age. I will never forget their screaming faces after I was done with them and left them in an alley."

My body stiffened, and my blood boiled and burned in blinding rage.

I was going to kill him.

Both warriors pulled a table forward and unshackled me—their first mistake. They sat me down on a chair, pulling my hands flat out on the table, and Evan to my left put a plier around my fingernail.

Melvin placed a fountain pen in my hand—his second mistake.

"Show us what you heard, or I'll do to you what I did to them," he threatened, pressing his disgusting beard near my ear.

The whites of my knuckles showed when I dipped the sharp metal pen into the ink tray and began to draw with the pointy tip.

"There you go. I knew you had some sense in you," Melvin grunted in my ear.

When I heard him close to me, I twisted my body and stabbed him in the neck precisely where Aris once taught me. I plunged the pen even deeper.

He screamed, and I felt Evan seizing my arm when I grasped the knife from Melvin's hip and swung to my right.

I missed Evan when he dodged to the left, letting my arm go. But I didn't stop. When I saw the surprise on his face, I took advantage of the momentary calculation and lunged once more, stabbing him in the chest, right in the heart.

Evan dropped to the ground. Blood sputtered from his mouth. Dead.

Turning around, I met my next victim, again.

Melvin was holding his bleeding neck, shaking and backing toward the door.

"*I will kill you*," I said with a calm, hoarse voice.

His eyes as wide as could be, he scrambled for the door, but I was much, much quicker than him. He gave me the energy needed to end his life. With swiftness, I pounced forward, raising my arms in the air and plunging it into Melvin's chest.

He howled as I plunged deeper and deeper into his flesh, blood splattering onto my hands and arms. I was surprised no other guards came in from the sounds as I let my crazy out. I pulled the dagger out of his spine and plunged it again and again until I was sure he was absolutely dead.

Chapter Forty-Seven

With the new tunic I stole from Evan's short body, I wrapped his leather belt around my tiny waist. The tunic hung on my body in an embarrassing way. There was a bit of blood at the top of his tunic I couldn't wash out. After rinsing my hair in the tub, the one I almost drowned in a hundred times, I sheathed two daggers on both of my hips hidden under the almost clean tunic. Knowing the bruises on my face and body still showed, I hoped I could still pass as a citizen as I planned my next victim's death.

I wrapped a nearby cloth around my hair, hiding again—but not for the same reasons as what felt like a year ago. I was hiding for a purpose far greater than insecurities.

This time, it was to attack, not defend.

Opening the door, there were no guards around. I stepped out and walked down a large hall. Was this normal? Must be since this place was death itself.

Something exploded nearby and made me flinch. I shook my head. This place did a number on people.

I straightened my spine and continued my way in the general direction of what had to be the main hall, where I was sure I could find Helon. He did this to me. He was the reason why I lost who

I was. He was the reason for the pain and suffering I had gone through. Passing large, dark tapestries and windows, I decided to take a moment to look outside.

Smoke filled the lands, more than usual. Chaos.

Interesting, but not interesting enough to stop me.

Hurrying my steps, I ascended a few stairs. I finally made my way to the main hall's doors. Taking what might be my last breath, I opened its large metal doors, sneaking in with a dagger in my hand, ready to die for this last kill, but instead, I froze in my steps.

They didn't hear me enter for their conversation did not cease, but I could hear them.

The words they barked back and forth wasn't the reason for my stuttering breath.

Aris was standing in front of me in his battle leathers and sword in hand. Lifeless warriors lay near the pillars to the side, one near him. It was only Aris, Malakar, Acantha, and Helon in the throne room. A family reunion, it seemed.

I was late to the party.

My head cocked to the side. How could I have forgotten the way he moved, the way his voice sounded, the way his being shone in every room he was in?

Remembering why I was here, I slipped to the side between the pillars where it'd be hard for them to catch my presence. I crept towards the dais—

"It's over," Aris said with lethal calm.

"How could you do this to us?" Malakar said in disbelief.

"It was time."

"What do you mean '*it was time*'?" Malakar shouted at his son, eyes going wild. "We didn't raise you to do this to *us*! We raised you to build *with* us, use your skills here, in *Stroka*. Not for some silly project you're rebuilding in the middle of nowhere."

Aris looked over to Acantha, whose brows were furrowed over fear-filled eyes.

"Come with me, Mother." Aris held his hand out to Acantha.

Malakar's laugh thundered in the room. "You're delusional. She's not moving a step towards you. She's loyal to *me*." He pressed his fingers into his chest as he shouted at Aris.

"It's over, Malakar."

"It's over when I say it's over, son."

I was close to the dais, hopping silently behind the different pillars.

"Not this time."

Breathing in deeply and before he could turn from the sound my feet made, I snuck behind Helon with lethal swiftness. Though I was weak, considerably, I placed a dagger against his throat.

I tugged the back of his tunic toward me, gaining more control.

I could *hear* their backs stiffen. All was quiet besides the screams of dying Strokan citizens in the distance.

I didn't dare look at Aris as I held death over his conniving uncle. Given the number of bruises, cuts, and wounds on my face and body, I wouldn't be surprised if Aris didn't recognize me.

"*Bitch*. How did you make it out?" Helon breathed shakily, trying not to move too much against the dagger.

"What did you do?" Aris' voice was barely a whisper. I could hear the shock in his voice. I could hear the pain.

"She came here, Aris, to Stroka. Sh—she told us your plans for invasion, and we couldn't trust her word so—so we kept her."

I laughed hoarsely, pulling his body closer to me, dagger pressing and breaking skin.

He didn't know I could speak for myself.

Blood leaked down my hand.

"She's no longer there, Aris," Helon breathed through the pain I dealt him. "She's useless to you now." He smiled nervously, knowing I could kill him by pressing one more centimeter into his skin.

"What did you do to her?" Aris' voice was controlled, though I heard a sliver of panic.

"He didn't *do* anything, Aris. Stop the dramatics." Malakar scowled.

I pulled Helon's neck towards my face. Looking in his eyes, I said, "*You* did this."

His breath caught in his throat, and he froze, eyes wide.

If the main hall could breathe, it held in its breath. Utter silence filled the hall. Not a single muscle twitched.

Helon stammered, "I—I—"

"You're not a mute," Malakar whispered, shocked.

"*Answer me.*" Aris' power rippled towards Helon.

I dug the blade in further.

"She—she's—Aris, she's—"

"*You* took me. *You* tortured me for information you never got," I hissed into his ear. "*You* killed me and my memories. *My life.*"

Two things happened at once.

Malakar swept towards me, grabbing my waist, but it was too late. I had slit Helon's throat, ending his wicked, pathetic life.

Now it was Malakar's turn to have a blade at my throat.

I let Helon's limp body drop to the floor. Blood dribbled from his neck and mouth before the fire in his eyes faded.

Malakar's arms pressed into my sides, not allowing air to flow. I didn't need to see it or to feel it to know that he had reopened the wound around my neck. Blood spilled on his blade, making it appear worse than what it felt like.

I didn't dare struggle against this emperor.

Aris had stepped forward but stopped when Malakar stiffened the dagger upon my neck. Aris' eyes remained cold and distant.

"She's *Insulatus* now, Aris. She's gone, for good." Malakar straightened his spine. "You always had a soft heart for the weak. Remember that one—the man I captured in the war? What was the name you kept telling me he was called... Something with a... Ah, yes. Jonam. Yes, yes, I think that's what it was. I thought I taught you a lesson not to get too attached to those people, Aris. And now you've done it again. I'm quite disappointed in you as a son. Except this one seems to be more than a brother-in-arms bond. Perhaps...something stronger?"

Aris' jaw twitched.

"*You* killed my brother?" I breathed.

"Your *brother*?" Malakar drawled. "Oh, Aris. This keeps getting better. No wonder you're so attached to this thing. Your guilt weakens you."

"What did you do to him?" I raised my voice, feeling the power from within.

"Jonam? He was the only one to escape the cages. I'll always remember him. What did he do with his freedom? He found me and tried to *kill* me. Spewing something about how I deserved justice for what I have done to Aris and to my people." Malakar scoffed and shook his head. "He was so enraged he didn't see my men come from behind him, and I ordered his execution then."

So that was how my brother died. By trying to end Malakar's life. That was something my brother would do. Instead of running and escaping, he fought.

Aris took a calm step towards us. Not caring anymore what he saw in me, I lifted my eyes to him.

He met them.

All of my feelings for him flooded into and around me, spilling into every cracked crevice. For a moment, I let him see all of me. The pain, the fear, the anger and hate, the change in me that Helon uttered, the part of me that I hid from myself, the loss of myself, the part that reminded me of him in the darkest of moments, and the love I had for him. I let him see the sweet, soft girl he knew that had changed forever, let him see how much I wanted to end his father's life. I let him see the part of me that didn't care if he hated me or was disgusted by me, because it didn't surpass how I felt about myself.

"Of course, we saw something in her. She knew something she wasn't telling us. We had to use some tools on her to get her to speak." Malakar shifted with me pressed against his body. He was using me as protection or leverage. I wasn't sure which yet.

"How did that work out for you?" I croaked while my bleeding throat moved against the blade.

Malakar laughed, looking at me. "You did fool us, but I wonder how long you would last."

"Until death."

He stopped laughing, but I didn't let go of Aris' beautiful dark eyes.

I could see the strong column of Aris' throat move. I would have died to keep his secrets with me, I told him through my eyes.

Malakar's rough, bearded face spoke against my cheek. "Enough. Aris, it's simple. Leave Stroka with your men, and I won't kill her."

"You're done, Malakar. Your infantry—is done. They're gone." Aris stepped closer. "Hand her over to me."

He still wanted me—the person I had become. He was delusional; he thought I was still here.

"She's dead if you don't let us go, son." Malakar chuckled but pressed the blade even deeper, piercing my flesh.

I glanced at Aris, and I saw the fear in his eyes. I shook my head as much as I could.

It's over, my mind told him. *It's over. Let me go.*

Panic filled his eyes and his face. He was no longer the controlled emperor I was so used to seeing standing in front of me.

He was breaking.

"*Kill* him," I whispered loud enough for him to hear me.

"Shut up, you bitch! I'll gut you to pieces." More blood slid down my neck. I flinched against the dagger.

I could feel the pain—

"I'll do it. I'll leave the city at once," Aris blurted. "Just hand her over to me."

"No!" I cried out against the blade. "I'm already gone, Aris. *End his life*. Finish what you came here to do."

"Hand her to me *now*," Aris growled, ignoring me.

"How will I know you won't kill me after?" Malakar grunted.

"I'm a man of my word, unlike you," Aris said through clenched teeth. "I promise I will not kill you if you hand her over."

Malakar loosened his hold on me and lowered the bloody dagger from my throat. Shoving me down the dais towards Aris, he reached for his wife.

But Acantha was nowhere beside him.

I scrambled on cool, hard ground on my hands and knees. Aris rushed to my side, grabbing my arm. His touch sent electricity through my veins, and I felt my heart beat stronger than it had in months. I lifted my head to meet Aris', which were dark, wild, and everything I now remembered. He turned and watched Malakar as he searched left and right for his wife.

Acantha was now behind us.

Malakar narrowed his eyes. "Come here."

Acantha stifled her sobs. "No, I won't do this anymore. I can't—"

"Do *not* make me repeat myself!"

"Enough!" Aris shouted. He drew a dagger from his chest. "You did this to yourself. You lost your family. You lost your people, your country. And now you'll lose yourself."

Aris flung his dagger with full force, aiming straight for Malakar's heart.

Malakar turned to his left just in time for the blade to plunge into his right shoulder, but we both didn't see the next dagger flying in his direction. Another perfectly aimed dagger diving into the center of his chest.

Silence fell in the throne room.

Malakar's knees dropped to the dais, echoing off the walls. He lifted his head and looked at his son. "You..."

He crumpled, and his open eyes turned vacant.

With a blank face, Aris took a deep breath and turned towards me. "Let's go home."

CHAPTER FORTY-EIGHT

Aris' words hit me. I didn't have a home. Especially not with him—not anymore. Not after...who I became.

The room felt too small, and the air from my lungs was disappearing. The wet, warm blood which had soaked the top of my tunic felt too sticky and smelled of metal. I was going to be sick. My chest tightened as I lifted my gaze to Aris. He didn't know me anymore. He didn't know what I'd been through. I took a step back on the cold, hard floor.

I had no home. The only home I now knew was the cage I'd lived in for months and the mental cage I'd lived in for years.

Aris narrowed his eyes as he approached me, as if he knew what I was thinking. Without giving him a moment to react, I spun on my heel and sprinted through the throne room's doors. I could hear him calling my name, telling me to stop.

If he knew, he wouldn't want anything to do with me. He would be disgusted. I was doing him a favor. He just didn't realize it yet.

I didn't register the steps I took from the palace as I dashed and stumbled through the dead garden into the streets of Stroka. My breath was already struggling from the sudden expended energy. The smoking buildings, the dead bodies piled upon each other, crates of fruits splattered on dirt roads became a blur as I sprinted through the short streets. My body was used to an empty stomach and hunger pains, but this type of nausea was a whole new level. Bile was on the verge of my throat, pressing to be released, whatever was left in me.

Aris' voice and steps faded into the distance as I bolted into an alley that looked familiar. I was running off of willpower, nothing more.

The freedom of being able to run without any walls or barriers was exhilarating.

I knew exactly where I was and where I was heading.

Back to the cages—to my home.

I rushed down the alley and into the square. Looking through the thick smoke, I made out most of the slaves were gone from their cages except for a few. They shouted and wailed, hands gripping the caged walls, begging for their freedom.

Without a moment's hesitation, I ran for them, picking up an axe from one of the dead Strokan warriors. My heart pounded from seeing where I lived for so long. Where my soul wilted and died.

I marched my way to the three enslaved men. Fear filled their crinkled eyes until they saw me.

"Over here!" One of them reached for me.

Rage swallowed me whole. Not knowing where my strength came from, I lifted the heavy axe with maximum effort, but it fell to the ground. My arms were so weak. The men screamed. Fire blew from a building near the square.

I lifted the axe once more and slammed it into a lock on the cage. It flung off, and the door creaked open. The mumbling slave scrambled out, and I barely heard a thanks as I hurtled for the next lock and bolt. And the next.

Once the rest of the slaves were freed, I placed my hands on my knees, finding my breath, unsure of what to do. I felt a comforting presence behind me, but I didn't need to turn around to know who it was.

I couldn't burn these metal cages. I knew that. But that didn't stop me from spreading my lethal fury on them as I hoisted the axe again, and it met the impenetrable metal. The clang was louder than the explosions nearby. I didn't stop hammering them with deadly strikes and I lunged for my own cage. Breathlessly, I swung my axe into my and Rubert's cages and its metal bars.

Again and again.

But it did nothing.

The *crack* snapped back at me, refusing to make a dent in these gods-awful relentless cages.

The last strike had me almost tumbling over with the axe. My shaking hands could not hold on to the weapon any longer as it slipped from my fingers. The air in my lungs had not returned, but only depleted more. I placed my hands on my knees and gazed at the burning square surrounding me. The sounds my throat made were sounds of panic. Blood dripped from the wound that encircled my throat into the dirt.

Calm, calm, calm.

I'm free, I reminded myself.

Breathe. Focus.

I was going to run as far as I could from this place, never see another being again, and live the rest of my days in peace. I would grab—

"Solei—"

My head snapped up to see Aris standing nearby, watchful and calm. I could still hear the screams of Strokan warriors pleading for their lives.

"Don't." I raised my trembling hand between him and me, shaking my head. He didn't listen as his large form was suddenly in front of me. "Please, Aris—"

He wrapped his arms around me, and I couldn't breathe. Not because he held me tightly, as if he were afraid I'd slip away again, but because the panic in my body wouldn't leave. My body trembled in his arms even though he held me firmly.

"Just breathe." Aris' low voice filled my ear. The screams from the streets, the fires surrounding us, and the warriors who shouted commands muffled as Aris spoke. "You're here with me. Just breathe."

"I can't—I can't breathe. It's too difficult," I cried against his tunic.

An explosion near us filled the air, and I flinched. Without time to think of where it came from, Aris wrapped his arms around my back and legs and lifted me up. He carried me through the square and alleyways.

I might have said the name *Fenrah* because Aris responded that he'd send a search out for her. Fenrah was alive, and I couldn't believe it. After all this time, she had found me. I needed to know she was going to be safe. I loved her. She was family.

I kept my head on the spot between his chest and shoulder that was created just for me, and everything became a blur—then went black.

I could feel Aris' throat vibrate and move as he barked orders to warriors with me still in his arms. I could hear the horses' hooves near me pound in preparation to leave, and my eyes lifted for a moment to see the commotion on the outside field of Stroka—then saw black again.

"Solei, I need you to drink this," a familiar voice said softly in my ears. I felt arms around me, and my body swayed side to side. "Wake up, Solei."

My eyelids rose. I was on a white beast—Pacha.

"There you are." Aris' arms tightened around me, as if he was comforted by the idea I was awake—alive.

How long had we been riding for? He handed me a tin filled with clear, liquid water.

"Drink," he ordered me. An emperor. A leader, a commander, the one who destroyed cities and villages. The one who opened his heart to me, a captive from a foreign land, and worshiped my body. The one who had killed for me.

The one who chased me down orchards and swore he'd always find me.

Darkness enveloped my eyes again until Aris shook my body aggressively. "I said wake up. Drink."

My eyes flung open, and I lifted the tin from his hands and gulped water down my throat as quickly as possible, ignoring the feeling of what it was like to be forced under water, barely alive.

"How long?" I rasped. I looked behind us, and I saw the large army behind him going for miles and miles. I could hardly see the end as their emperor led the way.

"We've been traveling for two days." Aris paused. "We have about fifteen more to go."

"No." I swallowed. "I'm not going back."

"Yes, you are."

My chest tightened, the air being sucked from me once again. "I said no, Aris."

"You'll be safe with me."

I almost had the energy to laugh, but I didn't. I simply stated as a matter of fact, "You said that once."

I saw his white knuckles holding the reins in front of my body as his jaw and chest hardened. He didn't speak another word for the rest of the afternoon.

Night had fallen quickly, and so did the weather. It was bitingly cool when Aris stopped Pacha and the rest of his infantry for rest. Aris grabbed my waist and pulled me down, letting go to prepare a fire for the night. He left for a while, most likely giving more orders to his higher-in-command warriors before he came back.

I sat at the base of a large tree and wrapped myself in the blanket Aris provided while he maintained the fire burning brightly. I sipped from the tin, replenishing the thirst I'd had for months. Even though the trees above us completely covered the starlight and the moon, I could still see his face in deep contemplation, focusing on placing sticks and larger pieces strategically in the fire.

Exhaustion hit me once again, and I closed my eyes, lying on my side on the mossy ground. I heard the crackling of the logs split, then I heard Aris step towards me.

He dropped behind me, his body gifting me his warmth. He wrapped his strong arms around me and pulled me close.

I could feel the hesitation in his body when I tensed. I hadn't had this type of human interaction in so long.

But I allowed it. It was purely for survival, the cold wind exposing the winter season approaching. This felt similar to the first night we had together. And maybe there was a chance that Aris wanted to be near me to remind himself that I was alive—that I wasn't gone. Little did he know, I was barely breathing.

I couldn't help but remember the last night we were wrapped in each other's bodies. I swallowed, and tears stung my eyes.

Only when I felt his breathing slow down, telling me he was asleep, did I whisper to him against the howling winds, "I'm gone."

I felt my heart shatter in my throat after I spoke those words, my chin trembling not from the cold but from the ache that wanted to be released. Tears fell from my face onto the wet ground.

When slumber almost took me into darkness, I heard his low voice reply, "You're here."

Fifteen days went by, riding with Aris on Pacha towards Siniya. The air was crisper and cleaner but just as cold since the time we started our journey away from Stroka. Aris and I barely spoke more than a few words to each other every day. I was mostly sleeping in his arms. And every night, he'd hold me as I cried and cried. He'd never say a word about it in the morning when we packed up and left for a day full of riding.

He wouldn't let me out of his sight for more than a few minutes to speak to his high-ranking warriors, who gave me glances like they pitied me. Pitied me—I almost threw up every other time. Aris had given me one of his tunics to wear, and I secured it with a belt around my waist.

Every time we saw the stream coming from the north, we'd stop and clean our wounds. My neck had been cleaned several times by Aris, who insisted he'd help no matter how many times I'd swat his hand away. He'd only grab a stronger hold of me, cleaning the infection, and didn't take my rejection seriously.

I knew I would have the scar for the rest of my life, no matter how many healing herbs I'd place on it.

"Continue as planned. Ensure they all get proper rest when they get home. I'll be back when I'm ready," Aris said to Justir, who rode nearby.

"Of course, Aris. We'll see you when we see you." Justir gave him a quick nod.

"Good luck." Aris hesitated. "And don't mention to anyone where I've gone."

"Not a word."

Aris clicked his tongue to Pacha, and we were veered into the forest, through branches, on a narrow road only one Pacha could fit through. The road was so narrow and so old that the ferns and grass were growing into the road. If I didn't know any better, I wouldn't know it were a road at all.

"Where are you taking me?" My heart pounded at the very sudden change in direction.

"A place where I used to go when I felt..." He paused, finding the right words. "Alone or lost."

"Why?"

"I don't want to bring you somewhere you're not ready for yet." Leaves kissed my cheeks as we passed the thick forest. "I built this place for myself when I needed time away from Malakar. I'd come here to think, to hunt, to just...be. I'd almost forgotten about this place."

We were silent for a few hours before my heart tightened at the cottage that appeared. It was simple, made of bricks and stone. There was a white fence surrounding it, protecting it from unwanted visitors and animals. There was a chimney on the roof that meant there was a fireplace.

"The serenity of this place was exactly what I needed at the time. It helped me process so much of the life I had in Stroka. I felt lost and broken and most of all, I felt stuck with what to do about Malakar and my position with him. Jonam had just died, and I left shortly after, unsure how much brutality I could take from Malakar."

Pacha stopped for a moment. The weight of Aris' arms felt safe as he continued, "When I built this place, it reminded me that there was beauty in life where there was such darkness. I focused on the light, the brightness that engulfed this cottage, and I let that fuel me. I found Siniya shortly after, and Malakar took it under his empire. I had asked him if I could rule Siniya as an emperor, knowing that I would build my own empire to eventually overthrow him."

Aris clicked his tongue, and Pacha started once more. "The cottage is yours now, Solei. You can burn it, leave it, or do whatever you want with it, but it's yours."

My heart swelled. I closed my eyes and took a shaky breath. A tear escaped the corner of my eye. I swallowed, and I believed, in that moment, wholeheartedly, I would find my healing in this life or the next.

It would feel warm like Aris' arms, bright like Siniya, and full of love for myself.

Thus, I began my healing journey.

Chapter Forty-Nine

Several days went by as Aris and I cleaned inside the cottage and cleared the outside space of its shrubs. I was adamant on helping, but I had a hunch that Aris felt I was slowing him more, though he hadn't put it in direct words. I'd argue every time he'd make an excuse—*you need rest* or *you can't afford to keep expending more energy*. Eventually he'd give in, telling me to do whatever I wanted. I knew I was thinner, much thinner than before.

Aris went through an old stash of his and found some dried-out seeds that he had left behind. He placed it on the table in the middle of the cottage, attempting to lure me into a less strenuous activity. It worked. I walked over and began to separate the seeds without saying a word.

The moment Aris stepped outside the cottage, I could hear his audible sigh, though I knew he didn't intend for me to hear. My shoulders dropped. I knew he was worried about me. I knew I was quieter than I had been the last time we were with each other, but so much had happened. I'd changed. I couldn't look at him. It *pained* me to look at him. Remembering everything that I'd lost.

While keeping my hands busy on my new task, my eyes flickered for a moment to find Aris taking his tunic off and grabbing a shovel.

He started digging holes for what I assumed were the seeds I would want to plant. He had cleared the space earlier today for my garden.

I dropped the seeds that were in my hands onto the table and rushed out the door. "That's too deep for the seeds, Aris!"

"I'm not a gardener. That's your job." Aris gave me a wink.

I felt the heat rise past my neck, and my eyes fluttered everywhere but him. I threw my arms across my chest and straightened my back. "Then why are you here?"

There was still a fight within me. Poor Aris.

"I wanted to help you, Solei."

"I don't need your help. I can do this."

"You can barely hold a shovel." His voice remained cool and controlled, but I noticed how his jaw tightened. He was also angry. He was also hurting. Probably hurting for me.

And that hurt me all over again.

I took a step forward and paused.

"*Leave me alone.*"

Even the birds became quiet.

"Is that what you really want?" Aris' gaze locked with mine.

"It hurts to look at you. I want to be alone." I leaned forward. "Preferably forever."

I turned around and slammed the cottage door. My body dropped to the ground against the door, and I muffled my cries as best as I could. I couldn't have him hear me; it would hurt him. This vicious cycle was going to be the death of me if he didn't let me go.

Wrapping my arms around myself, I cried myself to sleep right there against the doorway. A few hours went by, and the sun set over the trees as darkness crept in.

I peered over the window to find Aris had grabbed a blanket that was left outside, placing it in the clearing and was lying on it. Most likely he was asleep, though I wouldn't be surprised if he wasn't since I could feel the cool breeze seeping through the cracks of the doorway.

The door creaked open, and I hissed at the coolness of the ground on my bare feet, but Aris didn't move.

My feet brushed against the dirt, and I stopped where he lay.

"Aris, it's me," I whispered.

"I know. I heard you the moment you got up."

Of course he did. My body tensed, and all I wanted to do was leave. I wasn't even sure why I was out here talking to him.

"What do you want, Solei?" Aris asked plainly.

The clearing went still. I backed away, not knowing what or how to answer. I turned, heading to the cottage. Without another moment, I heard Aris jump up from his blanket, and he gently touched my elbow.

I froze.

Touch was not something I was used to.

But Aris didn't stop as he pulled me to face him.

"Say something. Anything," Aris said against the biting cold.

I folded my shivering arms, and I could sense Aris wanting to wrap me in his arms, but he was resisting. He knew I'd push him away even more.

I stared at him. "I—I don't..." I swallowed the lump in my throat. "I don't know why you're doing this for me."

"Because you're worth it."

"I'm not worth it anymore. I'm gone, Aris," I whispered, the truth I didn't want to admit out loud. "I told you to leave me alone because—because I don't want you to have to see this broken version of me. I want to be alone so you don't see the person I've become. I want you gone because I don't want to explain myself... I'm broken."

His throat moved. "Even so, you're worth it." Aris took a step toward me. "Every broken part of you is worth it to me, and I won't stop until every cell of your being knows that."

With his warmth near me, my body trembling became more noticeable, and it wasn't from the cold. It was from being deprived of something good—of something that felt a lot like...love.

"I can barely hold on to this reality with the thoughts that are consuming my mind." My voice cracked. "I can't think of anything else. I can't see anything else. I can barely *breathe*, Aris. I *feel* like death." The tears ran from my face as I searched for the breath that kept choking me. "Sometimes, I wonder if I'm even alive."

Aris' arms wrapped around me, pulling me close to his body, and I broke. I let it all out.

I screamed, and I sobbed, and I pulled his body and tunic closer to me. I needed this. At one point my legs gave out, and I fell on the ground, and he came with me. And he held me tighter as I grieved the pain of the life I'd lived for months. Aris rocked my small, weak body in his arms.

"I'm angry, Aris. I'm so angry. I betrayed my body and mind and hid myself in—in more ways than I could count," I stammered between sobs. "I'm angry I forgot who I was, the weakness I embodied for so long. My—my brother wasn't coming back, because—because he's really, truly gone and I—I hate myself for not grieving for him when I knew I should have. I lied and lied to myself—" I squeezed him, holding on for more than support. "And my family no longer breathes, yet here I am hardly breathing without them, and I feel so...guilty because of it. I don't deserve this. They don't deserve this. And Rubert—"

I broke again. Aris seemed worried for a moment I wasn't getting enough air in my lungs because he kept murmuring, "Breathe, Solei. Breathe."

I continued, "Rubert was my friend...and he's dead, and I'm here. And—and you've been so kind to me, and I've been so cruel to you." Aris brushed a thumb across my wet cheek. "I'm so angry, and I can't—I can't breathe."

A moment went by. I had never said so many words before.

"Focus on the air that goes in." Aris breathed with me. "What does it feel like?"

When the tears had dried and I couldn't force anymore to come out, I sniffled, his oakwood scent filling my nostils. "It feels cold." I chuckled softly through my sobs against his chest. I could feel his smile on top of my head, and I added, "It feels clean."

"What else?" he asked.

I took a moment before I whispered, "I can also feel my chest moving," I observed. "My lungs fill up, and I can feel that, too."

After almost an hour of crying in his arms under the cold moonlight and him talking to me through what it was like to breathe again—I felt a sense of relief, of freedom. I felt lighter in his arms.

A few minutes went by in silence.

"I'm sorry, Solei. Forgive me for what I did to you."

"This isn't your fault." I paused, bringing my head up to look into his eyes. "I didn't mean—I didn't mean the words I said about wanting you to leave..."

"No." Aris shook his head, his body tensing. He wouldn't meet my eyes and turned slightly away. "I can't imagine what it must have been like to be in those cages. I want to destroy Stroka all over again and again just thinking about you being there and I never knew… I would do anything to take those memories of yours away. How could I have not known—"

"You couldn't have—"

"And really what infuriates me the most is that this wouldn't have happened if I hadn't—"

"Aris, you'll have to forgive yourself the way I have to forgive myself." A pressure was building in my throat.

He slid his gaze back to mine. A long moment passed.

"We can do it—together," I whispered.

He must have found something in my eyes because his widened a bit. A spark casted above them. His lips parted, and he blinked.

"Together, then."

I grabbed his hand and pulled him into the cottage where he began a fire at the hearth. He had been sleeping out here by it on a couch while I stayed in his old bedroom. Once he finished making the fire, placing the logs in a strategic manner to ensure it burned strong and bright, I said, "Stay with me."

He pulled back slightly and looked up from the fire, meeting my eyes. His brows lowered, seemingly unsure.

"Please," I whispered.

He nodded once, grabbed the candlestick on the small dining table, and met me in my bedroom.

We crawled under the cold covers. Not a minute went by before I could resist it, and I found him under the covers, curling myself against his body and chest. My body relaxed and leaned into his.

CHAPTER FIFTY

Four months passed with Aris and I living a life out in this small cottage, a few days' journey from Siniya. Of course, Aris had to leave from time to time to ensure the maintenance of his empire, but he'd always come back. When he wasn't at the palace, his mother acted as regent for him. She was ruling in his stead with just and grace, the perfect person to take care of his kingdom when he wasn't there. He'd ask me every time if I'd want to join him back in Siniya, but I wasn't ready.

Each time Aris came back, he'd make sure to bring more herbs and seeds for me to plant. They were from Fenrah, who now shared the apothecary with Peter, and she'd shove bags of herbs, seeds, and letters in his arms before he'd leave the palace. Apparently, it was a whole show when he departed with gifts for me from people like Nirelle and Sebry. Everyone at the palace knew I wasn't there when he'd visit, so they knew he was staying with me somewhere else.

But the herbs and the letters I received from Fenrah made me happy, and the garden was now prepared for spring.

Pacha had a *lady friend*, Willow. Aris brought her home when he rescued her from an abusive owner, who he had flogged in the square as punishment. Willow and I learned our boundaries with each other, and in turn Willow grew fond of Pacha, who gave her time and patience to grow accustomed to him. Willow was letting Pacha come closer and closer with each day that passed, and that made me smile. I admired how brave Willow was and how she was open to trusting Pacha after all she'd been through.

Besides snuggling together during the colder nights and when we were stargazing, Aris hadn't once tried to touch me in an intimate way. I wasn't quite ready. I didn't feel comfortable in my own skin yet. But now...now, I felt like I was beginning to be.

At times, I'd look at the scar around my neck in the mirror longer than Aris would have liked. I'd feel the tension in his body almost like he wanted to shake my shoulders when he'd tell me it didn't matter. He'd say I was more beautiful to him now than I ever was and the spirit within me glowed more strongly every day.

And he was right—that I was growing stronger with each day.

He was waiting for me. I knew he was.

He'd been gone now for a little over a week, but I knew he'd be back either today or tomorrow. I hope he'd come bearing news and drama from the palace, things I'd loved to hear. It was one of the first things I'd ask as soon as he was back: *what's new, what's happened with so-and-so,* or *how is Peter doing with the apothecary.* The last time he had come back to the cottage, though, he had let me know he found Maeri in a nearby village. I knew he had some awful plan set for her. I saw it in his eyes. I panicked.

I *begged* on my knees he would not harm her. I didn't want her blood on my hands, either—I couldn't bear it.

"I don't blame Maeri for what she did—what she thought she had to do and that she had no choice. I forgive her. She was a friend to me, once, a long time ago, and I will never forget that."

Aris' entire being froze in that moment, but he gave me what I asked knowing that it went against what he thought Maeri deserved.

He swore he wouldn't bring harm to Maeri.

I couldn't believe it, but he kept his promise.

A few times, Nirelle was brought back to the cottage, and it was the sweetest reunion between. I realized that our friendship wasn't as quick as Maeri and I's, but ours was slow and tender in a way that blossomed into something so sweet and fulfilling. I cherished Nirelle, the light she was and the stories she would tell—her eyes lit up every time she'd explain her drunken moments with men at the pub or how incredibly jealous and territorial Justir would get when a man laid a hand on her. She made me laugh.

Since we arrived four months ago, I had become more at peace these days than before. During the first few weeks, I'd have terrible episodes and even nightmares thinking I was back in the cage, but Aris held me through them, reminding me he was here with me. He never let me go—no matter how bad those moments got. He didn't let me go until I pulled myself up again and a new day began. Each time got easier. I went through those episodes when he was gone, too, but I got stronger because of it. I was learning to pull myself together alone.

I had the courage to heal.

I had everything I needed, the tools in front of me, to pull through in this life.

My life was worth breathing, no matter how hard it got.

Willow made some sounds that brought me back to this world, and I looked over and saw the most beautiful man I'd ever seen. My heart stopped for a moment.

Aris rode Pacha into the clearing. He was home.

I slammed the book I was reading shut, placed it on the outdoor table, and ran to him. He climbed off Pacha, who neighed his happiness at being home, and opened his arms to my flying body.

"You're back," I murmured against his chest.

He squeezed me tightly, as if it'd been months instead of a week. As if he still saw that version of me on the dais. Almost lifeless. Almost gone. But not quite.

"I'm happy to be home." He closed his eyes and deeply inhaled the scent of my hair.

"Your *home*," I repeated against his chest.

"Yes...if that's alright with you," he said.

It was wild to think he thought of *this* place, a place of humbleness, as home when he had a luxurious palace full of servants who'd do anything and everything for him. This place where we made food together from the garden we worked so hard at, where he cut firewood from the forest for us to be warm at night, where he worked to keep this small cottage functioning and for some reason he thought it was the most perfect place for him to call home.

I lifted my head so I could look into his eyes. "Of course it is. I just never thought you'd think of this place as home like I do. I thought maybe you considered the palace your home."

He brushed a few hairs slipping from my braid away from my face. "It doesn't matter where the place is. As long as you're there, that's where my home is."

My heart felt warm in that moment, and I couldn't resist my eyes lowering to his lips. But I said, "I made something for you."

"Oh, yeah, what's that?" He winked at me, and I flushed.

"Zucchini bread."

Aris smiled in a full grin. "My favorite. You're the best." He leaned in and brushed those soft lips against my cheek.

I tried to hide the fact I was completely flustered while I helped him with Pacha, who was equally as excited to see his Willow. But I didn't think I fooled him since he tended to notice *everything*.

How annoying.

After eating a slice of zucchini bread, Aris leaned back on the chair and gave me this look. Like he was waiting. Like he knew what I wanted from him. He had this smile—a smirk—like he knew I *craved* him, and his arm draped over the chair, and he waited, patiently.

My neck burned insufferably hot, and I got up to place the dishes in the sink. After I rinsed them in the bowl, I turned—

He was behind me with no space between us, his face close to mine, reading me.

"Why are you so nervous?" he asked casually, narrowing his eyes.

"W—why are you so close to me?" I stammered.

He took a step closer. "Because you want me to be."

My breath hitched. "How do you know that?"

"The way your body is moving." His voice lowered, and his hands found their home on my body, grazing along the curve of my hips and waist. "The way your face is warm." He leaned down and brushed his lips along my cheeks. "The way your neck is warm." He traced his mouth along my neck, licking and kissing, and I almost forgot to listen to what he was saying. "And the way you're talking to me."

Every place he touched me, it created a burning sensation that I was his and he was mine.

His hand reached behind my neck, through my hair, and pulled me closer. My lips parted.

"So, what do you want, my quiet sun?"

"I—I—" I stumbled with quick breaths. "I want—I want you."

He traced kisses down my neck. I could feel his smile. "I'm sorry, I didn't hear you."

He licked the spot behind my ear and neck, and I melted in the heat of his breath. I had enough of the teasing, and I pulled his face into my hands and brought his lips home.

His lips were warm and soft. It felt as if I had reentered heaven. I never forgot how good it was. How sweet it was. The memory of his lips had been ingrained in my brain since the moment he claimed them in his chambers.

My mouth opened slightly, and his tongue swept in, and our kiss turned passionate and longing.

Damn, I'd missed this man. My hands mingled in his hair, pulling him closer. He tugged on my lower lip. His hands sat on my hips and tugged me a bit closer to his.

He was my home.

Aris pulled back from my lips and looked into my eyes. "What's wrong?" he whispered, brushing a finger across my cheek, catching a tear.

I stared at the teardrop. I hadn't realized I was crying.

"Nothing's wrong. I've just really missed you…" I looked back into his eyes, and they turned a shade deeper. "You're one of the few things that make sense in my chaotic world."

"I'll never let you go, Solei," Aris promised. "Even if you hate me and kick me out of this cottage, I'll never let you go."

I let out a soft chuckle. "Good. I'm counting on that." I pulled his mouth back to mine and kissed him fiercely. "Because you're mine," I said between our lips.

I could tell those words sung in his veins because he then grabbed my backside, and he leaned so far that we nearly tipped over the bowl I had washed the plates in. We both smiled at the mess we were making; it was time to change the scenery.

He lifted me carefully in his arms and carried me into our bedroom and onto the bed he'd been holding me in every night. My heart was thumping against my ribcage.

He sat me on the bed, tongues entwined, and I pressed my body against his. My hands fumbled, bringing his tunic over his chest and neck, and I grazed my lips over his body. He, in turn, wrapped my sleeves around his fingers and slowly, very slowly, brought them past my chest, stomach, hips and then—snapped the dress off me.

Oh, he was hungry.

I smiled, and that made him go wild. He closed my mouth with his kisses.

Gods, I missed him, I missed him, the voices in my head were singing. And I loved him, with every cell in my being, I loved him. Tears were falling from my face, and he kissed every one of them, and I laughed and then he laughed.

He laid my bare body against the bed, but before he could crawl on top of me, I twisted my body and pushed him into the bed.

His lips curved. "Have me however you want, darling."

I smiled as I unbuttoned his trousers and dragged them off his legs. My chest tightened at the proof of the pleasure he received from our bodies mingling with each other.

Aris pulled my neck back to his soft lips, and my own insides became a powerful current, flowing through my body. He pressed against my entrance. My mind remembered the night we had together, so long ago. So full of passion and love. But my body tensed for a moment as if it had forgotten, and then relaxed. I whimpered softly as he entered me.

I released myself around him, and the deeper he went, sounds I'd never made before left my lips. Our breathing synced with each other deeply and powerfully—unlike anything I'd ever felt.

His hands wrapped gently around my back, guiding me. It felt so incredible. It was so like him to guide me through anything. He'd always been there for me, showing me just how wonderful life could really be.

He moved his hands to my hips. "You're mine, Solei." He gripped them firmly, and I finally let go. I leaned more into him, he knew exactly how to—

My release rippled through me, and I welcomed it and allowed it to fully envelope my existence and stop time itself. Exhaustion hit, and he twisted my body flat against the bed.

Aris caressed my body from where he was above me. My hands grazed and explored his chest and his back.

His mouth began on my nipples, playing with it between his teeth, and then he dragged his tongue, slowly, to my mouth. I caught his lips, his tongue deep inside me as his hips began to move between my legs.

The feelings I had for him were so overwhelming, so powerful that another moment in time and space caused me to leave my body.

He worshipped my voice, my body responding, and finally release met him, too.

We held each other, bare, breathing deeply and heavily.

I was speechless. I looked over to Aris. He was in another world. Something in my chest swelled and expanded, as I had something to do with that look on his beautiful face.

He turned and met my eyes. They were clear. Magnetic.

My pulse sped up more than when we were claiming each other. I'd never felt this level of passion and intensity before. It had crept slowly, so slowly, and I couldn't ignore it anymore.

"I love you, Solei," Aris whispered. He traced the back of his finger against my flushed cheek. I never thought he'd say those words to anyone, but yet here he was, confessing his undying love for me.

Tears filled my eyes, and I whispered what I knew all along: "I love you, Aris."

He claimed my mouth again, and my tongue danced with his.

"Marry me, Solei."

It wasn't a question, I realized. There wasn't a choice.

I was his.

I nodded, and tears fell onto my cheek and splattered on the bed where we just made love.

EPILOGUE

ONE MONTH LATER

ONE MONTH LATER

The crisp spring winds flowed through the orchard, settling around Aris and me as we held hands together in unity. I was barefoot, toes embedded in the cool grass, and had a flower crown in my hair, dressed in an ankle-length beige dress. Aris wore his usual black attire with the top of his tunic loose, his black hair ruffled by the whispering winds. I could feel his heartbeat racing.

With our hands entwined, Justir guided the ceremony.

Nirelle was beaming behind me with tears in her eyes. Beshien, Peter, Sebry, Fenrah and Acantha were seated, watching the intimate moment between our two souls combine for eternity.

I began to speak. "My vow to you—"

Aris leaned forward slightly and whispered so only I heard, "Need I remind you, you tend to break your vows."

My ears burned, and I slapped his arm, forcing a chuckle to rise from his chest. I tried to hide my smile and continued out loud. "My vow to you is unbreakable even if I tried. This is my vow to you, that not only on this earth I vow my body and soul to you, but for the lives beyond, where you and I will find each other again. I am yours, Aris. My soul belongs to you and only you."

Aris' chest rose, and he blinked several times before he cleared his throat. "I vow my existence to you, Solei. I'm yours, until the end of times. Until our souls no longer beat to the rhythm of life and beyond. I will always protect you. I will always fight for you. I will always love you."

I couldn't stop the tears that flowed from my eyes, and Aris gently squeezed my hands.

"I'm glad you found me," I whispered.

Aris must have known what day I was talking about. The day from over a year and a half ago. "I'm glad I didn't let you escape that dreadful day, too. I couldn't bear not to see the little vixen that fixed me up in my sleep... I knew from that moment you were mine."

A smile escaped my lips, and I nearly laughed in bliss.

"I love you," I said.

"I love you," Aris growled as he pulled me into his arms and crushed me with a kiss.

THREE YEARS LATER

I wrapped the young girl's wrist as tightly but gently as I could. The girl had sprained her wrist while playing with her friends.

"Have her drink this twice a day with some tea. It'll help the pain," I informed the girl's mother in the apothecary. There wasn't much I could do besides helping the pain. Only time would heal this wound—like many wounds, physically and emotionally.

The mother said her thanks to Fenrah and I before the doors of the apothecary slammed open and Aris barged in. The bells rang violently.

I shook my head and smiled. What an entrance.

Aris smiled apologetically as the mother and young girl left, murmuring their greeting to the emperor. Fenrah placed a hand on my shoulder and gave a quick squeeze before she went back behind her small wooden desk to study some dried blood samples.

The people in Siniya had been recovering in a remarkable way from Strokan's deadly empire. Siniya was thriving in a way it never had before and expanded its traditions and cultural characteristics upon the neighboring countries who had reveled in this peaceful era. The countries that were sworn to Stroka were now sworn to Siniya. The people worshipped Aris and his strategies for rebuilding the empire, starting from within the family structure and stretched to building harmony between the different classes of people. He forbade slavery, and the price to pay wasn't pretty.

"Someone didn't want to take their nap today." Aris gave a nervous chuckle.

I lifted a brow but looked behind Aris.

A small black-haired boy, barely two years old, appeared behind Aris' leg. His thumb stuck into his pouting mouth. The moment he looked at me, his mother, with light green eyes, he nearly broke down at the sight of me.

I rushed over. "Oh, my baby boy." I picked him up and held his little body close to me, comforting him.

"Neo wouldn't sleep, no matter how tired he is," Aris explained.

"It's because he's teething. Aren't you, Neo?" I asked him, knowing he wasn't going to answer.

Aris placed a finger beneath my chin, lifting it up, and brushed a soft kiss against my lips.

I smiled and became speechless. Aris, after all this time, still made my heart race with butterflies in my stomach.

"Ma-ma!" Neo clapped his little chubby hands together.

Aris and I beamed together and nodded. "Yes, that's right. 'Mama'!"

"Can you say 'Papa'?" Aris asked enthusiastically.

"No." Neo pouted.

It was his favorite facial expression and favorite word.

I shook my head and stared at Aris. "I blame you for that."

Aris burst into laughter, the sound echoing in the small apothecary. He grabbed my hand and the three of us walked through the palace halls.

Regardless of how Siniya inspired me to dance more, smile more, and live more, Neo was the missing piece to accepting myself and where I was in life. Aris and Neo were everything I needed and more.

Aris and I held hands while Neo walked to the burnt orange curtains and played with the numerous plants living on the low windowsills exposing the vibrant outdoor gardens.

Aris stopped me in the middle of the large hallway and kneeled. He placed a kiss on my swelling middle. "What do you think it'll be?"

"A girl." I smiled. "I've never been wrong in guessing the gender of a baby."

Aris raised a brow. "Is that so?"

"Yes, I swear!" I laughed.

"If it's a girl, what will we name her?" Aris asked the belly, as if the baby was going to answer the name of its soul.

"I'm not sure, but we have time. About five months," I said softly. "What do you think? Have you thought of anything?"

"Yes. I thought maybe the name Fenrah. Maybe Fe for short."

I froze and melted in the same moment. "I love that..."

"She'll be a little healer like her mama, won't you?" Aris asked the swelling belly. He rose and looked into my eyes. "I have never felt so complete until this moment with the four of us." He shook his head slightly. "And yet, I thought I was complete when I found you. Then, when I made love to you, everything made sense to me. The next was when I asked you to marry me. My heart was filled with love. Then, when you gave birth to our son, I couldn't believe I had made space for another love. When I found out about our next child"—his eyes glistened—"I thought I was going to implode with love..."

He leaned his forehead to mine. "I had thought at one point in my life that I didn't have room in my life or heart for love or anything like it..." He held my face in his hands. "I've never been so grateful to be so wrong."

ACKNOWLEDGEMENTS

First, I want to thank my brother, 1st Lieutenant Jonam Russell, for giving me the courage to write when I was fourteen years old. Jonam, you made me believe in myself by being the one to believe in me. You told me I could be anything I ever wanted to be. I know you're in the skies, watching over me, and I can't wait to be in your arms again one day.

William Durlene, you are the love of my soul and the inspiration for this book. Thank you for being there for me, encouraging me during those late nights when I was writing, editing or formatting. Thank you for believing in my story, even though you never read it. Your faith in my abilities is beautiful, and I needed it more than you can ever realize. Thank you.

To *The Quiet Sun's* BIGGEST cheerleader since draft one, Kristin: I would not have believed in this story if it weren't for you! Thank you for being there and encouraging me that this story was meant to be read and meant to be seen.

To my mama, Sophia, and to the best librarian I know: I used to hide from chores in your walk-in closet (which was practically a mini library) as a child for years, reading all your Christian romance books. That's how my love for reading and writing began. Thank you for helping me find the name of this book. Thank you for always teaching me new words. I promise I'll never forget our Greek heritage.

To my beta team and friends: Mary, Lindsay, Syd, Lyndsi, Brieanna, and Rachel, and to my developmental editor, Shannon—thank you for all your hard work and the care that you put into understanding these characters and their story. Thank you to my copyline editor, Clara Abigail. And thank you once again to all of you for your creative ideas and for helping this book come full circle. This book would not be where it is today without each and every one of you!

Thank you to my friends, Clover, Lindsay (again—thank you!!), and Natalie, for all the hours you spent listening while I talked about my book. Your support meant everything!

Thank you, Fernanda, for seeing my vision, the recognizing the hard work I put it, and for letting me be me. Thank you for believing in me, for encouraging me, and for being the reason this book has seen the light of day. Thank you, Alexandra, for your creative input and for always being willing to see my next book cover idea!

ABOUT THE AUTHOR

Originally from Quebec, Canada, Noémi now resides in Phoenix, Arizona, with her fiancé and two adorable dogs, Echo and Bellagio. Noémi has dreamed of becoming an author since she was fourteen years old. In pursuit of becoming a full time author, she also loves conducting hypnotherapy sessions for her loved ones, exploring the world through her Traveling Sisterhood women's retreat business, and binge-reading a well-written book while cold plunging. She is also passionate about fostering healthy connections between the mind, brain, and body—talk anything related to neuroscience, and she's all ears.